I0612255

HIDDEN PRIESTESS
CITY OF TEMPLES
BOOK TWO

BARBARA LUND

LUND PUBLISHING

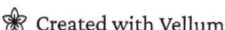 Created with Vellum

ACKNOWLEDGMENTS

Thanks to Alex at Addictive Covers for the cover.
https://www.addictivecovers.com

Thanks to K.V. Moffet, Offworld Press for editing.
http://www.offworldpress.com

Any mistakes left are mine.

For my blood family and my found family.

Dear Readers,
As with the first book, time gets a little wonky.
Some things need to be seen from two different points of view.
Good luck.

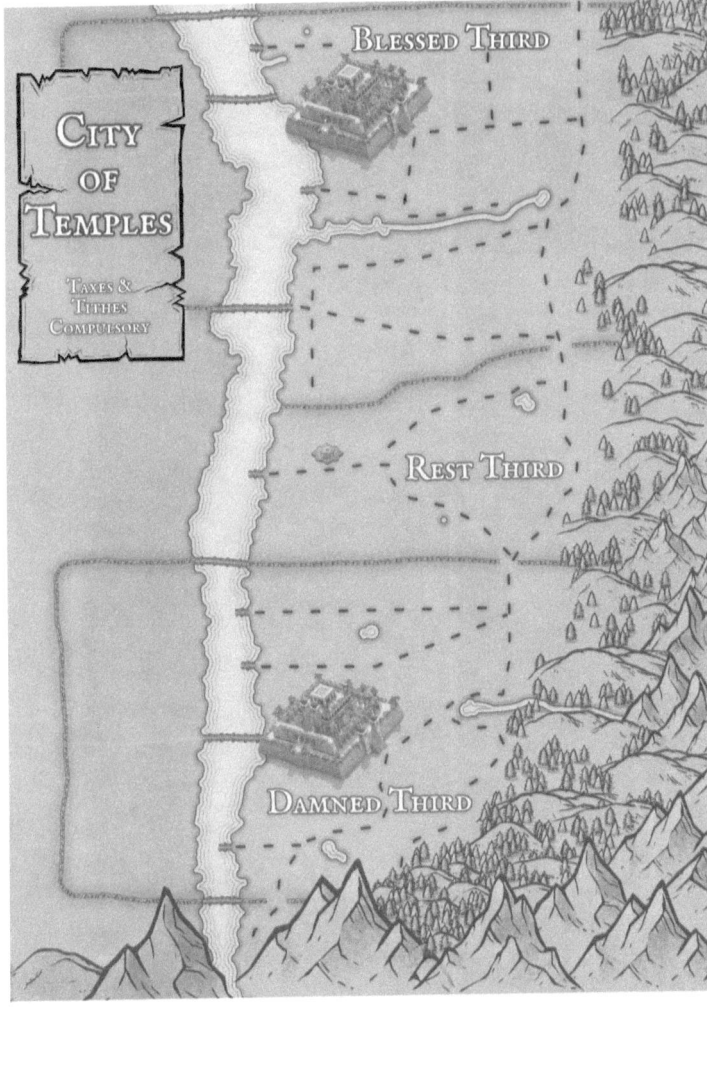

CITY
OF
TEMPLES

Taxes &
Tithes
Compulsory

BLESSED THIRD

REST THIRD

DAMNED THIRD

CHAPTER

ONE

S *umi*

Love is hard.

Love is especially hard in the City of Temples, where the city is divided into three. Two massive, opposing forces— the Blessed Third and the Damned Third, Bendita and Maldita, the bright and the dark, the kind and the cruel, though I had never seen evidence that either the blessed or the damned were kind, only cruel— and the Rest Third stuck between them, without goddess or temple, without power or influence, without magic.

It always comes back to magic.

I had been the high priestess of the dark goddess Maldita, steeped in blood and sacrifice, pain and power, my magic stronger than anyone's, my will standing between Her and utter destruction, but I had given it all up for love.

Now I was no one, hiding my magic from my beloved's family, from the dark goddess, from the world. They all thought the previous high priestess of the Temple of the Damned was dead, and I had to keep it that way if I wanted to live.

I very much wanted to live.

But coming back from nearly dead was a horribly slow process and if I hadn't been so tired I'd have been furious at myself and my circumstances all the time.

Now, for example.

The bed I shared with my beloved, Jay, was half the size of the one we'd shared in the damned temple, and he felt every shift and shudder. And I did shudder with every shift, held my breath and rolled to my side— darts of agony in my shoulder, hip, back. Tightened my core and braced my arms and pushed up enough to roll to my feet— spasm in my lower back, black spots in my vision. Then I stood, panting, at the side of the bed and waited for the worst of it to subside, opened my eyes and found Jay there, his shoulder-length brown hair disheveled from the bed, his honey-colored eyes wild with a need to help me, his muscles locked with the knowledge I wanted to do it myself.

I dredged up a smile for him. "Would you hand me my cane, please?"

He twisted in a way that had my back cramping in protest and handed me the smooth redwood cane he'd spent far too much of the family's money on when brownwood or yellowwood would have been serviceable... but would have drawn attention because it didn't match my Color.

Red— red skin on my hand, shaking, reaching, clutching the cane, no longer filled with black tattoos marking me as a priestess of the dark goddess Maldita. Red hair, long and tangled and wild, no longer streaked with thick ropes of black showing the degree of my power and control. Red and white eyes, currently blinking back tears at the pain, no longer high-priestess-red from lid to lid when Maldita was quiescent nor solid black when She took control of my body.

Once I had the breath to do so, I straightened, then walked slowly and carefully from our bedroom to the tiny necessary, all my attention on my aching feet, my twinging knees, my throbbing back, and the Brown man who followed me.

I'd *died* on a snowy night two months ago, and he brought me back, pounding on my chest to make my heart beat, breathing into my mouth to make my lungs work, sharing his life with me to remind my body and soul what it was to be alive.

Sometimes I suspected it had broken him— to see me dead — and not quite healed him to bring me back. The way he worried about me, about my blood-son Wilyam and heart-son Antero, about everyone... his time in the Temple of the Damned had changed him, and not for the better.

I used the necessary then washed my hands at the sink, particularly grateful both that I could manage this much on my own without sobbing from the pain— I was getting stronger— and that the house had this much plumbing, as most of the houses in the Rest Third did not. It was river water— not drinkable, but good enough to wash with accompanying soap— and around here that meant Jay's family was rich.

My hips and knees and back were starting to loosen up, so I crossed more easily through the main room of the house and the lines in Jay's face eased.

Jay's mother slept on the couch, her yellow hair and yellow face pale spots in the gloom of closed and shuttered windows. The boys curled up together under a pile of blankets in the far corner.

Dawn peeked through the edges of the shutters. The rest of the house would stir soon. Something twinged in my back and I paused to keep from falling.

"Sumi—" Jay's voice was quiet, desperate. He needed to

help me so much, but how would I get stronger if he did everything for me?

I shook my head *no* and concentrated on my boys while I waited for the spasm and the shaking and the tears to pass.

Wilyam, a Red like me, and strong in both *push* and *pull* magic, and Antero, a Purple boy and the blood-son of one of my few friends, Hana, who had died protecting me from an assassination attempt. My throat ached at the reminder she was gone, but my back eased and I continued my slow path across the room.

Antero was almost as strong in his magic as Wilyam, and only time would tell if removing them from the temple was saving them or dooming us all.

Jay folded back one of the shutters and let in the chill winter pre-dawn light. The boys stirred under their blankets, then burrowed deeper. Could I make it back to our bedroom before that bit of cold struck at me? Another difference from the temple— Jay's family house had no magi nor priestessi *pulling* heat from the desert in the winter, nor cold from the deep mountain lake feeding our river in the summer. They— we now — dressed for the weather, and I hated it.

My fingers ached from the cold and from my grip on the cane, but I was almost to the bedroom.

If I used my *push-pull* magic, I could fix the temperature, lift myself back to the bed, heal Jay's mother.

"Oh good, you're up." Robin, the older sister, poked her head out of the bedroom she shared with Dee, the middle. "We can't feed all of us. Especially not growing boys." It had the sound of an old argument, but new to me.

My steps faltered, but I wasn't sure I could turn and make it all the way to a chair. Better to take the last few steps through the doorway to our bed and sit.

Robin came out of her room and claimed a seat at the table.

She drew her sword and ran the sharpening stone along the edge, no thought to whether it would wake the boys or not. She wore guard grays and had braided her yellow hair tight to her skull, almost ready for work. She'd joined the Rest Third guard after she'd proved her lower-caste-Yellow worth to them by spying on the demon hunters.

Not fair, to by judged by Color.

"We can, for a little longer." Dee emerged and sat across from Robin, in the only other chair. Good thing I hadn't turned around. Dee had inherited their father's Brown coloring over their mother's Yellow.

Jay paused in his hovering over me and turned to face them. "She's still sick," he said softly.

Jay's mother's tiny snores had stopped so I wasn't surprised when she sat up on the couch and pushed her blankets back. *She* was the sick one. Her skin was more gray than yellow, her hair dull and thin. But Jay and his sisters were ignoring it as hard as they could.

"We *can't* keep us all *fed,*" Robin insisted. "The house, the taxes, and food for eight on three guard salaries?"

Maggie, the youngest sister, was a guard too, out patrolling the streets and city walls of the Rest Third while the older sibs had this discussion.

Mom— and it was strange to call a woman *Mom* after dealing with my own hateful, cruel blood-mother— blinked sleepily. "This again? I could—"

"No, Mom." Jay crossed the room to sit next to her. He put his hand over hers, and the shape of their fingers matched, even if his hand was larger, and the Colors different. "I'll go back to teaching at the guard. I just..."

"Didn't want to leave her alone." Dee shot me an apologetic glance, then rested her elbows on the table. "She's a grown woman, Jay. With two kids. And the boys have to help too."

My boys— I tensed, ready to leap up and fight for them... or rather, feeling the fatigue in my muscles, I clutched my cane tighter and pulled myself upright again. I stepped over the threshold from the bedroom to the main room and felt as if I'd run a race.

Bless my betraying body to heaven. My magic was the only thing about me that was strong, and I couldn't use it.

"They can fetch water," Jay's words fell heavy into the room. "They're both eight winters old now— old enough. That will save us the price of the waterseller." Drinking water, he meant, from the fountains, where the water was filtered clean. Several blocks away.

"Fetch water." I tried to sound neutral, but from the way Robin's shoulders hunched, I hadn't succeeded.

"We're not rich." Dee looked at me. "Sumi, you're welcome here. We're happy to have Jay back, and the boys are wonderful, but we need the extra salary." *And you're a drain.*

The words were unsaid but I heard them.

"I can earn my keep," I lied. I couldn't fetch water from the nearest fountain. I'd never make it that far. Couldn't carry the buckets empty, let alone full. Couldn't move fast enough to keep the water from freezing in the winter chill.

With magic, I could *pull* water from the river right to the house, pipes or no—

If I wanted Maldita to find me. To wreak havoc on Her previous high priestess, suddenly alive. What would the current high priestess, Aimi, my blood-sister, do if she found out? What would happen to this tiny, ramshackle, overfull house and its occupants? What would happen to the children?

Between my blood-sister and the dark goddess, Hell would snatch them all up in its jaws and I would never get them back.

I shivered, despite my layers. Lifted my chin. Lied again, like I wasn't still recovering from being dead. "I can cook basic meals. Clean a little. The boys—" Here I faltered. I wanted them safe, wanted them with me so I could protect them, but I couldn't protect anyone anymore, not without my magic. "The boys can fetch water."

Robin tested the edge of her blade, then nodded and sheathed it. "So that's settled. Jay teaches, Sumi cooks and cleans and tends to Mom. The boys fetch water and help clean until Sumi is fully recovered, then they can find other little jobs. That should be enough to keep all of us fed."

My knees were trembling. Dee and Robin sat at the table, the boys burrowed in their blankets, Jay and Mom leaned together on the couch, the cookstove warmed us all, and the room was full. So full it sucked the air out of me.

I retreated to the edge of the bed and sat again. How was I going to take care of Mom when I couldn't even take care of myself?

Robin slung her sword belt around her hips, nodded sharply. "Work calls. I'll tell Thom you can start tonight." She hustled out the front door, letting in a gust of winter chill before she shut the solid faded brownwood door behind her.

Jay opened his mouth to protest but she was already gone. His shoulders slumped and he nodded. "I'll be there."

Dee clapped him on the shoulder. "It's for the best." She disappeared into her room.

Envy prickled at my heart that they could move so easily. I hated feeling it— only a monster would wish to take someone else's health for their own. I dropped my gaze to hide it.

Faint black tattoos showed on my red skin.

Goddessi— Had I thought too much about my magic? "Do you see them?" I whispered, my breath short and shallow.

"See what?" Jay knelt in front of me.

I traced one with a fingertip. They felt the same— raised like a scar, but not painful.

"Oh." He took my wrist. Ran his hand up and down my arm. "No. I don't see them. Don't feel anything. They're gone. Your blood-sister took them from you."

Not gone.

Just as Maldita was not truly gone, but a quiet thread deep inside me I dared not disturb. She didn't give up anything that belonged to Her, and I belonged to Her, blood, bone, and soul.

She'd just... misplaced me for a while.

Jay cupped my chin. "You're all right. You're free of all that."

"I am," I lied, and leaned forward to touch my forehead against his. So many lies today. "We're free."

∽

JAY

THE SNOW HAD STARTED WITH FLURRIES JUST AFTER MIDMORNING, then changed into great fat slow-falling flakes in the afternoon. When the sun set, the mushy streets would freeze solid and make the roads treacherous. If winter was ending and spring was coming, Jay certainly couldn't tell.

The boys seemed to think fetching water from the fountain was the worst chore in the history of chores. Each swung a bucket from one hand and avoided the cleared paths to stomp through snowdrifts as if his life was ending. At least until they forgot they thought it a punishment and started to caper. Remembered, sobered and glared, stomped again.

This was the farthest either had been away from home, so they forgot more and more often.

Wilyam had grown during the winter months, giving him an extra handwidth over Antero, but other than the too-tight fit of his boots, neither seemed to have noticed. They chattered while they walked, or rather, Wilyam chattered. Antero listened, and threw in the occasional correction.

On their own street, they were fine— the boys had played outside often enough to become a common sight, but as they went on, stares followed them like ducklings following their mother. Jay raised his chin and pretended not to notice, but a Brown man escorting but not *serving* a Purple boy and a Red boy — not something the Rest Third saw, especially when the boys were obviously best friends. The Purple boys of the Rest Third played with other Purple boys, when they weren't learning to be rich, while the few Reds had been apprenticed to tradesmen.

Color and caste was pervasive in the Rest Third, but these boys had come from the Temple of the Damned, and they didn't understand. Didn't see any reason to change. They'd been friends longer than he'd known them, and Jay wouldn't be the one to force them.

In the damned temple, Jay had learned to love Wilyam for being Sumi's son, and Antero for being Wilyam's best friend, but during the past two months in the Rest Third, he'd come to love both boys for themselves— for their quick wits, their insatiable curiosity, for Wilyam's brazen assurance everyone wanted to know every thought that passed through his head, and for Antero's quiet wisdom.

Now, as they walked along the streets of the Rest Third, he tried to see this part of the city through their eyes.

Snow hid the scars and scrapes of the Rest Third and made it magical— the cobblestone street decorative instead of dirty and uneven, the candles in the windows festive instead of a desperate source of light and warmth, the families clearing their walks or righting wind-tipped rain barrels thriving instead of eking out a living at the edge of starvation.

Goddessi, he was getting cranky in his old age.

His parents' house sat roughly in the middle of the Rest

Third, a short walk up to the bathhouses and down to the nearest fountain. The streets nearer the fountain had terraced yards, the owners' effort to keep their precious gardening plots from washing away with the spring rains, and— of course— the boys found the raised walls too tempting to resist. Before Jay had thought to keep them off, Wilyam scurried up, Antero following behind.

"Look at me!" Wilyam raced along the wall, bucket and free hand windmilling as his boots slid on bits of ice. Antero followed more slowly, his balance more sure.

If they fell, they might crack open their heads, and then they'd need healers and he'd have to find money to bribe— er, *pay*— a healer from the blessed temple or the damned, and that would get complicated.

"Boys. Get down."

Wilyam glared and slipped. Antero caught him before he sank more than half-boot-deep in the mud. They both wrestled Wilyam free with curses meant to be under their breath but carrying in the cold air. A Brown woman and her bundled-up toddler crossed to the other side of the street to avoid them, and the woman stooped, pressed her hands over the toddler's ears and looked scandalized.

Jay opened his mouth to apologize but before he could say anything, the street opened up to a commons, with the water fountain at center.

"Woah!" Wilyam jumped down off the corner of the wall. His feet slid, but Antero landed soft-footed and steadied him. "Look at all the—"

The boy's words were lost as he turned his face toward the commons and the general noise level rose. Jay took longer steps to catch up.

The snow still fell but it couldn't stick— too many people passed back and forth for it to do anything but reluctantly melt.

If the commons hadn't been paved with cobblestones, it would have been a mire of mud from one side to the other. The majority of the people here were Browns and Reds and Greens — this was a popular area for guards and their families— but there were a few richer Blues and Purples and some poorer Yellows and Oranges. The Yellows especially had a tendency to hesitate and stare at their feet, which could be precarious with this many people about.

One bright-eyed Green woman was sugaring and roasting nuts, then selling them to anyone with coin to buy, and the line to her cart wrapped halfway around the commons.

The boys reversed course and came back for Jay, pleading with every line of their bodies.

He hadn't brought coin, and they didn't have it to spare... but if he'd brought it, he'd have spent it for them. "No," he told them.

They scowled, glanced at each other, then darted off again, buckets cracking against the shins of the less wary as they went.

Jay sighed. Compared to some other fountains in the Rest Third, this one was simple— a raised circle of stone with burbling water at the center. Pipes brought the river water, and by artifice or magic or both, the water in the fountain was clean enough to drink without getting sick, and never froze.

Wilyam cavorted along the far side of the knee-high wall encircling the fountain, oblivious to the angry glares. His boots were filthy and this was their *drinking water*. Jay winced. Whistled to catch the boy's attention, then pointed down.

Wilyam ignored him.

Jay scowled. He ducked his head and circled the fountain. "Get down," he snapped. Wilyam pivoted and walked away.

"You can't tell me what to do!" Wilyam yelled over his shoulder.

Resting betweens, if he didn't want a Purple or a Blue or

another Brown to punish Wilyam themselves, he had to get him down. Jay rubbed his forehead. "Wilyam, Antero, come on. We need to take water home."

"I don't *want* to." Wilyam scuffed his foot along the edge of the fountain, kicking water out in a spray.

It spattered Jay, a Red man, and two Yellows. The Red man scowled, but the Yellows just ducked their heads.

Jay looked down. Noted the water on his heavy overshirt. It was just water, but the sun would be down by the time they made it home, and ice would form on the cloth, and then it would melt in the house, then Sumi would have more to clean, and she'd be upset and she didn't deserve to be upset—

And now the boys were a quarter of the way around the fountain again. He followed after them. Growled, "Get down."

"No!"

Antero stood behind Wilyam, looking back and forth between them like he couldn't decide who to support.

Parenting was hard.

How would Sumi handle this? In the dark temple, she would have *looked* at the boys in that cold, quiet *I'm in charge* way and been obeyed. Now? Reason with them until they gave in from sheer exhaustion, perhaps. He took another step forward and reminded himself to be logical, but still appeal to a boy.

Then a tall, bony Purple woman pushed her way through the crowd. Marched up to Antero. Took him by the arm and hauled him down off the edge. "Who are you?" she demanded. "Who are your people?"

Antero stared up at her, his hands clutched around his bucket like it was a safety rope.

Wilyam stopped yelling and stared too.

Horror choked Jay. If she took the boys— or even just one of them—

"He's with us, Honored Purple." Jay let his hand linger on the pommel of his sword— as if he could draw on a Purple woman just for grabbing a Purple child.

Space opened up around them, and silence rippled out. Nothing good would come of this. Jay swallowed hard, took one step forward.

She ignored him. Gripped Antero's face and tipped it one way, then the other, toward the light of the setting sun. "You could be a Lunata or a Wescott."

"I don't know what you're talking about. Lunata?"

"You shouldn't be here alone."

"You're not making any sense." Antero stared up at her, baffled. "That's my dad. And that's my brother."

"The Brown man? The Red boy having a tantrum? Psh." The Purple woman shifted her grip to Antero's collar. "Come along."

The Yellows and Oranges had disappeared from the crowd, melting away like the snow. The Green woman was packing up her cart, casting frightened glances his way. A few Browns lingered, staring.

Jay reached for Antero, but he didn't dare yank him away. "Please, Honored Purple. He is ours. Please don't take him away."

"Yours." She looked down her long nose. "He is no Brown. This boy should be raised with his own Color."

Wilyam lept down from the wall. Charged forward, fists raised. Goddessi help them all, if he hit the woman, or worse, used magic on her— Jay darted between them and wrapped an arm around Wilyam's waist, lifted him off his feet. Wilyam cried out, struggled.

The Purple woman took several steps toward the river— the richer part of the city— dragging Antero with her. He finally came out of his stupor and swung his bucket wildly.

The woman jerked away, eyes wide. Her grip loosened, and

Antero ripped himself free. He ran toward them while the woman gaped.

Jay caught Antero in his other arm, then turned and fled. He glanced over his shoulder and saw the Purple woman staring after them, perplexed and muttering.

They rounded the corner and Jay dropped into a walk, then set the boys on their feet. "Give me the buckets," Jay said heavily. "I'll go fetch the water. You two stay here."

"You're leaving us?"

"*Stay here.* Out of sight. Stay quiet. Without the water, we'll have nothing to drink tonight and maybe no supper."

He snatched up the buckets and marched back to the fountain, looking for anyone who might cause him more problems. People scattered before him, fled the scowl he felt etched into his face.

But the Purple woman was gone, and with the boys out of the way, everyone seemed to have forgotten what had happened. He didn't see anyone he knew, and even if he had, he wouldn't have stopped to talk.

Resting betweens, he'd come so close to losing them both. If Antero hadn't gotten himself away from the Purple woman— if a Red had come after Wilyam— if Jay hadn't gotten them both away from the commons—

He *had* to protect them. No matter the cost. For their mother.

As quickly as he could without running, Jay returned to the boys and was relieved to find them pale and silent. "We must never tell your mother about this," he said, handing them each a bucket.

"Never," Wilyam promised.

With his free hand, Antero clutched Jay's shirt like he would never let go.

TWO

S *umi*

THE AFTERNOON BROUGHT HEAVY, SWIRLING SNOWFLAKES THAT MADE my stomach knot. When Jay took the boys out into the cold, I dug my fingernails into my palms to keep from protesting. Snowfall had been peaceful for me, until I died in a storm.

I am broken.

The only things that kept me upright were the sky, gray instead of black, and the knowledge that panicking would set my body back weeks— and then where would I be? Cleaning and crying, crying and cleaning.

If only I hadn't been Maldita's high priestess, I'd never had been killed, never have had to give up my magic—

Bah, what was I saying? People died every day. I was one of the lucky ones— I did have magic, even if I'd given it up to protect my family. I did have a found family, far better than my blood family. I could breathe and open my eyes and hug my boys after *dying*. So I had to clean a little to help make this household work. So I hurt. I *lived*, and I was grateful.

I could survive this. I'd survived worse.

I forced myself to my feet and left my cane behind— couldn't use a cane *and* a broom nor a cane *and* a scrub brush.

Footprints on the floor showed me who had been here and left again. Robin hadn't returned yet, after throwing down her ultimatum that Jay get his job back. Dee had gone out in the afternoon for her shift. Maggie had stopped by for a quick dinner, then left again. Then the boys left with Jay. Only Mom and I remained in the house— her, carefully propped up on the couch, away from the mud, and me in my layers of socks, the outermost filthy from the ghosts of everyone else's boots.

And of course the broom was on the far side of the room, near the necessary.

Me and my filthy socks crossed, dodging the mud as best I could. Once I clutched the broom in my hands, I swept myself a clean tile, leaned on the wall long enough to strip the outer-most socks from my feet, then started sweeping from there.

The scrape of the broom across the tiles was soothing after the... *discussion* this morning and the houseful of people since. I'd had no idea how much alone time I'd needed until I had none.

"What's that song?" Mom demanded from her couch.

"What?" I paused my sweeping and leaned on the broom, panting. My hands felt stiff already.

"You've been humming. What song?"

My throat tightened. The tune was one taught to the priestessi. Would she know that I was no escaped servitor from a simple song? No— surely not.

If she ever found out who I was, she'd despise me. Jay's whole family would. They'd said horrible things about Maldita's high priestess in my presence without knowing it was me— I'd taken Jay away from them, enslaved him, though he volunteered to save Maggie from her punishment. According to them I was responsible for all the bad things that had ever happened to them *and* the entirety of the Rest Third.

They could never know. They'd hate me. And it would break me to have my found-family hate me. My hands shook and the bristles rustled against the tile floor.

"N-nothing really. Just something I heard."

She gave me a look. I'd seen that look before when I was a servant and the priestessi didn't much believe a story I told. Heavens, I'd *given* that look to a few under-priestessi in my own temple when they lied to me.

"Mmm." Mom shook her head slightly. "Well, it was nice."

I smiled vaguely and turned my back on her, flexed my hands, then turned my attention back to sweeping, *without* the accompanying song, bless it.

How did I stop from doing something I hadn't realized I'd been doing?

What if I did it for something else? Something worse— magic?

No. I'd had better teachers than that. I wouldn't use my magic without knowing.

Scritch, scritch, scriiiitch.

For such a small house, the floor of the main room was enormous. My calf cramped. I flexed it, then the other, until the cramp eased. Anyone else would have been done by now. *I'd* have been done by now if I was the same person I'd been a year ago.

But I wasn't the same person. Wasn't a damned high priest-ess, nor even a priestess. Just a nobody, now. "Bless it," I muttered softly.

No matter how much I wished it otherwise, I couldn't

sweep this floor like I would have a year ago. Jay and his family would have to be satisfied with what I could do now.

I looked up and found myself at the back door with a pile of dirt and a heaving chest. I paused to catch my breath.

Goddessi, a little *push* and the dirt would be out the back door—

No.

No magic.

I could do this.

The broom seemed to think otherwise, twisting against me as I shuffled around to open the door, but I fought myself straight again and swept the dirt outside to mingle with the muddy, snow-covered backyard.

The trees sparkled in the light from the house and the mud was mostly covered by a fresh blanket of snow. It didn't look so bad from inside.

A sharp little wind cut its way through my layers and I slammed the door closed, then arched with a spasm in my back. I grunted to stifle a whimper and rode it out.

My broken body should have been healed by now. *Would* have been, if I'd been at the dark temple.

I chose, I reminded myself. Somehow knowing I'd made the choice and could unmake it anytime I wanted— if I could bear the consequences— made it all right. Maldita would take me back, I had no doubt.

How much She hurt my family in the process— that I could not abide.

The blessed floor drew my gaze. It wasn't as if I didn't *want* to wash it now that the sweeping was done— I did!— but getting down would mean I'd have to get back up, and I'd either have to crawl to the couch or a chair to drag myself up or wait for help. I *hated* needing help.

Moving even more slowly now, I set the broom aside.

Dumped warm water from the stove into a bowl I thought I could carry, added soap and a rag, then lurched my way to the table.

"Sumi?" Mom sounded worried.

"I'm fine." I meant it to sound confident, but it came out breathy with pain and tears. But I couldn't manage anything better right now.

If I didn't twist but went straight down... if I moved slowly enough, maybe...

Success. I reached the floor without bruising my knees or starting any new cramps. The ache in my back was getting worse, but it didn't have any more choice than I.

Tile. Soap. Rag.

Not the black-veined white marble tile of the damned temple sanctuary, nor the white granite of the temple bedrooms, but the sunbaked reddish-brown clay tiles of the Rest Third. Many houses had *dirt* floors, so I supposed I should be thankful to even have tiles to scrub.

Goddessi, this would have been so much easier with magic.

I scrubbed. Wrung. Scrubbed.

"Sumi? You're doing it again, dear. Humming."

I blinked and shifted just enough to see Mom.

"I just thought," she said softly, "if you didn't like doing that, you might want to know. So you don't hum in front of the others."

"Thank you." I'd *lied* to her and she was worried about helping me hide it from everyone else? My throat tightened for a different reason, this time— Jay's mother was the kindest person I'd ever met.

I scrubbed. My shoulders were burning. I scrubbed some more.

What about an Old Spell?

Maldita wouldn't notice that. She'd never been particularly

19

interested in Old Magic before, almost like it was a blind spot of Hers. It should be safe. Give me a small bit of magic to have and hold.

Carefully, I tightened my focus to the dirt on the floor, just a few tiles, then whispered the words, pushed my breath out to mimic a scream without the noise, wrung my hands.

Thousand Breaths of Wind ripped out of me—

A gust blew across the tiles, taking the dirt to the back door.

And I collapsed, straining to breathe.

"Sumi?"

My back spasmed, long and cruel. When it released me, my eyes were leaking, my middle hollow, my hands shaking, my lungs burning. What had I done wrong? I'd done this spell before, a thousand times, in the damned temple. And I'd tightened my focus.

But I'd only worked big spells when overcharged by the damned sacrifices. Spells use energy—

I remembered the emaciated forms of the demon hunters who'd tried to kill me over and over. Maybe the Old Spells took more energy than *push-pull* magic— had I just not noticed because I'd been well nourished, well rested, and full of the goddess's magic in addition to my own?

"Sumi? Are you all right?"

I laid on the floor and muffled my sobs in my arm. I could breathe. The cramp had lessened and the sharp needles would fade to a duller ache. The emptiness in my center would go away. I just needed something to eat. A nap.

Too bad I couldn't have either of those until the floor was clean.

I wallowed in my self-pity.

Mom sighed, then said, "Sumi, come here."

I wiped my eyes. Rather than stand— which sounded much too difficult— I crawled on my hands and knees to the couch where Mom was half-reclining. Pulled myself up next to her.

She reached, tucked her blankets around me and shared her warmth.

"It doesn't have to be perfect, you know." She patted the blanket over my knee. "A little dirt never hurt anyone."

I sniffled and wiped tears. "I made a promise."

"I'm not saying you shouldn't ever clean, but you're pushing yourself too hard, dear."

My blood-mother had never been kind; it was slowly becoming less strange to hear words of comfort from Jay's mother. "You think so?"

"You're not a goddess. Just one of us mere mortals."

I'd borrowed the power of a goddess once. Been able to do things no mere mortal could do.

I didn't regret giving it up— I didn't!— but sometimes it hurt.

"Thanks, Mom."

"Your bread is improving, Sumi, but if you'll let me help—"

"You're sick!"

"I'm dying," she corrected me. "My children will deny it, but you know it's true."

The touch of her skin on mine shouted that she was right. I didn't even have to reach with my magic— it was all right there, *pushing* at me, despite the aching hollow inside me where my magic had been before I'd used it up on a foolish cleaning spell.

"I've lived a good life. Loved well." She jutted her chin forward and I saw a hint of the determined beauty she must have been in her youth. "They're not ready yet, but I can't last much longer. Until then, I'm going to help you with your baking. First, though, you rest while I tell you about Jay as a baby."

How could I argue with that?

So I sat with her, bowed my head, and listened to the stories of a dying woman as if she were the highest priestess in all the city while the blessed floor dried around us.

~

Jay

JAY SAW THE CLEAN FLOOR AS SOON AS HE OPENED THE DOOR. HE removed his boots, crossed into the house. Took the buckets from the boys and poured them into the cistern for drinking water, then helped them take their boots off and join Sumi and his mom on the couch.

They looked so cozy, the four of them, tucked under blankets and leaning against each other. He wanted to stay. But if he put off begging for his job back for another night, he'd do it again the next night and the next until they starved, and Robin and Dee would never forgive him.

Bad enough he'd nearly let Antero get taken by a Purple woman. Bad enough they didn't have enough to eat because he couldn't constantly care for Sumi and provide for his family at the same time. Bad enough he'd not realized Sumi would need a healer after dying and being brought back to life... and couldn't have paid for one if he had.

Should have taken money from the Temple of the Damned when they fled. More shameful? Less?

He had no choice but to go, so he made sure there was plenty of wood for the stove, added blankets to the pile of his family, shoved his worries to the back of his mind.

He went to his room and changed into his best brown shirt and brown pants. The Rest Third Guard gray leathers gathering dust in his room were off limits until Thom gave him permission. Wasn't a guard yet. Probably should have taken them back to the guardhouse before, but—

Now he was going to ask for permission. He armed himself. Kissed his family goodbye. Walked through the city with his favorite twinned swords at his side and knives in his boots, and watched to see if a thief would try him. Smelled snow on the wind.

They'd get one more snowstorm before true spring, he decided. Then the snow would melt, the river swell, the fields flood, and the irrigation ditches run with life again.

He walked into the guardhouse, into the training room, as if the last year of his life had never happened. Nothing— and everything— had changed.

The room was larger than he remembered, brick walls, wood floor, baked-tile roof, all gray, gray, gray, and echoing with the hails of the guards.

So many new faces.

He climbed the stairs up to the offices and paused in front of Thom's. Feet stuck, shoulders stiff, heart racing more than the climb up the stairs warranted.

"Come in, Jay," Thom said. The man didn't raise his voice, but it cut through the clamor below as if he'd bellowed.

Jay swallowed. He *needed* this job to keep his family fed. He stepped in, stood in front of the desk, straightened. "Sir."

The room was the same. Graywood and simple, more graywood for the desk and chair. Parchment stacked neatly on the shelves along one wall. Thom, the only color in the room, a Blue man going gray.

"Dee says you want your old job back." Head of the Rest Third Guard, Defender of the Peace, Balance Between Light and Dark, Master Thom Yulian, studied him, blue eyes cold. "Why should I give it to you?"

Jay's hands clenched to fists. "I need this job," he said carefully, "and you need my training. I've been training with the Damned Third Guard. Picked up a few more tricks."

"Tricks."

Resting betweens, the man was being difficult.

He'd been like a father to Jay— before Jay's year in the Temple of the Damned, serving the high priestess of Maldita. But Thom had taken that service as an affront, though it hadn't exactly been Jay's fault. He had to make the old man see his worth.

"Sir, I trained with Lena, the Head of the Damned Third Guard. And the men and women who guarded the high priestess."

"Who died."

Snow falling down and Sumi still under his touch. Desperately breathing for *her—*

"Yessir." Now was not the time to think of the past. Lie with the truth... "At the hands of the new high priestess. Not a thing the guards get involved in."

"Succession?" Thom raised his eyebrows.

"Yessir."

"You might be more valuable for what you know of the temple." Thom ran one hand over his mouth and stubble, as if considering. The man looked like he hadn't slept for days.

Jay squared his shoulders. Chose his words carefully. "I will tell you what I can, *if* you hire me to train the guards again."

"You haven't been here since the big snowstorm. The night the last high priestess died. Haven't been training. I understand you brought a woman with you and she's been sick."

Goddessi. How much did the man know? He'd been at the house more than once, but Sumi kept to their bedroom when Thom was around, though Jay was convinced Thom wouldn't recognize her. Thom had met her when she was the high priestess, but now she had no tattoos. Lighter skin, no stripes of black in her red hair. No dark goddess possessing her. "Yessir," he said again. "She's been sick. But she's getting better. And I've been practicing when I can. I'm strong enough. Fast enough—" *to take you down.*

He didn't say the words, but Thom heard them anyway. His blue eyes narrowed, then the man came up out of the chair like he was young.

Resting betweens.

"Let's go then," Thom said quietly. "If you do well enough, I'll let you train 'em. If you don't—"

Jay dipped his chin, keeping his gaze locked on Thom's. A gesture of respect mixed with outright defiance. How he felt right now.

They clomped down the stairs and guards went quiet. Thom rarely left his office.

Maybe this was bigger than he'd thought. His only chance to show Thom he'd still be useful to the guard. His chance to fail — to *not* get the job back, to *not* provide for his family—

No. Jay shoved all of it to the back of his mind and focused on his heel hitting each step, his arms swinging loosely as he walked along the corridor of gaping guards, his jaw clenching, unclenching.

He could be a field worker, maybe, except the Yellows and Oranges fiercely guarded their low-caste job. They wouldn't allow a Brown to join them. The only worse job was night-soil collector. Jay shuddered. He couldn't do that. They'd all starve *and* he'd be miserable shoveling other people's shit.

The practice room brightened as the guards lit more lanterns— no one wanted to miss a single move. The air had chilled when the sun dipped below the horizon, but he'd warm soon enough.

"I need a practice sword." His voice sounded loud in the

hush around him, but he knew the rules. No live steel on the practice floor. Not since he was a new recruit and two second sons from wealthy families had shattered a fancy temple-made sword on a cheap Rest Third blade in a mock fight. Then the fight turned deadly and one of them had nearly killed the other before their unit leader could get between them.

That had been his first introduction to Thom— then the unit leader.

Thom eyed him, nodded. "At least your sense hasn't deserted you completely." He raised his voice. "Get the man a blade."

A Red boy young enough to be the newest recruit handed Jay his practice sword, then took Jay's belt reverently, as if his twinned swords and paired knives were made of gold.

"My name is Mal," the boy breathed worshipfully.

Jay nodded. "You have a practice knife? Can I use that too?"

"Yessir!"

Jay stepped onto the practice floor. Swung the wooden blade to get the feel of it. Flipped the knife so its blade lay along his arm like a shield.

"Throat guard," Thom said sharply.

Rest it— he'd forgotten. Now he looked foolish in front of all the guards he might be teaching tomorrow night.

I need *this job. Need to provide for my family*.

Jay turned to set down the practice blades and found Mal there, taking them from him. Handing him the stiffened leather neck piece. Grinning.

Hoped the boy wasn't going to be a problem.

He could be a healer. Apprentice to one of the Rest Third healers and learn to set bones, sew skin. Watch his patients die when he couldn't magically heal them.

Jay wrapped the leather around his throat, tied it, rolled his shoulders and wiggled his chin to ensure it was in place. Picked up his sword and knife again. Entered the floor and nodded to Thom.

Thom was an old man, for a guard, but he'd grown up wealthy, well-nourished, learning weapons-work as he learned to walk. His hair was graying and his joints bothered him when it rained, but it wasn't raining now. The snowstorm and a steady wind had cleared out the city smoke— torches, cookfires, trash fires— leaving behind a cold, clear sky.

Thom held a sword and a knife, like Jay. He'd been the one to teach this particular skill, so Jay wouldn't have an advantage there. They bowed to each other in unison. Circled.

Thom shifted his weight and they clashed together, their blades blurring— *block, block, block, strike.* Moves Jay had practiced over and over until he didn't have to think about them, intertwined with short bursts of thought.

Overhead. Left block. Twist the blade. Keep your knees bent— watch his left hand! Old man should be stiff from all that sitting but he's not moving like he's— rest it!

Jay defended himself, hoping Thom would tire. *Block, strike, block.* The practice sword was weighted wrong, too heavy at the tip. It dragged on his shoulder muscles.

He hadn't been practicing enough. He wouldn't be able to outlast Thom.

But this was the one job he wanted.

Thom's sword came in on the left and Jay blocked with his knife. The sword smashed into the knife and numbed his arm. Jay danced back, swearing under his breath. Feinted with his own sword while he waited for feeling to come back into that hand. At least he hadn't dropped the knife.

Focus.

They clashed again, trading blows. *Strike, strike, strike, push off—*

Jay spun, whipped his sword around. Thom ducked under it, thrust up from beneath. Barely in time, Jay blocked, twisted.

His feet were off now, and it was all over, but he wouldn't go easily.

Thom forced him back. Circled his sword, bound Jay's, wrenched it out of his grasp and flung it down. Jay saw his opening. He darted forward, inside the range of the sword. Slashed his knife across Thom's throat guard, hooked it on the back of his neck.

"You're dead," he said. He'd done it. Earned his place.

"So're you," Thom growled.

Jay looked down, saw the knife blade positioned to run up under his ribs into his heart. Tricky old man— a magus with a blade, though he didn't actually have magic.

They stood chest to chest, arms locked and straining, breathing each other's air. Jay felt the laugh start in his belly, couldn't stop it. Pushed away from the old man and guffawed.

"Your face," he said, crunching over to try to breathe.

Thom stared at him, then his own face creased and he chortled. Clapped Jay on the back. "Rest it, boy, it's good to have you back."

THREE

S *umi*

WINTER STRUGGLED TOWARD SPRING. THE SNOW MELTED, ICE THAWED and froze again. I missed the heat of the damned temple in winter, the slower pace, the time spent planning for the spring, but— for now— I was free of the dark goddess, and I would take every moment.

Jay had come home with a small gray flying carpet rolled up on his back and a triumphant grin on his face— he got his job back. He wore his guard grays at night when he went to train or to guard the city, and more than once, he told us the story of how the Rest Third Council finally found the money for flying carpets for the guards after the disaster to his unit. His sisters rolled their eyes, but they listened. Every time.

At least something good had come from that night.

Following Mom's suggestions, I made better bread and

cleaned when I could and let Jay help me when I couldn't. He spread himself thin, like a bit of fat over toast. Working with the guard, fetching water with the boys, helping me do everything I couldn't manage. His sisters' schedules were unpredictable and I learned I never knew when anyone would be home, though they all tried to coordinate at least one meal together every week, and usually Jay would cook it, despite Dee's ongoing chiding. She had no idea the grief Jay was saving her— my cooking had been described as *barely adequate* and being in the Rest Third hadn't changed that.

When the first flowers bloomed through the snow, Mom gave in to the inevitable— and her children's nagging— and asked the Rest Third healer to visit. She timed it so we were alone in the house— Robin and Dee and Maggie working and Jay fetching water with the boys.

The spare Green woman appeared in the doorway as if from nowhere. She brought an aura of confidence with her, even if she had no healing magic, and she poked and prodded until Mom waved her away. The healer dragged a chair close to the couch and sat, face grave.

I settled next to Mom and offered her my hand, and she took it, grinding the bones until she realized.

The healer said words, but they sounded far away. I didn't need them anyway— I knew.

She was always cold, despite heaps of blankets, trapped in the past more than the present, her appetite failing her. Dying, like she'd said, and the healer confirmed it.

I'd seen this sickness before, in the halls of the Temple of the Damned. Without magic, the body grew odd lumps and wasted away, but a proficient healer could *push* and *pull* the sickness out for a time— yes, even this far gone.

Without magic, death came hard, as it was coming for Jay's mother.

Jay would be devastated. He'd brought me back when I was on the cusp of dead and gone, but he could do nothing for his mom, and it hurt him.

If I'd dared, I might have been able to save her. I wasn't a particularly practiced healer; there were many more skilled than I. But those I knew resided in the Damned Third, and we in the Rest Third, and the damned and the blessed had already refused his sisters' petitions for help. It would hurt Mom— and how strange to call a woman *Mom* as if mothers were not another source of pain and shame, but this woman had become my mother in the way my own never was— if I used my magic on her, *pushed* and *pulled* out her sickness. But she would survive. At least for a short time longer.

She was old, for those of the Rest Third. How much longer *could* she live? Magic could extend life only so far.

The Rest Third healer left and shut the door behind her. Mom continued to clutch my hand, and we sat in silence until Jay came in. He poured drinking water into the cistern as solemnly as any magus performing a ceremony.

"Bluejay?" Mom blinked up at him and smiled. "Help me sit up."

"You feel better." His gentle hands lifted her, propped her. "The healer helped."

"Yes, I feel better." She took his hand and mine. "I am so glad you have each other."

A hint of blush touched her yellow skin, the whites around her yellow eyes brightened. I swallowed my tears and put on a brave face. I'd seen this before. The sudden surge of energy right before the end.

Time to say goodbye.

I went to the front door, almost reached for my magic, almost *pushed* my voice to the boys, snatched it back at the last moment. My heart thundered and sweat beaded at my hairline. Goddessi, I'd almost ruined it all, for a moment of carelessness.

"Wilyam." I cleared my throat and tried calling again. *No magic.* "Wilyam, Antero! Come talk to your grandmother."

They came thundering in from the street, smelling of little-boy sweat and spring, in layers of cotton and wool in browns and yellows, hand-me-downs from Jay's youngest sister. They kicked off their boots and ran across the floor and slowed to carefully lean against Mom, both of them babbling like a brook over the rocks.

"The snow is melting, just like you said—"

"It didn't kill your flowers—"

"—the white ones—"

"—and yellow—"

"They're perking up again—"

"And we swept the walk just in case—"

"—you want to go out!" they finished together. Wilyam peeked at me, inviting me along.

"Thank you," Mom said. "You're growing so fast. I think I can *hear* it."

We all paused, listening intently.

Mom beamed. "Do you hear it?"

"I did." Jay clapped them on their backs. "Next week they'll be as tall as me."

Giggles.

"Ask a neighbor to find Dee and Robin and Maggie." A good day like this was so rare now, they'd come. "And after them, Thom."

"Kisses first." Mom offered her cheek.

"Mwah." Wilyam kissed her cheek.

Antero clutched Wilyam's hand. He glanced at me. After that foul magus in the damned temple, we'd had the conversation over and over again that Antero could refuse to touch or be touched and I would support his choice. Even if Mom didn't remember.

Shyly, quick as a bird, Antero kissed her cheek, then ran for the door. Wilyam yelped and darted after. They were bright and curious and exhausting, and I was so glad we'd gotten them away from the Temple of the Damned. They deserved to live like this— in a family full of love. The room seemed darker with them gone.

Jay's mother sensed it. Her fingers shook. "Son."

"Mom, we'll get your garden in order—"

"Your father is so proud of you." His father had been dead for years, but she forgot sometimes, especially with her Brown son who looked so much like his Brown father. But even with her mind clouded, she was still kind. She took his hand. "I'm proud of you."

Jay kissed her forehead. "You'll love sitting surrounded by your flowers. A couple days and it'll be warm enough."

"That sounds wonderful. You'll take care of Sumi? She doesn't know the Rest Third."

I winced, but she was right.

"I will, Mom." He grinned. "She's mine."

He could never know I might have been able to heal her. He'd never forgive me.

"Sumi, my new daughter, you take care of those boys and let Jay take care of you."

"I will. Thank you for—" *sharing your home with me, loving me when my own mother hadn't, raising a son who would see past Maldita's tattoos and love me anyway*— "everything."

How does one say goodbye?

"Mom?" Dee burst through the door. Brown, like her brother, a city guard like her brother, hard over kindness, like her brother. She reminded me of Lena, the head guard of the Damned Third, not in looks but in bold speech and sly humor.

"Chickadee."

Jay shifted to stand behind me and Dee took his place. "Maggie's coming," she said, "but look at you. The healer came? She helped? You look better!"

"I feel better."

Robin came next— the only one who had inherited Mom's color— her bright yellow hair bound back for guard duty. She dropped to her knees next to the couch, her sword's sheath catching, then sliding across the tile.

"Damn the blessed and bless the damned." Robin brushed Mom's yellow-gray hair off her faded, wrinkled forehead. The words had the ring of repetition now, and a hint of defeat.

"Now, Robin. Cursing won't help anything."

"But *I* feel better."

"I know, dear."

The boys came in and Maggie behind them, bustle and noise. Wilyam came to me, touched my arm— as much reassurance for him as for me— then he and Antero fled for their tiny, curtained alcove on the back wall. Maggie shucked her sword and knives, then threw herself across her mother and sobbed.

Mom pressed her lips together, but the lines around her eyes deepened. I wanted to tell the girl she was hurting her mother, but Mom chose to let her stay. She stroked Maggie's hair. "My little Magpie."

"This is all my fault. They should have cured you." Maggie sniffled "If I'd just—"

"Don't say that." Dee sideways-hugged Maggie.

Robin said, "The damned made their own choices. We helped them with the demon hunters but—"

"There were... complications." Dee frowned. "With the change in leadership of Temple of the Damned."

34

"You helped them. You helped them and now they didn't help us. I hate them."

Jay and I kept silent. Another burden of guilt for us both, since *I* was the complication. My blood-sister had taken over as the damned high priestess, and she had no love for the Rest Third. I could take my place back... but I would have to admit I was still alive. Go back to the temple. Allow Maldita to possess me.

"They made their choices." Jay set one hand on my shoulder. "And we made ours."

"Good choices," Mom insisted breathlessly.

Maggie heard it in her voice and shifted to the side. "Sorry, Mama. Is this okay?"

"Of course. My babies could never hurt me."

"You're the best mom," Robin said.

Maggie smiled and wiped her tears. "Don't ever leave us."

Dee closed her eyes. Of them all, I suspected she best knew. "Love you, Mom."

"My family." Mom's eyes fluttered and she slouched deeper into the pillows. She kept stroking Maggie's hair, but her hand slowed. "I love you, my family."

Jay saw it. "Rest now, Mom. Don't push yourself too hard." He helped Maggie get up so she didn't hurt Mom further. "You're mid-shift," he said. "They'll expect you back."

Maggie pouted. Lifted her chin. Sighed. "You're right." She bent and gathered her weapons.

"Little sister, you've grown up." Jay smiled.

"Big brother, you've gotten old and stuffy," Maggie sniped back, but she didn't mean it. I'd learned that over the past few months— they never meant the barbs.

"Widowed, with a new wife," he said, shooting a glance at me, "and two kids."

Jay had sworn to me as my Shadow, which meant we were

married in the Damned Third, but the high priestess was *dead*, so widowed. Except not, because I wasn't really dead— and living with him in the Rest Third, so married again... Our lives were complicated by all the secrets we kept.

"I have to get back as well." Robin rose to her feet and hugged each of us in turn. "Maggie, stay safe tonight."

"You first."

They left arm in arm, and Dee followed behind. The lines in Mom's face eased and a tiny snore escaped her mouth.

"I love you," Jay told me.

I glanced up. I still hadn't gotten used to those words from him, so often, so easy. But I wasn't objecting. I'd *died* and now every moment was precious. "I love you too."

He held out his hands. I took them and let him help me to my feet. I leaned on him less and less each time, though I still had bad days along with the good. Since the boys had cleared the walk, I would dare a few steps outside, under the weak spring sunlight. Not too long— too much sun on my red skin might bring out the faint shadow-tattoos. Jay assured me over and over he couldn't see them, but I could. Could trace each line and curve over my skin. Could close my eyes and remember the feel of them drinking in the blood from the sacrifices—

"Hello?" Thom came in the doorway, rushed to Mom's side. "I heard—"

Before I could escape to the bedroom, before I could cringe away, before Jay could blink or move in front of me, Thom saw me and froze. I'd been so careful, over the months, to be in our bedroom whenever he'd been here with Mom and now, all that care was undone.

Master Thom Yulian, Head of the Rest Third Guard, Defender of the Peace, Balance Between Light and Dark— Thom Yulian of the Yulian Merchants, the richest Blue family in the Rest Third— Thom Yulian who had met with me in my former life as the high priestess of Maldita, knew how to look beyond the surface appearance and spot the person hiding underneath— *that* Thom stared at me as if he knew me.

Bless it.

◆

Jay

Thom stared at Sumi like he was seeing a ghost. Considering everyone thought her dead, he was. But her hair and skin were lighter red, her eyes no longer bloody lid to lid nor black when the dark goddess stole her body, her clothes no longer the brief halter top and shorts of the temple but a motley of colors covering her from fingertip to ankle, the little skin showing no longer covered in the black prayers of Maldita.

And those in the Rest Third couldn't change the shade of their skin or hair the way the damned could and did. Did Thom know that?

Jay held his breath, wondering if after three long months, Sumi's secret would be revealed.

Then slowly Thom smiled. "So you're the woman who captured our Jay's heart. They've kept you hidden, haven't they? Worried I might steal you away from this one?"

Jay whooped out his relief, covered it with an outstretched hand, clasped Thom's. "This is Sumi," he said. "Sumi, Thom. My— the head of the Rest Third Guard."

Sumi smiled weakly, more of a faint lift of her lips. "Thom. I'm pleased to finally meet you."

"They've told me much about you. Escaped the temple, nearly died in the storm. More fragile than I'd expected my boy to fall for."

37

"I'm not as fragile as I look." Sumi's chin lifted, but her words were even. "And I'm getting better."

"That you are. That you are." Thom smiled again, then turned to Mom, who had opened her eyes again. "You, though..." He crouched and took her hand. "You're as pretty as the first day I saw you."

"Liar," Mom gasped, but she smiled too, pleased.

Jay's heart twisted. That a Blue had fallen in love with a Yellow was a miracle, even if they'd decided to hide that relationship from the rest of the city, him at his house and her at hers. Their relationship had begun and deepened while Jay had been secluded in the Temple of the Damned. It had shocked him to return home and discover it, and now, when all he wanted for his mother was her happiness, his heart ached to see them like this. Would they lose each other so quickly?

Give them some privacy. He drew Sumi away to their bedroom, the only place they could be alone in his mother's house. As always, his weapons were displayed on the walls, stacked on the floor, but now what few clothes they had gathered for Sumi were piled next to his own.

She stooped to pick up a shirt. Swayed. Straightened.

He reached to support her if she needed it. Hated seeing her like this as much as he hated seeing his mother hurting. In the temple, Sumi'd had everything— servitors, new clothes whenever she wanted them, power. Now she had nothing of her own and no strength.

But she had him and he had her—

It had to be enough.

"Come outside with me today?"

Sumi glanced through the door to Thom beyond. "What if—"

Jay stepped close, brushed his lips against her ear. "He

didn't recognize you. If he didn't, no one will. Come outside with me. Please. You're strong enough now."

She rested her head against his chest. "For a few minutes."

Her body nestled against his reminded him how long it had been since they'd loved. He ached for it, but she was still too weak, so he stepped back. "Now? Since the boys cleared the walk."

"After we cut my hair."

"Cut your—" He ran one fingertip over the fall of red. Followed the curve of a curl.

Sumi arched against him.

Not helping.

For one long moment, he imagined she was strong and well and he could kiss every part of her body. Then he set her away from him. Thought of the boys and the neighborhood and a clear blue sky, waiting for them.

Fetched a knife and a trash bag.

"Do you want Robin or Dee to do this?"

"No." She finger-combed her hair, brought it forward around her face, then shoved it back. "No. I should have done this as soon as we left the temple, but I wasn't strong enough to bear one more thing." She met his gaze as if she were the high priestess again. "I'm strong enough now. Cut it off. A little ragged matches the new me."

He clamped down on a surge of emotion— guilt and love and desire. She could have everything— *everything*— but she'd chosen him. And freedom from the dark goddess.

As carefully as he could, he sawed through the strands. Evened them. Cut a little more until he was satisfied.

The Sumi who stared back at him was a different person from the high priestess of Maldita he'd met long ago. This Sumi seemed lighter, more alive, more joyful.

"Done." He set the knife down, ran his fingers through her chin-length strands.

She lifted her chin. "All right. Now." She followed him out through the living room to the front door, hesitated behind him on the threshold.

The boys rocketed past them, whooping for joy, jostling her.

Sumi's mouth tightened in pain, but she didn't cry out, didn't reach for him, didn't collapse.

Progress.

Still, he hovered, one hand on her elbow and ready to sweep her up into his arms if she started to fall.

The air was warming but still had a teasing bite of winter to it. Fine, powdery snow dusted roofs and walks. Wilyam and Antero slid across a bit of ice, much like they'd slid across the living room floor, whooping and hollering. Other children peeped out of their houses and a few even emerged.

He tried to see the neighborhood through her eyes. Shabby. Small houses crowded with too many people, small vegetable and fruit gardens stuffed into every bit of land, dormant for the winter. Mostly lower-caste colors here— Greens, Oranges, Yellows, which was why Wilyam— a Red— and Antero— a Purple— stood out. And why the other kids hesitated to play with them, still, after three months.

But their natural jubilance wore down the other kids, like it always did now, and soon enough the street filled with running, laughing, playing kids of all Colors. So different from the dark temple, where the kids ran and laughed and played only under the supervision of their teacher— no parents— while reciting Maldita's prayers.

Sumi closed her eyes and lifted her face to the sun, and Jay's breath caught. The light caressed her eyelids, her cheeks, her lips, and he wanted to kiss everywhere the light touched... but she was still fragile, so instead he drank her in with his eyes.

Her steps were slow and cautious, but they were steady, thank the goddessi. More than once he'd thought she hadn't really survived. That he'd dreamt sharing his breath— his life— with her and this Sumi was just a shade of the one he'd left behind in the temple. That she'd sickened again and died in the night and this was all a dream he'd escaped to when he couldn't face reality.

He sucked in a deep breath. The sky was blue, the air cold, smelling of snow and supper. His bad knee ached faintly.

This was real.

"What's— what's that?"

He looked where she was looking. Spotted paint on the neighbor's wall, a diamond shape, quartered, in red, orange, yellow, green. He squinted. Maybe even blue and purple, under the other layers. "Demon hunters," he muttered under his breath. No one else would dare. Despite all their losses when the damned high priestess had been killed— he glanced at Sumi and saw she hadn't heard— they still skulked about the city, the resting betweens only knew why.

"Nothing," he said more loudly. Smiled at her.

A neighbor yelled for her kid. Sumi flinched from the sound. Turned her head to locate it, then once she had, her shoulders came down. She shivered.

"That's enough for one day." He thought she might object— used to telling everyone else what to do rather than being told — but either she was even more fragile than he'd thought or the shout had frightened her. Maybe the paint on top of that, even if she hadn't understood *who* had marked the wall.

She looked around warily. Nodded.

The house seemed smaller when they turned. He caught Sumi's hand and held her back from opening the door. Lowered his voice so Thom wouldn't hear. "Do you miss it?" *The dark temple, the servants, the luxury, the power...*

41

"Miss it?" Sumi's brow wrinkled.

"Everything you had. Before."

"The—" She gazed off into the distance, toward the Damned Third, then returned her gaze to him. "No."

"Your rooms were bigger than this house."

She examined his face as if she'd heard more than he'd said aloud. Smiled. "Can't say I love cleaning. Sometimes I miss mangoes. But I don't miss *Her*. Ever. And here I have you, and the boys, and your family."

Maldita, the dark goddess— he didn't miss Her either. He drew Sumi into a hug. "It's good to see you outside."

"Like you said, it's time. I can't live my life afraid."

"I love you."

She twined her fingers in his and drew him inside the house. After the sun, the shadows were deep and his guts clenched with foreboding.

Don't be stupid, he told himself. *Everything will be fine.*

Thom looked up at their entrance. Made an effort to hide his sorrow, but it was obvious in the deep grooves on his face. He ran one hand over his graying blue hair. "Your mom's sleeping again." He pressed a kiss to her forehead. Stood. Jay and Thom clapped each other on the back. "See you at training tonight, Son."

"I'll be there." As soon as one of his sisters was home to stay with Sumi and Mom.

Thom nodded sharply and left.

Sumi drifted over to Jay's mom, ran her fingers over her forehead, frowned. She looked up at Jay, sorrow and shadows etching lines in her face. "I think—"

He shook his head. Rejected the very thought of it. "I don't want to talk about it." He'd seen death before, never more often or more ugly than in his time at the Temple of the Damned, but

— *She's dying*. Seeing his mother falter and fail... if they never said the words, maybe it wouldn't happen.

"All right." Sumi pressed a kiss to the corner of his mouth, then sat at his mom's feet.

He tucked the blankets around them both and started assembling dinner.

Mom never woke again.

CHAPTER
FOUR

S *umi*

JAY'S MOTHER SLIPPED INTO A DEATH-SLEEP. SHE WOULDN'T ROUSE TO eat or drink, her chest barely moved. Her children knew her time was coming.

Gloom shrouded them. They each grieved in their own way and in their own time— Robin going silent and grim, Dee pouring herself into her work with the guards, Maggie alternating false joy with weeping and wailing. And Jay wrapping himself around me night and day as if he could somehow prevent any more death.

The boys didn't seem to notice, except they rarely let me out of their sight.

I felt stronger every day, as if I was taking Mom's life from her— though I wasn't. Every time my magic rose, I buried it deeper, and every day I walked farther and farther under the sun with Jay, tangling his hand in mine.

The first time I saw the flying pallets— *pallets* for Maldita's sake, and boards and even once a bucket, though the bucket didn't make it up past the roofline— I'd ducked for cover. The second, I'd stared, horrified at the rickety, jagged paths the barely magicked boards had made. The third, Jay murmured that the wealthiest among the poor had to transport themselves and their goods *somehow*. After that, they became almost common place. Almost.

It rained in the morning, great blobby drops that filled the rain barrel and splashed mud up onto the paths, and grounded the blessed flying pallets, but after breakfast the rain lifted and Wilyam and Antero swept the walk. They spent a few minutes hovering over Mom but as soon as Jay put on his favorite double-swords and I my boots, they jammed feet in their own boots and burst through the door. We trailed after them.

Gray clouds parted, allowing shafts of springlight to fall on patches of gardens and roofs and sometimes my face. I spotted more of those multicolored, quartered diamonds on walls, sometimes discreet and sometimes bold, and had a nasty feeling that I knew what they meant.

Just because we'd left the temple, killed the demon hunters who had invaded it, didn't mean they were gone. And the way Jay's face had scrunched when I'd asked— But I was hidden and they wouldn't find me.

I walked faster, my strides longer. Sooner than I expected, we were poised to leave our little neighborhood for the next one over, a part of the Rest Third I hadn't seen before. Before we crossed the street— a ribbon of cobblestones narrower than the temples' largest flying carpets— Jay pulled me to a stop.

"Careful," he said. "Our closest neighbors all know you. They know me. No one out here knows you."

"What are you saying?" My arms and back were loose and I felt *good*.

"It's different in the Rest Third. You— we— are nobodies. Not low-caste but not high-caste either. Just..." He glanced at Wilyam and Antero. "Let's avoid problems."

Caste again. Even without Maldita screaming in my head that the only Colors that mattered were red for blood, white for bone, black for souls, I didn't understand it. What did Color have to do with a person's inherent worth?

But looking at the boys, I hesitated. As I was no longer in the guise of a high priestess with bloody eyes and black tattoos, Wilyam, a Red, looked like me. Antero, however, was highest-caste Purple—

"Should we send the boys home?" I couldn't bear it if anything happened to them. Either of them.

"No." Jay ran one hand over his brown curls. His hair needed to be trimmed again. His eyes darted back and forth, but he turned my own words back on me. "We can't live in fear. We'll be fine."

Had something already happened with them they hadn't told me about? They went every day for water— My feet felt stuck to the cobblestones.

The boys must have overheard us. Wilyam took Jay's hand and Antero— a little desperately— took mine and tugged.

We crossed.

Likely I imagined it, after Jay's little speech, but the air didn't smell as sweet, even if the houses were one room larger, in better repair. Men and women didn't smile as easily, even if their clothes were richer. Not much, but enough to notice.

Antero faltered, shrank in on himself.

Jay glanced at me, at him. "Boys, I was already mad for the guard at your age. Did you know that? My dad was a guard and I was going to be a guard and nothing else would do."

"Really?" Wilyam stared up at Jay. "I'm going to be a guard too!"

He would never be allowed. Not if either temple found out the strength of his *push-pull* magic.

"I don't know..." Jay curled up his arm, lifting the boy off his feet. "You have to be strong. Smart—"

"I'm strong! I'm smart!"

Jay set him on his feet. "Able to be quiet."

Wilyam stumbled. Yelped. Pretended to close his lips and lock them shut. The moment of silence wouldn't last long.

"You can't do it, Wil," Antero said, pulling me forward. "I know."

Jay grinned.

Wilyam's face turned bright red at his efforts not to speak. I giggled and he burst out laughing.

Sounds of work slowed my feet. We turned the next corner and strangeness met my eyes. The hair rose on the back of my neck.

I hadn't realized we were so close to the Blessed Third.

For a breath, I panicked, felt inside for any stirrings from the dark goddess.

But other than that faint sense that She would possess me if I came to Her attention, She was as still as if She wasn't there.

Instead of a sleepy row of houses, men and women dressed in white were working— one group smashing down a house, another group carrying away debris, a third group building a wall. Thanks to the rain, the air was clear, but the streets and the blessed servitors were mud to their chests. And it wasn't a small project... the line of new wall extended back toward the river, as if the Blessed Third had reached out and swallowed a chunk of the Rest Third.

"What in heaven is going on?" I whispered.

"Heaven is right." Jay scowled. He left us behind, approached a blessed guard, a Purple woman who rested one hand on her sword, pointed with the other.

Beyond her, a familiar Yellow-Orange man.

I squinted. Couldn't breathe.

Zerth—

Lightning from my hands. Maldita possessing me, out of control. It took all my strength to guide Her, to keep Her from striking my people.

That one, *I told Her. Showed her the demon hunters. Helped Her strike them down— until their leader, Zerth, fought me spell-to-spell.*

I grabbed his neck, nails gouged his skin, drew blood, then Maldita took him, burning him from inside.

Blood, bone, soul.

"No— he's dead."

"Mom?"

The man turned away, disappeared, before I could make my feet move— chase him or flee and I wasn't sure which.

"Mom?" Wilyam tugged on my arm. "Are you okay?"

Zerth was dead. I'd watched as the dark goddess took him. Whoever that was, I must have been mistaken. He wasn't here, in the City of Temples, less than a block away from me, because he was *dead*.

Antero and Wilyam both stared up at me. I blinked away my thoughts and smiled. "I'm fine."

Wilyam nodded, but Antero looked like he didn't believe me. "What do you think the guard is saying?" I asked, desperate to shift my thoughts.

"Most boring job ever," Wilyam muttered.

Antero cocked his head. He whispered, "Could we *pull* their words to us?"

"Yes," I said with a small grin. Too late, I thought of all the conversations they probably shouldn't overhear... but these two had never been sheltered, so I shrugged. "Too late, for now. Here comes Jay."

We watched the servitors build and destroy and chant their prayers to Bendita while Jay walked back to us.

He scowled. "The resting owners of the resting houses owed the blessed too much money, so the blessed took their homes. They're tearing them down to add to some sort of children's play area. Grass and flowers."

"The whole row of them?" My gaze wandered along the construction.

Jay nodded. Drew me away. "One of our guards used to live there," he said, eyes still fixed on the mess of mud and brick. "Good man. Didn't get into debt."

Ah, bless it.

The waste of it. They were tearing down *houses* to put in *grass*? When these people needed houses and food so badly? The Blessed were expanding their borders, pushing into the Resting Third, probably lying to do it. And I knew exactly who was to blame.

The high priestess of Bendita.

My blood-mother.

Bless her to heaven.

"Come on." Jay tugged gently on my hand.

I turned away, bringing the boys with me, and sudden exhaustion slowed my feet. I'd pushed too far, too fast, and then with this new realization...

"I need to rest a moment."

"Can you make it to the next block?" His mouth was grim. He didn't have the flying carpet he used for guard duties, didn't carry it except for work, and it wouldn't fit more than two of us anyway. "I don't want you here, so close to..."

To the blessed.

He was worried too. And he didn't know Maldita still lived inside me.

"The next block is fine." I pushed my steps as fast as I could, leaned on his arm. Put one foot in front of the other.

My back ached and my knees complained bitterly.

One more step, then one more after that.

"Jay!" Thom called out.

My head came up. Thom didn't have a carpet either. My entire body yearned for one. Perhaps even a blessed pallet, goddessi help me.

"Did you see—?" Jay yanked his hand from Antero's to point at Thom. "What in the resting betweens are those—"

"The blessed?" Thom looked confused.

"Why didn't you stop them?"

"Ah." Thom ran his hand over his short, graying blue hair. He offered his arm for me to lean on, and Wilyam abandoned me to run on with Antero.

Left with no choice but to touch a man who could ruin my life if he discovered who I was— who I had been— I gripped Thom's forearm and concentrated on the next step.

Scowling, Jay took my other arm and we continued on. "That's all you have to say?"

"The rest of us were holding everything together while you were parading around the damned temple." Thom matched his stride to mine, as if he'd done it before. Of course— he'd done this for Mom.

Jay growled under his breath. "I wasn't—"

"Then you spent all your time with your woman." He looked down at me. "No offense."

"She nearly died!"

Did die, actually, and he brought me back.

One more step, then another.

"Son— Jay." Thom's voice was harsh when he said, "When one of them decide they want a thing... When one of those high priestessi get a thought in their devious little heads... There's nothing the rest of us can do."

Jay glanced at me, the previous, devious high priestess of the damned, then looked away. "But—"

Thom would hate me if he knew. All of them would. I'd be alone again. It would break me, but it might kill Jay. He felt things so deeply.

Thom scowled as if he'd heard my thoughts, but his words — "I couldn't even save one man. How could I save a whole house? A row of 'em?"

I flushed. He'd tried to rescue Jay from the damned temple. I hadn't let him. I didn't regret it— I didn't!— but it hurt me that I had hurt this man.

So strange, knowing a previous adversary, now almost a member of the family, and worrying for him.

Jay's arm was tense under my hand, as if he wanted to hit something. Maybe he was remembering too. "I'm sorry I wasn't here," he said softly.

The boys yelled out greetings and I looked up long enough to see we were home. Thank the goddessi. Just a few more steps and I could sit.

We walked down the path. I wanted to tell Jay and Thom to go ahead, but I wouldn't make it without them.

I hated this. Hated being weak. Hated getting tired. Less than a year ago, I'd been healthy, at the height of my power. Now I couldn't even walk around the neighborhood—

"Were you looking for us?" Jay stopped.

My knees shook. "Jay—"

"I was." Thom patted my arm. "Come on. It's time."

"Time?" My voice was weak.

"She's going."

Jay slid out from under my arm, strode into the house. Left Thom to take my weight. "Mom?"

A few more steps.

Thom deposited me at the end of Mom's bed. I couldn't bend to undo my boots, I was so tired. Her breaths were shallow, with long pauses and an ominous rattle.

Jay loomed and Robin paced and Dee and Maggie cried and the boys clung to me.

Mom breathed and breathed, and then Jay bent to whisper in her ear. His voice was gruff with tears, but he told her, "It's okay, Mom. We'll be okay. You can rest now."

And, as if she'd only been waiting to hear that, Mom stopped.

Finally, after her long fight, she was gone.

My fault. If I'd only dared use *push-pull* magic—

But I'd made my choice.

And let someone else pay for it.

Goddessi help me, I was a monster.

~

Jay

His mother was gone.

He had duties. Rituals for comfort. He dismissed the moistness in his eyes as weakness, swallowed the ache in his gut down where it belonged. Caught Robin's gaze and nodded to her to start the death rituals.

First, send the boys around to the neighbors who would miss Mom. Tell them of her passing and the five-day mourning confinement. To the guardhouse— a trainer missing shifts wouldn't be a problem, but three guards and the head guard missing would, if Thom didn't have others ready to cover—

No, first discover Thom's intentions.

Jay tried to speak. Cleared his throat. Swallowed hard. Tried again. "Thom? Are you—"

"Staying." The man looked old, his normally stern face falling deeper into grief. "I'm staying, Jay. If you'll have me."

"Maggie can— or Dee—"

"I'll be comfortable on the floor."

"Very well." He ran a hand over his mouth, his chin. Ignored the stubble there. The head guard in grief confinement for five days might be a bit more challenging for the Rest Third guards, but what was a second in command for? So— now, send the boys to tell the world Mom had passed. "Boys?"

Wilyam scowled but Antero pushed him toward the door. "It's our job," he hissed. "As the youngest."

Dee wiped her eyes. Sniffled. Nodded. Wordlessly agreed she and Robin and Maggie would prepare the body.

The box from the foot of the couch seemed heavier now it was time to open it. Still, he hefted it, carried it to the back yard, set it down on the brick path.

He'd made these bricks with Dad, helped gather the mud from their own yard and sand from the desert to the west and straw from a local farmer, helped mix it all together. Begged the neighbor— a Blue family— for the use of their molds, then watched while the Blue man and his own Brown dad had filled the molds, talked together like equals. Had watched for cracks and discarded the bad bricks, then a week later, had helped Dad set the bricks into a path in the yard.

Had watched his father's funeral on these same bricks.

And now his mother.

Sumi made a sound behind him. He leaned back into her softness for a moment, then straightened.

There was an art to laying the wood. The frame of it— common brownwood— had to support the body while leaving space underneath for the funeral woods. Greywood mostly, symbolic of the Rest Third, some yellowwood for Mom's Color, brownwood and more yellowwood for her children. A bit of bluewood for Thom. Slivers of redwood and purplewood for Sumi and Wilyam and Antero.

No blackwood. No whitewood. Those belonged to the temples.

He set aside a piece of yellowwood. Built the bier. At some point, Sumi tired and returned inside, but he barely noticed. Continued placing each piece of wood just so and used wooden nails to fasten a few key pieces. Retrieved his knife and shaved the last piece of wood into kindling. Left the long-handled match in the box. Looked up at the clouded sky and scowled, then put the lid back on the box, just in case.

Stood and stared down at what he'd built. It was sturdy enough.

She'd lived a good life. Loved and been loved. No goddess had taken her, so her soul should go to the resting betweens and find his father's.

It had to— he had to believe that with all his heart... believe her soul would find joy, in the betweens, if they existed. Had to — for someone as wonderful as his mom.

His dad had wanted a yellowbush— yellow flowers in the spring and yellow and orange leaves in the fall— as a way to remind them all he had loved his Yellow wife with all his heart. The bush grown in his father's ashes sat at the corner of the house, near enough that even if they had to sell the back patch of ground, they'd still have his memory.

Mom wanted a brownwood tree, so the box nearest the yellowbush would never again bear vegetables. At least their ashes could be together, since he wasn't sure he believed anyone who said they knew what came after death.

Dirt on his hands and streaking his face, he went to the market and paid the last of his coin for a brownwood sapling.

The seller observed his silence. Directed him to the strongest tree in the bunch. Gave him a kind price when he couldn't argue against it. Jay bowed his head and brought the tree home and set it next to the bush.

He fetched a shovel, dug its hole.

Noted the sun dipping toward the western mountains. Returned to the house.

The girls had washed Mom's face, then mixed wash water with dirt from the yard and painted their cheeks and Sumi's and Thom's with vertical streaks of mud, reminiscent of tears. They'd wrapped the body in her favorite blanket. Jay stooped to pick it up.

Wilyam and Antero came in the front door and stopped on the threshold.

"We're done," Wilyam said solemnly. "The neighbors, and the guard too."

Thom nodded his thanks.

Dee shushed them, beckoned them in, streaked mud on their faces.

The boys shuffled their feet and Wilyam opened his mouth, but Sumi crossed to them, drew them both into loose hugs, and he subsided. This ritual would be new to them, coming from the Temple of the Damned where the rituals gave souls to the dark goddess Maldita, and sometimes the bodies too—

No, he couldn't focus on them now. They'd be fine. He had to focus on the ritual for his mother, to give his grief the proper outlet, to keep it from ripping him apart.

He'd never been without her before, even when he'd been far away, and now—

He lifted the body, cradled it, tried to remember this was what was left of his mother after her soul had gone on. She— *it* — was so light.

His family and Thom— though since he was staying for the

funeral and confinement, Thom was family now— trailing behind him, he carried the body to the back yard and set it on the bier.

Thom brought a chair for Sumi and helped her sit. The boys arranged themselves at her sides. Dee and Robin and Maggie tucked sweet-smelling herbs under Mom's favorite blanket and into the wood crevices.

They all stepped back and faced west.

Waited for the sun to touch the rooftops, since they couldn't see the horizon.

Then spoke the only words they were allowed for the next five days.

We commend this body and its soul to the resting betweens, out of the grasp of the damned. Out of the grasp of the blessed. Free from the pains and sorrows and debts of this life. To everlasting rest. May all be at peace, forever more.

As the funeral words flowed from his mouth, he had to wonder what the difference was between this prayer and the prayers to Maldita, Bendita. But no one believed in Them in the Rest Third, so who exactly were they praying to?

Knowing the others were doing the same, Jay touched his palms together in front of his heart then opened them outward.

Sumi smothered a gasp.

From her perspective, words and gestures... it looked like heresy— their own Old Spell, akin to what she used when she called fire or wind or—

No— not now, while his mother's body lay in front of him. He'd think on it later.

He turned and retrieved the match from the funeral box. Handed it to Maggie. She struck it. Stooped and set it to the kindling, then dashed it against the bier as if she couldn't bear it. Dee and Robin took her hands and the three of them watched, tears running down their faces. The kindling smoldered, then abruptly the body was ablaze, plumes of smoke and sparks drifting up into the evening sky.

The clouds darkened from sunset oranges and reds and pinks to purples and grays. The stench of the burning body rose up all round them. Thom and Sumi were stoic, but Maggie and the boys screwed up their faces like they were going to gag. Robin and Dee braced against Maggie, and Sumi gathered the boys close.

The cinders and the smoke and the smell reminded him of the sacrifices Sumi had made in the pits of the Temple of the Damned. Sat like a rock in his gut and he wanted to puke and punch the goddessi themselves—

Anger was so much easier than grief, but today and for the next five days, he needed to grieve. He needed to honor his mother.

Jay turned to put the sapling into the ground, but the fires shifted from yellow to bright white, casting shadows across the yard and burning his eyes.

He whipped his head around and stared at Sumi. She was ashen and horrified, her eyes darting back and forth. It wasn't her.

The boys.

Wilyam glared at the fire, tongue caught between his teeth. Antero glanced at it out of the corner of his eyes, but his fist clenched.

And now Jay knew their tells for doing magic.

He'd have to thank the boys for hurrying the process, even if it did put them at risk. Didn't know how he'd bear five days of watching his mother's body burn.

He cleared his throat. When Sumi looked, he glanced at the boys, then turned his back on the fire. She'd handle them.

He could pretend his mother's body wasn't crumbling in on itself.

He rolled his shoulders, hefted up the brownwood sapling, then settled it into its hole. Pushed half the dirt in around it. When the body had finished burning, they'd mix the dirt with her ash and fill the rest of the hole. And his mother would nourish her tree.

Rest, Mom, he told her soul. *You belong to neither Maldita nor Bendita, unlike the rest of us. Be at peace.*

CHAPTER

FIVE

S *umi*

THE FIRE BURNED HIGH AND THE MAGIC IN IT REACHED OUT TO THE magic in me, like hot sun on cold toes.

The magic might be warm, but I was cold. If I gave in, if Maldita found us— I fought it down, didn't let it win. I'd *pushed* back the dark goddess Maldita Herself in Her rages. But my fear was harder to restrain.

Would anyone notice two boys doing magic? It was careful and controlled. If I hadn't been so close, so sensitive, I wouldn't have felt it. Would Thom? He had no magic, but he was smart— would he realize the flames were too bright, too hot? Who would he blame? Living with us in the heart of our house, in the presence of their magic, how could he not realize who I was and where I belonged?

I wasn't going back.

I *deserved* this escape. The boys *deserved* it too, and they didn't understand how badly they were jeopardizing it.

Nothing to be done now— not with the entire family looking on— except think how to get them to listen to me, so I let the fire rage and pushed my own magic down, down inside. Then followed Jay and the rest back into the house.

Amidst the silent scrubbing of the couch, the bleaching and recovering the cushions, the wordless communication while trying to feed all of us in too cramped a space, Thom called no alarm. No guards came to the house, nor priestessi of either temple.

Perhaps we were safe.

Four long, tortuous, wordless, *grieving* days.

Sometimes, I worried the boys weren't *sad enough*— if that was a thing— because they didn't grieve Jay's mother the way the rest of the family did, and perhaps it was some fault of mine...

And then I remembered their upbringing, in the damned temple, where their own blood-mothers weren't allowed to care for them, and the priestessi in charge of the children changed out every year or so. No wonder they weren't so attached to Jay's mother.

Absolutely a fault of mine, because I'd allowed it. And perhaps we'd damaged them irreparably, but I was doing my best now to love them and give them someone stable to love in return.

When I could stand it no longer, I took the boys by their hands and brought them to the back yard, pacing along the stones, stepping past the ashes of the pyre. The dirt was ready to be planted but Jay and his family wouldn't start until after their grieving was complete, and I wasn't sure exactly when that would be. The beginning of the fifth day? The end? Not till the sixth morning? There were so many things I didn't know about the Rest Third—

I turned my back on the yellow flowering bush, the new budding brownwood tree, the house, the mid-morning sun and shadow, and broke their tradition of silence.

"What in blessed heaven do you think you are doing?" I hissed. "Magic, outside the temple?"

Wilyam glanced at Antero, then stared at his feet. "It was going to take *days* if we didn't help."

Antero nodded, his purple hair falling into his eyes. "Rot. Diseases. Ick."

They both needed haircuts as much as I needed patience. "And what if someone *noticed*? You want to go back?"

"No!" Wilyam looked over his shoulder at the house and lowered his voice. "No. Just, we couldn't— it wasn't right—"

"We are careful." Antero pressed his hand to mine and *pushed* quietly, gently.

My magic surged. I held it back. Fought my temper down, along with my magic.

Looking, he was right. He was being careful. His magic barely stirred against the rest of the world.

"It's harder, away from the temple. Takes more work." Wilyam's shoulder twitched. "But, like Andy said, we're careful. Quiet-like."

We *are* being careful, he'd said. They'd been doing more magic than this and I just hadn't caught them before. Because they'd been *quiet-like*? Hmm. *Focus on the now.* "Andy?"

Antero beamed. "Nickname."

"They do that out here. In the Rest Third. Like Jay is really Bluejay? And Dee for Chickadee and Maggie for Magpie? He wanted one, so he picked Andy. I'm Wil."

"Andy." I tousled his purple hair. "Wil." Tousled red. I didn't have a choice really. They were using magic will-I nill-I. Didn't want to stop. Maybe *couldn't* stop. And I couldn't make them, not without using my own magic and risking *everything*. So— "I guess we'd better start classes again. Writing and history and *magic* and all that."

Antero— Andy's eyes lit up and he grinned. Wilyam shrugged. Of the two, he was the more gifted but the less studious.

My boys, now that Antero's mother was gone and he had chosen us as his family.

They had so much energy, so much life, and it was my intention to protect that— to let them explore and grow without the shadow of either temple or goddess.

"Let's start now. How many layers can you *push* and *pull* through, away from the temple? Can you *feel* the yellowbush through the ground? Don't hurt it." I *looked*, a passive way to see the magic around me. Waited to be noticed by Maldita.

My heart thundered, using my own magic, even in this tiny, soft way, but I needed to watch them use theirs. When no lightning struck me down, I tentatively believed She hadn't noticed, so I *looked* some more. It was a little like a drug, this magic, this ability to *do* things others couldn't, and I missed it. Craved it. How much worse would that craving be for two young boys who didn't have my experiences? Away from Maldita's influence, they could use their magic for good, not ill.

Wilyam— Wil— concentrated, his tongue caught between his teeth. "Four? The air, dirt, stone, dirt... almost the roots. Like they're there but I can't quite—" He screwed up his face with effort.

"That's a good starting point. Anter— Andy?"

"Three. Air. Dirt. Stone." He looked up at me. "Harder. Outside the temple."

My own head swam a little— even passively *looking* used my energy.

Wil nodded. "It's much harder here. Like there's not enough magic or something. Makes it easier to be quiet-like, though."

And they were 'quiet-like.' I saw what they were doing, but only because I was looking. They created almost no ripple in the magic. My own magic stirred again and I was tempted— so tempted!— but they hadn't been sworn to Maldita, hadn't been Her priestess, didn't have the tenuous thread inside them I felt still connecting me to Her.

And it didn't exhaust them the way it would me.

No.

No magic for me. It wasn't worth the price.

"Good." With a sigh for the washing I would have to do to clean my pants, I settled down onto one of the stones of the naked raised beds. "I want you both to *push* and *pull* rocks up out of the boxes so the vegetables will grow better. Quiet-like. Put the rocks out here, on the paths."

"Yes, Mom."

They *pushed* and *pulled*, Antero with his clenched fist and Wilyam with his tongue poking between his teeth, and I counted the rocks that eased their way out of the ground to the path.

One, two... ten, eleven, and my boys were sweating as if it was the height of summer, and everything took longer.

As extended as my magic was, I *felt* Jay and the rest come out of the house. Nearly panicked. Cleared my throat to ask the boys to stop. Had Jay's family heard us break their silence? But Dee beckoned us over.

Jay scooped the ashes into the dirt next to the brownwood tree. He mixed them together, then set the shovel aside and crouched and thrust in his hand and brought out a fistful of ash and dirt, then tossed it over the tree roots. First Robin, then Dee, then Maggie mimicked him. After a significant look from Maggie, I followed, then the boys, then Thom.

Finally Jay took up the shovel again and finished piling dirt around the tree. Then he cleared his throat. "Resting betweens."

"Resting betweens," echoed his sisters.

He straightened, looked eased. "Thank you for joining us, Thom."

"Thank you for allowing me."

Jay held out his hand and I took it. "Fetch some water," I told the boys.

Wilyam opened his mouth to protest. Jay nodded, more a dip of his head than anything, but Andy lifted his chin in response. They scampered away. I followed Jay into the house.

Five days of silence was hard to shed. We wordlessly washed our faces and put on sandals, then he took me along the path to the water fountain, where we watched the boys until they had filled their buckets, headed home.

Then we went on to the market. It was as small and tattered as the Rest Third itself, but after the death ritual, it was bright and loud and exciting. I found myself shying away from the people, weaving between them and making an effort not to touch, ducking away from the whoosh of landing pallets. The sun shone high in the sky but the spring day was still comfortable, the awnings overhead all different colors, and someone had been experimenting with dye because one was several shades, all blotchy and running together.

"They grow herbs and small vegetables in their houses all year round," Jay said, pointing with his chin to a Brown couple. The women smiled broadly. "If you're tired, we'll get our starts for the garden now and go home—"

"More!" I controlled my breath, did my best to control my body.

Jay nodded, and we went on. My eyes drank in the sights and my nose the scents and if I flinched back, no one said anything about it.

"We'll come back later on our way out then," he said over one shoulder, as much for them as for me.

But other things had already caught my attention— shirts and pants and skirts and shawls in yellows, browns, oranges, greens. Small mirrors— the glass bubbled and flawed compared to what magi and priestessi could create, but mirrors all the same. Wooden swords and knives, for practice, and in the same stall, clever wooden puzzle boxes and games and carved animals.

Real animals, in their own pens at the edges of it, two horses and several pigs and a cow. Goats and chickens and squirrels everywhere.

Meat pockets and whole turkey legs and flatbread with melted cheese. Berry pies from last year's berries and spun sugar and custards and cakes and tarts. Raised breads and braided breads and sweet breads and salted beef and sausage and eggs and all of it made my mouth water.

People, mostly Oranges and Yellows and Greens, but Browns and the occasional Red, too. And an entire section of stalls run by Blues and Purples, some of them looking enough like Thom to be family, with imports from outside the city— castoffs from selling to the damned and the blessed, surely, but *here* and interesting and new.

All rubbing elbows with me.

The longer I was among them, the more I realized they had no idea who I had been, and the less I flinched from them.

For the first time in a long time, I was entranced instead of afraid, and I reveled in it, darting from offering to offering, laughing and delighted.

Perhaps if I hadn't just been *looking* at the boys' magic, I would have missed it, but someone *pushed* at me, a sort of look-away *push*, and then I felt ghostly hands at my waist.

I had no coin to carry, so the thief got nothing.

Whoever it was *pushed* against Jay next but the magic slid off him. A light Purple sharp-boned girl— young woman?— brushed her long fingers across his belt pouch and *pulled* and his hand clamped down over hers.

My gaze traced back to the other thief, the one using *push* magic, the young, squarely built Orange man just behind her, and if I hadn't *felt* them, I'd never have believed they were working together.

After Lena's and Jay's and Dee's stories about capturing criminals, I knew not to look at him directly. Instead I pretended I was interested in something beyond him, took two steps, and grabbed his hand just as hard as Jay had the young woman's.

Then, as if we'd practiced it a hundred times, Jay and I met each other's eyes, he flicked his toward a gap between the stalls, and we shoved our captives into the makeshift alley.

"You're thieves," Jay said flatly. "Tell me why we shouldn't call the guard."

I clamped down on my surge of fear. I couldn't say anything about their magic— shouldn't— these two might be smart enough to realize what it meant about *me*— but they had to *stop*—

The fear rose up in my throat again and despite myself, I blurted out, "Why are you using magic? Why aren't you at a temple?"

~

*J*AY

. . .

In the shadows of the makeshift market alley, the Orange man twisted his arm and escaped from Sumi's grip, but he stayed. Hovered near the entrance to the alley as if he was still captive too, blocking out the light, thanks to his wide frame. Jay bent the Purple woman's wrist so she would hurt herself if she moved.

"Wasn't stealing." The man flipped his orange hair out of his eyes. "No proof."

"Don't need proof to call for a magus," Jay drawled.

"Let's not be hasty." The Purple woman looked Danya's age — sharply reminded him of her— but sounded older than she looked. As if he didn't have her wrist captive, she casually leaned against one of the awning poles. "If you know we used magic, then *you* use magic."

The Orange man gaped at them. "My spell didn't work on you."

"You need to stop." The tiny muscles at the sides of Sumi's eyes tightened as if she was doing magic, then she wrapped her arms around herself, shook her head. "The thieving and the magic. Just stop."

"Why should we?" The Purple woman moved to cross her own arms, came up against his hold, changed her mind. "Woman's got to eat. You don't look that much better off than us. Are we cutting in on your territory?"

"What? No!" Sumi glowered.

The Purple woman grinned toothily. "You let us go and we won't come back to this market. Promise."

"Tash—"

"Shut up." The Purple woman tugged her arm, ground the bones of her wrist against his fingers, grimaced in pain. "Takes a thief to catch a thief, eh?"

"Tash," the Orange man hissed. "I can't get him off you. Like my magic don't affect him at all."

"Which he knows now. Thanks for telling him."

"I knew already." Jay snorted. Sumi had made him her Shadow— her magic-husband— while they were in the Temple of the Damned, and had given him a shield that made him immune to magic. Immune, he'd thought, just to the magic of the damned, but now he wasn't so sure. He gripped the girl's wrist, grinding her bones enough to get her attention. "Tash, is it? You look like you belong to the Yulian family. Thom is a friend of mine."

A spasm of fear crossed her face. "Call the guard then," she snapped. Sheer bravado. "You didn't call them at first, so I bet you don't want them involved any more than we do. What they gonna find on you?"

Sumi opened her mouth to protest, but Jay caught her eye and shook his head. They should have called the guards in the beginning, before all the talk of magic, but now— there would be awkward questions and Sumi was already terrified of being discovered.

Rest it. If it was so important Sumi would tell them to stop — admitting her own magic— then they needed to stop. But how to convey that?

"Thom will know you? He should know someone is using magic in this market." Jay watched his captive's face.

She blanched again. Brought her free hand to her captive. Sawed at his grip with both. "Call him then. Go ahead."

"Stop." He clamped his other hand down. "Stop fighting me. You're hurting yourself."

"Better than what Cousin Thom will do to me."

"You *are* a Yulian."

"A distant cousin. A poor one." She stilled, glared at Sumi. "You asked why I didn't get sacrificed to a temple? Now you know. The Yulian name. Enough to get me out of a death trap but not enough money to keep a roof overhead."

"*Tash* short for something?" Jay shifted, not yet ready to believe the Purple woman.

"Tasha Yulian," she muttered, sarcasm lacing her voice. "At your service. And that's Gui."

"You have to stop using magic." His Sumi looked a little wild-eyed. "You'll call them down on us."

"What?" Jay gaped at Sumi. "What?"

Tasha flinched. The Orange man— Gui— shuddered, stopped doing whatever he was doing that made Sumi so anxious. "Call them? Call who? How?"

She'd *pled* with them. The woman who used to be able to command, reduced to—

"You're *loud*. Like... throwing a rock in a pool of water. When you use your magic it ripples up against other magic and they can *feel* you."

Gui snapped his mouth shut, then drawled, "Nah. You're lying for sure. Or they'd'a already come."

"The damned have been busy," Sumi hissed. "Things... happened. But someone felt it. Someone— they're coming now."

"Let me go." Tasha stared up at Jay with big purple eyes. "We have to go."

If the damned and the blessed could feel their magic, he had one more thing to do to protect Sumi before he let these little thieves out of his sight. "Let's say this *is* our territory then, shall we?" Jay bared his teeth. Waited for their hurried nods. "Get out. Don't come back."

Then he released her.

The two thieves ran out of the alley and disappeared into the crowds before he could say another word.

Jay wrapped one arm around Sumi. Felt her suck in a deep breath. "Let's go."

She nodded and walked into the sun with him. Her eyes

darted back and forth as if everyone near belonged to a temple. Rest it, if she could feel *them* coming, if she could feel the thieves' magic, then she still had her own.

As long as she was free from the dark goddess, he didn't care.

She *was* free, wasn't she?

He guided her toward the little plant seller. Felt her stiffen.

"On your left," she said softly, ducking her head to his chest.

He stepped into the stall and picked up a baby tomato plant in a pot already too small for it. Hefted it and examined the leaves. Shifted so he could look.

They weren't subtle.

Guards dressed head to toe in white, hands on their swords, glared about suspiciously. They moved in formation, then as one of them bobbled a step, parted. At the center, the palest Purple woman he'd ever seen. Flowing linen, no weapons other than herself, white streaks in her hair.

Not a magus then. A priestess.

"Resting betweens," he swore.

"Bless it," Sumi mumbled against his shirt. "We're in trouble. Seems like they're tracking more on *where* than on *who*, or they'd have stopped Tasha and Gui."

"And we're coming from the area." His mind raced. "Will they recognize you?"

She shuddered. "Shouldn't. I don't look like my blood-family. Now."

He had to ask. "They won't feel your magic?"

Sumi peeked at the priestess, then gazed up at him. "Hope not. I'm hiding it."

"Right. She's looking this way. Kiss me— someone who had just done magic would be running away, not smooching in plain sight."

She winced, and he knew she *wanted* to run away. Then

stood on tiptoe and pressed her mouth to his. At first, obligatory. Then her lips softened. Parted.

Desire swept him, hard and fast. If they weren't in the market— weren't hiding in plain sight from a blessed priestess — if she wasn't still recovering from dying—

He could imagine exactly what he wanted to do with her and the way she nestled against him, ran her hands up his back, pulled him closer, he knew she'd agree. Had forgotten the blessed were anywhere near her.

Before his hands could do more than trace over her excellent ass, he eased away. Stared down at her and *needed*.

She blinked up at him, her luscious mouth swollen and demanding more kisses. He almost gave in, but remembered the blessed priestess. Guards. Who were spreading out through the marketplace, questioning shoppers.

"Come," he growled, taking her hand possessively. "Let's finish this someplace private."

Her eyelids lowered and her flush subsided. She'd remembered their audience. But then she smiled up at him like she hadn't and his desire surged again. He tucked her in beside him, splayed his hand across her lower back, shifted it to her hip, and tried to not think of sliding it down.

They walked together away from the sunset into the shadows. Let the blessed stare into the sun— make it harder to describe a Brown man and a Red woman other than their Colors.

A guard shouted. "Stop!"

Sumi tensed, but Jay muttered, "Keep going," as if they hadn't a care in the world. One step, then another, until he thought they'd made it—

A hand fell on his shoulder. "Stop," the blessed guard said again.

He dipped his shoulder and turned, putting Sumi behind

him. "Easy there, Brother," he said, leaning hard on the hope the blessed guard would not force him to draw his blade.

The guard backed up a step but had his hand on the hilt of his own sword. "You a guard then?" he demanded. The man was young and a Yellow, so likely looking to prove himself.

"I am."

"So you know to stop when I say stop."

Jay bit back his first reply and his second. "I know we aren't doing anything the blessed would be interested in," he said softly. Looked at the man's trousers until he flushed. "Unless you want to join us?"

"N-no. Just—" The blessed guard swallowed. "The priestess said to question everyone..."

"If she can keep up, she can join too!" Jay forced a hearty laugh. "Though I've heard the blessed claim not to enjoy matters of the flesh. Still, there are more of them every year, so they must engage in those matters whether they enjoy them or not."

Sumi moaned throatily behind him. Wrapped her arms around him and let her hands wander. "Joining us or not?" she murmured throatily.

He captured her hands. Walked her back to the nearest wall and pushed her up against it, pinning her hands overhead. Glanced over his shoulder. "Well?"

Sweat glistened on the guard's face and his mouth gaped. "No— Brother—" he gasped, shifting to hide his rising— ahem —interest. "Thank you for your cooperation."

Then he was gone.

Jay leaned into Sumi. Nuzzled her neck. Felt her arch against him. "Gone?" he whispered.

She trembled against him and he wasn't sure if it was arousal or fear or both. "Gone."

"Then we should be gone too." He eased back and adjusted his clothes. Thought of nasty things until his desire vanished. Used his body as a shield for Sumi to recover. Then took her hand and led her into the maze away from the blessed.

Eventually toward home.

CHAPTER
SIX

S *umi*

THE WALK BACK TO THE HOUSE WAS FILLED WITH SUNSET AND SILENCE, and I couldn't decide whether or not I was supposed to be the one to speak first.

I should have kept my mouth shut about the thieves' magic — but the presence of the blessed proved I was right. Their sloppy use of magic would endanger me.

It sounded so selfish, that way. But if the blessed found me, I didn't know what I'd do, and that endangered the boys and Jay and his whole family too.

"So." Jay looked over his shoulder and checked the street behind us. I could have told them they didn't follow— *felt* the distance between them and us growing— but I didn't know how to say it. He dropped my hand and I wondered if I should have told him anyway. He glanced down at me, then away. "You can still..."

I opened the door. This wasn't a conversation we could have outside where anyone could hear. It would only make everything worse. I drew him into our bedroom. The house was empty, so safe enough—

He stood behind me, hot and brooding and I *really* wanted the conversation to take a different path. *Needed* it to. But often I didn't get what I wanted. "I can."

He slammed our door— gently, so the frame didn't break. Controlling his anger. "You weren't going to tell me?"

I turned and lifted my chin. He wouldn't hurt me— he'd never been anything but gentle, no matter how furious he was — but I had given up my magic and couldn't protect myself that way anymore. I had to trust him even more now.

"I can't *use* it." I wet my lips. "*She* will know. She'll come for me."

"*She* knows you're alive?" He eyed my mouth.

"She knows." I wished he'd kiss me instead of interrogating me. But I'd known keeping secrets from him would be dangerous, would hurt him. I didn't want to hurt him. "I *think* She knows. We're still connected, but faintly. So faintly I thought it was gone."

"Your connection." Our room seemed smaller, darker. He rolled his head, releasing the tension in his neck and shoulders. The look on his face meant he was going to ask something I wouldn't like. Just when I was ready to break from the tension, he asked, "Are you sure She wants you back?"

Ouch. But he really didn't understand how the goddessi worked. "Blessed sure. She might not want me as a—" even here I wouldn't say it— "you-know. My sister is likely more biddable. But She never gives up what is Hers."

"Never?"

I let the trapped feeling show in my eyes, red and white instead of blood or black lid to lid.

Let that be answer enough.

He looked away. "All right. You're not doing magic. You talked to the boys, right? So they're not doing magic. So as long as those two— Tasha and Gui— stay away from us, you're safe?"

What would hurt him more— tell him the boys *were* doing magic, and I was not just encouraging them, but teaching them too? Or finding that out later?

They had to learn— they'd already proven they wouldn't stop. Jay wouldn't approve— magic frightened him, especially since it had killed me.

So... tell him, and hurt him when I couldn't stop teaching? Or not tell him at all? Which would hurt him least? I would do almost anything to avoid hurting him.

And now my silence had stretched on too long.

"Don't do anything foolish." That sideways look meant he suspected. "It killed you last time, and that nearly killed me."

Guilt rose up inside me, stronger than my magic. I'd made the best choices I could at the time, but it had cost me my life, and— in some ways— his; he was still recovering just as much as I was. My ribs twinged— remembered pain— and his eyes darkened.

"I'll try." I leaned forward to rest my forehead on his chest and told him the biggest truth inside me. "I love you."

"I know." He sounded so smug— I peeked up at him and confirmed it. Smug, but also grinning like he would never get tired of hearing it. He cupped my face in his hands. "I love *you*, Sumi."

As always, hearing my name on his lips sent an extra thrill through me. Then, even better, he lowered his mouth to mine. This time, though he was tender, there was an edge of desperation to his kiss. As if he believed our time together couldn't last. I molded myself to him— tried to prove I was his and he was mine with my mouth and hands. I rucked up his shirt, ran my hands up his stomach to his chest—

Robin and Dee came down the front walk, arguing loudly.

Jay jerked away from me, cursing under his breath. He fixed his shirt, glanced at me, then opened the door.

I tried not to feel hurt. Really, it wasn't about me, but about his sisters, his family, and his foolish belief I was still weak. Which— I swayed— I was. My knees buckled, but he helped me to the bed instead of the floor. The walk to and from the market had exhausted me.

His sisters came through the door, voices still raised as if we weren't tousled.

"I'm serious." Dee ducked into their room, but her voice carried. "Someone is stealing *stories*."

"Stories." Robin unbuckled her sword belt and disappeared into her side of their room.

"Like scrolls and paper and *words*." Dee, always the more practical of the two, had no use for books.

"Words are important," Robin argued back. "Paper and ink doesn't change. People do."

Dee emerged in comfortable, faded clothes. "That's exactly why words don't matter. Written down doesn't matter because it's not what people *do*. Actions matter."

Robin scoffed and walked past her, to the stove. She studied the bread cooling on the counter. "You need to travel outside the city more. There are places where the laws are written down and they matter to everyone—"

"It's still stupid—"

"What do you mean?" I felt like I was stumbling to catch up, to shift from being thoroughly kissed to stolen... writings? "Someone is stealing stories? Stories are free— just ask a traveler."

"*Written* stories. Old ones." Robin glanced at me, at her

brother, then back at me. She shrugged. "At least, those are the reports we're getting. Nothing new has gone missing, just the old stuff."

"Histories." Dee shrugged. "Books, scrolls, bits of parchment. Anything old. Anything that might talk about the start of our city. When the goddessi came. Stuff like that."

I bit my lip but my thoughts raced. Stories about when the goddessi came... *demon hunters*.

"Came?" Now Jay was baffled. "Weren't They always here?"

Dee shrugged. "Guess not. Someone— lots of someones— from the founding families wrote it all down and now their stories are being taken."

"How does a goddess just... show up? Why here?" Jay's question *felt* important. Why here? Why were we the City of Temples and not the City of the River or the City of Fields or...?

"Rest it, how would I know?" Dee swatted Robin's hands away from the bread. "Stew on the stove? I'll serve. Maybe those are the questions someone wants answered."

The stew I'd put together this morning from last year's roots didn't interest me. "*Stories*, you said." I tried to sound casual. "How many were taken? Who took them? Why hasn't the guard stopped them? Is there a way to get them back?"

Dee stared at me, so I'd managed *intense* instead of *casual*, bless it. She lifted her stubborn chin and held her ground. Irritation spiked through me— didn't she know who I was?— then a giggle— of *course* she didn't. She shouldn't.

"I'm not sure," she said. "Robin?"

"Lunatas, from a distal branch house." Robin's voice was crisp. "Wescotts from their main house. Every scrap of history they had, and they're furious. Thom will take care of the Yulians, but Stonefields are demanding we make arrests before anyone gets to them."

Jay blinked— if I hadn't been watching them all so closely, I'd have missed it. "From a main house?"

Robin took bowls from the shelf and handed one at a time to Dee. "They must have been in the house for *hours* to go through everything. Left a huge mess, so it took them a day to discover what was missing, then another day to decide to call us."

"Why?" I tried to rise, but my legs shook and my knees ached, so I stayed slumped on the bed. I'd forgotten to listen to my body and now I would pay.

"You're interested." Robin set a full bowl on the table, then stared at me. "Really interested."

"Mmm." I should have been able to hide it better. "I suppose."

Robin quirked one eyebrow at Jay. He shrugged. He wouldn't be able explain my interest. *I* wasn't even completely sure.

"Sumi, if this is important to you, you should talk to Thom." Dee set the last bowl on the table and started cutting the bread. "He'd know all the details."

Jay scowled. "It's not just who *has* these stories. Who *wants* them?"

All right. Did I say it? Did they not see it? I should say it. "Elementals."

"No!" Dee paced around the table, thrusting slices of bread into each bowl. "I thought we were done with them."

Robin snorted. "You've seen the marks."

"So those are them." I knew it.

Jay scowled— he'd known. But how many demon hunters inhabited our city? Why were they stealing the histories? What did they hope to find?

Could we find it first?

Jay shook his head *no* at me.

I *wasn't* thinking of sending his sisters to find out. I *wasn't*. Robyn had spied on the demon hunters last year and they both had fought against them that night. The demon hunters might recognize them, and then—

No.

"Yeah, they're still here," Robin confirmed. "But you're safe with us. They're only interested in the high priestessi."

I winced, then tried to guide the conversation properly. "We don't know why they want those histories?"

Robin shifted uncomfortably. "I could—"

"No," Jay snapped. "Until we know they don't know you were our spy—"

"I'm a grown woman!"

Maggie and the boys came in. Maggie looked at her sisters' faces, ruffled the boys' hair, and left again with a wave. Robin retreated to the corner with stew and bread and ate like someone might take it away. The boys toted their buckets of water over to the cistern. We all waited silently.

Wil beamed and poured his water into the cistern. As always, a few splashes escaped, but this was drinking water, not river water, so it would only make the counter cleaner. "An old Brown lady, an *ancient* one, paid us to carry her water home. That's what took so long." He stepped out of the way for Andy to pour his bucket— not a drop spilled— then set his bucket down and thrust one hand deep into a pocket. He opened his hand and displayed a coin. "It's for you." He handed it to Jay. "To help buy food and things."

Jay put his hand on Wilyam's shoulder and squeezed gently. "Thank you."

Antero's smile faltered. He looked at each of us in turn and then grabbed Wil and dragged him out the back door. "They're *talking*," he hissed, then closed the door behind him.

Dee dunked her bread in her bowl, then stared at it. "If they remember you, Robin," she murmured, "remember you fought with us at the temple, they'll kill you."

Robin slurped the last of her stew. "It's my choice to make."

Jay spun on her. "We're family—"

"That doesn't mean you make the choice *for* me, Brother. I'm an adult."

Dee nodded her agreement.

"I—" Jay waved one hand expansively. He wanted to protect her so badly, but she was right. She was an adult and she had to choose.

"We're worried about your safety." I wanted whatever the demon hunters wanted, but not if it cost Robin's life. I put a calming hand on Jay's arm. If I'd had my magic—

No.

"My choice." Her tone was grim and her shoulders square when she stepped in front of Jay and glared at him.

His jaw bunched and the muscles under my hand tightened, but he nodded incrementally.

"Demon hunters don't like to kill us normal people," Robin said.

So I wasn't normal? Ouch.

"But I won't spy on them. For now."

"For now." Jay pinched his nose. "I'll take for now."

I had killed people, I reminded myself. Wantonly at times, when the dark goddess took control of my body. No one else knew how much I fought Her, held Her back. No one else truly understood. Robin hadn't meant to hurt me.

Something inside me *knew* whatever the demon hunters were looking for was important. Possibly deadly— for us.

When Jay handed me a bowl of stew, I murmured, "We have to get those writings."

∾

Jay

SUMI WAS EXHAUSTED FROM THE INCIDENT IN THE MARKET. IT SHOWED in the lines of her neck and around her eyes. Jay made sure she ate, then tucked her into bed and told the boys to read to her. They didn't have many books in his house— really only a handful, the kind his mother had loved, about pirates and adventure — but the boys could practice reading and keep their mother company at the same time.

By the time Jay left for work, evening cloaked the city in shadows. As always, looking into the dark for whatever might be hiding there brought him wide awake, even if he was supposed to be teaching, not patrolling. Couldn't help himself.

He grinned.

Sumi was safe, the kids were safe, his sisters were as safe as they could be, considering their jobs were dangerous.

Mom, though— guilt hit him hard. He shouldn't be happy when he'd just lost his mom.

The rest of the walk to the guardhouse was solemn and hurried. Once in, he cornered Thom in his office.

"Jay?"

"Dee said something about extra security jobs?" He eyed Thom. Clenched his jaw.

The old man opened his mouth. Looked like he wanted to ask Jay about his *feelings* or some garbage, then changed his mind. "Yes. The list is posted."

Jay nodded. He'd hoped he could get that resting job for Sumi. Guarding rich people's books. Make Sumi happy. But if the list was already posted— "Thanks."

"You dealt with magic-users in the temple." Thom leaned forward. "Some blessed priestess was in the Rest Third today, searching for a magic-user. Any guesses on how to spot 'em?"

Jay blinked then stilled his face. What could he say that would keep Sumi and the boys safe if they decided to use magic? What could he say to keep the people of the Rest Third safe?

"They usually have a tell," he said slowly. "But if you don't know them well, you won't have time to discover it. Each one is different." Rolled his shoulders. "I'll think on it though— what a guard might be able to see..."

Someone acting like they could steal from you without you noticing. But no one else *would* notice because no one else had been shielded by Sumi, so that wouldn't help.

Thom steepled his fingers. Looked tired. "Please do. Last thing we need is magic-users in the Rest Third. At least when they're attached to the temples they follow some rules."

Jay winced. He'd seen up close exactly what rules they might or might not follow. "Thank you, Sir."

"Dismissed."

Jay descended to the practice floor and saw the sign-up paper was nearly full. Sumi would *not* be happy. He snatched up the quill. One of the other guards— Purple, nightshift, Litka— jostled him, spattering ink across the floor.

"Rest it." Jay dashed his name across the paper, then dropped to wipe up the ink.

"No jobs for the damned," she sneered.

"What?" Jay stared up at her, the rag in his hand forgotten.

"Spent all that time in the damned temple, right?"

"I'm here now."

She snorted. "You belong to them. Once you've gone in—"

Jay stood, his jaw clenched. "I belong to myself."

"There's enough of us who stuck it out here who need the money."

He was about to answer when he felt the silence around them. Paused and looked.

The other guards— the ones he was supposed to train tonight— had fallen silent around them. Some heads were nodding, some ducked down, others avoided his gaze. Seemed like most of them agreed with Litka.

How in the resting betweens was he going to get what he needed for Sumi *and* train the guards *and* do it without busting any heads?

Litka had gotten tired of waiting. "You think you're special? Because Thom let you come crawling back to us? Because you *train* us?"

Jay rose, using every fingerwidth of his height to his advantage. He looked down his nose at the Purple woman and realized he felt no need to defer to her Color. His time in the Temple of the Damned had done him *some* good. "Crawling back?" Deliberately kept his tone mild.

"Crawling. Begging. *Simpering.*"

The whole room was quiet now, the new arrivals alerted that something was going on by the low murmurs— probably bets— and lack of normal greeting shouts. Jay felt every eye on him, demanding he prove himself.

"You think Thom went easy on me." He smiled lazily as he traded out his favorite blades for a practice sword and knife. Latched his throat guard.

"I do." She mirrored his movements.

"And when I prove you wrong?"

She smirked. "I'll let you take my place on The List."

Jay smirked right back. "Done."

"Witnessed!" Mal, the kid who tended to worship him as a hero shouted it, but the others around them said, "Witnessed," more raggedly.

"And when I win?" Litka stepped into the center of the room.

"Bragging rights." Jay moved to stand across from her.

"Not enough."

"No training for a month."

"Done."

Again, the other guards witnessed.

With no other warning, Litka threw herself at him.

But he'd been expecting it, and slid aside, parried her blade. *Think of it as a training opportunity*, he cautioned himself, *so you don't hurt her badly.* He *wanted* to break her, and shame pricked at him for it, but he pushed that down into his legs so his muscles bunched. He hadn't had a good fight since Thom, and suddenly all the frustrations of the past months bubbled up inside. Sumi. The kids. Money. His mom.

Jay swung.

Met her sword and turned it aside, leaned away from the sinister knife. Rest it, she was fast. Jammed his own wooden knife into her side hard enough to bruise her ribs. "Dead," he told her, and spun away.

She screamed— roared, rather— and came at him again in a flurry. *Parry, parry, parry, block*— a hard block, blade to blade and crossguard to crossguard so all he had to do was twist— *like that*— and her blade went flying. Again, she followed up with the knife— *good, good, keep coming*— but he sucked in his gut, shifted to a two-hand grip, smashed the flat of his blade into her upper thigh where the muscle could bear it. "Dead again, or missing a leg. Can't keep a job without a leg."

Litka snarled. Paused. For a moment, he thought he was getting through to her, but no— she came at him again, but slower and smarter this time. Moved like he'd been training her. Fast and smart.

But he *had* been training her, and he knew her weaknesses. Knew his own and how to hide them from her.

He allowed her to pursue him around the training ground,

tiring her without tiring himself. Decided she might be his successor when he was gone. She was that good.

If she could get over her own Color.

Could any Purple? She was here, working with every other Color, so that was a start.

Her blade slid along his arm, but she danced away. "Light," she panted.

He nodded his respect. Honest. She might be able to replace Thom, when he was gone. The head of the Rest Third guard had to meet with other high ranks across the city, and being a high-caste Purple would be more helpful than hinderance.

She nicked him again.

Time to stop *thinking* and end this.

Instead of retreating as she expected, he advanced, with a flurry of strikes pretending to be blocks. He bound her first blade, threw it aside. Bound her second. Stepped back to give himself the correct reach. This time, when he put his second hand on the hilt of the blade, he put his weight behind his swing.

Bunched his muscles. Channeled his rage into it. Saw her eyes widen. Flexed every muscle to stop the blade when it kissed her neck.

"Beheaded." He panted and his muscles quivered but the wooden blade was steady. "Dead thrice."

Litka stared at him over the edge of the wooden blade, her purple eyes wide.

"Do you yield?"

She nodded. Her chin touched the wooden blade. He withdrew it. Bowed, eyes still fixed on her.

Litka dropped her gaze. Bowed back. "Thank you for your time, Guard Trainer. You have educated me."

"Thank you for the workout. You are very skilled with your sinister knife."

A flicker of a smile crossed her face. Litka bowed again and stepped off the floor. The other guards clapped her on the back.

Mal approached Jay, beaming. Jay sidestepped his congratulatory blow and muttered under his breath, "You work with her, right?"

"Yeah."

"Get your ass over there and tell her how well she did. You *work* with her. You work the same shift, you work the same neighborhoods. She's good— and you have to have each other's back."

Mal blinked at him.

"Come talk to me later tonight. Not now. Now talk to her."

Mal ducked his head. Shuffled away.

Jay racked the practice sword and wiped sweat off his face. Out of the corner of his eye, he saw movement. Looked up.

Thom glared down from the balcony outside his office. How long had the old man been standing there?

"Get up here, boy."

"Yessir."

Jay vaulted up the stairs, leaving the rest of them and all his anger behind.

Thom looked him up and down, examined his split lip. Sighed. "Feel better?"

"Yessir."

"No broken bones? Not on you and not on her?"

"Correct, sir."

"Understand Litka bet you her place on The List."

"Yessir." Adrenalin— as much as during the fight— thrummed through Jay.

"Five nights from now. The Stonefield manor. Front gates. Someone will meet you."

"Yessir." Jay bowed, short and sharp. Somehow, without

saying anything else, he felt he'd won not just the fight with Litka, but the old man's respect as well.

Before he could ruin it, he spun on his heel and left. Success carried him all the way down the stairs before reality caught up. He'd earned the job, could get a look at whatever it was the demon hunters wanted... but Sumi read better and faster than he did.

She'd want to come along.

How would he get her in?

SEVEN

S umi

THE NIGHT HAD BEEN COOL, WITHOUT JAY BESIDE ME IN BED— THE man was a furnace and I missed that heat. He'd returned home late in the night and I'd woken enough to curl around him, to run my hands over his skin, but he shifted away with a pat and a murmur, "You're still healing."

Then he'd gone to sleep, leaving me to stare into the darkness and wonder how healed I had to be for night games.

I'd finally risen to sweep the floor. As I worked, the day started and eventually the sun warmed the house to the point where I opened every window but his to get a hint of a breeze, with little success.

Another thing I'd never done as a servitor— open and close windows. One of the first tasks for an underpriestess was to keep the temperature in the damned temple comfortable, to *pull* cool to the temple from the depths of the river or the tips of the mountains and offset the heat, or *pull* heat from the desert to offset the cool. Spring and Fall were particularly good training times, since the temperatures fluctuated so much. With no magi, no priestessi, I was learning that the Rest Third sweltered and froze by turns, and that was as frustrating as the endless chore of cleaning dishes and floors.

Through the back window, I saw the garden was sprouting, bits of green showing that life went on, despite magic and the lack of it. The world went on, and I was here to witness it.

And, honestly, I was happy, chores or no. Healing, setbacks or no. Loved, sex or no. I missed Jay's mother— an ache in my heart— but she'd also shown me a different kind of motherhood, and I needed that example.

Maggie sneaked in the front door and paused to remove her boots. Her uniform looked as clean as when she'd left the night before and her boots still shone, which was strange. Occasionally she came home bloody— if there'd been a fight or a riot— but often she had sweat stains, and always scuffed boots.

She straightened, smiled at me and offered a chipper, "Good morning!" but the smile didn't reach her eyes.

Maggie was lying about something.

It wasn't my business. She and I had never grown close, and whatever was happening at work was Thom's to worry over. Though I hoped his grief didn't blind him to it.

"Toast?" I offered.

"No, thanks. I need to get to bed." But she lingered, her eyes too bright.

The boys roused themselves, rising out of their nest of blankets like birds on the wing. Wilyam flung his arms around me in a haphazard hug while Antero rubbed his eyes. This time, when Maggie smiled, she did it with her whole face. "Good morning."

"Auntie Maggie!" they chorused raggedly together, then tumbled into her for a hug.

Yes, taking them from the damned temple had been the right thing to do. They were *loved* here, and confident with it.

"I'll take them to fetch water," Maggie said with a glance toward my bedroom. "Let big brother sleep."

"Thank you." She needed to learn to lie better. Though I would not be the one to teach her.

The boys pulled on boots, snatched up buckets, and were towing her away before I could say anything else. Good kids, all three, despite how much Maggie had grown up.

I smiled to myself and swept the last of the dirt out of the main room. Even this was getting so much easier. I'd never again take for granted bending or standing without pain.

Before I knew it, the boys were back and Maggie had slipped past me into her room. I shooed Wil and Andy into the front yard so Jay could sleep, then set them to spelling words in the dirt on the walk. At least when they tried to stump each other it was still a game.

They were falling a bit behind, according to temple standards, but I didn't care. If I had my way, they'd never go back.

Two things happened at about the same time, and they twisted up in my brain so I can't remember them apart. One of the neighbors, a Green woman about the same age as Maggie came from her yard into ours, towing a pair of girls who shared her hair and her eyes and the shapes of their mouths— daughters— and a squad of guards, some in Rest Third gray and some in Blessed Third white, rounded the corner and surrounded the neighbor at the end of the street.

Fear slammed into me and my back spasmed in a wash of blinding red. When it passed, Wil held me up on one side and the neighbor on the other.

"Easy now," she said soothingly. "I'll wager you've been

pushing yourself too hard. A body doesn't get over nearly dying too fast, does it?"

I slowed my breathing from panicked pants to smooth inhales. "You... know about that?"

Wil eased away from me with a doubtful look, but I nodded for him to go. The Green girls had joined Antero, who was helping them sound out a word.

"A neighbor hears things. And I've been watching you teach your boys and meaning to ask you to teach my girls for a while now, but I don't want to be a burden to you."

"Teach?" Dark goddess, she didn't mean *magic*?

"I expect they're behind your boys in letters, but about the same for numbers. They've helped me in the market a time or two."

"Helped you." I couldn't seem to think anything more than *not magic*.

The guards left the first house and moved on to the next. They weren't shouting, but they were questioning the residents. What would they ask when they made it here?

"They're good girls and I'm willing to trade— your teaching for some charcoal sticks. Or they can help you clean. Ain't a body alive that enjoys cleaning every day."

The guards left that house and came closer. One more house and then us. The Green woman lived on the other side. For one moment, everything went magi-glass clear.

If I was teaching the neighbors' children their letters, we would blend in better. Me as just a teacher and the boys as just two more Colors amidst a bunch. To the parents, I'd become familiar instead of unknown, and familiar is always harder to see clearly. They'd be less likely to believe it if one of us slipped up.

"Of course." I squeezed the Green woman's arm gratefully. "I'd love to teach them. It would do the boys good to have some competition. Other neighbor children are welcome as well... though we will have to find—" not *paper*, a rarity, but— "*parchment*. Since you would be willing to trade charcoal sticks."

"Just the thing." Her green eyes twinkled at me. "Charcoal sticks write well on flat rocks. That's how my girls started their learning, anyways. And Suann across the street makes candles on the regular, and she would love for *her* daughter to come learn."

"Honored Red, Honored Green." One of the Rest Third guards approached us. "Have either of you seen anything unusual—"

A Blessed Third guard pushed him aside. "Who else lives here?" she demanded. "Who among you is using magic?"

We all gaped at her. The boys side-eyed me and I sent them the look that told them to go back to their words and numbers. "I live here, and this is our neighbor—"

"Dansy," she said cooly. "I live in the next house. And none of us is using magic, as you very well know, or you'd have taken us away by now."

I nodded my agreement. Dansy had bravery to spare, standing up to a guard, and a blessed one at that.

"*I* live here as well." Jay's sharp tone could have peeled the skin from either guard and I felt his heat at my back. "With my sisters, who are guards, my wife, who you see before you, and our boys."

The Rest Third guard paled. "My apologies, Guard Trainer. We— we're just following orders."

"I understand that," Jay said more kindly. I half-turned to see his face and was amused when he glared at the blessed guard. I'd been a bad influence on him. "You can follow orders without being brutish or nasty."

"Yessir." The resting guard tugged at the blessed guard's arm and pulled him away, whispering frantically in his ear.

The blessed guard only looked back once, his mouth tight. He executed a half-bow— half an apology?— and the whole group of them went on past Dansy's house to the one after that.

"You're handy to have around," Dansy, smiling though her hands shook. "I'm just glad you were here since my Nydia ain't."

"Happy to be of service." Jay grinned at her, then went back to glaring at the guards. "Following orders is one thing," he muttered. "Stirring up neighbor against neighbor when they have nothing more than the same questions they always have—"

I stepped into his arms and hugged him. "Good morning."

"Afternoon," he corrected me absently, then kissed me on the forehead, his eyes still on the guards. "You shouldn't have let me sleep so long."

"Barely past, and Maggie took the boys for water, then we were working on letters."

"All's right." Dansy beamed at us. "You two— I remember that time. When we couldn't keep our hands off each other."

I stiffened but kept my smile in place. Jay let me go. If only she knew—

Private matters.

"Who do you think they're looking for?" I asked idly. I knew exactly who— Gui and Tasha, for using magic in the Rest Third. And to a lesser extent, the boys. They weren't looking for me, because I was dead.

Dansy rolled her eyes. "They come through every once in a while and stir things up. Asking their questions and deciding if they have enough to take you away. Right foolish of them. They stir hard enough and something will come up—"

"Peace, Dansy." Jay sucked in a deep breath of warm air. "You and Nydia and the girls are well? You have everything you need for the next few months? Suann and her father and her daughter too? Anyone needing something to make it through?"

"We're well." Dansy patted him on the shoulder. "You can't take care of all of us, Jay, though you sure try."

Inexplicably, Jay's mouth tightened. Then he grinned and I thought I'd imagined it. "You'll let me know if that changes."

"Yes, sir, Guard Trainer, sir!" Dansy laughed and Jay laughed with her.

And for the moment, like Dansy had said, all was right.

∿

Jay

"Why don't you fetch Dansy some tea?" Sumi suggested, "while the girls and I get to know each other?"

"You're going to teach them?" The words slipped out before Jay could stop them, and he realized his shocked tone was even worse. She'd be offended— or worse, hurt— by his belief she couldn't teach. But she'd been so aloof from the children of the Temple of the Damned!

She wrinkled her nose. Laughed instead of getting angry, thank the resting betweens. "I can."

Before he could embarrass himself further, he smiled weakly at Dansy. "Tea?" he asked and led the way. Pretended his gut didn't tighten at the thought of leaving Sumi and the boys outside with guards in the area. Even if it was their own yard.

Maggie met them in the main room, deep circles under her eyes. She looked so much like Mom, but in Brown instead of Yellow. Her face, her hands. Whatever the girl was up to— out all night and day before and after her shifts and only showing up to the required trainings and thought he wouldn't notice?—she was running herself ragged.

Should be sleeping now, but instead she filled a pot with water and put it on the stove. "Dansy," she said warmly. "How are the girls?"

"Out front with Sumi." Dansy smiled back and Jay remembered they were about the same age. "She's going to teach them. Improve their letters and numbers for me. Resting betweens, *I* don't have the patience, nor the time, anymore."

"Sumi?" Maggie faltered.

Jay bristled. Caught himself. What did Maggie know? Or think she knew?

"Anything wrong with that?" Dansy's words were casual, but her eyes were sharp. Nothing would hurt her girls if she had a say.

"No, of course not." But Maggie dropped her gaze to the water on the stove. Lying. "This will be ready soon enough. I need to go. Jay, can you—?"

Had she met someone? Fallen in love? Fallen in love with the idea of being in love? He opened his mouth to ask, realized she might be embarrassed to answer in front of company. He'd corner her later. "I know how to make tea. Have done for years. Dansy and I are fine."

Maggie grinned and it took his breath away. In that moment she looked nothing like their mother, but only like herself. Years ago. Carefree, spoilt, happy Maggie. "You used to make tea for me."

"Before you decided you were all grown up." He wrapped an arm around her. Hugged. Enjoyed a moment of silence and knowing the sister in his arms was safe. Then he stepped back. "Go. Do... whatever."

She grinned again and only the water boiling on the stove made him stop staring after her.

He concentrated on making three perfect cups of tea. Appreciated Dansy's silence. Handed one to her.

Dansy sipped. "Can't believe she went to the guard and stuck with it. She wanted such different things when we were children."

Jay nodded. "She had to grow up fast when—" *When he went to the Temple of the Damned. His fault.*

"She talks about it sometimes." Dansy sipped again. Watched him with deep, serious eyes. "She stole from the priestess on a lark and you saved her life by taking her place. She never forgets that."

Jay blinked. Took the time to think about it. Sipped and found he had emptied his cup. "It changed so many things. She still had to go into the guard—"

"But she didn't have to serve at the temple. We've all heard how horrible it is. It would have killed her." Dansy patted his arm. "You're a good big brother."

"I wish—" Jay cut himself off. No matter how much he liked her, Dansy was a neighbor, not family. And he had secrets he could not share. He shook himself like he was shaking off water when he was really shaking off the feel of all the secrets.

Looked up when Sumi came in and closed the door behind her.

Sumi, twice his lovely Red wife. Once by her choice in the damned temple and again by her choice to stay with him here. How he loved her quick wit, the feel of her skin, her inner strength, the scent of her—

Sumi smirked like she knew what he was thinking. "The boys went with the girls to fetch water—"

"You sent them off by themselves?" Goddessi, what if someone tried to take the boys? What had she been thinking?

Dansy cleared her throat. "Thank you for the tea..." She

trailed off. Realized he wasn't really listening to her. Murmured, "I'll just go," and slipped out.

Sumi blinked at him. Waited until the door shut and they were alone. "They know the way. If they don't by now—"

"What if something happens?" His feet took him back and forth across the floor, stomping as if they would break through to the earth below.

Sumi's gaze followed him. She frowned. "Nothing is going to happen. They're kids. This is what kids in the Rest Third *do*."

"I would have gone with them."

"You can't be here every time they fetch water."

"I can—"

"Dansy's girls go by themselves all the time."

"Those aren't *our* kids," Jay snapped.

Sumi pursed her lips and though they were arguing, he wanted to crush her to him, kiss those lips and tangle their bodies together until they were one.

Until she was safe.

"I don't understand. Did something happen you're not telling me about?" Sumi crossed the room and wrapped her arms around him. Looked up, trust in her eyes. How could he tell her? Especially now?

"No." His hands found her hips. Pressed her against him so he could feel her. Wanted to sink into her softness. Wanted her.

But she was still healing and he couldn't bear the thought of hurting her. He was too big, too strong, and she wasn't well enough yet.

"They'll be fine."

He wrestled his thoughts back to their conversation. The kids.

"They were coddled in the damned temple, but—"

"Different circumstances." He buried his head into her neck.

Imagined the boys growing up there, surrounded by death and darkness. Shuddered.

"How will they learn responsibility if we never give them any?"

She sounded so resting reasonable. Wasn't actually wrong. He'd been fetching water by himself when he was a year younger than the boys. But their Colors... that Purple woman. "I worry." His voice was muffled, his lips on her skin.

She didn't seem to notice. Further proof she wasn't ready to make love with him. "I know. I do too. But running yourself to collapse is not the answer."

"Collapse?"

"You think I haven't noticed?" She leaned away, so he loosened his grip. She gazed up at him. "Working into the night. Cleaning with me in the day. Going for water with the boys in between—"

He released her. Shrugged. "I want to do all those things."

"I want you to sleep."

It was like having Sumi the high priestess back, but without the dark goddess. He straightened. Felt the pull in his muscles when his shoulders squared. "You do?"

"I want you healthy."

"Oh?"

"I..." Now she blushed. "I *want* you."

While they had the house to themselves— a rare occurrence — maybe they could play a little.

"You do?" He circled behind her. Trailed his fingers down the line of her neck.

"Yes." She stilled like she would frighten him away if he moved.

He contained his snort. Turned it into a nuzzle below her ear. Kept his hands away from her, though his fingers curled at the need to touch her. "Tell me," he whispered, nibbled on her earlobe, "if you feel any weakness. If your body—"

"Please—" she gasped.

"As you wish." He grabbed her hips, brought her body back to his, her back still against his front so he could support her, keep her from falling.

That and it was sexy as heaven.

Her red skin was as smooth as if she'd never had a damned tattoo. He ran his hands up her sides, under her shirts— she was still wearing two or three layers because she chilled too easily. Bit gently at the muscle between her neck and shoulder. She was getting her muscles back, and her curves, and he wanted to touch them all.

She moaned and he froze. Rest it, he *knew* it was too soon!

"I'm fine, I'm fine— don't stop!" She pressed her hands over his, but it was too late.

He would do anything to protect her. Anything not to hurt her. And he'd just hurt her. His body ached for release. He'd take care of *that* later. Alone, rest it.

Gently, he untangled his hands from her.

Just in time, too. The boys came up the walk, chattering like large, hungry birds.

Jay adjusted his pants, then moved to open the door.

"Wil, Andy. Everything go all right?" *No higher-caste Colors making any trouble*, he meant.

The boys nodded in unison. "Tara and Nathy are fun. We can go with them every day... if you want." They peeked around Jay to look at Sumi.

Jay sighed in mock surrender. "But where is *our* water?"

"You..." Wil faltered. "You want to go with us? Back?"

They are safe. They are safe. Away from his protection, was anyone safe? He wouldn't know anything happened until... Jay bit his tongue and said what he least wanted to say. "You can go. By yourselves. We trust you to get the water and come back and be smart." The words dragged out before he could stop them. "Be safe."

Sumi hovered behind him. He turned away from her so she wouldn't ask.

She didn't ask.

EIGHT

S *umi*

A WEEK PASSED IN RELATIVE PEACE.

The days grew longer and warmer. The boys fetched water, mostly with the neighbor girls, but also on their own, and whatever catastrophe Jay expected to happen, didn't. We all took a rare day together to plant the garden, and then the boys' water duties doubled— the rain barrel ran low between summer storms and the pipe that brought river water to the house came from the street, so the boys carried water all over the yard, from Jay's father's memory bush to Mom's memory tree through all the raised beds to the back of the yard where the squashes grew.

On clear days, the Green girls came to our yard in the morning before breakfast. They brought enough charcoal sticks to teach ten children, and the spares I put carefully aside. I taught them and the boys from sunrise until it was time to break our fasts. When the Yellow girl from across the street joined us, she brought an Orange boy, a Green boy, common-gray slate tablets, and two sweet-scented candles.

They ranged in age and all the kids had the look of being there because they were told. None of them had a hunger for learning. If I could give that to them, I would consider myself a success.

I started asking questions and not giving them answers.

"How much stone does it take to build a bridge across the river? How many mules to carry supplies for a caravan across the desert? Does it matter if the caravan contains weapons or spices? Who put the Purples in charge of the city? Why does it snow in the mountains sooner than in the valley? Why does the river carry drinking water to the fountains and gray water to the houses here? Why not drinking water to every house in the city? How much does it cost you and how much does it cost a healer for the healer to set a bone properly? Why have temples to the goddessi? Why does the sun rise in the east and set in the west, why not the other way around? How did we come up with the word 'west'? Why—"

Finally, one of them asked me— "Why? Why learn all this?"

The boys glanced at me like I would rain Maldita's wrath down on the Green girl for asking, and I had to admit, the magic surged and churned inside me, but I pushed it down, as I always did.

I sat. The boys had watered this morning, but I still put my butt down on the damp walk right in the middle of them, knowing I'd have a mark on my pants in the same places they had marks on their pants. I needed to be at their level for this discussion. "What jobs can you have when you grow up?"

"Anything!" Wil said with a smile.

This might break his heart. "Not *anything*." Jay had explained it to me once and it had broken mine. "In the Rest

Third, Antero can grow up and lead the guards or lead a merchant house or captain a ship. You could head a farming business or a small trade house. Perhaps lead the guards, but perhaps not."

Wil gaped at me, but the worst was yet to come.

"Trade," one of the Green girls said, and her sister and the Green boy nodded their heads. "Not lead anything."

"Farm." The Orange boy raised his head proudly, brave kid. "Not trade, only farm."

The Yellow girl hung her head as we waited for her to speak. "Sell our candles," she said softly. "Maybe only collect night soil."

"What if—" I wasn't sure how the adults of the Rest Third would take this, so I checked for anyone watching us before I continued, directing my words at the Yellow girl. "If you know your numbers and your letters, you could join the guard. There are Yellows in the guard."

She glanced up at me, a hopeful, frightened look. "That's what Mama wants," she admitted, almost too low for me to hear. "I just want a fair price for the candles. I don't like fighting. I *like* candles."

"What if—" now the true mind-breaking subject. "What if one day, Andy was running a shipping business and he knew you knew your numbers and letters and worked hard... what if he hired you?"

"I would!" Andy jerked his chin. "You're smart. You're my friend."

Wil still gaped at me, silent and hurt as he realized what the other children believed their future to be.

"Or what if Andy and Wil together run a merchant house because they can't be separated anyway. What could happen then?"

"We can hire anyone we want." Andy's voice was firm.

"But if they don't learn their letters and numbers and history, they won't know how to compete with anyone else's trades. They won't know how to get the best prices and the best products or *why* some other city won't trade with them. Won't know how to figure out supplies for their caravans."

"Then they can't hire us." The Green boy said, his eyes bright.

"And if you don't learn your letters—"

"They won't *want* to hire us." The Yellow girl.

Crack. Wil's slate tablet. Antero shifted his on top so no one else could see the damage. They could fix it later.

"You all—" Dangerous, so dangerous. The same dangerous things I'd been trying to teach in the Temple of the Damned. "You are *smart*. You can change the future. Change this city into what you want it to be."

"Really?"

"Really. But sometimes people don't like to hear that, so be careful."

As if we'd summoned him, Jay came up the street, his guard uniform gray and official, his stride long. The children hushed around me and we all stared at him.

A child dressed in rags rounded the corner after him. He caught my gaze and I flicked my eyes away from his— at the child. He'd have heard the footsteps, but this way I could make sure he knew the child was coming after him.

Jay slowed, then turned. He talked with the child, exchanged a coin for a scroll, then resumed walking toward us.

"Lessons are over for today."

The children gathered their charcoal sticks and their slates, retreated to their various houses, still solemn, even Wil and Andy. Jay came up the walk and waved for me to go ahead of him into the house.

105

Whatever the child had brought him, he was worried. Worried enough he hadn't noticed the kids being worried.

I stepped into the dark and blinked my eyes furiously until they adapted, strained my ears, then *listened*.

No *push-pull* magic users nearby. No magi-guards. But still my guts clenched.

Jay turned, his sword brushing my leg as he closed and latched the door behind him. Then he turned back to us, the boys on the couch and me next to the table, unsure if I should sit or not. I backed up another step to give him space. To give that terrible look on his face some space.

"Boys, fix the tablet. Be quiet about it." Give them something else to do, something to concentrate on.

"I don't know who this is from," Jay said. "No one who knows me well enough to write to me knows *how* to write. Except Thom, and he'd speak to me in person."

"Wait." Oh goddessi, what if—

I thrust my hand out. *Felt* for magic. Let myself breathe again. "It's safe. Or at least, there is no magic in its making."

The boys shifted and the couch creaked. They joined hands and bent their heads over the tablet, *pushing* and *pulling* the two pieces back together in a process I knew so intimately my own magic reached out and I had to snatch it back. Stuff it down.

Jay examined the plain wax seal, then broke it. The scroll unrolled into two sheets of paper. The first said only, *You'll know who this is for.* That sheet he laid carefully aside, reminding me again how dear paper was for those of the Rest Third. He scanned the first few lines of the real letter, then passed it to me.

"Sumi..." His voice lowered to a whisper. "It's from the Temple of the Damned. From the head guard. For you."

I staggered. My magic roared. I only barely stopped it from breaking free.

106

Lena knew I was alive. Knew the prior high priestess was alive and hiding in the Rest Third. Knew *where* I was hiding—

Jay's hand on my elbow steadied me, steadied my magic. I sank onto the nearest chair, then tipped the letter toward the daylight. My heart thundered at her handwriting and I had to remind myself to breathe again.

My dear friend, Lena wrote—

I hope this letter finds you well. We've all been a bit busy here, with the death of the old high priestess and breaking in a new one. I shouldn't speak of them that way, I suppose, but did you know I've seen three... now four different high priestessi in my time as a guard? And another two before that while I was in training. It's a different point of view, no?

Goddessi, she was right. To watch so many high priestessi come and go, and all of us believing only we knew best...

Speaking of priestessi and guards, now that she's gotten the temple duties arranged, the high priestess has instructed our guards to find the stirrings of magic they all feel in the Rest Third.

The boys were quiet— so quiet I could barely tell they were working magic right now, fixing that tablet. Probably it had been the two thieves who gave us away— Gui and Tasha. I'd *told* them they were loud.

I've delayed her as much as I could. We don't need the blessed and the damned picking over the rest for magi, but we can't just let the blessed take them all.

True. Despite what everyone outside the Temple of the Damned believed, the damned treated their people better.

Be careful— if there is someone out there using magic, they may be feral. I know you'll do what's best for the city.

You always do.

Did I though? I'd only escaped because I'd died. Was it selfish, not to stay and defend the others against my sister's wrath?

Yours always,

Lena

She wasn't coming for me. She wasn't bringing priestessi and magi to trap me and chain me and drag me back.

Lena, the dear friend who had let me go, was warning me the guards were looking for rogue magi.

The boys picked up water buckets and slipped out, leaving the now-mended tablet behind. They were good boys, and so quiet.

The blessed were already meddling in the Rest Third. If the damned came too— if they confronted each other—

The only people they would hurt were the rest.

We couldn't afford any mistakes.

Not if we wanted to survive.

~

JAY

HE HATED TO SEE HER LIKE THAT— PALE, EYES WIDE, HANDS SHAKING. The letter fluttered to the floor. Sumi curled in on herself.

Pick up the letter? Read it? Or let her tell him why she was so frightened?

Rest it, he'd be the one to lose either way.

So when Sumi stared and stared and stared into the distance, he finally decided. Scooped up the letter and scanned it. Cursed Lena.

The Purple woman could have left them alone.

Should have.

If she'd meant what she said about wanting Sumi to *be well*, which directly contradicted *do what's best for the city*. He'd thought she understood that when she let them go—

Snowflakes falling out of the dark, Sumi in his arms, so cold—

No.

Jay tossed the letter up onto the table, scooped up his woman. Carried her into the bedroom and settled onto the bed with her in his lap. They were alone in the house— the boys fetching water, his sisters working or out— but he still kicked their door shut. "You're free," he reminded her.

She jumped. Blinked. "Am I?"

"Yes. She can't control you. No one can."

Sumi smiled, a tiny quirk of her kissable lips. "Not even you?" She leaned toward him until his breath caught and all he could think of was touching her.

"I don't control you," he murmured, cupping her face in his hands. "I just love you."

"Mmm." Her lips touched his and he was lost. Found her waist. Dragged her closer. Trailed kisses down her neck, then remembered she was fragile— still recovering from being *dead*.

Stopped himself.

She felt him withdraw. Stiffened. Turned her face away.

"I want you so much." He ran his finger down her arm, all the contact he could permit himself. "But I don't want to hurt you."

"You won't."

He thought she would turn toward him again, convince him, but she didn't. So she really was too weak still.

With a sigh, he stood, straightened his clothes, and just in time because Wilyam came barreling in.

"Mom! Mom mom mom—"

"Wil!"

"I need you— Andy— he—"

"I'll go." Before Sumi could protest, he was out the door, running after Wil.

Rest it, what had happened? They'd been fine for over a week, by themselves. He should never have left them alone—

never let them fetch water by themselves. Anything that happened to them— and happened with Sumi because of this —was on him.

He followed Wil past the fountain past the bath houses that meant they were nearing the river, down to the docks where a ship had docked and workers scurried to move boxes off and on. Sweat showed on their shirts as they hustled under the early afternoon sun.

"Wil—"

"He's there." Wil pointed. His words jumbled together. "That boat. They offered some extra money. To help. And he wanted to. And we started, but then they— cause he's a Purple they said he belongs with them. He told me to run. Find you. To—"

"All right." Jay settled his hand on the boy's shoulder. It sounded an awful lot like they'd been hired as day labor to load and unload a ship, but then Andy's Color had caught someone's attention.

Again.

Goddessi, he couldn't protect them. But he couldn't lose these boys. How to keep Wilyam safe while he rescued Antero? "Stay here."

Dread clutched at his guts as he moved toward the ship. And it was a ship— built for running the river. Deep keel for cargo storage, though sailors spoke of shallow-keel boats for other shallower rivers when they'd had too much to drink. Large sails to catch the winds and a magic-user on board to help move them back upriver against the current. Plenty of coin to offer day-laborers and plenty of exciting stories to entice them to stay.

He dodged sailors and children and boxes. None of the kids were Purples. Made his way to the first mate, shoremaster, a wiry Purple man with short hair and old eyes. Opened his mouth and only then realized Wilyam was tucked in behind him, standing in the tiny bit of shadow the sun allowed.

Told you to wait, rest *it*. Change of strategy. "Honored Purple, First Mate. This is my boy, Wilyam. He and his brother Antero were helping unload the ship. He says Antero got... lost."

The first mate lifted one eyebrow like he knew exactly what Jay meant when he said *lost* in that tone. "Brown boy?" he asked. "None of them lost, so far as I know."

"Purple boy." Jay let the man feel the weight of his words and worry, let the sounds of the docks fill the silence between them.

Finally the first mate heaved a sigh. "Shoulda known the boy was trouble. Purple boys always are."

Jay let a tiny, relieved grin cross his lips. "All boys are trouble, First Mate."

"That they are. That they are." The man whistled, waved, and another man came running. "My cousin," he said, probably as much for the newcomer as for Jay. "He'll take over the docks while we go aboard."

Jay nodded sharply. "Thank you."

The first mate stepped onto the gangplank. "Don't thank me yet."

His guts twisted sharply, but Jay followed anyway. He had to get to Andy. Before anything bad happened, because the boy likely had magic enough to get himself into real problems if he was frightened.

He could still picture the magus Wil had killed— with only his magic— in the damned temple. The man had deserved it. These boys were just trying to survive in a harsh world. But if Andy killed with magic here, in the Rest Third, the priestessi would know. Would come for them.

Up onto the deck, aft all the way to the wheel, beyond it to the door of a cabin. "Captain Rafa Lunata. Keep civil and... perhaps you'll keep your tongue." He knocked on the door.

Wilyam tugged at Jay's jacket. Gave him a panicked look.

"It's all right," Jay murmured. Ruffled the boy's hair to take his mind off it.

"Is it?" A large man— tall and wide— filled the doorway, his purple skin flushed, purple hair long and strung with bead and bone. "Is it indeed, Brown man?"

Jay caught a glimpse of Andy behind the captain. "Honored Purple, Captain—"

"They've come for the boy." The first mate scratched at his beard. "I told you a Purple boy wouldn't be out and about and not belonging to a family."

"This man's Brown. Browns have no claim on him." The captain's voice boomed across the deck. "The boy's a Lunata."

The first mate sighed. "Or a Westcott. Or a Yulian."

"Honored—" Jay tried again, but the captain brushed aside his speech like it was a mosquito buzzing around his ear.

"He's working the docks. That means no family."

"He's got a family!" Wil piped up. "He's got us!"

Jay rubbed his hand over his face. The boy never did know when to keep quiet. Good thing he was a Red and not an Orange or Yellow— low caste and that mouth would have killed him years ago. Still, he let the boy's words stand.

"You?" Captain Lunata gaped. "A Red boy? Claiming a Purple?"

"Yes Honored— Captain." Wil stepped forward to stand next to Jay, and Jay let his hand fall on the boy's shoulder to keep him there. "He's my brother. Just ask him."

"Ask him? Ask the boy who was doing manual labor when he should be spoiled by all the goddessi have given us?"

Jay winced. As long as they spoke of the goddessi and not Their priestessi, no one would know the boys had magic—

"Captain?" Andy's tiny voice made it around the bulk of the man. "That is my brother. Please let me go back with him."

The captain turned to look at Antero, and before he could close the gap, the boy darted past the man and knocked into Wil. Hugged him and held them both upright.

"You're telling me you'd rather be with these... ragtags... than with my family? With riches pouring down on your head?"

"Yes, Captain. Sorry, Captain." Andy looked up at the Purple man, *earnest* written in every line on his face. "Thank you for your trouble, Captain, but this is my family."

Captain Luntata looked like he'd tasted something rotten. "That so."

Andy lifted his chin. "That's so. Captain."

"And why didn't you say so before?"

"I—" Antero's mouth opened. Closed. Opened.

"You're a *ship captain*." Jay let a tiny smirk cross his lips. "All boys are mad for ships and here you are, larger than life, a *captain*, paying him attention. It was probably just a bit much for him."

The captain gave a raised eyebrow that said he didn't believe it, but Antero was already nodding. "Captain," he said in that small, earnest voice of his. "Please, may we go home?"

"All right. But, boy, if your family ever has troubles, you come to me, you hear? I'll take you on as crew. Raise you up as one of my own."

"Wow!" Antero's eyes were huge. "Thank you, Captain!"

"Captain!" Wilyam attempted— and failed— a salute, but the captain seemed more charmed than angry.

Jay turned to go.

"You, Brown man."

He stiffened. Half-turned back. "Captain."

"Take good care of the kid, yeah?"

"Honored Captain." Jay met the captain's eyes, didn't lower his gaze, let his experience as a guard show through.

The captain nodded slowly, just as challenging.

Then they got the resting betweens out of there before anything else could happen.

Down on the deck, safely off ship and away from any crew who would take matters into their own hands to please their captain, Jay found a convenient half-wall and perched on it. Dragged the boys into a hug and realized his shirt was as worry-damp as if he'd been working the docks.

"You both all right?"

"Sorry." Antero wriggled until he got free, then dropped his head. "Sorry, Jay. He was just so—"

"Big! Amazing! Incredible!"

Andy elbowed Wil in the side and— miracle— Wil quieted. "He was all that," Andy said softly. "But it was more. The things he had, the things he promised me..."

"We don't have much." Jay winced, remembering the boys' lives at the damned temple. Fumbled to say what he wanted— needed to say. "But we love you. We are your family."

"Family." Andy grinned slow. "Thank you for coming for me."

"Family!" Wil shouted. "Family sticks together!"

Yeah, Jay nodded. *Family sticks together. Despite goddessi and river captains and whatever else life might bring.*

Family sticks together.

Goddessi, he could have lost them both. Had come so close.

Had to do better.

NINE

S umi

Jay was quiet and snappish for the rest of the afternoon.

He wouldn't discuss where he'd been or what had happened, and when I turned to question the boys, they disappeared like mist in a wind. So I let him alone and wondered if he was as glad to leave for his shift as I was to see him go.

Disagreements were rare between us, perhaps all the more jarring when they did happen, but he would work out whatever he was gnawing on and tell me eventually. Or not.

I hoped he'd tell me.

Despite the sun sinking toward the western sky, the heat barely let up. All the windows were open in the house to catch the breeze, but I couldn't go back inside yet. Maldita's *breasts*, I hadn't realized how much I would miss the ice-cold of the dark temple in summer.

Thunderclouds rolled across the fields, reaching for us

before they bumped against the mountains, but they made the air muggy instead of providing a cooling rain, bless them. My magic reached out, ready to *push* a little more moisture into those clouds, to make them burst and soothe my parched skin, but I yanked it back.

I was in control and a little heat wouldn't kill me. Returning to the Temple of the Damned might.

With the boys avoiding me in the backyard and Jay and his sisters gone to work, I was alone in a way I hadn't been for far too long. I couldn't bear the stickiness of the house so I walked the streets of the Rest Third, in any direction except toward the bright temple.

Unabashedly curious, I peeked into windows as I passed. Most had their shutters open and curtains back, as we did. Most were simple and plain, as ours were. One neighbor had plants inside, filling one room. She was known to have the best, freshest herbs, especially during the winter. Another neighbor had as many weapons on his walls as did Jay— he belonged to the guards too. Another had drawn fanciful images on their walls; the bright colors drew my eyes.

Every bit of land in every yard was in use. Now that the plants were taller, I could name most of them. Tomatoes, peppers, carrots, peas. Lettuce, watermelon, all kinds of squash. Ever-present raspberry bramble divided the yards. The occasional flower or decorative tree more often than not was a memory.

I glanced back, imagined Jay behind me, hands casually in his pockets. He wasn't, of course, but it was nice to imagine him there while still having time to myself. I'd been used to so much of it before he entered my life. For now, I set my face to the sinking sun, squinted against its brightness, and continued my meander.

Two corners later, I found a whole patch with no house.

Apple and cherry trees, apricot and nectarine trees, with corn and wheat and a small patch of oats.

"We have a community garden," Mom had confided one afternoon, not long before her death. Her eyes had shone when she talked about it— she'd missed being part of it. "We all add in what we can, when we can. Take when we need."

I'd stared at her. "Your jarred cherries? You get cherries from there."

She'd nodded. "A Blue neighbor gathers the cotton and spins it. A Purple neighbor dyes it. The rest is open to whomever needs."

"You take care of each other."

Even now, looking over the neat rows and paths, my throat closed. I bent to tug out a weed. Swallowed hard. The temples — bright and dark— had so much to learn from the Rest Third, if only they would listen.

A smatter of rain touched the dirt— the warning before a storm. I chose a path under one of the trees where I wouldn't get as wet, then stood, looking out. The skies opened up with giant drops and the noise of them pattering down was loud in my ears. Two people dashed across the street and crowded in with me, a Purple and an Orange together in the Rest Third—

Gui and Tasha.

Tasha flipped dripping purple hair out of her face. "Fancy place to meet you."

Make a run for it? Or stay and hear what they had to say? They'd obviously sought me out.

"Stay," Gui said, blocking the path.

I turned to go the other way, but Tasha had circled around behind me without disturbing the growing crops.

"We just want a word," she said, holding out her hands. "Please."

If I pushed her out of the way, she'd damage the corn. If I

went off the path, I'd harm it. Unless they were going to hurt me, I chose not to take food out of the mouths of our neighbors. "Not long," I said. "I'm expected back."

Gui raised his voice over the rain. "Jay lived here before. He worked for the Rest Third Guard before. Then he went to the dark temple and now he's back where he belongs. But he brought you with him. You..." Gui's smile turned sly. "You don't exist."

My hand found the hilt of my knife. Their magic didn't work on me, and this close to them both, I could draw the knife fast, maybe plunge it into Gui's throat faster.

Do what I needed to stay free.

"Wasn't so hard to figure out *you*," Gui said, as if he wasn't a hair from dying. Tasha looked a little more wild-eyed, unsure what I would do.

She was the smart one.

I swallowed hard, turned back to Gui. Wished for the thousandth time I could use my magic, but it wasn't worth the price. Maybe. "Wasn't it?"

Gui grinned wider now, and rain dripped off his nose. "You was a servant he stole away. Prolly the night of that big fight with the demon hunters and the guards and the priestessi and everyone."

Yes. I relaxed. *A servant.*

"We want you to teach us." Tasha's words tumbled out. "You know magic. You said we're loud. Teach us to be quiet."

My hand convulsed on the hilt and Tasha flinched. "Teach you?" My voice was raspy.

"Teach us to be quiet."

Thank the goddessi they don't know anything about the temples or they'd know I wasn't a servant. Not with my magic. So ignore their request and have them keep blundering about, keep bringing the damned guards to our door, or teach them and risk them knowing too much, about magic—

About me.

I wished Jay was here, then I was glad he wasn't. This was between me and them— the magic users— just as his teaching weapons was between him and the guards. But I'd learned from my time in the Rest Third— they'd pay me back in kind. Somehow.

"All right. I'll teach you. But you must teach me things too."

"Yes!" Gui punched the sky. Then he faltered. "Teach you? What would we have to teach you?"

"Think of something. But not here. Not now."

"You sure about that?" Tasha's magic brushed up against the tree's leaves, dumping rain on me.

Loud.

I grit my teeth. Forced myself to relax. "Fine. Here and now. First lesson. You're using too much power to do what you're doing. You must use the least amount possible."

"The least—" Tasha frowned, concentrated, *pulled* at the water in my hair.

I *reached*—

Restrained myself from slapping at her with my magic.

No magic.

No goddess to contend with.

Freedom.

A drop of sweat rolled down my back, indistinguishable from the rain. "Better. Less than that. Imagine you are threading a sewing needle instead of... oh, swatting a rat. And magic your own blessed hair."

Gui's orange eyebrows drew together, then smoothed. "That's a head picture, innit? Our Tash, swattin' a rat."

My eyes flicked back to the street. Still empty, but the priestessi would have felt that. The blessed would come, and maybe the damned, even in this downpour. "Gui? Try it. Think *small*. Tiny. Barely enough power from you to *push* the water away from us."

He frowned. Lifted one hand above our heads. *Pushed.*

Still too loud.

"Better." I risked a glance up and caught a raindrop in my eye. Bless it. "But still too much. Time to go. Before the guards get here. You work on using the least amount of power you can to do things. Think precision."

"Instead of swatting." Gui chuckled. Tasha eeled around me like I wasn't there and Gui tousled her now-dry hair. "Rats. Our Tash."

"You've raindrops on your eyelashes," she murmured, facing him, one hand half-raised as if she might touch his cheek. Her lips parted, but then she jerked back and stuck her hands in her pockets.

Gui had looked just as entranced. Now he flushed.

All right. So they were interested in each other, but something was keeping them apart. Not my problem. I turned and tried to sneak away— as much as one can when sloshing and squelching through mud.

When I reached the cobblestone street, I fled the guards and priestessi who might be coming *right now*—

What was I going to tell Jay about teaching those two magic?

Was I going to tell Jay anything at all?

I skidded to a stop in front of our house. Splashed my way up to the front door, then used a ladle-full of fresh rainwater to rinse my feet before going in. Dried my feet, then dashed around closing windows, then checked on Jay's weapons... then stopped to think again.

He wouldn't kill me, of course, for leaving the windows open during a storm. Not for letting his weapons get wet nor for teaching Tasha and Gui how to control their magic. Not even for keeping secrets from him. He adored me, which still surprised me. Watching his sisters and how they all interacted as a family—

A pang of guilt hit me. I might have healed his mother if I'd only dared, but I hadn't dared. I didn't know for sure I could have healed her, and I *did* know for sure the dark goddess would have come for me.

I missed Mom.

He was keeping secrets too. I'd seen that on his face, more than once. But I trusted him to know what he needed to tell me and what he didn't.

And that was it. I trusted him. And I trusted him to trust me. So I would tell him I was teaching Tasha and Gui.

For now, I looked out on the thundering rain filling our water barrel and splashing down on the yellowbush and bathing the small but steadily growing brownwood and enjoyed the sound of rain and the cool it brought.

~

Jay

JAY HAD HANDED THE BOYS OFF TO SUMI, THEN WENT TO GUARD practice where he took all his fears and frustrations out on his fellow guards. It felt good to fight until he was exhausted, let everything go.

After his shift, he left the guard training grounds stinking of honest sweat. Walked the streets in the deepest hours of the night, muscles moving easily now, but if he sat long, he'd stiffen up. It had rained while he'd been training, and everything was cleaner now.

Robin had the early shift, so she'd left work when he'd arrived. Dee had watched him with knowing eyes— she'd want to know what was eating him. Maggie was supposed to be working, but he hadn't seen her. Started early? His youngest sister was convinced she was all grown up and didn't need to tell anyone where she went or with whom, so he shouldn't ask, thank you.

Jay wanted to go home to Sumi, but he also didn't want to answer her questions, see the doubt in her eyes, or worse, have her look at him with disappointment. He should have kept a better eye on the boys. Headed off that whole incident with the riverboat captain.

Especially when Dee would be waiting to have her go at him once Sumi was done.

His eyes moved, watching the shadows and one hand swinging near his sword hilt, but he wasn't expecting any trouble. It was late enough most of the Rest Third had bedded down for the night, though if he'd been in the Damned Third, they'd have been up until dawn.

A skinny Yellow boy darted out of the shadows, bold as brass. As if he were invisible, he ran up to Jay, reached out for the money purse hanging off Jay's belt, grabbed.

As if he were invisible— or using magic.

Jay latched on to the boy's wrist, jerked him to a stop. He pulled the boy into the light, realized *he* was a *she*, with delicate hands and a stubborn chin. She twisted her wrist frantically, her eyes wide and desperate.

He should drag her to a cell, charge her with theft, but from the hollows in her cheeks and the dingy gray rags she wore, she was living rough.

They'd send her to a temple.

"Hey, stop. I'm not going to hurt you."

"I didn't— I didn't do anything!"

He laughed. "No, but only because I caught you."

She continued to saw her arm back and forth until he thought she'd hurt herself. "Stop," he said a little more forcefully.

This time she did, but she panted, watching him like he was a snake about to bite.

"What's your name?"

The girl ignored him, bit her lip.

"You can either come with me to find a guard or come home with me."

The girl yelped. "I ain't gonna do none of that—"

He flushed, stepped back so she had all the space she could while he still held one wrist. "I don't want you for sex and no one else in the house will either."

Her lip curled. She didn't believe him.

What would she believe? Obviously not that he wanted to help her, get her somewhere safe. "I want you where I can watch you," he said slowly. "While I figure out what to do with you. Decide to give you to the guard or to a temple or... not."

She cocked her head, her yellow eyes cynical in the torch-light. "Or... not?"

"Maybe just let you go." After he'd fed her, at least. Figured out why she was out stealing in the middle of the night instead of sleeping at home with her own family.

"Let me go now!"

"No. My house or the guardhouse."

She bared her teeth at him, but then her shoulders slumped. "Yours," she said sullenly.

The breeze changed directions and her stench overwhelmed him. "First a bath," he said under his breath.

She heard him. Looked panicked again.

With a sigh, he towed her up the street as gently as he could manage, over a street, and up again to the nearest public bath house. He didn't have the coin to pay for private rooms with tubs and hot water, but the owner would drop prices a little because of the recent rain, and that would be enough to get them both a shower.

The torch was burning, so he knocked, still surprised when the door opened immediately. The wide Brown woman planted herself wordlessly in the doorway until he showed his coin, then she moved aside with a gap-tooth grin.

"Single?" she asked with a leer.

Jay scowled. It was *that* kind of establishment then, at least this late at night. He corrected her, "Two waterspouts and the loan of soap."

The Brown woman shrugged. Named the price and accepted his payment. "Watch yer step," she said, nodding at the wet floor.

He followed her, tugging his reluctant prisoner over the rough tiles. Noted her wince when she stubbed a toe. Felt a pang of guilt, but couldn't do anything more about it than he was doing.

The Brown woman guided them to the first room on the right. "Five minutes," she said with a cackle, then shut the door behind them.

The room was tiny and plain, brownwood walls and ceiling with pipes and two waterspouts showing. Hooks near the door for belts and boots. The floor sloped gently toward the door so the water would drain out to the tiles. There was no other door, so Jay pushed his prisoner into the room, shucking his belt as he went. He crouched to rip off his boots and socks, then took the spout nearest the door. "Hurry," he said.

"What—?"

He gestured up at the spouts. Grabbed the chain and pulled. The usually tepid water was resting cool, thanks to the rain. "You've never bathed under waterspouts before?"

"No. How does it work?"

Jay let the water run over his shirt and chest. Snatched up the soap and started with his hair. "We only have five minutes," he said, turning his back to the girl. "We're near the river. They pipe in the water from there. Catch rain in barrels on the roof when they can. Filter and clean it. Run piping into the rooms to bring the water to the spouts."

He peeked. Water ran over the girl's clothes and she soaped her short hair grimly.

"The temples have pumps and magic so their water is hot or cold. However they want it."

"Truly?"

He soaped his neck, shirt, skin. Thought about his pants but decided he wouldn't have time. Rinsed while he still could.

"Rinse," he told the girl, though he could feel the heat of her glare. Rinsed the last of him and enjoyed the clean water on his head for ten breaths. "Time is almost—"

The water shut off.

"Up." He scowled. The woman had shorted them, but not by much. He stood, dripping. The latch turned and the door cracked, but the Brown woman was courteous— or cautious— enough to let them be.

Jay ran his hands through his hair, squishing the water out. Stripped off his shirt and wrung it out, then put it back on. He side-eyed the girl who stood dripping, her chin up as if daring him to comment.

"Hungry?" he asked. Needed a way to bring her home without imprisoning her again. "I know a place that sells meat pockets."

"This late?"

"This late they mostly sell to guards. That won't be a problem... so long as you stick with me."

Unlike Sumi, every thought the girl had crossed her face. Avarice, dismay, resolution—

"All right," she said.

He hid a grin, picked up his boots in one hand and his belt in the other, nodded for her to precede him through the door.

She scowled, but set her hand on the door knob, closed her eyes, cocked her head as if listening. Listening with magic? She opened the door and sailed through it like a high priestess.

He chuckled and followed after her.

They dried as they walked and ate, and he noted her eyes wary on the other two guards who ate with them. She didn't talk to him, but she stayed. Propped herself up in a corner when she had finished and he hadn't. He exchanged pleasantries with the guards— Mal and Litka. Mal had listened to him and made friends with Litka, so they were fine. The Yellow girl was asleep on her feet.

He took a moment to put on his boots without lacing them and cinched on his belt, then lifted the girl in his arms. She murmured a protest, but settled and went back to sleep.

He took her home, fumbled at the front door, and brought her into his house. Toed off his boots and stopped to think what he'd done.

Taken a thief, cleaned her fed her, brought her to his home—

Sumi emerged from their bedroom, her feet bare and her red hair wild around her face. It was sleep-mussed, the way he liked it best, and he ached to touch her.

But first he had to deal with the girl.

He shifted her, tried to think of where to put her. Robin's bed for the night? Dee's? Resting betweens, they both had weapons in their rooms—

"What is that?" Sumi rubbed her eyes, a furrow growing between her brows.

He swallowed, reconsidering. "She's just a kid."

"A kid." Shadows hid her expression, but her tone was flat.

He didn't want to admit this could have been a mistake. "She's been living on the streets. I, ah... came across her this evening. Bought us both five minutes under a waterspout and soap." He turned. Took a step. "I think Dee's bed."

Sumi's horror stopped him. "Five minutes is *not* long enough to put her in Dee's bed."

"We washed our clothes too."

"I can see that." Her gaze lingered on his wrinkled shirt, twisted belt. "Still not." She shuddered and tugged her thin nightshirt down as if it would protect her. "The house is too small." *We can't keep her.*

He heard the words she didn't say as clearly as the ones she did. "So we build another room. There's space."

"For a closet," she scoffed.

"For a small room." He rolled his shoulders, shifted the girl. Why was she being like this? She had fought the dark goddess to protect her people but wouldn't allow another child in *his* family's house? "If we build up to the edge of our land."

"It would kill the brambles."

"They'll grow back. Or we go up."

"Up. A second story?" Sumi rolled her eyes. "Look at her. She's feral. Worse than our boys."

He frowned. Admitted she was right, but only in his head. Strengthened his resolve. "I don't have it in me," he said.

"In you?"

"To let her keep living out there. On the streets. In her own filth. The things she thought I was going to do to her—"

Sumi flinched.

"And... I think she's a magic user. She was too brazen. Expected something to happen that didn't."

Now Sumi was the one frowning. She knelt. Stirred the coals

in the hearth. Rose. Her eyes unfocused and she *looked* at the Yellow girl. Touched her arm. Muttered, "Blessed heavens."

"She has magic, doesn't she?"

"How did I become the teacher of half the Rest Third?" Sumi glared at the girl. She wasn't just talking about the boys, so there was a story there, but it would have to wait.

He needed to believe he could save this girl. He had failed the boys— again— and his sisters didn't *want* to be protected. "Please, beloved."

Her eyes squinched up like he had said something horribly embarrassing, but the quirk at the side of her mouth meant she liked being called *beloved*, even if she would never admit it.

"Fine." She pushed her red hair out of her face, flipped her hand. "Put her on the couch. We can start building a room in the morning."

"The couch?" His eyes cut to the door. "She'll bolt."

"She'll stay." Sumi rolled her eyes. Stood. "The girl's awake. She knows a soft touch when she finds one."

"Awake?" He looked down at the Yellow, saw her face relaxed, her breathing even.

Sumi snorted. Retreated to their bedroom.

She was right, he was sure she was right, but— He laid the girl down on the couch, covered her with a blanket. The same blanket he'd covered his mom with, time and time again. He swallowed hard. Mom would appreciate her blanket being put to good use.

He smiled, in the dark, looking down at this girl who had magic yet lived on the streets, now sleeping— or feigning sleep — on their couch.

Another puzzle. And he enjoyed puzzles.

And enjoyed *helping*.

CHAPTER

TEN

S *umi*

THE NEXT MORNING, THE YELLOW GIRL WAS STILL ON THE COUCH, JUST like I'd told him she would be, all curled up and snoring faintly. Maggie, Dee, and Robin were all home and no one yelling, which meant she probably hadn't stolen from them. The boys had slept through it all and they had nothing to steal.

The crumbs scattered across the floor would entice the bugs if I didn't get them up. Half a loaf of bread was missing from the cabinet, so the little thief had eaten well enough in the night.

Well enough not to leave.

The girl had both *push* and *pull* magic. Strong, but hard to see until I touched her skin. Could I learn to hide like that?

If the girl stayed past waking.

Bless it, how had things gotten so complicated? I should ask Jay to get one of his sisters to take her to a temple... but as he didn't have it in him to let her live in filth, I didn't have it in me to let her be broken by the high priestessi or the goddessi.

We were both fools.

I swept the crumbs out the front door, then when I heard the boys stir, poked my head past their tiny blanket divider and shushed them. Cocked my head and thought hard, then tipped my head toward the back door.

We slipped outside into the dawn. The air was pleasant still. It wouldn't get too hot to bear until the afternoon. The birds singing in the trees would be after our ripening fruit soon enough. The brownwood tree had shot up taller than the boys — Antero had outpaced Wil this time, and they both had small-but-almost-man hands. They waited for me to speak— rare for Wil— and that reminded me.

"What is going on with you two? Jay knows. Wilyam, you've never been this quiet, and Antero..." The Purple boy had always been quieter than my Wil, but now he was skittish—

I gave them the Look. I'd practiced it in the mirror as a priestess and then refined it when I'd become the high priestess of Maldita. It said, *I already know so you might as well tell me*, and *if you don't there will be more trouble*.

Then I waited.

An inability to be silent being Wil's greatest weakness, he broke first.

"There's been... um... trouble. Because of our Colors."

I pressed my lips together and waited for the rest. Finally it came tumbling out of them, the Purple woman trying to take Andy the first time they went to the fountains, the Purple captain the night before— as usual, Wil told the story and Andy corrected him when he needed, and at the end of it, a bright bubble of anger lodged in my chest, expanded, then popped.

Why they'd kept it from me— they were *trying* to prevent

me from worry. Which the three of them should know was impossible.

Jay, though— Jay was still hurting, and none of us were allowing him to look after us the way he wanted. We were all too independent. Even the boys, when they remembered they had magic.

"Thank you for telling me." I reached for their hands and they let me take them. "If you're ever in trouble, real trouble, you can use your magic to protect yourself. Like you did in the temple."

"But we're not supposed to!" Wil clutched my shirt. "You said."

"If you have to protect yourself," I said, letting my sincerity show, "you do *whatever* you need to."

Andy nodded, then ducked his head. Somehow, despite growing up in the Temple of the Damned, the two of them still had soft hearts.

"Jay brought home a Yellow girl," I told them slowly. "She's still sleeping."

"She stinks." Wil wrinkled his nose.

Andy nudged him. "You would too if you didn't have a house."

"Oh. Yeah."

"She has magic. Did either of you notice?"

Andy shook his head. Wil stared at me, wide-eyed. "But she's not in a temple and she's *old*— not like *mom* old but..."

Something half a sigh and half a laugh caught in my throat. I hadn't been so young in such a long time... and even then, I think I'd been older because of how my blood-mother had treated me.

"She's older than you, yes. I'm not sure how strong she is. It's hard to tell when she's sleeping. She's very quiet though."

"That's our trick!" Now Wil was offended.

"I don't want to send her to a temple—"

Andy shook his head fiercely.

"But she doesn't understand our rules. Not the rules about magic or about living with a family, I think. She ate half the bread."

Wil scowled. "That was for us!"

"It's all right— she needs it more than we do and we can get more, but Jay wants to help her."

"Keep her?" Wil was scandalized but Andy looked thoughtful. "In *our house*?"

"Jay's family's house, yes."

They glanced at each other, communicating in a way I couldn't follow but wasn't *magic* per se, then nodded. Antero said solemnly, "We keep her."

"Thank you." They were good boys. "You watch her for me, all right? Let me know if she's loud when she uses her magic."

Wil scowled. "She better be quiet. I don't like those guards around."

"Me either," I said, and meant it.

Andy whipped his head around and stared at the house. "She's awake," he said. "Jay too."

"Our students will be waiting out front. Will you start lessons for me? I'll be there in a moment."

"Sure, Mom!" They beamed up at me, brighter than the morning sun— perhaps because I called the neighborhood kids *our students*— and then they ran for the house, their charcoal sticks and their tablets.

Good boys.

I followed more slowly. How to convince the Yellow girl to stay, for Jay's sake— someone to coddle— and for mine— ensure she stayed quiet, so she wouldn't bring the guard down on us all?

By the time I made it into the house, the Yellow girl was

sitting at our table with a hunk of bread in her hands and another in her mouth and crumbs all around again. Jay stood behind her, looking guilty.

"Morning," he said. "Ah, she was still hungry."

At some point, we needed to talk about the secrets he was keeping... but not now. Now was about the Yellow girl.

"What's your name?" I asked her.

She shrugged and stuffed another too-large bite into her mouth.

Right. If she wouldn't tell us then... I could give her one to try on. "You remind me of a mouse. Small and hungry. Shall we call you Mouse?"

She shrugged again, but looked pleased.

"Mouse it is." Like her namesake, the girl would panic and run if she felt trapped. I'd never dealt with children who had that kind of a choice before— once committed to a temple, always committed to a temple. Which she should have been years ago, but somehow she'd been missed.

But she'd been living without shelter, with what food she could beg or steal, without family. If her blood family was anything like mine, *family* would not be a draw for her. Food and shelter though— "She's feral." I let my dismay at her table manners seep into my tone.

"So?" Jay stared at me like I was speaking a different language. He was so ready to protect this little lost child.

"She should be at a temple."

The girl curled in on herself, her fingers making claws and her eyes going wild.

I couldn't see her magic use *at all* right now. Last night I hadn't seen it until I touched her. How much of that was instinct and how much true control? Instinct could fail when it was needed most. "She's dangerous."

"I'm not going to a temple." Mouse's voice was soft but furious.

"She can stay here." Jay folded his arms across his chest and set his jaw. "You can teach her anything she needs to know about her magic."

"Don't have magic," Mouse scoffed.

"You do." Denying it, ignoring it, wouldn't help anyone.

"Sumi, you can teach her."

"No one can know." My words warned him as much as her. "Not your sisters, not the neighbors, not the guards. Not about her magic, not about me teaching her."

"You can't keep me here." This time, her interruption was more a question than a statement.

Can. I turned my high priestess glare on her before I remembered I wasn't that person any more. Bless it. It had been so much easier when people just *did* what I *wanted.*

But that time had passed.

So I said the things that would get her to stay. Kept my tone light. "You're right. And when you go, we won't have to feed you or keep your things safe."

Her face blanked and I could almost hear her calculating thoughts, most of them starting and ending with free food. *Fresh* food.

Jay opened his mouth to protest. A tiny shake of my head and tilt of my chin told him I was up to something. Between Mouse and the neighboring Green girls, I shouldn't have to clean the resting floors ever again, and that would free me to teach... and perhaps spend *fun* times with Jay. "I *suppose* you could stay, if you sleep on the couch," I said, playing up my reluctance, "but you must rise with the sun and fold the blankets so others can use it during the day. You may eat our food, but you must clean the dishes."

"So... not *free* after all." That made her more comfortable. I wonder what she'd been offered for *free* in the past.

"Nope." Now I let the weight of my gaze press on her, all my experience behind it. Just because I wasn't the high priestess of Maldita anymore didn't mean I couldn't use my power to push at her... just not to *push* at her. "*I* don't care if you stay or go. You're one more mouth to feed." I examined my fingernails—filthy again— as if I had no interest in her. "But if you go, take that blanket. It's too full of holes for us anyway." It obviously wasn't. But I wasn't letting her leave without something better than she had now.

Not that I would let her leave yet. I just had to let her *think* so.

"I can choose?" Her eyes were wide and she clutched at the blanket. "I can take this?"

"No one will bother you here." I raised my eyebrows to see if she understood exactly what I meant by bother.

By the sudden paleness of her yellow skin, she did.

"Why would you do this?" She glanced at Jay, then back to me. "Offer me this?"

"You're a *person*," Jay said sharply. "You deserve better than the streets."

"Tell that to all of *them*." Her gesture somehow incorporated the whole city.

"We can't *house* all of *them*," I snapped. Softened. "You can stay if you really want to. But you have to help out. Be nice to the boys."

She looked at me. Looked at Jay. Looked back at me. Shrugged and tucked herself more firmly into the couch.

So... she was staying.

෴

135

JAY

HE'D FORGOTTEN HOW DECISIVE... COMMANDING... *STRONG* SUMI WAS — once she decided she wanted the Yellow girl to stay, she made it happen. He wasn't sure quite how. She'd been telling the girl to go and then—

Or even *why*, though he thought she might have done it for him.

Sumi was *complicated*. Important to remember that.

Maggie peeked out into the main room. Her gaze flicked between each of them, lingered on Sumi. Then she disappeared again.

Sumi lost all expression— reminded him of how she used to look in the Temple of the Damned when she was trying to hide that something or someone had hurt her. "Ever since the funeral," she muttered. "Her and Thom." She escaped out the front door. Shut the door behind her. Through the window, he heard her thank the boys for starting class for the neighborhood children.

Maggie came out of her room dressed for work. Before Jay could say anything, his youngest sister had slipped out the back door. He rocked on his heels. Mouse needed attention. Sumi needed a hug. Maggie needed to be scolded. Why the resting betweens was she avoiding Sumi? Thom too? Now that she mentioned it, he hadn't been back to the house since Mom died.

It hit him— the ache where his mother had been, and now she was gone. Made him crankier.

Dee strode into the kitchen rubbing sleep from her eyes. "Morning."

"What's Maggie's problem with Sumi?"

Dee blinked at him. Noticed the Yellow girl at their table still shoveling food into her mouth. "Who's this?"

"Mouse."

"As in *quiet as a...*?"

"So far. She'll be staying with us for a bit. Don't change the subject."

Dee shrugged. "You're going to have to take that up with Maggie. I have work to do."

Jay lowered his voice. "You tell her I want to talk to her tonight. At the guardhouse."

Dee grimaced. "You woke up on the wrong side of the bed."

"I'm fine."

"Sure."

"Dee—"

"I'll tell her! Resting betweens. Go back to bed, Jay. Better yet, take Sumi."

Jay winced. "Too late." He turned to Mouse. "When you're done eating, Sumi is teaching the neighborhood kids to read and write. You could ask her to teach you too, if you want."

Mouse shrugged, but the muscles in her back jumped. She wasn't as indifferent as she was pretending.

"Not all mornings are as exciting as this one," Jay muttered. "Mouse, this is my sister, Dee."

Robin chose that moment to appear. Did an exaggerated double-take of the girl at their table.

"And this is Robin." A headache bloomed behind his eyes. Maybe he should go back to bed.

"But..." Mouse whispered, "she's Yellow."

"Mom was Yellow, Dad was Brown." Jay shrugged. "We're mixed."

Mouse stared, the last crumbs of food forgotten. "And... she's a guard too?"

"I am." Robin sat down next to Mouse. "You can be too if you want. If you work hard. My brother and sister had it easier, but I've proved myself. It's better than any other job in the city. For Yellows."

"Woah." Mouse looked between them. "You all work."

"Yes." What had the girl's home been like? "Remember how Sumi said you need to clean to earn your keep? She teaches, the boys fetch water and run errands for the neighbors. We all work so we all eat."

"Huh."

"Cleaning isn't so bad in exchange for food and shelter. Clothes. And a chance to learn how to read and write. Is it?"

Mouse jutted her chin and looked stubborn.

"We're not holding you captive," Jay reminded her, though he desperately wanted to— her and everyone else he cared about.

"Robin, you're off today? I'm to introduce this one to Maggie." Dee shrugged.

"I'm off today," Robin agreed. "Best wishes with that. You know how our Magpie is. Might be better if you *don't* tell her."

Dee smirked. "Might."

Jay growled. He loved them, but sometimes—

Robin disappeared back into her room, then came out with an old shirt and pair of pants. "Here, Mouse," she said. "Since you're staying. If you want them, they're yours."

Jay hid a smile. The Yellow girl gaped at his sisters. She would stay. She had to. And he could leave her safe with Robin and Sumi.

He broke his fast and tidied up. As the morning came to a close and the afternoon started, Dee waved and headed for work, and Sumi came in from teaching. He made sure she had a large plate of food— she needed to put on more muscle— then kissed her thoroughly. Wished they had more alone time. Dressed in his guard-grays and belted on his favorite swords. Headed in to work.

His baby sister was in the weapons room. Maggie tried out first one blade, then another. Thom adjusted her grip and watched to see which fit best.

Good. He could yell at them together instead of having to do this twice.

"Out with it." Jay kicked the door closed behind him. Trapping all of them in with this many weapons wasn't ideal... but none of them needed weapons to hurt each other. "What is your problem with Sumi?"

Dee popped her head up from the back corner, where she'd been polishing an axe. "No one has a *problem*—"

"Bullshit. Resting bullshit."

Thom took the latest sword from Maggie— too long, too heavy— with gentle hands, but his words were sharp. "Watch your tone."

"You first." Jay folded his arms and leaned on the door. "You spent the mourning week with us, Thom, and we haven't seen you since. And now Maggie won't go anywhere near Sumi. So what the resting betweens is going on?"

Maggie studied her feet as if they held the answers. Dee opened her mouth, looked at his face, and shut it again. She settled back into the seat that hid her from the door and went back to polishing the axe. Thom scowled.

Maggie broke first. "The uh— the demon hunters think the damned high priestess is alive. Not dead, not murdered—"

"The previous one," Dee corrected mildly. "Not the current."

"The demon hunters. Uh huh." Jay scowled. Goddessi, of course they did. They were probably looking for her. A sudden need to run for home clutched at him, but he pushed it down. One threat at a time. And why would Maggie know what the demon hunters thought?

"You're spying on them," he said flatly. Then rounded on Thom. "And you approved this?"

"I'm not a little girl anymore!" Maggie's shrill voice contradicted her statement, but Jay heroically ignored it.

"She's doing well." Thom said.

"You sent my *youngest sister* in to spy on the demon hunters. The same people who nearly killed Robin last year—"

"They had no interest in killing Robin, and still don't so far as we know. Their interest is all on the dead high priestess."

"The one they think isn't really dead." Dee again.

"Not helping," he snapped at her.

"Not a child either," she said, her tone pleasant but firm.

"You're okay with our baby sister spying on these people?"

"Okay enough." Dee racked the weapon and chose another. "She's all grown up now and nothing you or I say could stop her."

"*Thom* could." Jay tried to strangle his bitterness.

"Thom is her commander."

"Thom is standing right here." Thom snorted. "The two of you are like dogs over a bone. Your sister volunteered and we need the intel."

"Fine." Jay slashed one hand down for emphasis. Anything *but* fine. "So Maggie is spying on the demon hunters and they've decided the dead high priestess isn't... and you've decided Sumi is somehow involved?"

"She came from the temple." Maggie pouted. "With you."

Jay rubbed between his eyes. "You think Sumi is the *high priestess*—"

"Retired! Ousted! Murdered?" Dee sang from her corner.

"— of the *dark goddess*. One of the two highest powers in this city. With the most *magic*."

"Maybe?"

"In our house."

"Er—"

"Our tiny, little, drafty house."

"Well, yes." Maggie blinked. "If you put it like that—"

"You really think the *high priestess of Maldita* would live in rags? Share a bedroom and wear your castoffs—"

"*Ousted* high priestess," Dee inserted.

Jay rolled right over her. "With no magic, no servants, crap food, half-starving and *scrubbing our floors*—"

"Um—"

"Thom, you met the damned high priestess. Had conversations with her. You saw what she was like. You think *Sumi* is the same woman? They don't even look alike!"

"They're both Reds." Maggie raised her chin.

"You and Dee are both Browns and *you* have the same parents. You look more alike that the damned high priestess—"

"*Ousted* high priestess—" Dee again.

"— than Sumi and the woman who took me as a servitor—"

"All right, all right—"

"She scrubbed the floors while *you* were with us in *mourning*. Does that sound like a damned high priestess to you?"

Thom winced. "You've made your point, boy."

"Have I? She's noticed. Maggie especially, but she's noticed and you hurt her feelings. Does *that* sound like the damned high priestess? Because I'll tell you, I *served* that woman and—" *forgive me, Sumi*— "it doesn't. The damned high priestess was the coldest woman I ever met."

Maggie stuffed her fist in her mouth.

Guilt hit Jay in the gut. Goddessi, they had guessed exactly right and here he was, hurting *them* to protect *her*. But if they guessed about Sumi—

His guts twisted. They'd send her back, and that would kill her or kill him or kill both of them and he couldn't let it happen—

But Maggie.

He pulled her into a hug. "It's all right. Just... stop avoiding her. She wants you to like her."

Maggie sniffled into his shirt. "I'm sorry. I just thought—"

"I know. It's all right. She'd tell you the same. It's all right." He could feel Dee's eyes on him. Dee wasn't as easy as Maggie — she was older, more experienced, and her thoughtful gaze made him wonder if he'd convinced her too... or made it worse.

"My apologies." Thom's hand landed on Jay's shoulder. "She has been nothing but kind to me, and it's obvious she loves you. I'm sorry if I caused her pain."

Jay nodded, his throat tight. "You know you're welcome at the house any time," he said gruffly. "You're family now, and we don't give up on family."

"Thank you, son. I—" Thom sighed heavily. "I have been avoiding it. The house without your mom in it. I'll make some time soon. Come for a meal."

"Happy to have you."

Maggie wiggled out from Jay's hug and wiped her eyes. "I have to go."

She was going back to the demon hunters. He couldn't keep her safe— "Be careful," he said sharply. "If they suspect you at all—"

"I'll be fine, big brother."

"She will." Dee smiled. "She's playing it smart."

Rest it, if he could just gather them up and keep them all together, safe in the house all the time, he would.

But he couldn't.

Could only do his best and try to trust them to keep themselves safe. It was tearing him apart.

"Back to work then," he growled, and turned away from them all. Could take his frustration out on one of the more skilled guards who could handle it.

Just had to find one brave enough.

ELEVEN

S umi

THE NEXT MORNING, I *INVITED* MOUSE ALONG TO CLASS WITH THE neighborhood children with nothing more than a pointed look and a jerk of my head. She rolled her yellow eyes but came along.

Wil gave her 'his' seat and charcoal stick and tablet, then hovered over the girl as if she wasn't at least five years his elder. He showed her a letter *A* and set her to tracing it before the others were all seated.

"No Tara today?" The Green girl was missing from beside her sister.

"She's helping Mom." Nathy bounced as she spoke. "One of the merchant houses, and if Tara shows her skills..."

"Maybe they'll take her as an apprentice?" I arched my eyebrows. "That is exciting."

The rest of the children nodded and some grinned. They

may not have had a desire to learn when we started, but more of them had that spark now.

"Let's start with a story, then we'll go on to letters." I thought back to my time in the Temple of the Damned, reading books from other cities, scrolls from our own city's past, and decided on an adventure from Vindas, to the northeast.

Wil nudged Mouse to listen, and then as the sun rose from behind the blue mountains and the shadows shrank and the light touched the children's eyelashes and cheekbones and knees, we began.

"Change is hard, in Vindas City, but one fine summer day, it came looking for the youngest daughter of the king—"

"What's a king?" interrupted the Orange boy.

"A king is like a high priestess, but he rules the whole city, not just a Third."

"A *boy*?" He sounded scandalized.

"Different places have different customs," I reminded him. "Women rule here. Men rule in Vindas." That seemed to satisfy him, so I continued. "The youngest daughter of the ruler didn't want to learn her letters and instead went exploring in the nearby wood…"

I wound a story of magic and adventure with a happy ending never truly jeopardized; these children laughed and gasped and clutched at each others' hands like they'd never dreamt such things, and likely they hadn't. I loved every moment.

At the end of it, I reminded them, "You can make up your own stories. A tale is as true as its meaning, and once it's written down, it's forever."

"I'm writing a story!" Nathy again, her green hair bouncing along with her. The child wasn't meant to sit still.

"Good! Let's jump up and down with the alphabet song.

Then we can practice our letters so we can all write stories if we want to."

With boundless energy, they jumped. Then Wil helped Mouse and Andy hovered over Yellow Cori, so I shifted toward the Orange boy, Kass. I knew I enjoyed teaching— when I had the patience for it— but I hadn't expected to come to love each of my students, hadn't expected my own glow of accomplishment when they learned something new.

Didn't expect the dart of fear and the rise of my magic when a pair of blessed guards came down the street, because it was as much for these children as it was for myself. I clicked my tongue to warn the boys, who stiffened but showed no other signs they had noticed.

No one stood up to the blessed— they could take whoever they wanted as long as they claimed the person had magic.

And why were they in this neighborhood again? Had they felt Mouse's magic? Wilyam's and Antero's?

I wouldn't allow them to take any of these kids... but how could I stop them? If I unleashed my own magic, the dark goddess would come, and She would be even worse. I couldn't do anything but freeze and wait for them to come.

Run away, coward.

My breath rasped. I controlled it, inhaling to three and exhaling to three. Clenched my jaw to keep my chin from trembling. Couldn't do anything about my heart, thunder in my ears nor my hands, cold despite the summer sun. I couldn't even fight them physically. I had no sword, had no right—

They passed us by.

Thank the goddessi.

Still, I watched them go, watched them until they were out of sight, *felt* them and their tiny gifts circle back to the Blessed Third.

I couldn't— shouldn't— use passive magic to *feel* everything all the time. It would not just exhaust me— even without *pushing* or *pulling*, it was like standing in a crowded room listening to hundreds of conversations— but wouldn't do any good. What could I do if they came for any one of us? Nothing without unleashing my magic. Even the boys couldn't do much without being discovered.

Bless it.

Yellow Suann appeared in the doorway of her house and Cori, her daughter, straightened and looked at me for permission. Time for breakfast. I nodded and the children scattered.

Wil, Andy, Mouse, and I went back inside and found Dee waiting with bits of sugared fry bread. "A treat," she said with a shrug.

Mouse gaped at her, but the boys fell on the bread like ravenous desert cats and soon enough our newest family member joined them. I scavenged a bit for myself, but I couldn't eat yet. Not with my stomach still twisted. Instead I eyed Dee.

She raised her eyebrows. "Yes?"

How would I convince her? Not just for me, but the boys, too. I could still feel the panic fluttering in my chest and wondered if they felt the same.

"I'd like training. To defend myself." I pushed the words out past my dry throat, past all my *shouldn't* and *can't*. Would a servitor in the damned temple be allowed to learn weapons? No — so she couldn't know Jay had taught me a little. "And for the boys. Mouse too, if she wants it."

The boys and Mouse stared at me.

Dee stared too.

Why didn't she say anything? Had I given myself away—

"You surprise me," she admitted.

"I'm sorry— I know your time off is precious, but Robin is never here and Maggie's avoiding me and Jay... Jay can be too kind." I lifted my chin. I might have hated Andy's mother Hana when I was learning magic from her, but I'd learned more from her than I'd learned from other teachers who had been too cruel or too kind.

Not that I could admit that to Dee.

"Robin is with— Robin has found love." Dee leaned against the counter. "Maggie should behave now. But I understand *what* you're asking. I don't understand *why*."

Robin? Love? Wonderful— but how would Jay feel about that?

I swallowed hard, brought my wandering thoughts back to what I wanted from Dee, considered my words carefully. "The boys— did Jay tell you? They've had some problems because of their Colors and I want them to know how to get away, to run away, to fight if they have to."

"Mmm." She wasn't convinced.

"I—" Took a deep breath and told my lie with the truth, "I want to be healthy. Stronger."

Dee raised one eyebrow, looking so much like her brother that I blinked. "You're more than a little afraid of guards," she said softly. "And I can't blame you. I'd be afraid to be taken back to a temple too."

I nodded, speechless.

With a little shrug, she pushed off the counter. "All right. Tiring out the boys should give us a few moments' peace, anyway."

They grinned at her, unrepentant, and she grinned right back. "Fetch us some water first," she said. "We'll want it after."

They went, and dragged Mouse with them.

I thought back to the cool of the vault, the feel of a sword in my hand, Jay's body behind mine— and flushed. All right, maybe not Jay. The sword. I enjoyed learning the movements, having my body respond to my command.

Dee led the way out to the backyard and waved at the pathways, mud tiles baked hard under the sun. "You've been walking a lot," she said. "How far can you go without stopping?"

"To the community garden and back. Maybe to the border of the Blessed Third, but... I avoid that direction."

Dee nodded. "Not bad."

"Not good enough."

"No, but this is where you are now. Accept it and work *with* what you've got."

I grumbled to myself. Accepting where I was— *not* my strength.

Still, my body would betray me if I wasn't careful, so I would be careful.

Like I had the children earlier, Dee had me jump up and down over and over until sweat ran down my back, and then she showed me how to lift heavy things, told me to do it correctly or not at all.

The boys and Mouse returned, and she had them running and jumping and falling, and I almost changed my mind. All this would make Mouse a better thief... but if she was stealing because she needed to eat, and we kept her fed, then she wouldn't need to steal anymore.

Dee taught well. She stopped me after a shorter time than I wanted, but she gave me a knowing look and I bowed my head and accepted her instruction. I settled onto the edge of one of the raised garden beds and watched her teach the boys, faintly glad it wasn't me.

My hands, resting on my thighs, shook.

It was this sudden breathlessness, the hollow feeling that still reminded me when I pushed too far. I loved it for telling me how far I'd come and hated it for telling me how far I had yet to go. I leaned forward and found my legs had stiffened.

When Dee finished with the kids, they took turns laying on

the paths and spooning water into each others' mouths. Which, of course, turned into *dumping* water on each other, which turned into dumping *all* the drinking water all over the yard as they mock-fought each other, which then turned into another chance to fetch water from the fountain.

When they'd gone and the yard was quiet if not clean, I tried to push myself up and groaned.

Dee offered me her hand.

"Thank you," I told her, meaning more than just the hand up.

She heard it in my voice. "You remind me of one of my favorite recruits. He's an older Blue man, content to learn from a Brown and willing to do all the running and fighting he's asked to, but he's also smarter than the rest of them. If there's a more efficient way, he sees it. Does it."

I huffed. Moved slowly toward the house. "Is this your way of telling me to be smart?"

"It's my way of saying you did well, but don't expect to keep up with the boys. Do what *you* can do, and do a little more, but not a lot more. I don't want you dying on me."

"Yes, pries—" Shut my mouth fast. Swallowed. *Not* a priestess. "Got it. Dee. Thank you."

She looked at me like she was seeing all the secrets I wasn't saying, then nodded, and held open the door into the house. "I hope one day you'll trust me."

Bless it. I did trust her, much like I trusted my secret-keepers, but I didn't know that *she* would trust *me* if she knew the truth. I looked down at the faint tattoos on my arms, black lines against the flush of my red skin. The ones Jay still swore went unseen by everyone but me.

After all, how often does a woman who used to be the High Priestess of Maldita show up in your brother's bed?

What could I say? "I—"

"Some day," she said, and disappeared into her room.

~

JAY

THE HOUSE WAS BURSTING AT ITS SEAMS.

Dee and Robin split the big bedroom and Maggie used the smaller on one side of the house, Sumi and Jay in the added-on bedroom on the other side of the house, the boys in their own little corner in the main room and now Mouse on the couch— it was too much, and Jay saw it in the tension that gripped each of his sisters when they were home.

Which they all were, right now— a rarity. In the middle of the day, when it was already sweltering. Adding all the bodies didn't help.

At least Maggie was behaving decently again. Sumi already looked happier, though it had only been two days since he'd taken his youngest sister to task.

Jay sacrificed one of his oldest shirts for mending, and as soon as he did, the vultures came round to rip it to pieces— as intended. He took his own piece of faded brown— a bit of shoulder?— and tacked it to the inside of the worn knee on his second-best pair of pants. Needle, a bit of thread, and he could mind his family while he mended.

Sumi swore under her breath as she darned a sock. He watched her— competent if irritated. Dee folded a blanket, put it down on the floor, then lowered herself down and knitted winter socks as if the sun didn't beat down on their roof. No swearing from her— knitting seemed to be a form of medita- tion. Robin patched three spots on a shirt in the time it took him to patch the knee of his pants. Maggie—

Maggie was the surprise.

She plopped down onto one end of the couch. Would have been on top of Mouse's legs if the girl hadn't jerked them out from under her. Shoved aside Mouse's blanket, then handed her yarn and a hook and started teaching her to crochet.

Mouse looked as stunned as the rest of them.

Maggie was spending so much time away from the house he hadn't been sure she knew Mouse had moved in or was avoiding her, but watching Maggie decide to teach the still-feral Yellow girl how to crochet— Jay hastily swallowed the lump in his throat.

Good girl.

Wil and Andy looked from bowed head to bowed head and muttered to each other. Stared at Sumi.

She didn't seem to notice them at all, still bent over her mending, but as Jay watched, she glanced at them. Nodded slightly.

Like arrows from a bow, they were out the front door, before he could do or say anything.

Jay scowled.

"Don't." Sumi glanced at him, nothing more than a flicker, but he saw it all in her face. *Let them go. They'll be fine. I talked with them and they'll be smart, be safe.*

She knew.

She knew about the times the boys had been in danger and still she let them go. Knew he'd almost failed them.

Something dark and dangerous roared inside him. If he was there, he could protect them— could fight back the danger— but she let them go—

His breathing rasped. The last time he'd left Sumi alone, she'd died. But the boys were in danger too. How could he choose between them? The edges of his vision went dark.

All he could see was her face, gray and still—

Sumi touched his arm. Her hand burned against his skin. She didn't say anything, just looked at him.

The little noises around him came back. His vision widened again to include his sisters, Mouse. He concentrated on his breathing. Slowed it.

Groaned and sank back into his seat. And the dark, dangerous part of him grumbled, subsided.

Sometimes his Sumi was so aware of every little thing and sometimes... not. He didn't quite understand it. Suspected it had to do with her magic.

But he didn't want to think of it.

So he focused on his mending— made each stitch perfect. Heard Sumi resume her swearing. Felt her knee touch his. Drank coffee to wash the iron from his mouth.

It wasn't getting better or going away. The darkness inside him. But if he focused on each stitch, he could ignore it a little longer.

Wondered, in the main room of his parents' house with all his sisters, his love, and Mouse all jostling for space, which of them would bring it up first. Maggie for sure—

"Hot out there," Dee said between counting stitches. "Tight in here."

"We need a bigger house," Maggie muttered.

"Or fewer people in it." Robin opened her mouth to say more, but that dark thing inside Jay rose up to cut her off.

"No." If they left, he couldn't keep them safe— He scrabbled to fight the darkness back. Sumi's knee against his helped. And — he reminded himself— they were just talking. No one was actually leaving.

Steered his thoughts away from the boys, out there in the streets of the Rest Third. Without him.

"We're doing all right." His tongue felt large, scraping in his mouth. He swallowed the last of his coffee. "We are, right? All of us together, the way Mom and Dad wanted."

Robin and Dee exchanged a quick side glance. "It's just a lot of people in a small space," Dee said. "It's only working because we're never here together."

"Like now." Sweat beaded at his hairline. He *had* to convince them—

Dee grinned, quick and bright. "Now is nice. Too resting hot, but nice. But if we were all here, all the time, it would be untenable. Just like it would be torture to pack all the guards into the guardhouse at the same time. We'd be on top of each other. Miserable."

"But you said it—" Made himself sound reasonable. "We're not all here together all the time."

"But we each need our own space." Robin's nostrils flared.

"You're right, it's crowded." Jay set his mending down on his lap. Took a deep breath. Leaned forward. "But what if we expand?"

"The house? That's expensive." Dee's eyes flicked to Mouse, then back to her own mending.

He knew what she meant. They'd just gotten back to a comfortable place, with Sumi cleaning and teaching and taking services in kind, the boys fetching water and running the occasional errand, and Jay working again. Mouse upset that delicate balance. One less day of work and they would have to skimp on food for everyone.

He wanted to take care of them all. If only—

Jay realized he'd crumpled his pants in his fists and made himself relax, press the fabric back out. Control his darkness. "It is expensive, but—"

"I can move in with—" Robin stopped short. Looked like she had swallowed her own tongue.

Move in with—? What in the resting betweens? "Who?" Jay demanded. Stood. His half-mended pants fell to the floor.

"Don't be mad." Robin slid off her chair and backed up a step. "I've been spending time with someone. After spying on the demon hunters, some of the things that happened... I needed to talk to someone and I found someone who listens to me and—"

"*Who?*" She hadn't talked to him. She thought he wouldn't listen to her. Goddessi, he was a resting shitty brother and now she wanted to move *out*—

"Lena." Robin lifted her chin and met his gaze even though hers wavered.

Dee rose and stood beside her. Supporting her.

Against him.

Sumi put her hand on his back, a touch of cool against his sweaty shirt.

"Lena?"

There were no women with that name in the Rest Third Guard, none in the neighborhood. Who—

"*Purple* Lena?" Sumi choked. "Head of the Damned Third Guard?"

Jay gaped at his little sister.

Robin flushed. "Yes."

"You and *Lena?*" Sumi seemed just as stunned.

"She's a *Purple*. And twice your age!" Jay clenched his fists, considered punching a wall. If that woman was taking advantage of his sister—

"She's not. She is a little older, but she's smart and wonderful and *beautiful* and I l-l-love her." Robin's voice caught and tears welled in her eyes. "And there's nothing you can do about it, Brother. I'm of age. And I'm moving in with her."

Resting betweens. The darkness loomed again—

"No..." Jay scrubbed his face. "Wait. Please. Don't move out yet. Let me get used to the idea. Please."

"Lena," Sumi said softly, still blinking in shock.

"I won't get between you." Jay held out his hands. Begged. "You deserve to be happy and if she makes you happy..." He swallowed. "Then that's great. Just— please. Don't move out yet. I'm not ready."

Dee nudged Robin. "You made him say please."

Robin choked on her laugh. "All right. I'll stay. A little longer."

"You knew," Sumi accused Dee.

Before Jay could process that, Dee smirked. "Of course I did. Who do you think introduced them?" Then, again before Jay could recover from *that* blow, she stepped nose-to-nose with Jay. Brought Robin with her. Lowered her voice so only the four of them— Dee, Robin, Jay, Sumi— could hear. "How are we going to pay for adding a room to the house? We're stretching thin again with the extra mouth to feed."

"We'll have enough money after—"

"After?" Robin raised her eyebrows. Shifted away so it didn't look like they were excluding Maggie. Smart. Goddessi, she regained her equilibrium fast, Jay marveled. He was still reeling. But before he could stop her, she went on, "That's right, you took Litka's place on The List."

"List?" Sumi looked back and forth between them.

Maggie snorted. Mouse peeked at them, scowled, and tore out a stitch.

"*The* List." Robin grinned. "Easy work, easy money, guarding rich people's stuff so nothing happens to it."

He'd wanted to tell Sumi himself. But he slumped, couldn't find the words.

"Guarding—" She bit her lip and tried desperately to not look hopeful.

"Guarding their records." He turned to her. Let a tiny smile play on his lips. "Their *stories*."

"Then we'll be the best guards ever." She started thinking, imagining it— he could see it on her face.

"Jay—" Dee warned, but he cut her off with a sweep of his hand.

The other guards didn't need to know about Sumi joining him for this job. They'd have a tantrum if they knew, but as long as no one found out, it would be fine.

Everything would be fine.

It was worth it to see the smile on her face, that look in her eyes.

His Sumi was back.

CHAPTER

TWELVE

S *umi*

JAY'S REACTION YESTERDAY WORRIED ME. THE THOUGHT OF ANY OF HIS sisters moving out had infuriated him, and the man I knew didn't anger easily. He was becoming obsessed with protecting us all.

I'd thought convincing Mouse to stay— give him someone younger, more passive to protect— would help, but I couldn't say it wasn't making things worse.

Lena— the woman Robin apparently *loved*, and that was going to take some getting used to— had talked of something similar to me once.

It was a guard thing, she'd said, but could apply to anyone in the temples. When one of them had seen too much, got stuck on something they'd experienced, they'd be hurt, but hurt in their souls. Become angry because anger was so often easier and more acceptable than hurt. Close off themselves to the good things— like I'd done for a time before meeting Jay.

But falling in love with Jay had healed some of my hurts. His loving us seemed to be the *source* of his hurts. And as protective as he was of his sisters, he wouldn't talk to Lena about it. Especially not if she and Robin were spending time together.

I didn't know how to help him.

Thom— perhaps Thom could help.

I'd risen, taught the children, then come back to bed and fallen asleep. Now I lay in bed with the man I loved and watched him wake. He woke fast, like I supposed all guards did, and when he saw me watching him, he smiled. I loved him just awake, hair tousled and brown eyes warm in trickles of afternoon sun.

Perhaps I was wrong and love was enough to heal this obsessive need to protect us.

"Robin let it slip. The job is tonight." I traced a finger over his arm, and watched bumps rise and flatten under his lovely brown skin.

"Mmm." He sprawled, granting me access to his chest.

And I took advantage. Ran my hand over his muscles. "A job. The List?"

He froze— an awkward word in the heat of the afternoon and our bed. Then his hand captured mine and moved it off him. He turned away. "Maybe you should stay here."

My stomach flipped. I hadn't imagined his need to protect us. Me. "I won't," I said. Sat up and tried to remember to be patient, compassionate. The things the high priestess of Maldita *wasn't*. "If you go without me, I'll go out tonight too. Find something else to do."

His shoulders bunched. What a pity we were wasting our time together with a fight. But he needed to remember I was my own woman and made my own choices. Could take care of myself—

Until I'd refused to use my magic.

So... I could still use my wits. If I allowed him to steal my choices now, I would end up hating him. I couldn't bear it.

I crossed the gulf of our bed and ran my hands over his shoulders. "Trust me," I told him. "Trust me to be safe with you as I trust you to keep me safe."

His shoulders slumped. "You are safer *with* me," he admitted.

I shifted my hands lower. "So we steal the histories—"

"No." Jay jerked away from me and stood. "We *read* them. We don't steal them. Rest Third guards don't steal what they're guarding."

I blinked at him. He had a point. But the demon hunters... "But—"

"No. No stealing or you don't come."

I winced. His face told me this was non-negotiable. Going up against his guard training so often was.

"So we protect their stories from the demon hunters and *read* them ourselves and hope our enemies don't steal them."

"Yes."

I shrugged. "All right."

He leaned over and kissed me and for a moment I was as lost in his kiss as I'd ever been— Then he stepped back. "I brought you a new shirt, new pants."

He fumbled under the bed, then handed me a red tunic and red trousers. They weren't silk and leather, but they were cotton and clean and new. "How much—?"

"Don't worry about it." He smiled. Leaned over again and teased me, his lips nearly touching mine. "I like that I was able to buy you something. Even if it's not as good as the temple."

"Better." I shifted, but he turned his head, and his mouth

found the corner of mine, then trailed down my neck, and then his hands were in my hair and—

He stepped back yet again.

I was going to murder him. Slowly.

"We have an appointment with Thom."

I growled. But then remembered Thom might help him with the overprotectiveness. "Fine."

"Get dressed."

"Fine!"

He smirked and headed out into the main room. Closed the door behind him.

Leaving me *frustrated*. As I'd be until he believed me *completely well*. But to be able to read the stories the demon hunters were after— bless it. Every time I thought I could forget about them, they resurfaced.

So I dressed and braided what was left of my hair out of my face and told the boys to listen to Jay's sisters.

"Want a ride?" Jay hefted his guard flying carpet.

"I'd rather walk."

He slung it over his back and held out a hand. We walked away from the house to the Rest Third guardhouse and as soon as I stepped inside, it felt like everyone turned to stare at me.

So, really no worse than stealing the high priestess position from my sisters— naked.

I lifted my chin and avoided everyone's eyes and followed Jay like I belonged. He took me upstairs, then knocked on a closed door.

"Come." Thom. His voice was distinctive, even through the door.

"Sir." Jay stood stiffly, reminding me of how he used to stand when guarding me. Whether or not I'd asked him.

"Sumi?" Thom's brows arched up high on his face, and it didn't crack. I hadn't been sure he could show that much expression— which wasn't fair. He'd grieved for Jay's mother. Maybe I was just used to being afraid he would figure out who I was.

Jay nodded. "Yes. She's coming along."

Thom's eyes flicked past us as if he were looking at the city behind the walls.

"They won't like it."

The guards? The family who owned the stories? The demon hunters?

"Don't tell them. It'll be fine."

They were talking code in front of me like I could understand it. On the one hand I was flattered, on the other, furious.

"Don't tell the client about the person they're hiring who is bringing along another person they *didn't* hire."

"We'll be there before your runner can brief them anyway." Jay grinned.

Thom looked at him.

"Almost?"

Thom sighed. "Your job to lose. The Stonefields own all the fields across the river."

"*All* the fields?" I knew better, but some demon made me say it anyway.

"All not owned by a temple." Thom examined me in a way that made me regret opening my mouth. The less he thought of me in conjunction with a temple, the better. "They own the grain silos too. They're the backbone of this city. The river is its heart."

Right. *Now* he was treating me like a simpleton. Now that I had his attention.

I knew the founding families better than most as I'd had to deal with them all for the damned temple's sake. Next though, next he'd tell me about the merchants—

Thom smiled at me gamely. "The Purples and Blues— the merchants— are its lungs."

Any other sad metaphors about the city? I kept the words in my mouth. This was the man I wanted to ease Jay's need to protect us. His anger.

And then my mouth opened again— "The Yulians."

Thom flushed at my tone. I shouldn't trouble him— his family served the city not just as merchants but as guards as well, evidenced by his position as the head of the Rest Third Guard.

He cleared his throat. "And the Lunatas and the Wescotts—"

"Sorry." I waved one hand. "I apologize. A demon has gotten into me today."

"I hope not literally."

Now he was twitting me, and I liked him better for it. I laughed. "Not that I know of."

His mouth quirked.

"Fascinating as this all is..." Jay leaned forward. "What do we need to know for tonight's job?"

Thom sobered, and leaned forward as well. "At sunset, you'll present yourself at the front gates of the Stonefield Manor and be shown the items you are guarding. Guard everything all night. Done at dawn."

"All in one room?"

"They've been instructed to centralize their histories."

"Good." Jay turned to leave.

My feet stayed rooted to the floor. I hadn't thought this through. "Ah, may I have a word?"

Jay paused at the door. His shoulders bunched. He knew I knew something and didn't want to hear it, but he didn't leave.

Thom just looked at us.

I fumbled for how to explain it without giving myself away.

"In the dark temple, I... saw things that lingered. Hurt me to think about. I... wonder if Jay is feeling—"

"No," he said from the door, his back still to us.

"He's angry. Angrier than he was in the damned temple, and that's not right. It... frustrates him to let the rest of us out of his sight."

"I'm fine."

"Talk to him," I told Thom.

He nodded sharply, his eyes fierce.

Thank the goddess.

I dredged up a smile and went to Jay.

"Ready?" We descended the stairs together. I ignored the hostile glares sent my way and focused on leaving the building.

Once we were outside, despite the stifling heat of summer, I could breathe again. "Are *you* ready?" I teased Jay.

He smiled. Only the brackets around his mouth showed his tension at the exchange I'd had with Thom. "Let's go earn some easy money."

Tension fizzed up my spine and I savored it. "Stop the— um — bad guys."

The Rest Third changed as we walked northwest, toward the river. Larger houses, larger gardens, more Browns and Reds and the occasional Purple or Blue. Jay tugged gently at a lock of my red hair— no black, still no black. "You're sure you need to come along? It could get dangerous if those *bad guys* do show up."

"Anything the demon hunters want to see, we need to see." I couldn't quite explain it, but I knew, inside. We had no choice, really.

I watched the people as we walked. Now that we were in the midst of the richest area of the Rest Third, the Purples and Blues and Browns far outnumbered Reds and Greens. Cleaner hands, newer clothes and more of it imported instead of homespun. No Yellows nor Oranges. The Reds and Greens wore gray trimmed Purple or Blue or Brown, and a house placard as well.

Jay noticed me watching them and muttered, "Servants."

Suddenly aware of eyes on me, I twisted to murmur in his ear, "What does Color have to do with serving someone?"

He shrugged. "They're high caste. Who understands how they think? This is what it is."

My brain felt like I had stubbed my toe against a threshold, and the memory of Maldita's voice played in my ear— *Red for blood, white for bone, black for soul are the Colors that matter.*

Power didn't follow the Colors— obviously, since the current high priestessi were all Red, not Blue or Purple, and some of the most powerful priestessi and magi I knew were Rahel— Yellow— and Adan— Brown. Orange Eya had the potential to be very strong, once she learned some discipline. The color of the skin didn't matter to *push-pull* magic.

But telling people that hadn't seemed to work. *Showing* them, making them work with the people they thought they despised worked— sometimes.

My thoughts carried me the rest of the way to Stonefield Manor.

The brick wall stretched past us in both directions, meeting the other houses' walls in one seamless line. Between the wall and the trees, I couldn't see the manor at all. That piqued my curiosity. We presented ourselves to the front gate where a Brown woman blocked our way.

"Jay from the Rest Third Guard." He nodded to me. "And Sumi."

The woman checked a list, then nodded. "Come inside the gate. Move to the left and wait there. Someone from the house will come for you."

Jay nodded. The gate swung open. We passed when we were told and stood where we were told.

Once inside, I could see more of the house. It had started large and only grown larger; older brick gave way to newer as wings were added, and the second story was wood. I wondered how much magic had been used to raise it, if any. There were windows everywhere, and the front area where we waited felt more like the damned temple gardens than a private house. Voices came from the back, and I wondered what a manor had behind it. More gardens? Fields? Something mysterious I couldn't imagine?

"You there. Guard." The man's voice boomed over the sounds of children playing in the backyard. He'd approached from the side and made me jump. "You ready?"

We turned. I clutched Jay's arm, trying to not betray my shock.

The big Brown man looked a heaven of a lot like an older version of Jay, and I could see them both noting it— the line of their noses, the shape of their ears, the same brown hair, though Jay's had some yellow in it.

They were related, somehow.

Ah, goddessi, we were going to lose this job before we'd even started it.

∾

Jay

THE BROWN MAN LOOKED LIKE HIS DAD. JAY HEARD HIS HEART thunder, nearly missed the man's words.

"You're Ren's boy." The Brown man beamed. "Look just like him."

"You— knew my father?"

He sobered. "Dunno what Thom was thinking, sending

you."

Jay's chin came up. "He was thinking you wanted the best."

"If she sees you..." he shook his head. "Best go the long way round. Might tickle her to see her nephew working for her. Might not."

"Nephew?"

"She had five boys and him smack in the middle, but Renfreth always was her favorite. That's why Ma took it so hard when he left us for the girl." He side-eyed them. "Your mother."

"You're..." Jay shook his head. "You're saying you're my *uncle*?"

"The old harridan never could abide anyone having thoughts of their own. Still," the man threw over his shoulder while leading them down a long hall, "once she's at rest, you'll come. Bring your siblings. Meet your cousins and their cousins."

"Cousins..." Sumi nudged him along like he was dazed and wit-wandering— which he was. Three sisters and no one else to uncles, cousins, a grandmother. "Come meet them?"

"Fair horde of us, when we all get together. I'm Nick. Nickard. Second oldest, just older than your dad." The man grinned.

Jay almost missed the guard at the double doors. The guard who groped Sumi with his eyes then sneered at Jay. "'Bout time you got here."

"Excuse me." Nick— his *uncle*— handed the guard a bag of coin and jerked his head. "You can find your own way out?"

The guard inclined his head. "Yes, Honored Brown."

"Then go on."

Nick waited for the guard to go, grinned at Jay, who still couldn't think past *his father had belonged to this family.* Opened double doors to a towering room filled with books and scrolls and tables and chairs and more books. "Welcome home, boy."

That snapped him out of it. This wasn't his home. This was a job. And a scam on top of it. They'd never forgive him if they found out, but he wasn't about to forgive them for casting off his father for loving his mother.

"And the particular items you want guarded?" he asked coolly.

The Brown man noticed. His smile faltered. He shifted to business as well. "These," he said. Waved one hand over a pile on a table in the center of the room. Watched them carefully.

Jay nodded. "They'll be here come morning."

His *uncle*— Nick— nodded sharply. "Three doors, and that unlocked one's a necessary." He pointed. "Windows locked shut. Despite that in other houses, they've been getting in. But not here, because of you guards. I'll be seeing you in the morning."

The man closed the doors behind him. Turned a key in the lock.

Sumi went to the necessary and showed him it was much more like her necessary in the damned temple than the small sink that filled the pull-flush night-soil pot they used at Jay's house. Here— too many pipes, a real toilet, and a bathtub and probably all the water drinkable, despite the waste. She arched an eyebrow in appreciation. "I'd no idea you belonged to such a wealthy family."

"I don't." It came out surly, and he knew it. He tried for a more even tone. "I didn't know they existed. And after what they did to my father—" He shook his head. "I don't belong."

She nodded sympathetically. Left the necessary and crossed to a table between the two locked doors. "Water and weak wine," she said, sniffing at the pitchers. "Crackers and *fresh* bread and olives and berries." She stopped long enough he turned and saw her clasp her hands to her chest reverently. "*Cookies*," she breathed. "I could get used to working for your

—" She pinged the side of a temple-made glass. Smiled. Poured wine into it. "For rich folks."

If his... alleged *family*... saw him now, they wouldn't continue to employ him. He wiped the scowl from his face. Made himself cross the room and accept wine from Sumi. Sipped.

Not as good as he'd had in the Temple of the Damned, but pretty resting close.

He entertained himself for two minutes, thinking what it might have been like for his sisters to grow up here, to not have to work so hard every day, to do whatever it was his *cousins* did... then sneered and put that thought away. "Focus on the job," he reminded Sumi.

Reminded himself.

She nodded. Settled into a chair like dusk was settling into the room. Nibbled at the food and sipped the wine and wiped her fingers on a napkin as if she didn't miss all these little luxuries every day in his home. They had a few more now, with Sumi teaching and the boys running errands. But nothing like this.

The house quieted around them until the majority of what he heard were creaks and groans of wood and plumbing. The family had gone to bed, or at least retreated. He cautiously checked the doors to make sure they were locked, checked the windows. Sumi lit all the fancy lamps scattered around the room— the ones his *real* family could never afford. On the table next to the fireplace, she set out playing cards while Jay braced a chair under the door latch. He eyed Sumi and received her nod. Went to the pile of scrolls and unrolled the first.

Her eyes unfocused, *looked* for magic. Her kissable lips thinned as she read over his shoulder, then quirked in a not-smile. "No."

Not what they were looking for. He rolled, set it precisely

aside, and moved on to the next. "You really think the demon hunters' answers are somewhere in here?"

Sumi shrugged. "*They* think they are."

At the shake of her head, he moved that scroll out of the way. "And their answers are so important we have to stay up all night?"

"We might learn something to keep the goddessi far, far away from us." She smiled hesitantly.

He stilled. Swallowed. Touched the next scroll. "Worth it then."

As the hours whiled on, Jay moved all the scrolls to the next table and started in on the books, paging through them one at a time. There were many fewer books, but so many more pages. Eventually, he settled into his own chair, decided his *family* were a bunch of blowhards— all these scrolls and books they thought were so valuable had nothing of use.

And then Sumi hissed.

This time, Jay was flipping through the pages of a book, thank the resting betweens, because his hands convulsed around it in a way that would have crumpled a scroll.

It was a large, heavy thing, bound in leather and scribed in long, loopy letters that made Jay's head hurt, though Sumi seemed to read it well enough. "Look at this," she muttered, her finger running along the words.

"So they *do* have something useful." Jay looked at the size of the book. "That's... pages and pages of words. No one could remember them all."

"There was a desk..." She held up a lamp, headed to the far side of the room. "Pen. Ink. Paper." Brought all of it back while he held the book open. Then she sat down and started a copy.

He watched her— her hair shifted blood to shadow to blood in the flicker of the lantern light and his guts clenched, reminded of the Temple of the Damned— and marveled when her neat letters shifted to loops. She set out the first page and he looked back and forth between the copy and the original.

After the first paragraph, he couldn't see the difference in the writing.

Goddessi, the woman was a natural forger. He turned the page for her, watched her go on. Thought it was a resting good thing she hadn't been found by the criminals of the city when she was a child... then remembered the little she'd told him about her childhood with her blood-mother and winced.

She copied. He turned pages and wondered about the choices he was making.

The lamps guttered, oil almost gone, and dawn sneaked through the windows. Jay replaced the books where he'd gotten them while Sumi finished writing out the last page. She glanced at the lamps. Scowled and took the ink and the pen back to the desk. Set them just so, then took a pinch of fine sand from a dish. Scattered it across the papers to dry the ink faster. Picked up one paper after another and folded them, shoved them down the sides of her boots, into the waist of her pants.

The lock turned.

Jay ran for the door, spun the chair out from under the handle back to the table he'd taken it from. Sumi stood over the last paper, desperation on her face.

The handle moved. Couldn't be helped— Jay thrust the last sheet of paper into his shirt while Sumi dumped the drying sand into her sock. He winced for her and again for himself when he felt the grit of the freshly sanded paper rub against the skin on his gut. Threw himself back into a chair, trying not to crumple anything vital. Flipped a card.

The Brown man— *dear* old Uncle Nick— poked his head into the room and for a moment it was like seeing his own dad brought back to life, peeking into Jay's bedroom to wake him in the morning.

Jay's heart thudded. He shook himself clearheaded. Rose stiffly as if he hadn't just sat. Held a hand out to Sumi. She scooped up the cards as if they'd just been interrupted in their game and thrust the deck at him.

"Morning," Jay said neutrally, pocketed the cards. Carefully lifted his sword belt off the table and buckled it around his waist.

Nick's gaze went between them to the scrolls on one table, the books on another.

"Got bored," Jay said, rolling his shoulders and settling his blade. *Sound uneducated.* "Tried to read some of these things, but I don't read that well and *she* don't read at all."

Sumi stared as if she were addled. Jay stifled a chuckle. "All there, if you want to count. Kept safe for one more night."

"Reading? To stay awake?" Nick sounded baffled, as if they should have been making love on the floor instead. "I suppose that's all right. Since you're family."

Jay schooled his face to simple sincerity. "Thom said you'd have them all safe after tonight, yeah? No need for us to come back?"

"Yeah— yes. A priestess coming to put magic on them. Prevent them from being taken from the room."

"Good. I, ah..." Jay studied his boots. "Perhaps I will come. After Grandmother is at rest. If you'll send word through Thom."

Nick smiled. "I will, son."

With the feeling they were escaping a sleepy but still deadly moose, Jay followed his uncle out of the room and out of the house. Tangled his fingers in Sumi's when they were clear of the front gate.

Breathed a sigh of relief.

They were free.

THIRTEEN

S *umi*

UP AT DAWN AFTER COPYING JAY'S ESTRANGED FAMILY HISTORIES ALL night was not my favorite time to teach a bunch of kids *anything*. I could feel the exhaustion pulling at me, blurring my focus, but numbers— always the same, two plus two equals four— were solid enough to ground me in the here and now. The copied pages went under our bed, safely hidden and for now, out of my thoughts.

Tara and Nathy continued to be the fastest at their numbers, but they were cheerful little souls who were happy to help the others. Suann's daughter, Cori, struggled when left to herself, but bloomed under their tutelage. Andy and Wil spent most of their time helping the Orange boy and the Green boy, and practicing magic in tiny ways at the same time— they needed to be able to split their attention.

Mouse... when it was a story, Mouse could remember things

word for word. When she had to write her numbers, even the youngest child far surpassed her.

I was making up a silly story about the number seven so Mouse could remember the shape of it when Andy hissed. I looked at the children first, checked to make sure they were where they were supposed to be, no one injured, then—

Tasha and Gui sauntered down the middle of the street, as confident as a high priestess in her own temple. Staring right at me. Coming toward us. Me, the boys, the neighborhood children—

The neighborhood would never forgive me if I let their children associate with thieves, much as a relationship between an Orange and a Purple would do them good to see.

I kept my gaze focused on my two newest recurring problems, but directed my words to the kids. "You all head home and practice your numbers. Tomorrow we'll have a test to see how much you can do. Run along now."

Perhaps they heard it in my tone, but— miracle— they did as they were told without any extraneous questions. Wil and Andy side-eyed me like I was mad. I didn't want Gui and Tasha to know about the boys, but it looked like it was too late for that.

Mouse, though—

Mouse looked like she'd seen a ghost.

Gui was walking slower now, staring at Mouse. Tasha noticed, and her step faltered.

This had all the makings of a giant mess, right here in the front yard in front of Jay and the neighbors and the goddessi.

"Wil, Andy, you two have been all over this city," I murmured, for their ears alone. "Is there a place we can all talk in private?"

Wil stared up at me. "You're letting us—"

Andy nudged him with a sharp elbow. "Yeah, Mom. It's close, too. Follow us."

Mouse ducked like she was going back inside but I grabbed her collar. "You too. Looks like you're a part of this."

I met Tasha's eyes, then Gui's, and jerked my head, then followed the boys, towing Mouse along with me. They took us down and over a couple streets to a building taller than those around it, with fallow yard space and far too many shadows under the early morning sun.

"What is this place?" My words fell like rocks in the shade of the building as the boys led us around to the back. The maw of an empty doorway gaped like the mouth into hell.

"Abandoned." Wil shrugged. "No one ever comes here. Not for a long time."

Andy nodded, then scurried inside.

Once my eyes adjusted to the gloom, I saw a large room with a balcony around its edges and a couple small rooms coming off it. Down low, the windows had been broken out and boarded up again, but up high—

In the peak of the roof to the east shone glory— a massive round window composed of lead and bits of colored glass, all bright with the sun shining through them and down onto us. The wonders we could make, when we wished— I swallowed hard, then twisted to look behind me. A matching window sat in the west, in shadow.

Red and yellow and green and blue light fell down onto boxes and partial walls that made the main room into a kind of maze. The floor was fairly clean. A broom leaned drunkenly against the wall by the back door where we'd come in, and when I glanced at Andy, he blushed and ducked his head.

My boys had been spending a lot of time here.

"Why'd you bring us here?" Tasha demanded as soon as she crossed the threshold.

My magic surged raggedly inside me, but I shoved it back down, holding tight to my temper. "You came to my home. Either you want more lessons or you want to yell at me. Either way, we shouldn't be within hearing distance of a house full of guards, should we?"

Gui bumped against Tasha, pushing her further into the room. "Lessons," he confirmed. "You ain't been around much to hold up our bargain."

"Yelling might be nice," Tasha muttered.

Belatedly, I let Mouse go. She scurried into the darkness like her namesake and I felt a pang of shame for dragging her along after me. But she needed to deal with whatever was going on, and if it involved these two, she needed to do it far, far away from Jay. "All right. A lesson, then."

After another look around— lacking both a cheap lamp and my ability to *pull* daylight from outside in— I located the stairs to the balcony and cautiously made my way up. The balcony was just as clean as the room below. The boys had been up here too. I tested my weight against the railing before I leaned over to locate my students. Sure enough, Gui had cornered Mouse, and I could hear every word.

"Mari—"

"Don't use that name. I hate it. I'm Mouse now."

Gui rolled his eyes. "Sure, Cousin. As you say. But how would Daddy Enzo feel if he knew his baby girl was running around in the city he's trying to purge? And what about Grandpa Zerth? He's haunting you for sure."

"Shut up!" Mouse glared back at him, defiance in every line of her body. "Grandpa Zerth didn't do nothing for me and my father don't *care*. Just like Mom. No one *cares* where I am or what I do. This Red and her family... they might be nutters but they ain't preaching 'bout demons and they give me food an' a place to sleep and they don't *touch* me like dear ol—"

"All right, all right." Gui held his hands up in defeat. "Sorry, kid. You just... surprised me, is all. But this 'un is taking care of you?"

"As much as I let her." Mouse jutted out her chin. "She don't tell me where to go nor who to marry, so that's a start."

"Yeah." Gui ran one hand over his face. "Yeah, that's a start." He glanced around until he found me, then glared. "Righto, eavesdropper. Let's get to our lesson then."

Our houseguest was related to the leaders of the demon hunters. Not just distantly. Zerth was her *grandfather*. It was the farthest thing from *fine* I could imagine. But what could I say? I was the missing high priestess of Maldita, and so far, being away from the temple to make my own choices was the best thing that had ever happened. "Let's."

Mouse put her hand on Gui's arm. "You're all right too? You're with that 'un cause you choose?"

Gui smiled. "I am."

Now that they'd settled that—

"What is this place?" Tasha was directly below me. She'd been eavesdropping too, but she hid it better.

"Abandoned church," Andy said from next to me. The boy appeared out of the shadows like he was part shadow himself.

Wil— as expected— popped up next to him. "Neighbors say it's old. Hasn't been used for a long, long time. They also say it's haunted." He sounded thrilled.

Couldn't really be a church— it wasn't shaped like a temple of the goddessi, didn't have the feel. Maybe an outlander church, but not one of ours.

Tasha squinted up at me. "You don't believe in ghosts?"

I remembered blood flowing through the air to me, the dark goddess sucking it in through my tattoos— *I believe in much much worse things.* I scrubbed at my arms. "No."

Tasha snorted. "So... you going to teach us or not?"

"We're going to play a game. Mouse hides, you and Gui find." I smiled grimly. "You all keep your magic quiet or we'll have guards on us quick. The blessed are... two streets over? And they'll feel anything loud."

"And your boys?"

Was that a subtle threat? I couldn't decide, so I treated it like it was not. "They'll observe. Watch for too much magic."

"So they can do it too." Now she was satisfied. I'd given something away, bless it. But she'd have figured it out eventually.

"Careful," I told her. "They might decide to help. And they like Mouse better than you."

She laughed.

Thus began the strangest game of hide-and-seek I'd ever seen.

Mouse was fast and crept through shadows like she owned them. She always knew when any of the others were near— always. And when I checked, I could *feel* subtle shifts in *push-pull* magic, but they were so delicate, I almost didn't believe it.

Without any training, she was using magic to avoid Tasha and Gui, who were both actively using their magic to try to find her.

They crept around each other in a strange dance that had me holding my breath more than once. And then one of the boys would throw something down— magical or physical— and completely change the game.

The first time Andy threw down a scrap of board, it clattered off a partial wall and all of us jumped. Mouse was fastest to take advantage of the distraction and darted halfway across the church before Tasha realized she'd moved. Gui glared up at us, but Tasha just followed grimly, her magic reaching out in front of her like a pair of spectral hands.

The next time, the chunk of wood barely missed Gui's head

and he was the only one who jumped. I did spare a moment to glare at Wil. He winked at me, and the game went on.

It went on, in fact, through breakfast into the afternoon, until the boys flopped down beside me and gave up all interest, until Tasha sprawled on the stairs, until only Gui and Mouse were still at it, and I didn't think either one of them would— or could— voluntarily give up.

"That's enough for today." My voice projected throughout the building and I wondered if anyone outside was close enough to hear it and whisper of ghosts.

The boys bolted down the stairs and out of the building before the rest of us had mustered the energy to move.

"You've learned some things, I trust?" I eyed Tasha, then held out one hand to help her up.

"I did." She took my hand but barely leaned into it to climb to her feet. "Gui, though?"

The Orange man snarled when Mouse emerged from where she'd been hiding— in the fireplace. She had soot across her face and for an instant, I flashed back to the many nights over the years the dark goddess Maldita had consumed her sacrifice blood, bone, and soul, until only the smallest ashes were left.

Being tired was no excuse for letting my mind wander. I jerked it back to attention and nodded cordially to all my students. "Practice, practice, practice," I offered them, "but do it quietly."

Then took myself out from abandoned building in the hope I might find a nap at home.

~

JAY

· · ·

OF ALL THE GUARDS HE ASKED TO HELP OUT TODAY, ONLY DEE AND Robin and Thom showed up. Even Maggie had disappeared, claiming she was *working*.

About the time Sumi dismissed the neighboring children— blessedly early— and took the boys off somewhere, they were ready to start. At first, Jay was irritated none of the neighbors came to help, but then he thought of their children running wild and broke into a sweat.

The neighbors *were* helping— by keeping their kids away.

So today they'd remove the roof slates, pry up the trusses, and extend the house upward. One more room where it wouldn't cover up precious dirt. That was all they needed. One more resting room.

Then put the roof back together and hope it didn't leak.

"You've confused them." Thom carefully pried up the fixing nail, then a tile. He scowled at both. "I don't think your roof would have lasted through another storm. It's a good thing we're taking all these off now."

"Confused who?" Jay took the tile and the nail, crept over to the side of the roof, reached down and handed them to Dee who handed them to Robin.

Robin and Dee would straighten the fixing nails the best they could, would pile the slate tiles to the side where they could use them again once the new room had been added.

"We're going to need to use glue with the nails when we reroof your addition." Thom pulled up another tile, this time with no nail. "This one stayed up on sheer luck."

Jay sighed. "Glue will help. And we'll buy the nails we need. More nails and tiles we can reuse, more money we'll save." He squinted across the city toward the river. "Surprised Mal didn't show up."

"Mal's covering for Litka today. But the rest of them... the guards..."

Jay faltered. Nearly dropped the tile off the roof— which would have been an expensive mistake. "What?"

"There are rumors."

"Like always."

"You brought Sumi along to a job."

"Yeah. I did." Jay raised his chin, felt the stirring of darkness inside him.

Thom handed him another tile, but held onto it until Jay met his gaze. "You put your family first. Ever since you went off to the Temple of the Damned— even, resting betweens, *going* off to the temple, you put your family before them." He raised his eyebrows. "As you should."

"Job won't be there for you if you can't pick up a sword," Jay grumbled.

"Nope." Thom bared his teeth. "They don't want to admit that they do the same. They're young. But they'll learn."

"Rumors—"

"Don't worry about that. Guards'll talk. That's what they do. And they'll keep learning from you, like it or not. Won't back-talk you either, not since you took on Litka like that. Thank you for not breaking her. She's a good guard and we'd've been short for however long it took her to heal."

Jay grunted. Rolled his shoulders. Walked another tile off the edge of the roof.

"You've always been a protective sort," Thom said solemnly, "but now like your woman said, you're angry about it. And that's not the man I remember."

"Things happen. People change." Jay took the next tile and turned his back on his mentor.

He didn't want to think about it. Didn't want to talk about it. Didn't want to give the darkness inside him any more strength.

"Things happen, yes." Thom was quick, always ready with another tile and nail. "Are you sleeping?"

Jay scowled. Thought of all the time he *wasn't* sleeping, too worried about his sisters or Sumi or the boys. Thought about all the times he closed his eyes and saw his dead around him, accusing. "I'm fine."

"Not what I asked."

"I can still do my job."

"But sleep would help." Thom nodded sharply. "If I were a betting man—"

"You are."

Thom grinned. "I'd bet you have nightmares about the people you think you've failed. Then you stay up worrying about the ones you think you *will* fail."

Jay flinched. Walked the tile to the edge of the roof and took his time handing it off to his sister. This time, as he walked back across the slant of the roof, he concentrated on placing his boot just so for every step. Frowned at Thom. If there was one man in the city who had seen death, failed his people, yet done his best for them, it was the man on his roof, handing him another resting tile and nail. "You think you can help."

"Me? No." Thom grimaced. "But I can give you some pointers and you can help yourself."

Jay made several trips back and forth with Thom's words churning in his guts. When he couldn't bear the silence any longer, he said, "So? Spit 'em out."

"Right." Thom took a deep breath, but Jay hauled away another tile. When he returned, Thom said, "These things are going to sound pithy. But think about them and the more you think, the more complicated they'll become."

"Uh huh."

"Feel the feelings, son. Probably the hardest thing, but let yourself feel them. Then realize they're just feelings."

Jay snorted. His resting *feelings* could go shove themselves up someone else's orifice for a change.

"Let go. You can't control your sisters, your woman, your boys. You keep trying to control their every move, you'll lose them. But you can control yourself and your reactions."

"Right. Those reactions you say are problematic."

Thom sighed. "If you're not sleeping, then you're not controlling them. Just stuffing the feelings down till they leak out other ways. You feel the feelings, step aside and watch them go by, then they won't leak."

Jay paused to scrub his hands over his face. "Replacing the roof on my resting feelings while we replace the roof on this house?"

"Whatever it takes, son."

"Uh huh."

"Focus on the here and now. What you've got. What you can do."

"You don't understand. I can stop them. The bad things."

"You know that's impossible, son."

"I do. But—"

"But you can't stop thinking about it." Thom nodded. "Happens."

"Not helping."

Thom got that look in his eyes— the faraway, hurt one that meant he'd seen some shit. "I suspect most or all of us have the same feelings. Sure, some people go into the guard for the money, but more often it's a desire to protect. Their family, their neighborhood. But we can't stop every bad thing from happening. Not every single one. People make their own choices."

Jay scowled.

"You're afraid something will happen again. If you don't protect them. But what do you think will happen?"

Jay's hands went cold, his throat tight.

"What happened before?" Thom stopped his work on the roof to wait for an answer.

Jay coughed. Forced the words out. "Sumi died. Because I wasn't there," he admitted hoarsely. "Gray and still and cold—" The terror of it gripped his heart and squeezed so hard he forgot to pay attention to his steps.

Thom's head swiveled like he was looking for her. "But—?"

A shingle slid out from under Jay's foot and he sprawled on the roof, grunting and cursing, fingers digging at anything to keep himself from sliding off. If he hit the ground like this, he'd crack bones.

The loose shingle slid down.

Who was below? He bellowed, short and sharp, "Ware!"

An entire row followed the first shingle, one after another.

Dee cried out, "Wil!"

Shingles made meaty thuds and Dee made one agonized noise after another. Jay clung to the edge of the roof. Craned his neck to look down.

Saw a scene from his nightmares— Dee, hunched over Wil. Broken shingles all around them and tile marks up her back.

Blood seeping through her shirt.

Jay bent his knees and dropped. Hit hard and felt the jolt all the way up. Fell onto his ass, then crawled to his sister. Didn't know where he could touch her. What to do.

What to say.

CHAPTER
FOURTEEN

S*umi*

I CAME AROUND THE SIDE OF THE HOUSE WITH THE KNOWLEDGE THAT something was wrong, was about to go wrong, and saw Andy and Wil staring up at the roof just as tiles started coming down.

Falling tiles that would destroy faces and gouge out eyes.

My magic billowed up inside me and I *reached*—

Dee yelled. Shoved Andy away, grabbed Will and fell on top of him.

—I *yanked* back all my magic so hard it burned—

Tiles hit her back, thin edges and sharp corners and she flinched but held on tighter.

— my magic settled into pain that came up my neck, wrapped around my temples, sparkled around lights and sank nausea into my stomach. Still there, but I couldn't reach it.

Jay dropped from the roof, cursing.

My knees buckled and I faded to the ground.

Sounds started coming back, yelling. Wilyam apologizing through his sobs. Dee crying but in that hitching, moaning way that meant she was trying to be strong but was in agony she couldn't hide.

And every bit of sound made my head hurt.

My stomach churned. I could barely open my eyes. Had to see—

Jay and Robin and Thom circled Dee. Andy pulled Wil out from under her, but every move made her hiss or moan and none of them were coherent.

Andy clenched one fist, using his magic somehow. Perhaps to support Wil or stop any other tiles from coming down off the roof.

I could do nothing. *Nothing.* Andy looked at me, tears running down his cheeks, and tears pricked my eyes.

What was he asking? Tiniest movement— shook my head *no.* Paid for it in starbursts and a surge of bile.

His focus shifted back where it belonged.

Jay and Robin carried Dee into the house. Wil came back for me, his words bubbling in his throat.

"It was my fault, Mom. But I can't fix her back. It's too much. I can't. *We* can't..."

"It's all right." Carefully, I wrapped one arm around him. Held him tight. She'd saved his life. I *owed* her. "It'll be all right."

"Wil. Andy. I need you." Jay's voice cut through my brain like a knife. "Run to the market. To the temple messengers. We need a healer. We'll pay."

Wil wiped his face on his sleeve. Blinked at Andy. They joined hands, squinted at the roof. Fast, rough, magically tacked the tiles in place. Then nodded and bolted.

Sooner than they should be, they were back. Time was doing strange things around me. Andy blurted, "The dark temple healer won't come."

"Bright neither." Wil came to my side and tucked himself under my arm.

"But we'll pay!" Jay clenched his hands into fists.

Wilyam helped me to stand, and Antero came as soon as he saw me sway.

"I'll go." Jay's gaze flicked over me, over the boys. "I'll make them see reason."

Goddessi, I hoped he didn't get himself killed.

"Careful," I said, and I didn't know if it was to him or to the boys or to me, but it didn't matter because he was already gone.

We went into the house and the shift from daylight to gloom helped settle my stomach. I made it to a chair and breathed carefully through my nose, so I wouldn't throw up.

Dee lay on the couch, face down, limp. Robin pressed cloths to her back.

"It's not just the cuts," Robin whispered. Sweat beaded her forehead. "The way those tiles hit her..."

"I know." My voice was thick with tears.

Robin licked her lips. "She'll never walk again." Her voice rasped.

"Wait for the swelling to go down," Thom said from the doorway. He hid a shudder. He knew better, but said it anyway, "It might not be as bad as you think."

Desperate hope lit up Robin's face. The boys turned to me and I could see in their eyes they knew he was wrong.

If there was one person who couldn't be here for what I was about to do— "Thom, would you help Jay please? Make sure he doesn't..."

"Do anything stupid?" Thom nodded and disappeared from the doorway.

"Robin, there's a Rest Third healer, isn't there?"

"Yes. But—" *Not as good as magic.*

Her words went unsaid, but I heard them. "Go get them please."

She looked at Dee. Looked at me. Looked back at Dee. "You're getting rid of me." Her eyes were shadowed. "Why?"

"I can't tell you." My magic grew and grew in great surges inside me, demanding action. I fed it my headache, soothed the edges of it with a promise, but it kept growing.

I'd need it all anyway.

"This is some kind of dark temple thing."

"Mmm."

"You'll help her?"

"I'll try."

"Fine. Send the boys if you need anything." She fled.

"Don't let anyone in, boys." I swallowed my ebbing nausea, crossed the room, knelt by Dee. She blinked at me, face ashen.

"Thank you." I brushed hair out of her face. "Thank you for saving my sons."

She stared at me with glassy eyes. She could breathe on her own, which meant I had some time. I sat with her. Matched my breathing to hers, then slowed mine down. Hers followed. Bit by bit, I coaxed us both into a meditative state.

Then I reached for my magic.

Carefully. Quietly.

Goddessi, it was like touching sunlight after so long neglecting it— hot and fierce and *beautiful*. And *mine*, not Maldita's. Unlike an unused muscle, my magic came to my hands easily, eagerly. Still cautious, I started with my own body — *pushed* the upset out of my stomach, *pulled* the last of the pain out of my head. I could feel my limits, unlike when magic belonged to the dark goddess and I had no limits, but I had so much more than when I had tried using magic to clean the floor, months ago.

I *reached* for Dee.

My breath hiccuped but I smoothed it out again. Broken bones, crushed blood vessels, crumpled nerves— *Breathe*.

I could do this but we both had to be still.

Using the tiniest amount of power I could, first I *pulled* some of the pain into me. *Pushed* it through me into the floor and then the dirt below.

Interior only. She had to keep the scrapes and shallower gashes on her skin or it would be obvious someone had healed her, and then there would be questions—

Sweating from the need to be so still and quiet, I *pushed* and *pulled* the largest bone fragments back into place. Then the smaller. *Pushed* and *pulled* at them until they started to set.

I faltered. In the time I'd been denying it, my magic had grown stronger, more sensitive, but I hadn't used it this way.

Andy's hand then Wil's found my shoulders, quieted my magic for me, taking half the work.

Inside and around the bones, I soothed the nerves, ensured the proper connections. Eased the blood vessels back to where they belonged. Broke apart blockages. Channeled blood flow and healing and looked and looked again until I was sure I'd done everything I could.

For Dee.

Let myself fall away from her.

I blinked, back in my own body. My magic was gone, used up in the healing, but the shadow of it was still there, taunting me. It would grow again. Demand to be used again.

Dee was staring at me.

I said, "Don't move."

"You've magic," she whispered. "You—"

"Like Thom said, once the swelling goes down, it might not be as bad as... well, as bad."

"Resting betweens." Dee curled her fingers, then her toes. "I couldn't move my toes before. I couldn't bend my fingers—"

"Trauma lies—"

"No. It feels different. You— we met you once. When we brought Maggie to take his place and the high priestess— that was *you*. You said no. Jay fell in love with *you*? You're no servant."

I stared at her. Wished I could take her memory. Wondered if that was possible with *push-pull* magic, the same way one of my students had discovered she could put pictures into my head to 'talk' to me.

"Dee—"

"*Resting—*" She swallowed hard. Had to say the words out loud, bless her. "You were the *damned high priestess*."

"The high priestess of Maldita died the night the demon hunters attacked the dark temple." Goddessi, the risk— I had to make her understand. "If she didn't die, then people might come looking for her. Might do horrible things to the people around her, the ones who hid her. Whether they knew or not. Do you understand what I'm saying?"

"We've had the *high priestess of Maldita* living in our *house* for *months*. Washing our *underthings*. Cleaning our *floors*."

"You, Robin, Maggie, the boys— none of you are safe if... if she lives."

She blinked and blinked. Then shook her head minutely. "I — I understand. It's just a lot."

"It is. But you wanted me to trust you. I am trusting you with the biggest, most dangerous secret I know."

"You did *magic*. To heal me."

"You're not healed." She *really* needed to understand this part. "Dee, you *need* to rest. Stay still. I fixed some things—" *a lot of things*— "but you can't get up yet. You have to heal the rest of the way on your own. The bones—"

"All right." She closed her eyes. Then, raggedly, asked me the question I dreaded most. "You couldn't heal Mom?"

189

Guilt nearly bent me in two. I could have. I wouldn't have known *how* to be quiet with my magic, hadn't been this strong, hadn't been this sensitive, and the boys wouldn't have known how to quiet the magic for me— "That was different," I half-lied. "Her bones weren't broken."

Dee curled her fingers over and over. "Thank you for healing me. I don't know what I would have done—"

"You'd have figured out something. You and your family are the strongest people I—"

Someone pounded on the door. I glanced at Andy.

"Robin," he announced. "With the healer."

"Let her in."

Andy and Wil released the door, opened it to Robin.

Her eyes went to Dee, but her words were for me. "I brought her."

The person who accompanied Robin into the house was the same Red woman who'd been unable to do anything for Jay's mother. She was the oldest person I'd ever seen, with a pooch-belly and stick-thin limbs and red-gray hair and wrinkles around her eyes and mouth and joints.

I was up and moving toward a chair before I registered how utterly exhausted I was— my knees gave out and I lurched the last bit, and hit the seat only with help from the boys. Despite being hollowed out, my blood hummed— goddess, it felt good to do magic.

Now, like Dee, I had no choice but to wait. But not to heal. To learn if I'd brought guards down on us all.

Robin dragged another chair over for the healer, tucked it under the healer's slowly descending body— no plopping for her. The Rest Third healer sighed and I could swear I heard her bones creak.

The healer wiped the sweat from Dee's forehead. Peeled bits of cloth away from the ruined skin on Dee's back. Watched Dee move her fingers and toes. "Not so bad as you said." She shook her head. "If nothing gets infected, she has a chance. Wrap her up and hope for the best."

Robin held out something and I realized she'd brought the healer's bag. The healer fished out a linen wrap, peeled the last of Dee's clothes away from her back, plucked more bits out of the wounds, then started laying the wrap across the whole thing like it was as fragile as a hummingbird.

Which it was, for now.

Jay flung open the door, then hit it again when it rebounded. Thom caught it and Jay pushed past him. Jay's face flushed and the cords in his neck stood out.

"They won't come," he ground out. "No matter what I offered. Said we *didn't matter*—"

Feeling stronger now, I rose and wrapped my arms around him. "It'll be all right."

"I even went to my— to Nick. Begged him. He apologized but said *his mother* was the only one who could get a temple healer. I *begged* him. I—"

"Jay. It will be all right."

He heard the weight to my voice, stared at me, blanched. "You—"

"The healer says we need to give it time."

"Sumi—"

"Time," I said firmly to all of them. Stuffed down my fear and my guilt and my stirring magic. "Let's give it some time."

"Go work on the addition," Dee said suddenly. "While you're all here."

The healer nodded. "She needs rest. You all are not restful."

I hid a surprised grin. Truer words were never spoken.

Jay ducked his head, rolled his shoulders, hugged me hard, then went out the back door. Thom followed after.

With a pointed look, I sent the boys after them— they'd not

be able to get the tiles loose until the boys took their magic off them.

I thought I would go after them but when I tried, my knees wouldn't hold.

So I stayed in the house with Dee, the reek of magic in my nostrils and the marks of goddess tattoos faint on the backs of my hands.

∾

JAY

BETWEEN THE AFTERNOON SUN BEATING DOWN ON HIM AND HIS OWN internal, spiteful voices haunting him while he worked, Jay sweated. Those nasty little voices pointed out he should have stopped the tiles from falling, should have called out sooner, should have protected the boys and his sister— resting betweens, his *sister*... either she would never be the same or Sumi had done something so foolish—

Jay ripped into the last few tiles on the roof with the same ferocity he castigated himself, taking perverse pride in the nicks and cuts on his hands and the bruises building on his shins.

Thom watched from below. Shook his head dolefully, reached up and took the tiles then stacked them while the boys gaped. Jay wasn't ready to face any of them, not yet.

He came down long enough to consult with Thom about how and where to cut into the under-roof and found Wilyam and Antero sobbing.

One Purple boy, one Red, crying like their hearts were broken. Hadn't seen Jay yet, curled in on themselves and facing away.

Jay's hands made fists. Skin pulled and gaped, mostly at his knuckles. One cut started bleeding again. He ignored it, strained to hear the boys talking to Thom.

"We're sorry," Andy said. "We're sorry."

"Jay will hate us forever," Wil said. "We should have known. Stayed out of the way."

He couldn't let them believe that. He knelt on the tiles he'd helped his father make. Held out his arms. "Boys."

They came. Snuggled into his dirty, sweaty, bloody chest. Sobbed harder.

"We didn't mean to be in the way." Wil's entire body shook. "It's all our fault."

Andy nodded, his nose rubbing against Jay's shirt.

Knees started to ache, but he wouldn't stand, not when it would tell them they were right. "Wasn't your fault," he said heavily. "You didn't know the tiles would come down. You didn't know your Aunt Dee would save you— though I don't think she could have done anything else."

"We shouldn't have stood there. Should have used—"

Andy, still more cautious than Wil, sobbed over the top of him, so Jay couldn't be sure he heard Wil say the word *magic*— "We're sorry. Please don't hate us."

"I could never hate you." He gathered them closer. "This wasn't your fault, and I'll tell you that until you feel it in your bones." His fault, yes, theirs, no. But would they believe him? "None of us knew those tiles were loose. That they'd come down just then. My foot slipped—"

"Not your fault either," Wil said, untucking his chin and staring into Jay's eyes. "You didn't know either."

The boy was brave, speaking up like that, with his jaw jutting out and snot running down his face. Jay couldn't tell him how wrong he was, so he nodded. "I didn't know the tiles would come off either." He reached for words of comfort.

"Sometimes things happen. Things we can't control. But this thing, this was not your fault, you hear me?"

"Yes, Honored."

"Yes, Honored."

"Get up in the tree so you can watch without being in the way." Jay squeezed them, then set them away. Shifted and stifled a groan, pushed himself back to his feet. Stripped off his shirt, fit for nothing but the rubbish heap.

"That was a kindness," Thom murmured to him. "What you said. Do you believe it?"

They made their way back up onto the roof, started the first cut with Thom's borrowed saw.

"That it wasn't their fault? Of course." Jay shoved his own guilt down to focus on the saw in his hands. Borrowed, expensive, needed.

"It wasn't your fault either, son."

Jay stopped, braced himself on the roof. Buzzing filled his ears. He shrugged it away. "Not doing this right now."

"Jay—"

"No." He sawed carefully, hyper-aware the last time he'd let his attention falter, his sister and nearly his sons had paid the price.

"But—"

"No! We're not at work. You're not my commander here. You brought the tools, but you're in my home—" He looked down through the hole they were making. "On top of it anyway. I can tell you to leave."

Thom sighed heavily and they worked in silence for a long time.

The boys wanted to help, so— though it was more hindrance than help— Jay sent Thom down to help them lift boards, one at a time, up to him. Under Thom's watchful eyes, Wil and Andy grunted and pushed *physically*. Who knew what they could do if they used their magic? Not him— and they were being smart enough to keep their efforts purely mundane while Thom hovered.

They'd cut the posts and boards tongue-and-groove as much as they could, to spare the price of the nails, so he accepted the last of the new frame from the boys and banished them back to the tree. Then hefted the first post and angled it into place.

Thom grunted. Knelt. Guided the post. "Do you believe in fate? Believe you were destined to meet Sumi and fall in love? Or do you believe we choose our own fate?"

"What?" Jay felt the groove catch and jiggled it just enough to get it to go in the rest of the way.

"Fate? Or choice?"

This time Thom hefted the post and Jay guided it in. "Choice, I suppose. I don't think the goddessi care about a man like me or you, or the boys." *Sumi, though*— The dark goddess cared a heaven of a lot about Sumi, and if She had any say in his fate, She would have steered him away from Her high priestess.

"Interesting."

Thom was baiting him, and Jay didn't have the patience for it, now that his rage had subsided. "Out with it, old man."

"If you don't believe in fate, how can you affect it?"

"Say what you mean!"

Thom side-eyed him. "You say you believe in choice, but you're resting bent on taking it away from others. Not allowing them to make their own choices."

"Bullshit." If he had his way, he'd wrap all his beloveds in magic to protect them from the world— but he didn't. Couldn't. Allowed them their own resting choices every resting day.

"If you can affect every little thing they do, every conse-quence, then you believe in *fate*, boy. Your mere presence isn't enough to influence every person in this city to do exactly what you want to get exactly the outcome you want. Your desire, your *need*—"

"Fine! Fine. You're right. I can't make everyone do what I want." That was half the problem. "Are you happy now?"

"If you can't make them do what you want, you can't take responsibility for their choices."

"Resting betweens I can't."

"You don't make the choice, you're not responsible for the action. Unless you really *are* all powerful. Then you're responsible for Litka challenging you, and you're responsible for her arrogance in the first place. And you're responsible for Fitz's failure to show up for work yesterday, so I should punish *you* instead of *him*."

"No—!"

"So you're not? Responsible for Fitz's carelessness? Or Litka's arrogance?"

This he knew. "No."

Thom handed him the next pole, but then didn't let go. Made Jay face him. "The same way you're not responsible for your mom getting sick. Or your sister saving a *child* she saw was in danger."

"Old man—" Jay wretched the post away and wanted to throw it, but then he really *would* be responsible— for wherever it landed and whatever damage it did.

Thom knelt next to the last hole in the roof and cradled his hands, waiting for the post. "It wasn't your fault," he said. The words were quiet, but they sounded like shouting to Jay, and Thom didn't stop there. "Just like you didn't know the tiles would fall the way they did. You didn't put the boys there. You didn't make your sister rescue them. You didn't cause any of that to happen."

Jay's throat closed. Every muscle in his back was tight

enough to snap, and each one protested as he slid the post into the hole. "My foot slipped. I should have paid better attention. Should have—" The words came out raggedly before he cut himself off.

"No." Thom rose. Laid a hand on Jay's shoulder as heavy as his words. "You didn't know the tiles would fall. Sometimes things happen we *have no control over.*"

Resting betweens, the words rang true— his own words, but Jay didn't know if he could force himself to believe them.

He swallowed the bile churning in his gut.

"Not your fault," Thom said again. "You're not a goddess, boy. You don't control the world."

Jay's hands clenched. He forced them to relax. Thom's logic was sound, but it stung, all the same. He felt wet on his cheeks and realized he was crying.

Swiped away the tears and opened his mouth to bellow at the old man, then glanced over at the boys watching him.

He'd tried to be a good example to his sisters, tried to live up to what Mom and Dad had been teaching them, tried to take care of everyone he loved, and now these two precious boys who weren't blood but were his sons watched him the way Maggie had for so long— like they would do anything he said, *anything.*

Could they hear Thom's words?

If they could, Jay had to listen, because that was what his mother and father would have wanted him to do. Because those boys needed to know *things happened* they couldn't control, and a stupid accident wasn't their fault.

Because they deserved to grow up into strong, smart, *good* men, and being guilt-ridden— *ashamed*— wouldn't help.

Maybe he would have felt differently if Dee's back was still crushed, the way it had been when he'd carried her into the house, before Sumi had healed her. But because she'd used magic and nothing bad had happened yet, he had to believe they were safe, had to believe Dee would walk and run and fight...

It felt as if tiles were sliding off his own back; horrible, heavy tiles that had been pressing down on him from all sides, and for the first time since he'd heard Dee's scream, Jay drew in a deep breath.

Sometimes accidents happened.

Not everything was his fault— he just wasn't that powerful.

Maybe it didn't change what *had* happened, and maybe he couldn't bear to think about fault and guilt and shame as they had to do with other things— things like his mom's death or Sumi's death or his dad's death— but maybe just this once, he could let his fault and guilt and shame for Dee's injury go.

He hadn't kicked the tiles off the roof. Hadn't put the boys under that one, most dangerous spot. Hadn't made Dee save them.

But Dee had saved them and then Sumi had saved her.

Like he'd told them, sometimes things happened. Maybe— *maybe*— it wasn't his fault this time.

And for now that was enough.

FIFTEEN

S *umi*

BEFORE DAWN THE NEXT MORNING, I TIPTOED TO DEE'S SIDE AND *FELT* her injuries and wanted to shout— for someone with little experience at healing, I'd done a blessed fine job on her back.

While I stared at her, she woke, so I helped her sit up and hovered while she hobbled from the couch to the necessary and back, cursing and weeping and smiling. Spots of blood showed through her bandages, but she told me again she could feel her fingers and toes.

When the boys rose, they stirred the house, and Dee demanded we go to Temples Day without her. It only came once a year and we weren't all going to miss it to loom over her.

Robin had taken Dee's shifts in addition to her own and Mouse had disappeared during the night, but Maggie was home and the boys latched onto her, demanded she come too.

No teaching the neighbors today— even though the Rest

Third didn't have a temple, didn't *want* a temple, they still celebrated the founding of the city, and that meant festivals, filling the larger streets.

I couldn't imagine it— having only seen the Temples Day from inside one temple or the other— but I'd seen the preparations during my walks through the neighborhoods, and I was almost as excited as the boys.

Jay sat on our bed, blinking sleep away. I rebandaged his hands and thought very, very quietly about using magic to heal them, but he looked at me with his honey-colored eyes and clearly wanted me to keep my magic to myself.

Wil and Andy couldn't contain themselves any longer. They dragged Maggie into the streets, the three of them giggling together like siblings instead of adopted aunt and nephews. Jay lingered long enough to cram down a piece of bread, then followed after them, his bandaged hand in mine, winding this way and that through the crowd until we stopped in a little square, with a fountain at the center.

Unlike the other fountains of the Rest Third— plain, simple things only for drawing water— this fountain had a statue of two women twined together like sisters or lovers. Water gushed from under their feet into a pool. The pool's bottom glittered from all the coins covering it.

"A wishing pool?"

Jay smiled. His eyes flicked over the crowds and I knew, though he had brought us here, he was still alert for threats. My Shadow. He pulled me into his arms, my back to his front, so I could hear him over the chaos. "Thom's family— the Lunatas— built it years and years ago. Once a month, they gather all the coins, and once a year they use what they've gathered to pay for an apprenticeship for a kid whose family can't pay. No one steals the coins because even the most desperate know someone who has benefited—"

"Friends!" called a loud voice, too low for a woman but too smooth for a man. "Friends, listen and you shall hear a tale of the birth of this glorious city."

I craned my neck but couldn't see who was speaking.

The speaker leaped up on the edge of the fountain— lithe and graceful and ageless, too old to be a child but too young to need a cane. He— she? I couldn't decide which— dressed in layers of light brown silks as if she— she for now— had come from the western desert only this morning. She grinned, sky blue eyes bright in a sun-darkened face, and twirled about, flinging wide waist-length hair, dyed brown and red and yellow and green and blue and purple.

She— he? that seemed to shift with every moment— demanded of the crowd, "Have you heard this tale?"

Some in the crowd called back.

The would-be tale-teller bowed. "You have! But I shall tell it better than anyone before me, so listen close."

As if she had magic— she again? but I could *feel* she used no magic— the crowd quieted for the storyteller and she launched into the story.

"This city had begun, of course. People had fought over the river and the grasses for as long as there was a river and grass. But it wasn't until a certain day on a certain year that everything changed and this valley and these grasses became your City of Temples."

Heads nodded. Even the children in the crowd went quiet, though I could still hear selling and buying and laughing and yelling from the streets around us. *Your* City of Temples, she'd said. The story-teller was an outsider, and I wondered where she was from.

"That day, that year, when everything changed—"

"*Which* day?" demanded a Blue child.

Not to be outdone, the Purple next to her spoke up as well. "Which year?"

"Ah, good questions!" The story-teller's gaze went from face to face, as if seeing every person in the crowd. "Does everyone want to know?"

The adults around the inquisitive children nodded.

"But no one knows this answer!" The story-teller's voice had gone soft, but somehow reached every ear.

The crowd groaned and I groaned with them. I had to admit, this story-teller was the best I'd ever heard.

"It is all right," she continued— flickered from she to he and back to she, still impossible to be sure. "We do not need to know the precise year and day to know what happened. Will you listen?"

"Yes!"

"We do not know if it was sunny, like today, or raining. We do not know if it was morning or night. We do not know so many things, but this we *do* know. The Colors were all equal before that day."

Probably not. After all, the Browns had controlled the fields for a long time, and the Blues and Purples, trading.

"On that fateful day, someone summoned a demon."

I braced myself, but the thread that was Maldita inside me remained quiet. She paid me no heed, just as She had for months now.

"This demon came in fire and lightning and *ate* up its summoner in one gulp, just like demons do."

"Eeeewwww!" the Blue and Purple girls chorused together.

"Then..." The story-teller stalked around the edge of the fountain in a display of grace that held every eye. "Then the demon attacked and ate up the next person it met. And the next. And the next after that!"

The girls gasped. So did everyone else. I glanced up at Jay. His face was alive, but his eyes still flick, flick, flicked.

"Did it eat up everyone?" the Blue girl asked.

"No!" The Purple girl scowled fiercely. "Then there'd be no city!"

"Or the city would be named City of Demons instead of City of Temples!" The storyteller went still and silent, and every watcher mirrored that stillness and silence.

I shuddered.

The goddessi were bad enough I didn't even want to *think* about a city of demoni.

"The next person the demon found was *two* people. Two sisters— twins— who were also best friends and *also* had magic."

"Magic!"

The story-teller spread her fingers dramatically, lowered her voice. "The two sisters fought the demon. They *pushed* it away from others in the city, *pulled* it back toward them when it wanted to flee. But the demon wasn't easily hurt."

Jay's arms tightened around me. I wrapped my hands around his, mindful of his cuts and bruises.

"So there they were, the two sisters, battling the demon with their *push-pull* magic. They fought it back and forth and back and forth again, protecting the people. They fought it back and back to this very spot, pinned it down right here, where this fountain stands today, when it was just a patch of dirt."

Adults and children alike leaned forward, mesmerized.

"One sister on one side, and one sister on the other, and the demon between them. The sisters *pushed*, making the demon smaller and smaller. But then the demon stopped. It could only get so small and they only had so much power. They were at a stalemate."

The Purple girl shout-whispered to her Blue friend, "What's a *stalemate*?" The Blue girl hushed her.

I scanned the crowd for pickpockets, thought of Tasha and Gui and half-grinned. They'd love this crowd— drift through like smoke, take what they wanted, and be gone before the story was over.

"The demon tired, but the sisters tired too. They *pushed* and *pushed* but they were stuck. Finally the demon said it would go, but only for a price. The sisters' lives. They agreed, and *pushed* one last time, and then it was gone."

The children sighed in relief. A few adults, too.

But the story-teller continued, and her eyes sought mine as if she spoke only to me. "The sisters couldn't even say goodbye. They dropped down dead. But the demon erred because the sisters found grace in their sacrifice and became goddessi, one bright and one dark. The sisters were Purples, which is why we set our Purples higher than any other color. And their first devotees became their high priestessi, and they were Blues which is why the Blues are the next highest regarded. Though with our current high priestessi both Reds—"

I froze against flinch before it could start. *Give nothing away.*

"The Reds are overtaking the Browns." The story-teller changed then, dropping her serious mein for a playful face, flickering between male and female again. "Where we go from here, my children, is entirely up to you."

The children scattered, towing their parents after them and the story-teller disappeared into the crowd. I couldn't see her— him— her, bless it, not without using my magic, which I wouldn't do.

An unsettling ending to the tale I thought I knew well.

Jay shifted and I slipped out of his arms, ready to explore the vendors' stalls all around the square, but someone stepped sideways toward me. "An interesting story," the man said. He stepped closer, hemming me in. Lowered his voice. "Some truth, some lies. Wouldn't you agree, *high priestess*?"

I went still, so still that may have betrayed me more than if I'd reacted. I ducked my head and gave him my back, trusting Jay to protect me. "You have mistaken me for someone else."

"Have I?" the man hissed. "I *felt* you working your magic."

He *felt* me— bless it to heaven—

I spun. The man I'd seen briefly in the early spring, the one I'd mistaken for Zerth, alive again. This man was younger, the shape of his face subtly different. Still, I breathed the name of the leader of the demon hunters— "Zerth."

"Zerth was my father." He bared his teeth at me. "I'm Enzo."

"Father—" I felt like someone had hit me in the head. The old man I'd killed had a child who was now a man, and this man looked at me like he hated me.

Fair, since I'd killed his father.

Jay edged around me, his hand on his sword hilt. "Problem?"

"This man has mistaken me for someone else."

Enzo wrapped claw-like fingers around my arm. "Don't dismiss me, High Priestess, or I'll tattle on you. I just need you to do one thing for me." He shook me. "You *owe* me. For the life of my father."

Jay started to draw his sword. What if Enzo had magic like his father, Old Magic, and loosed it in this crowd? Goddessi, Jay's friends and neighbors would die.

I touched Jay's hand— no blood, *please no blood*— and his sword stayed in its sheath. "What do you want?"

"Nothing much." He lowered his voice so I had to strain to hear it. I refused to lean any closer, though I thought that was his desire. "Only some stories from the temples."

"You?" I lowered my voice. "Or the demon hunters."

He smiled slowly, with too many teeth. "All of us. But especially me, as I was forced into my father's place."

"Forced." I waved a hand, dismissing his own tale. That story wasn't important. I made my face cold and hard, though I was thinking of all the stories he and his demon hunters had already stolen, the stories we'd guarded— "You want stories."

"Stories such as the one we just heard. Origin stories, let's call them. The kind that might help to prove to you the goddessi you harbor are indeed demons."

Maldita was still quiet inside me. Jay watched me, his hand still on his sword and dots of blood seeping through the bandage on his hand.

I swallowed. "Not spells, not treasures. Just stories." To prove the goddessi were actually demoni? The man was mad.

He nodded slightly, his eyes bright. "Just writings. Just stories. What harm can stories do?"

"Plenty." Especially if he *could* prove the goddessi were truly demoni. I shuddered. "But I can't help you. I can't return to the damned temple. Can't even go near the gates of the Third."

"The bright then."

"That's no better, though at least they won't recognize me if I did. How would I get in?"

"You'll find a way."

"And you'll give me your silence for these stories." I missed Lena's ability to *pull* truth. I had to rely on my ability to read a man's face, and I hated it.

"My silence." He nodded. "Your debt for killing my father. After all, someday you and I will work together to rid ourselves of these demons."

"I doubt that." His assurance grated on me. I owed the man nothing— had only killed those who had come to kill me. If he shouted to all around us that *I* was the high priestess...

These people wouldn't believe him. As Dee had said, I'd

been washing my underthings in the same places they did, and taught their children letters and numbers. Time to prove my theory... I raised my chin. "No. No we won't get these *stories* for you."

His nostrils flared and now I saw how deeply angry he was. Still, he held all that rage in check and did not strike out at me, didn't shout my true identity to everyone around us. "You will," he hissed. "You have people you care about now, *High Priestess*."

"That's not me any longer. Just ask the *real* high priestess. Only you won't, because she'd kill you faster than I would."

He snarled. Turned and elbowed anyone too close. Then snapped over his shoulder, "We'll see," and disappeared into the crowd.

I watched him go, my hands shaking and my guts twisting. Goddessi, what had I done?

Jay watched him too, then turned to me. "Was that wise?"

"Probably not. He's right. I do have people I care about." But he hadn't *done* anything other than threaten to expose me, then not done even that.

"We take care of our own." Jay looked at me, and the light of the sun caressed his face, brightening his honey-colored eyes and sending shadows under his chin. My Jay. My heart swelled so much it hurt and I had to stop and put my hand on his chest to remind me he was alive and mine and *happy*.

"You're right." I smiled, dared a quick kiss.

His protest was muffled by my lips, but then his hands circled my back and dragged me closer and I told him with my mouth how much I loved him.

When he pulled away, we were both breathing hard, but instead of suggesting we return home— to continue our love-making— he said, "We should find the boys."

So we continued on into the festival as if nothing had happened.

~

JAY

THEY PRETENDED THE DEMON HUNTER HAD NEVER FOUND THEM—spent the bit of money they'd saved just for today on flavored ices and drumsticks and sugared nuts. One new shirt each and two for the boys and one for Dee because she wasn't with them. Talked about a hair ribbon for Mouse, but decided the girl wouldn't wear it.

Maybe next year.

The neighborhood children ran wild. This day, their parents didn't expect help... at least not until later, when their energy had been exhausted. Caught glimpses of Wilyam, Antero, and Maggie, as wild as the other kids.

Jay and Sumi investigated every table, every offering. Picked out a candle to exchange for more morning lessons, and a new bit of soap, then escaped from that square and headed for the next.

They cut through a rougher part of the Third, and Jay dropped Sumi's hand, resting his own on his sword, and watched for anyone who might give them trouble.

Sumi noticed and put on a more serious face, but he could still see the smile in her eyes. At least until they passed an alcove piled high with scraps of worn-thin fabric gone washed-out gray-brown, guarded by a nasty little dog, all dried mud and bared teeth. The pile of detritus next to the dog was actually a human being.

"Jay—" Her eyes weren't smiling anymore.

"Later."

Sumi kept pace with him, but gnawed at her lip. They

walked past more human debris and he saw her noticing them too. "So many."

He shrugged. Mouse had come from a situation like this, but as much as it tore at his heart, as everyone kept reminding him — he couldn't save them all.

"Are they all from those homes the blessed took?"

"Possible," he said. "We— the guards— took care of our own. Others went to their families. I don't know what happened to the rest."

"So why? How?"

"Some don't have families to fall back on, or their families are worse off than them. Some were injured." He shook his head, imagining Dee here. Swallowed hard.

"Can't work, can't eat," Sumi said softly, like she was remembering something someone had told her a long time ago.

"Some turned to drugs. Some can't be indoors. No one truly knows all the ways you can end up here."

"This is horrible."

"Some of them prefer it."

She wrinkled her nose, the first time she'd reacted to the stench. "Living in their own excrement? They must be getting sick from it."

"Can't force them." He sighed. "We'd fine them for their... refuse... like we fine everyone else, but they haven't got anything left to take. The next step is banishment outside the city walls, and that desert is a death sentence. We can't make them—"

"*I*—" She stopped herself. Visibly remembered she wasn't the high priestess anymore. Deflated. "Going to a temple is better than *this*. But these won't go?"

He shrugged again, though it hurt inside to act so indifferent. "We— the guards— know most of these. Those who refuse help. Would rather live like this."

209

"So they live in their own filth."

"Not sure which is more compassionate." He touched the hilt of his sword. "Let them choose to be diseased and starving or force them to be part of a temple. Turn here."

They turned the corner, and it was like they were in another city. The street was clean, the buildings repaired, the people fat — or at least not wasting away to sinew over bone. And the buildings and the people were decorated for the Temples Day festival.

Shocking, to go from one street to the next like that.

Sumi adjusted more quickly than he did— dived into the crowd and let him trail after. Not that she didn't care, just that she could transition from one hard thought to the next so much more quickly, while he tended to linger.

He watched her eat a tart, fondle a soft, filmy fabric, laugh at a puppet's antics. Felt his heart swell up in his chest that he had it so good— a smart, thoughtful woman, two kind boys, healthy stubborn sisters...

Sweat trickled down his back under the hot summer sun, and even that reminded him to be grateful— to be alive, able to swing a sword, build a room, make love to a woman.

Goddessi, it had been a long time.

Soon— too soon, but he suspected she'd worn herself out healing Dee— Sumi developed a pinched look around her eyes, so he found them one of the temporary tables set up in the square and sat her down with another ice. Lemon this time.

Watched for Enzo and rested his hand on his sword hilt. The man might find Jay more of a challenge than he thought, thanks to Sumi's magic shield.

Their table was tiny, barely more than a tall stool, but that made it easier to take Sumi's hand. He remembered one of the tattoos that had marked it. Traced it how he remembered it, then scowled. Was there a shadow? Did it darken when he touched it?

She smiled at him across the table and he forgot about her hands. Wanted her mouth.

Wished he could kiss her senseless right here, in front of everyone.

Decided he'd better ask the thing that had been nagging at him then braced himself to ask it. "What you did yesterday—" the magic— "Was that... wise?"

Sumi had been watching everyone around them but now she focused on him. "I don't know." She scowled. "We did what we could to keep it quiet, and no one came looking for us."

Jay raised his eyebrows.

Sumi dropped her gaze to her hands. "Until just now," she admitted.

"He didn't *do* anything."

"Yet."

He wasn't making things better. Invited her to talk technical instead of strategic. "Quiet, you said?"

"It's mostly passive. Watching while the boys do things. Listening for others nearby."

Watching the boys do *magic*, she meant. Listening for other *magic users* nearby. He had to unclench his jaw to speak. "Mostly."

"Mostly." She looked away. Looked back and lowered her voice. She was close enough to kiss, but her words drove that thought out of his mind. "Your sister... She saved the boys. I had to do something. Her back was *shattered*. That kind of injury... she was lucky she could breathe on her own."

"I'm doing a poor job of thanking you for it." Jay brought her hand to his heart. "I appreciate it. I just thought you... couldn't."

She shifted and dropped her eyes. Tugged her hand free. "I

didn't think I could either, without... causing problems. But I had to. I owed her. And I kept it quiet and the boys helped me."

"So does this mean you're going to—" He checked his words as a Brown family passed by, the children chattering to the parents about ices and pastries and a carved wood puzzle. Wondered briefly if they were some of the cousins he didn't know. Reminded himself he didn't care. "Going to do *that* again?"

"Would you have her crippled? Lose her job? Her ability to contribute to this family?"

Shame pummeled him. An hour on the roof talking to Thom wasn't a cure-all, as much as he'd have liked it. But— *no*. He had to remember what they'd talked about. Sometimes bad things happened. He wasn't in control of everyone and everything. Couldn't be. "No, of course not. But we would take care of her."

"You would." Sumi bit her lip. "And she'd hate herself for it. Probably walk into the desert and not return."

Jay stilled. His heart skipped at the thought of losing his sister. "Probably," he said hoarsely.

"Now she doesn't have to. You saw her this morning."

"I can't believe she got up. Walked."

"She still needs rest. A lot of it."

"But she'll heal." He scrubbed a hand across his face. "And you'll do what you must. I can't make your choices for you. All I can do is be here when you need me."

"I need you." She reached across the table. Found his hands and held them. "I wish you hadn't done this to yourself."

"I'll heal too. Thom—" Resting betweens it irked him to admit it, but— "talking with Thom helped."

She smiled, bright and quick. "Good. You know I'm always here if you want to talk about it."

"I know." Jay reached out. Brushed Sumi's hair off her forehead. "I worry about you."

"I'm fine. Look around. I'm in a place I never thought I'd be, with friends and neighbors around me I never dreamed I'd meet. With the man I love. And somewhere out there are our boys. Running around a festival I've never before enjoyed. Without any blood." She touched one of his bandages. "Almost no blood."

He grinned. To hear this woman echoing the same feelings he'd had earlier... what a wonderful thing. Then he frowned. "Yeah, but that man—"

"Can't do anything," Sumi said confidently. Too confidently.

But he couldn't bear to see her afraid, so he'd worry for the both of them. Let her enjoy the day.

The crowd ebbed and flowed around them, more Greens and Yellows and Oranges than the other Colors, but all had at least a few representatives and everyone was excited. If there were more demon hunters here in the Rest Third, he couldn't spot them— didn't want to. The sun beat down on them from a blue sky. The boys ran past, glanced at them long enough to catch Jay's nod, then went on through the crowd.

A jostle of people came from the direction of the river, a Blue, a Purple, two Browns. The Blue woman snagged a stool from another tiny table. Headed toward them and sat near enough to be at the table but not so close they touched knees.

Not enough space to get past her, but enough to take her measure and feel the breath catch in his lungs.

Lena, not in her black Damned Third Guard uniform but in tired mis-matched blues still too clean, too pressed, for the Rest Third. Lena with her blue-gray hair tight in braids, and her piercing eyes, and her ability to *pull* truth out of people. Lena, one of Sumi's secret-keepers while she was in the Temple of the

Damned. The Blue who knew *everything* about Sumi and the damned temple and the damned guards—

Lena, here in the Rest Third, sitting at their table. Perched on the tiny stool as if she wasn't a threat. Crossed her arms as if assuring them she wasn't going to attack, and said softly, "Hullo, Sumi."

CHAPTER
SIXTEEN

S *umi*

BREATHE— I COULD REMEMBER HOW TO BREATHE, REALLY I COULD. No touching my throat or whimpering— that would give away just how panicked I was. My still-tired magic surged and faltered and my back spasmed— a small one, a shadow of the spasms I'd had over the winter.

I bit down hard on my lip. Tasted blood.

The so-familiar taste steadied me.

This was *Lena*. She wasn't in uniform. Didn't have a complement of Damned Third guards at her back. Probably not surrounding the open square and all the people celebrating Temples Day, either. She'd always been my friend before, and if she wasn't now, we'd already be in shackles.

"L—" I swallowed hard and tried again. "Lena." I shifted closer to her and she shifted closer to me, and then I hugged her hard and felt her hug me back.

58 9

She gripped my upper arms, examined me, nodded. "You look good."

"You too." When she released me, I eased back down, glanced at Jay, and raised an eyebrow.

He shrugged minutely, looking a bit nauseated. He hadn't been expecting her and wasn't taking it well. First the demon hunter, now the damned head guard—

"You found us," he growled.

Lena eyed Jay. "Rest easy, Honored Brown," she said. "I'm not here officially."

He didn't relax.

She shrugged minutely and went on, "You made it easy. Whatever happened yesterday... you were quiet enough to avoid *Her* attention, but not *her* attention, hear me, girl?"

"Bless it," slipped out of my mouth. First Enzo, now her—they'd felt my magic. I shouldn't have healed Dee— but I *had* to heal what I could—

A passing Yellow woman glared at me, muttered, "Cursing in front of the children?" and hustled her brood out of earshot.

Lena smirked. "Your sister has people looking for... what you did. She felt *something* and she wants answers." She leaned in and lowered her voice. "My source in the... other Third says your mother does too. You don't want either of them to find you."

I swallowed hard. My blood-sister, Aimi, had taken over as the current high priestess of Maldita. My blood-mother, currently the high priestess of Bendita, was even worse.

Not found family. Not loving family. But blood family.

"Your sister seems to think you might still be alive." Lena frowned. "Doesn't really believe it, no, but she sent me out with orders to hire someone to find her."

"Her." My head was swimming. Too many people had felt me heal Dee, even with the boys helping, even without drawing on the magic of the goddess. Now the damned and the blessed were looking for me, and the demon hunters had found me.

"Her," Lena said firmly. "So I'm here to offer you both a job. Find the previous high priestess. All the current one knows is that she's a Red, is spoiled, pampered, and has oodles of magic she 'stole' from her. So that shouldn't be too hard. Find the Red woman that's out of place, rich in the poor Third."

The tangle of *hers* who were not *me* was making my head hurt. Still, that description sounded nothing like me, and Lena knew it.

Jay put his hand on top of mine. "What are you doing, Lena?"

Her mouth twisted into a sardonic grin. "I'm doing what I was told. Hiring out work. If it happens to be to a friend unassociated with a temple, then so be it. It's nice to catch up."

A bag hit the table and the muffled clinks made the contents apparent. Heads turned. Money drew attention in these parts. More money than I'd seen since we left the damned temple, more money than any of these people had likely seen in their entire lives.

Damned money.

I licked my lips. We could buy flour without bugs in it. Maybe some sugar. Buy the boys new clothes, boots for winter. Get some honest-to-goddess clean water— drinking water— pipes put in, maybe, and still have enough to tide us over until Dee was working again.

But it was blood money— from tithe and tax and sacrifices to the dark goddess— and I didn't want to touch it.

Lena rested her hand on her sword and glared past us, showed her willingness to fight over the money and the bubble of empty space around us grew a bit. "Don't be stupid about this. I'm *hiring* you for a *job*. Take the blessed money."

I looked at Jay. He was watching me, maybe reading my face, trying to guess what I was thinking.

"Take it." Lena nudged the bag closer. Turned to my beloved. "Tell her, Jay. Help me help you."

"How do we find someone who's not missing?" My voice was hoarse. This was going to be a mistake, I knew it. But I didn't know how to turn it down.

"Same way you find someone who *is* missing." Lena's shoulders relaxed, though her hand stayed on her sword. She knew she'd won. "Ask around. Talk to people. See where their answers lead. Just... with less success."

"Less success."

She leaned in close. "We don't want you to actually *find* you, do we?"

I choked.

"No," Jay answered for me. "No one at this table like you described." He glowered like he had taken her suggestion as an insult.

I shoved the money bag into his hands and he made it disappear.

"Buy us an ice—" I forced a smile in Lena's direction— "since you're paying. Tell us what's going on."

Blank-faced, Lena stared at me until I thought I had offended her, then she smiled, lightning quick. "Be right back."

As soon as she'd gone for the ices, Jay murmured, "Do we run?"

"No." I swallowed hard, managed the words. "She found us here, in the middle of a festival in a square we weren't sure we'd be at. She sent that letter. She knows where we live. Running won't do us any good."

We sat in silence under the heavy summer sun and I thought of the cool hallways and rooms in the Temple of the Damned. The power, the politics, the blood—

Lena came back and handed out red ices. For a moment, they looked like blood, and my stomach churned.

"Strawberry," Lena announced.

Of course. My brain was just playing tricks.

She sat again and started to lean her elbows on the table, but it shifted like it was going to collapse, so she straightened and licked her ice. "Aimi's not doing too badly. She didn't even try to replace most of us. Knows we know our duties."

"How is she treating everyone?" By *everyone*, I meant Danya and Yssa, Lena and Adan... the people I cared most about and had left behind.

"Actually, better than I thought she would."

"*Aimi?*" Almost shouted, compressed it to a whisper.

"Being responsible for *all* the decisions— whether or not you make them— has steadied her. She's ignoring Danya and Yssa, which means they're treated well. Apprentices usually are."

"Adan?"

Grooves etched the sides of her mouth.

The strawberry ice was marvelous, not washed out vaguely fruit, but fully strawberry and tart and sweet. I bit at it, savored it on my tongue, then realized she hadn't answered. "Lena, what about Adan?"

She leaned back. "He's well enough. Grieving the last high priestess, I think. But Aimi has started to listen to his counsel."

"Really?" How could the woman I'd grown up fearing and hating— who'd poisoned me, who'd stolen the goddess magic from me, who *killed* me— turn into someone responsible?

"She and Nori are planning—"

"Nori?" She was dead. I'd seen her fall, saw her stop breathing. "Nori's dead. Aimi killed her too. That night."

Lena blinked. "I thought you knew. She's alive. Aimi didn't kill her, only nearly. Viktra healed her along with the rest."

"Nori is alive?" I dashed tears off my eyelashes, sucked in a breath and didn't cry. "I'm so glad. And her hothouse? Did Aimi—"

"It's nearly complete. They're waiting on some glass panels that didn't come out right the first time."

"She's really letting her do it." I smiled through my tears.

"She is. Aimi has grown up."

I'm so glad. But I'd already said that, and I didn't want to repeat myself, so I kept it behind my teeth. My sister was alive!

"I'm sorry you had to live with that the past few months." Lena rested a callused blue-skinned hand on my red-skinned hand. She'd never have dared touch me in public when I was the high priestess of Maldita, but here, she dared. And her touch felt close, and right. After a long moment, she took her hand back. "How are your boys?"

Jay grinned. "They're great. Growing like weeds. Sumi's still teaching them and half the neighborhood too, making them practice their letters and numbers."

"Both of them? Antero—"

"Of course both of them!" Jay touched my arm, reassuring. "Wil and Andy— as they asked to be called— are doing just fine. Better, outside the temple."

"What about...?"

She meant their magic. I swallowed. "I'm teaching them," I said softly. "They're getting stronger, developing better control."

Lena nodded as if I'd answered an important question. "You kept their power under wraps while you were with us, so none of us know what they *feel* like, but there has been an upswing in magic in this area, so either they're not as controlled as you think or there are others out there."

Secrets stopped my voice in my mouth. Gui. Tasha. Mouse.

Who really knew how many others were hiding in the Rest Third?

Lena nodded again. "Be careful. Neither temple nor goddess take kindly to losing their power."

I dropped my eyes, hoping Lena couldn't see Gui and Tasha and Mouse in my gaze. I didn't want guards in the Rest Third. I'd warn the others and make them even quieter.

I didn't think I could stop them completely.

But Lena had information we desperately needed— especially after this morning. I licked my lips, tasting strawberry and tears. "What about the demon hunters?"

Lena looked at me like she was putting my question together with our location and not liking the answer. "Still here. More careful than before. Something changed when you — er, *the last high priestess* died. It's like they're rethinking their strategy."

"Killing m— *her*— didn't work last time." *That's why they need the origin stories.*

Lena's hands clenched and she blinked fiercely. "Thank the goddess."

I set down my spoon. Put my hand on her arm. I'd made them all grieve for me. "I'm sorry. I—"

"It's fine," Lena said gruffly. "I knew. I saw you that night. You needed to go."

"But I didn't mean to hurt you all."

"*You* didn't."

"I did... by dying. Then leaving."

"How did that all happen, anyway?" She leaned forward again. "I missed it, during the fighting."

Jay and I took turns, each filling in parts of *that night*. How we fought and I died and Jay brought me back. By the middle of the tale, my stomach was upset and I regretted the ice. By the end, I was shaking and so was Jay.

221

"Bless it." Lena looked stunned. "You were meant to go. So many things went wrong, but so many things went exactly right."

Jay nodded. "Everything went wrong. But we made it, and that was all that mattered."

"And no problems with controlling the..." She gave me a significant look. *The magic.*

I ducked my head and lowered my voice even further. "It... churns inside me, like it wants to come out. But it takes more effort, here."

Lena cocked her head. "Interesting. You've used it. And the dark goddess—"

"Not yet." I plucked at the skin on my arm. At the tattoo shadow no one but me could see. "She—" I winced, but Jay deserved to know too. "She's still connected to me. But it's like shouting across the fields. She's too far away to reach me."

"Ah. I'd hoped She'd let you go, but I'm not surprised." Lena tucked some stray hairs back into her braids. "Be careful. You don't deserve to get pulled back in... to all of it." Then she rose, threw down more coins, and left without a goodbye.

Fair. Last time, I'd left without the goodbye.

For a moment, I had an urge to go with her, but I'd left that life behind, and though every moment with her had been a gift, it had still been dangerous. She'd hired us to find *me* for goddessi sake.

"Let's take the long way back." I held out my hand for Jay. "I just want to walk in the sun with my beloved."

He smiled and joined his hand to mine, the little tension lines between his eyes relaxing. "You trust her?"

"Absolutely."

But my mind circled. Lena wasn't the problem. My blood-sister Aimi wasn't even the problem, though if she knew I was alive, she could be. My doing magic— apparently *any* magic was. If the damned high priestess and the blessed high priestess *and* Enzo the demon hunter could still feel it, as careful as I'd been, I could never use magic again.

They could feel Andy and Wil and Gui and Tasha and Mousie's magic too.

By teaching them, I'd put us all back into deadly peril.

But I had no other choice.

They had all been using magic, would all continue using magic, whether I *permitted* it or not.

So I had to teach them to be even quieter.

Jay

IT RAINED OVERNIGHT, AND COME MORNING THE CLOUDS WERE STILL tight and dark. Unusual for summer.

Despite the late morning hour, their room had a cool, damp breeze blowing through. Jay shifted Sumi off his chest and eased out of bed. She stirred. Looked at him with sleepy red eyes and tousled red hair. He wanted nothing more than to tumble back into bed with her, drive his fingers into that hair and kiss that mouth—

"Would you buy some wood? Cheap stuff? Enough that the boys can build something oh... bed-sized?"

Obviously *she* wasn't thinking about sex.

Jay sighed. "Do I even want to know?"

She smiled, but her eyes had already closed again and her second breath turned into a tiny snore.

So he went out into the gray morning and found what she'd asked for, left it on the pavers in the backyard. Climbed up the new ladder to the new second story of the house. Untacked the waxed hide from a window and slipped inside.

He and Thom had gotten the exterior walls and the roof up, but the inside was rough. Jay started on the walls and soon enough had two little helpers.

When they came down for breakfast, Sumi was awake.

"Morning." She wrapped herself around him and he seriously considered carrying her back to bed.

But the breeze had died and the thought of skin on skin in a shut up, muggy room— no.

Still, when she stepped back, he groaned. He wanted her so much— but she was still healing. Thought he hadn't noticed how tired she was after yesterday. How her body hurt after the walking and the stress—

"How fares the addition?"

"Coming along." He grinned at the boys. "I've had excellent helpers."

"Wonderful. If you can spare them for a bit, they have a project of their own."

"Of course." He emptied his cup and took a piece of bread with him. "I'll get back up there then."

He kissed Sumi. Patted Wil on the shoulder. Caught Andy's eye and nodded. Then climbed back into the addition that would soon enough be one large bedroom. Started finishing work on one wall, then heard their voices out back and let curiosity distract him. Leaned on the window ledge.

Watched.

The boys laid the wooden planks flat on the ground, one next to another; enough to cover a patch of ground a bit larger than a child's bed. Shoved until the pieces touched, but the wood was rough-hewn and uneven, with gaps and gnarls, and he wondered what they were going to do with it.

"Quiet now," Sumi said. "Even quieter than before. Make

sure no one will notice you. Balance each other out. Smooth the ripples."

What ripples, Jay couldn't see, but she had to be talking about magic. Having the boys *do* magic, even though both Zerth —no, *Enzo*— and Lena had found them yesterday and said they could feel it.

Resting betweens, she was courting disaster.

He had to trust her. Had to believe she wouldn't bring them all down on his family.

"Quieter." She leaned forward like she wanted to help.

Antero placed one sun-darkened purple hand down on the board farthest from Jay. Wilyam copied him, only his hand was red.

If these two could work together, couldn't all the Colors? Of course, they were being raised as siblings, but even before that, they'd been friends... Jay rubbed the knot of pain between his eyes. The caste of Colors didn't make sense— just ask his now-resting parents!— but he didn't know how to do anything about it.

Sumi said, "Remember what we talked about. What you practiced. This isn't any more complicated, just give it more time. Keep it small. Keep it hidden."

Wil's tongue poked out between his teeth. Andy's fist clenched.

Nothing happened. He was wasting time, watching them. So much magic happened invisibly.

Then the wood... *grew* together. The gaps filled. The boards smoothed until the whole thing was one piece of solid wood.

Sumi nodded. Handed them something.

The boys unwound bits of twine, measured them, then did *something* to cut them. Wil set an end of his twine on one corner and Andy set his on the nearest corner. Jay couldn't see how they were going to tie the twine to the board, being nowhere to anchor it... but the boys did another *something* and the twine stuck. They tugged gently, then pulled with all their might and the twine held.

Goddessi.

They were creating a flying pallet. At least, the *pallet* part. He wasn't so sure about the *flying* part.

"Set the spell into the wood and the twine," Sumi whispered. "It doesn't have to last forever. Just one good trip out and back."

The boys nodded. Glared at the board even more fiercely. Then sat on it. Each gathered a piece of twine. The thing rose knee-high into the air and hovered there.

They'd done it.

"They want to see the desert." Sumi looked up at him as if she knew he'd been watching all along. Held out her hand. "Come along?"

Jay snorted. "Yes, but wait for me." He climbed down from the roof, belted on his twin swords, filled waterskins, gathered travel-food into a small basket, then went back out.

Sumi was up on the board, her face alight. She held out her hand again and he took it and stepped up. Their flying board was just comfortable for four, the boys in front with matching grins, the food and water in the middle, and he and Sumi in the back.

As soon as he was situated, the board rose into the sky, straight up, smooth and fast. The air traffic was light today. Though their flight was smoother, their *pallet* more refined, they stayed with the other flying pallets, far below the clouds. Wouldn't fit in with the flying carpets and would draw too much attention if they tried.

They flew west, the boys' eyes wide as they tried to look at everything— the looming clouds and flying carpets above, the city below, the other pallets to either side, while Sumi cuddled next to Jay and he decided this was his favorite moment so far today.

They crossed the river and the other fliers went other directions, until they were the only ones flying west, high above the fields. The clouds thinned as if the fields were sucking away their water— resting betweens, what did he know? They probably were.

From up above, the fields were peaceful and green, as if those of the Blessed Third didn't allow the Rest Third to cultivate their own fields then take what they wanted at harvest time.

The line between the irrigated fields and the desert was almost as harsh as his anger for the blessed. The clouds disappeared, leaving only hard blue sky. He swore he could feel his skin drying out as they flew over the first brown and sand-touched hills, then farther into the desert until he felt like they were the only things alive.

Robin told stories of all the creatures that lived in the sand, so he knew the feeling wasn't true, but it *felt* true.

They flew over brown and cream and tan and white and occasional rocks that were striped all the colors of this desert. How far to the desert of reds and whites and odd rock formations only the caravans saw?

They kept flying until Sumi pointed. "There."

Jay couldn't see anything about this patch of sand that was better than any other patch, but with Sumi and the boys smiling next to him, he didn't care.

He'd do anything to make them smile.

The board descended smoothly, came to rest on a patch of pristine white sand, the high point of a small hill. Cerulean sky stretched all around them. Heat pressed down. Nothing moved.

Sumi grabbed the food basket and Jay the waterskins, but before the boys could get too far, Sumi cleared her throat.

"What?" Wil squinted all around him.

"Two more things before you play. One, *push* the board up and set it in place. High enough we can sit under it— without using the twine. Can you? Do you have enough power?"

Andy nodded and Wil scowled. They came back to the board. Touched it.

Slowly— so slowly they must be tired after the magic they'd already done— the board rose. Stopped. Stuck in the sky like... *magic.*

The boys turned to go.

"Two— stay in sight!"

They ran, whooping. Their footsteps marked the sand. Still calling and pushing each other, they tumbled down the gently rolling hill.

"Why...?" Jay gestured to the board.

"The shade is nice." Sumi crawled underneath, dragged the food with her.

He joined her. "But why with new magic?"

"Ah." She looked up at the board above their heads. "Every time they push themselves farther than they think they can, they get stronger, and then they know they can do it. Also, the flying magic can get tired. If we make it hover now, it might not fly us all the way back home."

Home was good— this far out they didn't have enough provisions to walk back to the city.

Sumi's eyes crinkled and she held back a laugh. He wasn't sure if she was teasing or not. He was just happy to see her smile.

"Sounds good to me." He leaned it and kissed her.

It was too hot for anything else, but her lips on his were heaven.

Soon enough, she broke away from him to check on the boys. "It's nice out here. Simple. Quiet."

Wil's particularly loud yelp broke the silence.

"Mostly," she laughed. Then she sobered. "We can talk out here. About anything."

"No one to overhear?"

"Not even magically."

Ah. The trip suddenly made more sense. Not just a getaway but a planning session too. The discoveries yesterday weighed on her as much as they weighed on him.

"We could go." Sumi ducked her head and Jay knew his guess was right. "Leave the City of Temples. Leave the goddessi behind. Leave the demon hunters behind. Get so far away no one would know who we are."

He nodded. He'd wondered if she'd been thinking it. Sweat trickled down his back. The very thought sent a dagger of guilt through his gut. "We could."

"But your sisters. Our friends. Even Mouse... I don't know if she'd come with us or not."

"We can't take everyone." He forced a chuckle, but it was as dry as the air around them. "We'd have to leave my sisters behind."

She looked out at the rolling sand. Breathed in the heat. Watched the boys. "It wouldn't be right. Not for the boys. They need their aunties." She met his eyes. "Not for you. You need your people. Your sisters, your friends at the guard."

He swallowed hard. Swigged a mouthful of water to clear his throat. Said his truth. "I'd leave for you."

She smiled, her eyes and lips turning up, but it faded into a sigh. "It wouldn't be right for the city. We don't know what the demon hunters are up to, and even if my blood-sister is a decent high priestess, my blood-mother is not. We can't abandon the Rest Third to her."

"Shouldn't."

"What?"

"*Shouldn't*, not *can't*. We are not trapped." He tucked a strand of her red hair over one ear. Thought of how much he loved her, this woman who— after everything— still worried about the resting city. "We have the choice. We *can* go. We *can* stay. Nothing and no one is forcing us."

"You're right." She dug her toes into the sand. "We *could* go. Thank you for reminding me." Squinted at him, then that little smile came back. "We have a choice. It helps. Not trapped— that helps."

Goddessi, he would miss his sisters if they went, but he would still go with her. Anywhere. "What do you choose to do, my love? Do you choose to go? Or to stay?"

He saw it in her face. Knew before she knew. His heart broke a little for her when she said the word.

"Stay."

CHAPTER

SEVENTEEN

S *umi*

Flying out of the sunset into the dusk, from the desert to the city, brought us back sunburned and relaxed, even me. Until we crossed the river. From up above, I could see the way the Blessed Third was eating into the Rest Third, the Rest Third pinched between the temples and goddessi, and slowly losing that vital access to the river.

As difficult as it was, the City of Temples was *my* city.

I'd been born here— at least according to the harridan who gave birth to me— and I intended to die here, hopefully old and gray and side-by-side with Jay, watching Wilyam and Antero and their families, and Jay's sisters and their families...

So we would deny the demon hunters what they wanted and forge our own path.

In the morning after teaching the kids, I slipped away into

the streets of the Rest Third. If we were staying, there were things that needed to be done.

How the heaven to do that while hiding?

Very, very carefully... I had to protect my found family. Had to.

So, first, *feel* for Tasha and Gui.

The summer storm had passed, leaving the sky clear and the heat once again heavy. As I smelled the decay of the tanneries and hot metals and pungent dyes and the sweat and frustration of this tiny neighborhood pushed against the hills, I wished I'd enjoyed the clouds yesterday instead of haring off to the desert with Jay and the boys... but we'd needed the break and we'd needed to talk plainly and without my magic it was almost impossible to ensure we wouldn't be overheard.

So— the tanneries and the tailors and the tinkers in the poorest part of the city. Were Tasha and Gui stealing from these folks too? Had I misjudged them so much?

My leg muscles burned and sweat gathered under my arms, but I made it to the tinker neighborhood where Reds worked metal and glass right over and *into* open flame and kilns— my heart jumped, then I remembered they had no magic to *pull* the heat from the flames to the metal, and burn-scars on their hands showed the danger of it. The priestessi and magi might make larger, clearer mirrors and stronger swords, but these people made *courage* solid.

I kept on. Next came the Greens, tanning animal skins into leather and molding the leather into shoes, and carding and spinning and dying Blue-owned wool into yarn and thread.

The Orange neighborhood held stacks of woods of all colors, as the Oranges built pallets and cabinets and chairs and bed frames. I stopped for a moment to catch my breath and admire the canny ways a man cut notches in a piece of blue-wood to fit a corner together without any nails.

Past the Oranges, the Yellow neighborhood, and the only things past them were the hills where the rest of the Greens tended Blue-owned sheep and goats, and then the blessed-owned and damned-owned caves and mines.

Where the remainder of the Third had gardens, the Yellow neighborhood had compost fields, and all the Yellows old enough to hold a shovel turned table scraps and weeds and dead flowers and used tea over and over nightsoil. And along the edges of the compost fields, their own narrow strips of vegetables grown large.

Sweat plastered my hair to my head and I longed for the cool of the damned temple if not the temple itself, but in the center of a rather fragrant square, I finally found Tasha and Gui.

Gui had a group of Yellow children clustered around him— no more than five and six years old and one as young as three— listening to a story. Tasha sat nearby, her Purple head bowed over mending, and what she was mending wasn't for her... unless she wore yellow tattered lace and I hadn't noticed.

Gui's story stopped my feet.

He told the children of a nomad people— Yellows and Oranges— who found the valley and the river and settled, living peacefully until discovered by Purples and Blues from the north.

"West!" one of the yellow women corrected.

"South!" another told her.

"North," said an oldster so faded it was hard to see he was Yellow at all, and his voice silenced the rest.

"From the north," Gui said, and went on with his tale. "The Purples and Blues stayed in the mountains for a generation—"

"Two!" A different voice this time. And this was the difficult part about histories passed down from voice to voice— no one agreed on the details.

"For two generations." Gui wriggled his fingers like spiders.

"Then they started creeping down into the valley. At first, they were helpful, with their stone waterways and metal pipes and their fountains to expand the reach of the river, but then they wanted more. It was a fine spring day—"

"Summer!"

"Winter!"

Gui hurriedly skipped ahead, "—when two Purple women each bound themselves to a *cari*, a mischievous spirit that gave them magic. And that magic gave them power over the settlers' children. And then the Purples and Blues divided the waterways and pipes and fountains between them. And two generations after that—"

"Three."

"Three generations after that, people started to worship them and so they became the blessed and the damned."

I did not want to interrupt. The Yellow adults, for all their inserted comments, obviously enjoyed having someone else entertain the littles while they worked, but I was going to make their life harder. I should be used to the weight of guilt on my shoulders by now, but no.

Tasha noticed me and whistled low. Gui glanced at her, followed her pointed gaze to me. His shoulders tightened, but he finished what he'd started to say, then told the children to shoo.

Accusing Yellow childish glares turned my way, but I'd been glared at by worse. I waited. The children scattered and Gui stood and Tasha set down her mending.

Once we were as alone as we could be, while surrounded by curious Yellows working the compost and their children, I stepped close to them both and said, "You need to be careful. Quiet— even quieter." I gave them a significant look.

Gui scowled. "We're trying. Been practicing."

I nodded. "I had a visit from someone who was looking for

recruits in the Rest Third, so if you're going to keep at it, we need to continue refining."

Tasha paled. "Looking? For us? What did you—"

"I told them nothing." They had few reasons to trust me and learning that Lena had hired us to find the previous high priestess— me— wouldn't help. "But if we keep drawing their attention, they'll bring in reinforcements."

Tasha exchanged glances with Gui. "Resting— all right. We can pull back some."

"Do that. I have something else for you. And I'll pay. Not much, mind—"

Gui's eyebrows rose and his lips thinned. Tasha kept her face still, but her neck muscles twitched. Suspicious— good, but difficult timing. They didn't yet understand that once they were my allies, they were always my allies, until they betrayed me or mine.

"There are demon hunters in the Rest Third."

"Resting—" Tasha looked around, then back at me, and lowered her voice to a murmur. "We're not going to track down every Yellow and Orange—"

"That's not what I'm asking. Not at all. There's one specific man. He... found me in the market. Threatened me."

"One man." Tasha rubbed between her eyes as if she was getting a headache. "You want us to find one man in a city this size?"

"Yes. Find him. Follow him. Tell me what he's saying, to whom. What his plans are for this city."

Tasha side-eyed me. "How will we know him?"

Ah, bless it. How would they? Nothing about Enzo shouted for notice. Unless— what Yssa had figured out while spying for me—

Bless me for a fool, I was going to use magic. But we weren't near my home, nor Tasha's and Gui's— they might think I hadn't noticed, but they'd started sleeping in a corner of the abandoned church— so even if the guards came looking for it, they wouldn't find anyone. "I'll... show you."

I slowly reached out, touched one finger to his forehead, her forehead. Then gathered up my power and carefully, delicately *pushed* a picture of Enzo into their minds. Exactly how Yssa had done it, how she'd taught me— but a thousand times gentler, quieter.

I wasn't sure it had worked until Gui gasped.

"You—"

"Shh." I slashed my hand down, *silence*. A sweat bead slid into my eye. Stung. I scraped the back of my hand across my eyes, then cautiously looked at Gui and Tasha.

Emotions chased across their faces, Tasha astounded and Gui furious.

Time to remind them they had a job to do, no matter what I'd put in their heads. "Now you know what he looks like."

"No," Gui snapped. He glared at me. "Enzo is family to me, even if distant. A third cousin once removed, and we don't spy on family."

Ah, bless me, I'd forgotten. How could I have forgotten his conversation with Mouse? She was Enzo's daughter and Gui reminded her of home. Bless, bless, *bless*.

I needed them to do this for me. The boys couldn't— if he realized who they were, he'd do something awful to them. Jay couldn't— he already had too much with teaching and working and finding histories. His sisters couldn't— Dee was still healing, Robin working and being in love with Lena, and Maggie... I couldn't trust Maggie.

I had to convince Gui. "I need you." I tucked my hands under my arms. "The demon hunters already attacked the damned third. Your cousin is here, destabilizing the city. Maybe preparing us for an invasion. You've seen the marks on the walls."

Gui glared at me, his mouth clamped shut. He knew.

Tasha put her hand on his arm. "I *like* this city. As messed up as it is. My family is here, you're here, your family is here..."

His gaze moved past us to the Yellows around us, and his fingers twitched. Were his parents, his siblings, his local cousins, surrounding us? Composting? Listening to his stories?

My voice so low it was more the shape of my mouth than the words, I told them, "He wants me to steal from the temples. I *can't*. It's not possible. Please. I told him I can't. I just need to know what will happen so we can prevent it... or prepare for it."

Gui bowed his head.

Around us, the stench rose up and the birds sang and the children chattered.

When he raised his head, Gui had more lines in his face and his eyes were tired. "How much will you pay me to betray my family?"

"No, not blood money." Tasha shook her head. "I want *that*. What you did to show him to us. Teach us that."

I swallowed hard. "I don't know if you can—"

"I can."

"It takes a particularly strong and delicate—"

"I can."

She wasn't going to give up. But this ability in the hands of thieves— what if they *pushed* a picture of a tax collector into a merchant's mind and took the money? Or goddessi-forbid, made people in the market see a monster and leave their wares behind? Really, they would only be limited by their imagination and their skill— what had I done? "Maybe." I'd find something else she wanted more. I had to.

"No maybe." Gui's brow furrowed. "Teach us that or we won't help."

Ah, bless it to heaven. I really didn't have a choice. "All right."

"Go." Gui stepped away from me. "We'll find him and see what we see. Then we'll find you. Don't come back here.

I ducked my head. The high priestess of Maldita could go wherever she wanted whenever she wanted and none could touch her— but I wasn't her anymore, so I let my feet carry me away.

They would find Enzo— they were good thieves to have lasted this long without being arrested, and they had contacts all over the city. But when they did find him, what would they discover?

Were the demon hunters planning another invasion? The last one had killed me. Literally.

I couldn't go through that again.

≈

*J*AY

SUMI HAD COME BACK TROUBLED FROM HER MORNING WALK. WHEN HE arched a querying brow, she shook her head, indicated she didn't want to talk about it, so he let her be.

The new upper room needed paint anyway, but Jay needed to inspect every fingerwidth before the boys could take it over. They would come to no more harm on his watch.

But when he set the ladder into its braces, Sumi gathered up a twine-tied roll of parchment and stood. He climbed the ladder and she followed him up.

"What are you—?"

"I want to spend time with you." She looked around the empty room, almost as large as the main living area below, then settled in the square of early afternoon light on the sanded yellowwood floor. Untied the twine and rifled through the parchments.

Sunlight poured in and caressed her. Her hair would be soft and smell of sunlight and woman, winding around his fingers, and her skin even softer under his lips— No. He was here to work.

To keep his hands to himself, he started in the far corner. Turned his back to her and examined each spot, looking for ways his and Thom's work could come undone, ways the structure could fail, ways the boys could hurt themselves.

Each board sat flush against the next, and when he tested them, none gave under the pressure of his hand.

He remembered Andy and Wil magicking the flying board. They'd been up here, done *something*, bless them.

"What did they do?"

Sumi didn't pretend to misunderstand. She set her hand down on the floor and closed her eyes. The corners of her eyes wrinkled in that way that meant she was working magic... or at least *listening,* as she called it. After a moment, her lips quirked. "It's safe," she said. "No way in the world this room will come apart from the rest."

"*What* did they *do?*" He wasn't mad— exactly— just frustrated none of them felt the need to communicate with him about their own safety. Especially when it touched on their magic.

She side-eyed up at him. "They fused the boards. Nothing but catastrophe will bring it down."

He pinched the bridge of his nose. "Let's not invite anything catastrophic, then." He was no magus or priestess— couldn't do anything but accept it. Understand they were completely safe, even if not how he would have liked it. "Fine. Just paint then."

"When you say *fine* that way..."

He made the effort to smile. Sumi was safe, the boys were safe, his sisters were as safe as they could be. "It is fine. Really. What are you reading?"

"Those histories I copied. That night." She looked relieved he hadn't asked about her errands. Her eyes twinkled at him, invited him to remember *that night*.

He grinned. Grimaced at the thought of his "family". Grinned again at outsmarting all of them. "And?"

She ran her finger along one line. "This... doesn't make any more sense than it did before. Some of this is tax information, some of it stories about the family, some of it stories about the city, but it's all jumbled together like one person didn't wait for the next to finish before taking the pen away."

He compared it to what he knew of the rich of the Rest Third, and blinked. "That's... odd."

She nodded, confirming his suspicion. "None of our— I mean, the *damned* records are like this. We have coherent stories, not this... mess."

"Wait— you *remember* the damned stories?" All this resting time the demon hunters had been stealing Rest Third stories, and she remembered the stories of the damned?

Sumi blinked at him.

"Of course I do. I studied them and I have a good memory."

Aggravating— she could have been writing down what she remembered all this time. Enzo had demanded she get the histories from the damned, but she had them all in her head. A chill ran over him, despite the heat. If Enzo ever found out... Rest it, he could never know. The things that man might do to her just to get those stories—

She still looked baffled, so he gentled his tone. "Write them down," he said softly. "Then we can compare your stories to the rest."

"Oh! I can do that."

"And never— ever— tell anyone else. If that gets back to the demon hunters, they won't just be following you around. They'll take you and you can't use your magic and they'll—" *torture you and maybe kill you and I couldn't* live *with that.* Jay realized he was clenching and unclenching his fists.

Sumi watched him, waited for him. She didn't run from his anger, trusted him to control himself. And no trace of pity in her eyes— he couldn't have borne it if she'd pitied him.

I will protect her. From them. From everything. He breathed like Thom suggested: in count to ten, hold count to ten, out count to ten. Smelled the fresh wood all around him, felt the sun on his face. Equilibrium.

Then he remembered what she'd started to say. "What's—" he swallowed hard— "*my family's* take on the origin of the goddessi?"

Sumi rose and hugged him, her body warm from the sun. "*Your* family is here, in this house, with you. No matter who your blood-family might be, your *found* family is who you love and who loves you."

All the fury went out of him. Resting betweens, he loved feeling her arms around him. Loved *her*. He pressed a kiss to her forehead. "Thank you."

"Love you." She pressed herself against him and he wondered for the thousandth time if she was well enough for them to physically love each other. But no— her knees hurt after her walk this morning. He could tell in the way she moved.

Gently, he dipped to kiss her mouth, then eased away.

She bit her lip, and he wanted to bite it, but he *would* control himself.

She tucked her head, slouched back over to her spot on the floor, slowly sat. Hunched over the sheets of parchment. Her voice sounded normal when she finally spoke. "Your blood-family seems to think they prayed so hard that the local farm and hearth goddessi were bound to the temples. So the fertility of the valley and the presence of the damned and blessed is entirely due to them."

Jay rolled his eyes. "Of course they do. Do the damned priestessi claim credit in their records? The magic users did in that story from Temples Day."

Sumi scowled. "And the Yellows have an oral history that tells of Purples invading and coveting power and then binding *mischievous* spirits to themselves."

"So we have goddessi or spirits or demoni and prayers or spells or some other mysterious *binding*..."

Sumi smoothed the parchment absently. "Maldita and Bendita are—" She waved one hand— "*present* in a way most other religions' goddessi aren't."

"None of it makes sense." He loved the little crease between her eyebrows. Reached out and stroked it.

She batted his hand away. "What the heaven are they looking for?"

"Who?"

"The demon hunters. Just knowing *who* was responsible won't be enough. *I* would want to know *how*. *How* might help get rid of them— if I believed they are demoni. Maybe I'd want to know *why*. Just to satisfy my own curiosity."

"Should we warn them?"

"Who?" She blinked up at him. "The demon hunters?"

"The blessed."

Sumi snorted. "About what?"

"That the demon hunters want their writings."

"Why?"

"Makes sense, doesn't it? If they're going after *all* the writings?"

"Yes, but *why*? They don't— Wait, one thing at a time... even if we wanted to warn them, *how*?" She shook her head, tidied the pile of parchment. "The damned we can work through Lena, but the blessed? They won't believe us if they don't know who I am, and if they did— they still wouldn't listen, just try to keep me for themselves. Or kill me." Sumi paused, chewed a lip. "I'm really not sure which."

"No." Jay's jaw clamped down. Ached. All the fury was back, filling him up and ready to explode. *Breathe. She is here where I can protect her.* "Neither."

"So what do we do?"

"They're the priestessi of the goddessi," he growled. "They're on their own." She looked a little smug, so he threw out something she hadn't thought about. "You know you have a talent to be a forger, right?"

"What?" That smug look was gone, replaced by bafflement.

"A forger. You're a natural."

"Forge... metal?"

"Writing. Exactly like someone else did. You copy someone else's writing and then sell it as an original."

Still baffled. "Why?"

"Money, my love. Easy money."

"But... that can't be legal."

He laughed. "It's not."

"But you're a guard! Why are we even talking about it?"

"Because you're a natural. Even if you never use the skill, you should be aware you have it. I watched you that night— you just... fell into it. Your hand moved different and the shapes of the letters changed to look like the ones on the page you were copying."

"A natural criminal." Sumi leaned back, her eyes dancing. "At least that's something to fall back on if poverty doesn't work out for me."

"You have your teaching."

243

"Right. Poverty."

He laughed. Sidled up next to her. "You have me."

"That I do."

She wrapped her arms around him and rested her forehead against his muscled belly. Desire struck him hard and fast, but he leashed it yet again. "Mmm."

"And I wouldn't give you up for all the money in the world."

"We're just as greedy. All your found family. Sumi, wife of Bluejay, mother of Wil and Andy, sister of Robin, Chickadee, Magpie..."

She laughed, just as he intended.

EIGHTEEN

S umi

TWO DAYS LATER, MOUSE FOLLOWED US TO THE ABANDONED CHURCH.

The sun beat down on everything. The air rose up shimmering from the stones in the road and the garden boxes and the houses. Almost expected to see flames from the nearest thatched roof. Sweat pricked at my armpits and trickled down my back. More than almost anything, I wanted to *pull* cool from the depths of the river to surround me and cushion me from the summer heat of the Rest Third— but I didn't.

No magic.

Not since fixing Dee's back, and only barely *feeling* the people around me, despite how it made the hair on my neck stand up, but we'd decided to stay and if I wanted to stay— and protect my family— *no magic.*

Brown canes ran along a dilapidated fence. Might have been raspberry bushes when the churchgoers still watered them, but now the dead sticks rustled. Something small crawled under them. A rodent, perhaps.

Mouse shifted, and caught my eye. She was crouched on the roof of the building behind the church. The building itself was small and square and might have been a shop or a storage shed, but had been abandoned with the church. The tile roof must be burning hot. How did she suffer it— and why?

Stepping over the threshold of the church into the shade was a blessed relief, but Maldita was a jealous goddess, and no matter whose this church was, I wasn't about to pray to anyone but Her.

I turned, silhouetted in the doorway, and beckoned Mouse.

She jumped.

Landed squarely and walked toward me, none the worse for her leap.

My knees hurt, imagining it, but she'd used magic to cushion herself.

When I'd been the high priestess of the Temple of the Damned, I'd been able to lift others and then myself off the ground, but it had taken me years to figure out how to do it properly— and this child did it as easy as breathing.

I stepped further into the gloom and waited for my eyes to adjust. Wil had already climbed up to the balcony, while Andy knelt and fiddled with something. With the sun high overhead, neither colored-glass window cast a second version of itself down onto the floor.

Still stunning.

The debris that had littered the main room had disappeared; the broken boards were leaning against the wall next to the front doors and the bricks had been piled into a small hill at the back. The building still smelled a bit of unwashed bodies, but not so strong, nor musty.

Someone had been busy.

Andy stood, and I realized he held a mousetrap.

Mouse— heh. I side-eyed the girl hesitating in the doorway.

Wil poked his head over the rail and scowled down at us. "Someone is overnighting here."

I choked back my first response— *it's not your church*— and went with something more neutral. "Oh? Do you know who?"

"How would I know who?"

Andy rose and stared at me, then his face lit. "You can identify people from their belongings? When they're not here?"

Sometimes. "You tell me."

He thundered up the stairs.

Mouse waited until he had climbed nine stairs, then side-eyed me. "What?"

"Why are you always following me around?"

"Not always." She looked away.

"Often enough." I'd *felt* her, all through the markets on Temples Day, never close enough to pick out of the crowd but never more than a shout away. "I thought you would follow Jay—"

"You're more interesting than him. He just goes into the guardhouse and stays there all night. You go to the neighbors and to the markets and to the poor areas and talk to interesting people."

"*Interesting*. Good word for it." I hadn't *felt* her yesterday when I'd sought out Tasha and Gui, but I should have.

Mouse dropped her gaze and studied her feet, or the floor. "I won't anymore, if that's what you want."

"It's fine." Not that I really believed she'd stop, just because I said. Perhaps be more careful. Since I wasn't in the habit of sharing my secrets within her earshot, her presence was a waste of time, not a threat. "If you have time to follow me around, you have time to do me a favor and practice your magic, too."

Her head came up. "I don't have—"

"Please." I loaded the word with scorn. "This thing you do — following me around? Out of sight but you always know which way I turn? Magic. Jumping down off the roof just now, without flexing your legs? Anyone else would have popped a knee. Magic."

Mouse blinked. "No. That's not possible."

"Perfectly possible. Remember when you first came to stay with us? I touched you. Felt it. Magic."

"I thought you forgot about that. Thought you was crazy." Her eyes widened until white showed all the way around the yellow. "I don't. I *can't*."

"Why?"

"My family— my dad. He'll kill me if he finds out."

"Finds out?"

"That I have your kind of magic." She rocked onto her toes, ready to run. "He'll kill me."

Her dad. Enzo. I made a point of looking around the church, as if seeking him. "He's not here, is he? He's not feeding you, not clothing you..." Careful. *Tread lightly here if you want her help.* "I'm not going to tell him anything. Are you?"

"No." She swallowed hard. "No, he's not here." Slowly her panic faded. "Okay."

"You can *feel* it, right? That he's not here inside the church?"

She nodded *yes*, then caught herself and shook her head *no*.

I smirked. "Magic."

Mouse groaned.

"When you said *your kind of magic*..." I kept my voice casual, examined a ragged fingernail instead of her. But if she knew *my kind* as compared to *her kind*, she knew Old Spells. "Your family has a different kind?"

She shivered and tucked her hands behind her back. "I don't want to talk about it."

She did know— tucking her hands away told me, since every Old Spell I'd encountered required some words, a sound, and a *gesture*.

If I was a horrible sort of person, I could start a spell— *Thousand Tongues of Flame*, perhaps, since it was easy. See if Mouse ran away into the shadows like her namesake.

Could I stop the spell, once I started?

And if I couldn't— I was stronger now, but was I strong enough? Completing the spell might half-kill me, outside the damned temple, outside Maldita's influence. Or at the very least, exhaust me beyond walking home.

My back twinged and I flinched away from the memory of agony, thought of another reason not to—

Would the demon hunters notice— the way the priestessi and magi could feel *push-pull* magic?

Best not to try.

"Right. So. *Our* kind of magic. Remember when we came here to hide and find? Gui and that Purple woman— Tasha— They were using magic to find you. You were using it to defeat them."

"Was not." She jerked back, offended.

"Yeah. You were. Remember, I can *feel* it all. And I watched you— from up there." I pointed to where the boys were peeking over the balcony railing.

They ducked back.

Someone else I didn't really mind spying on me.

Mouse clenched her jaw.

"I doubt you use it consciously. If you don't know when you're using it, the only way to learn is to practice using magic on purpose. If you can."

"If?"

"If. Sometimes if you've never thought of it, then you start thinking about it, everything is harder for a little while." We'd had a trainee or two like that in the damned temple. Skilled while unconsciously *pushing* and *pulling* and then once lessons came around— blocked. But we'd worn them down. They'd learned.

Just like Mouse would learn.

She looked sick. "You're not fibbing? I really do use your kind of magic?"

"You really do."

Her shoulders shifted under her thin shirt. Come fall, we'd need to get her some warmer clothes. Some of the money Lena had given us would go toward her winter shirts and pants. And the boys, too. They kept growing, as boys did.

"Guess I don't got much choice." Mouse straightened, decision made. "Gotta learn to control it."

I nodded. Now for the trickier part of the conversation. And considering the pitfalls of the first half, it would be rough. "You mentioned your blood-father..." I cleared my throat. "Enzo. The leader of the demon hunters."

The boys hissed and Mouse stiffened. "So?"

"You followed me through the markets on Temples Day. Did you see him talk to me?"

She looked away. So she had seen it.

"Did you hear what he said?"

No, or she'd have been more frightened of me. But I didn't need her to know that I knew— this was getting complicated. Still, I waited for her to shake her head *no*.

"He threatened me." *True.* Better to lie with the truth. "Us."

She paled, and her lip trembled. "No. He wouldn't do that."

She didn't sound convinced.

"He did. He threatened to tell the neighbors terrible things about me." Exactly *what*, I wouldn't tell her, or she'd be gone faster than flavored ice in summer.

I grinned briefly, imagining the taste on my tongue. My

words would need to taste as good, to tease out the information I needed. "We need to know where he's staying, what he's doing. What he knows about our family."

"*Our* family?" She blinked, and her yellow gaze flicked to the boys and back.

Wasn't sure why that was such a surprise. "Our family."

Her body was stiff, muscles tense. "*Our*? You including me in that?"

As if Jay would have it any other way. Nor me, though I wouldn't admit it to her. The scamp had grown on me. "Of course. You're part of our family now."

Her mouth fell open. "I am?"

"Yes." I let a smile bloom on my face, small, then larger. "You're family, Mouse. We feed you, we clothe you, we give you chores."

"Not sure how that shows you're family." She scowled and hunched up, defensive.

"We care about you. We want to help you learn how to work, to follow instructions, so if you want a job other than stealing, you can get one. We want you to learn you can be proud of your hard work. We want you to know you're safe where you sleep, and *we* want to know you're safe. We want to take care of you. You're part of our *found* family."

"But—" She leaned forward. Good. She wanted to belong to us. Her mouth gaped and no other words came out.

"Ours." I nodded sharply. "We won't give you up now."

"But..." Some of the tension went out of her.

"But your blood-father found me in the market and threatened to turn the neighbors against me. We need to know if he knows where we live, if he's started telling people lies—" *or the truth*— "about us."

Her mouth worked like a landed fish. Would she join us or run away?

"O-okay." She collapsed suddenly into herself, but her gaze met and matched mine. She had more strength then she knew. "And you'll teach me magic? How to... *not?*"

"Yes. If that's what you want."

She stood a little straighter, a little firmer. "That's what I want."

She would change her mind. She used her gift too often to do without it.

But I'd been wrong before. People were tricky.

"I'll teach you. But first, find Enzo." I smiled grimly. "And don't get caught."

She scoffed.

~

JAY

OUT OF NOWHERE, THOM DECIDED JAY HAD BEEN OFF THE STREETS TOO long. Told him to take a shift tonight instead of training the guards. He had his pick— but Litka would be too abrasive for a full shift, Mal too fawning, Maggie too talkative, even if she wasn't off spying for Thom. He had a sinking feeling every time he thought about her job spying, so he put it out of his mind. Dee would have been a perfect partner for the night, but she had just started retraining. That left Robin.

The sister who only came home to sleep anymore. He wanted to talk to her anyway.

The guardhouse seemed quieter tonight. More foreboding. Probably just because it was the late shift. Most of the guards were out already.

For the first time since he'd been back, Jay didn't shed his swords or his knives or his flying carpet next to the practice floor. Didn't remove the box of matches. Didn't remove the flare or the whistle that would tell other guards if he needed assistance. He did touch everything to make sure it was in its place, then picked up an unlit torch that at need could double as a club.

Solemnly, Robin watched. Jerked her head. And they went out into the evening.

The sun had dipped below the horizon and the last glow was fading. Most of the streets were cloaked in shadow— the main thoroughfares had torches, and the richest parts of the Third, lanterns, but the poorest parts had no extra money for light. They barred their doors and waited for morning.

Robin was one who left her torch unlit past the area of the guardhouse, and Jay grinned. His night vision had always been more important than lighting up an armwidth around and he was glad she thought the same.

They'd climbed a couple blocks toward the hills when they heard the first whistle.

A long blast, not the staccato of urgency, and still Jay felt his heart speed up and his palms go clammy. It had been *years* since the night so many of his unit had been killed, but he felt their ghosts pressing on him anyway.

And still his feet carried him forward at a jog.

Robin outpaced him, but not by much, so when he arrived, she was just lighting her torch. Guard Fitz held his high, and Jay took in everything at a glance while he caught his breath.

An Orange on the cusp of adulthood sat on the road. The pair of blue-dyed leather boots beside him and broken-latched door ajar behind him told his story. A Blue man— likely the owner of the animals and the leather— towered over a Green woman— the owner of the shop— poking at her with a stern finger.

"Your fault," the Blue man yelled. "If you had a better lock—"

"If you *paid* more, I could afford one!" the Green woman shouted back.

The thief side-eyed the shadows. He could sneak away while they were arguing and the guard distracted by them. Too bad for him Jay and Robin had arrived.

Jay took a spot behind the thief, whose shoulders hunched miserably. Robin stood with the other guard, Fitz. The Blue man's yells quieted, but he still towered over the Green woman.

Until he spun and pointed an accusing finger at the thief. "Cut off his hand," the Blue sneered. "That'll keep him from stealing anymore. Or maybe his feet, so he won't be needing boots at all!"

Jay fought the urge to step in front of the cringing Orange boy. The kid had only wanted shoes— Jay peeked inside the shop to confirm— he hadn't damaged anything else.

"Please, no. Please—" The boy broke into tears.

Fitz shook his head. "Honored Blue, you'd have to take that up with the Head Guard. For now, the boy will come with us. We'll assess the damage with Honored Green and then make our determination."

Jay loomed a little taller over the boy while Robin rested her hand on the hilt of her sword.

The Blue man deflated. "Fine," he snarled. "But I want the little shit to pay for the boots he ruined and the new ones I'll have her make. You hear me, Ada? I won't be paying you for remaking my boots. *He* will."

The Green woman— Ada— scowled but dropped her gaze. "Very well, Honored Blue."

The Blue man nodded sharply. Waited. When no one else spoke, he marched away, muttering under his breath.

"Why was he here?" Fitz asked. "It's *your* shop. You sleep in the back? Or above it?"

"In the back." The Green woman sighed. "He doesn't sleep much. Likes to check on his investments in the middle of the night. He's the one who caught the boy. Woke me with his shouting. He's caught a couple of them, sneaking around in the dark."

Fitz nodded. "My mom slept above our place. My older sister's place now. How much does the boy owe?"

"I can give him a discount on the lock because my oldest married into a Red family— decent metalworkers. Can't do anything about the boots though. He'll have to pay for the leather, the dye, and my time. Honored Blue will want the full price on two pair." She calculated, then named a sum.

Jay winced. He grabbed the boy by his collar and jerked him to his feet. "Come on, boy. You'll be working the fields for a long time for this. Unless you apprentice to the guards, and we'll work you even harder."

"No!" the boy squealed. "Don't hurt me!"

Jay shook him. "No one's going to hurt you." He set the boy on his feet but kept a hold of his collar. "Not from around here, are you?"

The boy's gaze darted from guard to guard to shoemaker. "No, please. I've only been here a few days—"

"Sure," Fitz rumbled. "Long enough to know where the shoemaker lives but not long enough to know we don't cut off hands or feet or anything else."

"Not the first time, anyway," Jay joked.

The boy nearly collapsed.

Jay rolled his eyes— a bad habit he'd picked up from Maggie. "Come along. We'll find you some shoes. Not blue, nor so well made—" he nodded to the Green woman— "but something that'll cover your feet."

"Softy," Robin mouthed.

With a shrug, Jay towed the boy downhill toward the guardhouse. Robin fell in beside him, her torch held high. Fitz remained behind to finish with the shoemaker.

"He can work harder, faster, if he has shoes," Jay said.

"Uh, huh." Robin didn't believe him.

Fair. He couldn't bear the thought of the boy working his feet bloody in the fields and they couldn't fit another stray in the house.

The questions that had been eating at him slipped out. "Where are you all the time? You're never at home any more."

"Out," she grunted. Avoided him by examining the street around them.

"Robin—"

She turned, brought the torch over his head, giving her face evil-looking shadows. "Why are you bothering me about this? And in front of a thief?"

"He's just a kid. Down on his luck."

"He's a thief who'll be working in the fields for a long time to pay for what he did."

"He needed shoes."

"But he didn't need *blue* boots. He could have picked something less showy.

"You're right." Jay tightened his hold on the kid's collar. At least his shirt was thick enough not to tear easily.

The kid stumbled but didn't yelp. Acting tough?

He needed to protect her. From everything. "You're my sister."

"I'm an adult."

"Yeah, but—"

The boy stumbled again, then tried to pull away. Jay jerked him back. His collar held.

Robin sighed. "I'm an *adult*."

"You're making money on the side and you don't want to share it?"

She rolled her eyes. "That's it. Because I've always resented us taking care of each other."

"You're tired of being a city guard? Want to go back to caravans?"

"No."

"Then what?"

She sighed. "You're not going to let this go."

"Nope."

"Didn't even occur to you I might be in a relationship?"

Now Jay stumbled. "A relationship?"

The guardhouse rose in front of them, well-lit and beckoning. Robin dunked her torch in a barrel of water. Opened the door for them, then followed inside and put the torch on the rack to dry. Picked up a new one. "I don't want to talk about it here."

"Thief," Jay told the cell guard, and shoved the boy inside. "Fritz's."

The cell guard nodded.

As soon as they were back on the street, Jay murmured, "A relationship?"

Robin rolled her eyes— she'd pick up the habit from Maggie too. "A relationship. A lover. A potential wife."

Jay scowled. His sister... with a wife? Leaving their home, leaving him— "I don't want you to go."

"Go where?"

"Out. Away." He waved one hand dramatically, even if she wouldn't really see it in the dark. "From us."

"Brother," Robin sighed. "It's not going to be today or tomorrow."

"But—" The words didn't come. She was his baby sister, and she had a *lover*?

"But what?"

"You— I— But—" He stomped next to her. Remembered the first time Mom had let him hold her as a baby, nearly as big as him and so heavy his arms ached but he'd been so proud. Remembered the first time she'd fallen out of a tree and knocked the breath out of herself. He'd felt like he couldn't breathe then either. Remembered teaching her how to hold a sword, holding his breath while she worked and worked and finally got it just right—

And now she was in a relationship. With who? "Are we going to meet her?"

Robin snorted. "You can't even think about it without cringing."

"I— I'll work on that. But I do want to meet her."

"Some day. Not tonight."

"A farmer? A shepherd? A tinker?"

"What?"

"Who is she? What does she do? What does she look like?"

"No." They walked under the lone torch on the street and he glanced at her. Robin's face pinched like she'd bitten something sour. "We're not talking any more about it. And don't harass the guards about her either. Or I will move out tomorrow. You understand me, Jay?"

He gaped. "They know?"

She rolled her eyes again. "Can you keep your mind on the job?"

"They knew and they didn't tell me."

"Leave them alone. Or I'll move out."

"You're serious?"

"As a temple after a magic user."

Rest it. She'd grown up so much. Enough to stand up to him. He hated it— was proud of her, but hated it. "All right."

She side-eyed him. "All right?"

"All right." What choice did he have?"

A flare burned up into the sky and exploded overhead. His throat tightened—*please, don't let any of our people be hurt*—but his body moved into a run.

It was going to be a long night.

NINETEEN

S umi

I'D SET MY SPIES ON ENZO AND SLEPT WITHOUT DREAMS FOR THE FIRST time since the demon hunter had found me in the marketplace. Morning classes came and went without problems; the boys went to get water and Jay and his sisters left for work, and I wrote down one of the damned stories Jay had asked for, and with all that done, the house echoed emptily around me. Even Mouse had gone, her face set in lines of discontent, perhaps at the thought of her magic.

Poor girl— to have Enzo for a father and not fit the family mold.

I at least fit the mold with my blood-family... or had, until I'd fled the temples.

Early afternoon sun streamed in through the windows. I wanted to curl up on the couch to study the Stonefield stories some more but I *should* clean the house. My feet were restless and before I knew it, I found myself at the market with a few coins to spend.

Little Tara had mentioned her grandmother was struggling.

I wanted Dansy and Nydia to like me— even more now that we'd decided to stay— and choose me over the demon hunters, if it came to that. So I bought a loaf of bread for grandma and some jam for the girls. The next time someone paid me in coin or trade, I would buy something for Suann. I could work my way around the neighborhood, house by house.

Maybe not a great plan— but it was the plan and coin I had.

I caught Purple movement out of the corner of my eye and spun, my heart thundering in my ears, my magic surging up inside me.

Not Tasha or Gui. Not Mouse. Not even the blessed, marching in from the far side of the market— worse.

Damned.

And two who knew me.

Danya and Yssa, my erstwhile apprentices. Danya, the Purple girl with the long, elegant nose, who— after months spying *on* me for the blessed temple— ended up spying *for* me on the demon hunters. Yssa, the pale Green girl who'd been terrified of herself and her powers in the beginning, but had learned so fast and been so curious and in the end, discovered how to *push* an image into my head—

I needed so much to speak to them, my apprentices I'd abandoned, to reassure them that I was still alive, but to do so would invite Maldita to find me.

I dropped my gaze— Danya was a Purple, after all, and Purples in the Rest Third could take offense at the direct gaze of a Red— then sidled behind a group of Green women, and purposefully stubbed my toe to change my gait.

Hid behind the shield in my mind. *Pushed* my magic down deep.

Walked away.

Why were they here in the Rest Third? Had they felt my magic when I healed Dee? Did they think I was alive?

I wished I dared walk closer and listen to them talk, but the closer I went, the more likely I'd be discovered. Still, I peeked at them again.

They wore their Colors— not damned black— so they weren't here as priestessi, but more likely spies. Looking for me. Or other magic-users. Were they full priestessi yet? Had I missed that too? They wouldn't recognize me— my hair, my skin, even my eyes were different. Not my voice, though.

I sneaked another look, then walked on.

They focused on a young Red woman carrying a Red baby. I couldn't decide if I should be hurt that they hadn't recognized me— the woman who had been the high priestess of the goddess Maldita and their mentor for all things magic— or relieved because they hadn't.

Relieved.

I should be relieved.

Should *not* want to reach for them— physically or magically, bless it. I'd started a different life, and had no way to bring them into it.

It was better this way.

Really.

My feet carried me toward home. All along the way, I blinked and dashed away tears. Foolish, wishing it didn't hurt me to see them, wishing I could sit down and talk with them like they were still my students, or neighbors, and nothing magic had ever happened. Foolish, foolish feelings.

With an effort, I put them away— gathered all the little bits of them and put them in a box in my mind, then closed the box and shoved it into the back, and dried my eyes on my sleeve.

I was here, now. Needed to focus on here, now.

The sun on the top of my head. The patch of beans growing along the road. The battered front door of our house, and the neighbors' pristine green door. The bread and jam in my hands. My plan to keep them liking me.

Dansy and Nydia lived directly across the street from us, in a small, patchy wood house, built with remnants of greenwood and yellowwood and orangewood with a red clay brick roof. Their mothers were slowly painting a bit at a time, they'd told me proudly, starting with that door.

I shifted my burdens to my left hand, then raised my right to knock at the door.

Tara opened it, beaming. "Teacher! Come in and see my room! Mama is away but Mom is here, so it's okay. Do you want to see my drawings? I'll show you. Come on—" She grabbed my free hand and towed me inside.

I almost dropped the bread. Stifled my halfhearted curse. Followed her in. "Dansy? Nydia?" I wasn't sure which mother was Mama and which one Mom.

"Mom! It's Teacher!" Tara hollered.

I'd never been inside before. The inside of the house was as patchy and charming as the outside, with a yellowwood table, one yellowwood chair and one greenwood chair. A distressed graywood rocking chair heaped high with quilts completed the seating of the room, and I wondered if the guards had sold it to them when they were done with it. Charcoal drawings— different kinds of flowers but mostly the faces of the girls straight on, the girls in profile, the girls somber, the girls laughing— lined the walls. Nydia's talent or Dansy's?

"Sumi?" Dansy came in the back door and wiped her hands off on her pants, leaving prints of dirt behind. "Everything all right?"

"Everything is fine. Tara is excelling on her numbers and Nathy on her letters. I just wanted to..." *bribe you to like me.* No, that sounded bad. At a loss, I handed her the bread, then gave the jam to Tara. "Here. These are for you."

Tara whooped and bolted for a spoon, but Dansy stood still and looked at me. "Ain't a holiday," she said. "Ain't Tara's birthday, nor Nathy's either."

"No. I just—" I waved one hand around as if that would explain.

Dansy smiled gently. "I've known you long enough now, I feel like I can say this to you, despite your Color..."

My throat closed. I forced out, "Mmm?"

"Sumi, you ain't got to buy our love."

Now I couldn't breathe *and* I had no idea what to say. "I-I-I'm not—"

She handed me back the loaf of bread. "We're after loving you because you're beloved of Jay and his family. We're loving you because you cared for his mother while she was dying. We're loving you because you teach our daughters and the neighborhood daughters and sons just like your own boys, though they're not so high-caste." She put her hand on my shoulder and it was so, so heavy. "We're after loving you for you."

My eyes stung and I blinked at her, still missing the words to respond.

"So you don't need to buy us things. Be a friend, trade with us, teach our children. No matter where you came from, you're ours now." She hugged me around the bread, sent a rueful look toward Tara who had a spoonful of jam in her mouth, then shooed me out her door.

"Bye, Teacher!"

I blinked in the midday sun, smelling the bread in my hands, hearing the pallets whoosh overhead, feeling my heart thud in my chest.

"Teacher, Teacher, Teacher—!" A little Orange boy raced to

me, ran into me and clutched me around my thighs. "Cori's gone!"

The Orange boy— Kass— lived next to Cori and joined us in the morning for numbers more than letters. Cori's mother, Suann, took care of her aged father and didn't get out much. "Suann looked in the house? You looked in the yard? You're sure she's not asleep under her blankets or up a tree?"

"We've looked!"

Now Suann followed after, her green eyes huge and haunted. If she'd left her father alone, she was terrified, and her uneven breathing confirmed it. "Sumi! You haven't seen Cori?"

I shook my head *no*. "I just came from Dansy's and she wasn't there. How long has it been?"

"Since this morning. What if the blessed took her? She's too young. Our family has no magic, not a speck of it. She won't be able to—"

"No." My spine straightened. Not these kids. Not this neighborhood. I would find a way to take that little girl back from the blessed or damned themselves if I had to.

"We'll find her. Jay and the boys and you and I will find her."

∾

Jay

SUMI CAME RUNNING INTO THE HOUSE LIKE THE DAMNED WERE AFTER her. "You're back, thank the goddessi. Cori is missing."

"Cori? Suann's girl?" Jay tossed his mending onto the bed, hefted his twin swords. "Where? When?"

Two heads poked down from their room, a tousled Red and a tidy Purple.

Sumi glanced at them, swallowed, looked as stricken as if their own boys had gone missing. "They haven't seen her since this morning."

Jay didn't let himself imagine anything. "Let's check her house first." He fastened his belt around his waist and nudged her out of the way. "Most kids are found curled up in a place no one would expect them to be." Didn't want to think of all the kids they *didn't* find. He'd heard other cities were different—Robin said it all the time and she would know from her time as a caravan guard— but here, in the City of Temples, the children taken to "serve" the goddessi, whether with magic or with work, were most often not found at all.

"Jay—" Her voice shook and her eyes drowned with memories.

"Shh." He went back. Held her. "Don't think about it yet. First we check the house."

She melted into him, rested her head against his chest. Wil and Andy clambered down the ladder and pressed against them both. For a brief moment, his family surrounded him and all was right with the world.

"All right." Sumi pushed herself away, calm now. "Let's go."

He followed her out to the yard where Suann waited. Noted the brittle edge to the Yellow woman's control, and resolved not to say anything to break her. The sun was high overhead, making the shadows small, and a faint breeze whisked by, smelling of the river and the fields beyond. The best time to find a child, really.

Much better than night, when the shadows pooled and most of the Rest Third retreated indoors.

"Suann." He took her hands briefly. "Let's start at your house. Will you let us start our search for Cori there?"

The Yellow woman nodded, her mouth moving but no sounds escaping. No wonder Sumi had been picturing it—

He had to keep them calm. He matched his breathing to Suann's. He turned with her, walked with her back to her house, slowing his breathing as they went. The house perched in the center of a half-sized bit of land like a baby chick among foxes. The color reinforced it— they'd somehow managed to mix yellow clay in with the more common local red, so the house and the paver stones were red, yellow, and orange swirls, which suited both Suann's and Cori's personalities. As if to make up for its size, each stone fit perfectly into the next and it looked as if no single grain of sand had dared escape its place.

When she was ready, he asked, "You saw her this morning? Anything unusual?"

"She went to class." Suann glanced over her shoulder at Sumi, who nodded. Suann focused on his question again. "I took my father to the bath house. I had to carry him. He's gotten so light, and she begged so hard to go play with Nathy after—"

"You checked with Dansy and Nydia?"

"Nydia is caring for her aged mother. Halfway across the Rest Third. But I checked with Dansy."

Jay side-eyed Sumi, but she was already turning to Wil and Andy and Kass. "Kass? You haven't seen Cori since this morning?"

Kass shook his head. "No, Teacher."

Tara came out of her house and met them in the street, jam smeared on her chin. "Teacher? What's wrong?"

"We can't find Cori. Is she with Nathy?"

Tara shook her head solemnly. "No. Nathy is with Mom and Granther."

"Go make sure," she murmured to them, and the kids were off, running down the street.

The inside of Suann's house was... full.

The main room had a bed and a pile of blankets in it, and so they started there, picking up and folding each blanket to assure the girl had not fallen asleep in her own bed and simply been missed. They looked over and under every space that could have held a child half Cori's size, because Jay had found children in cupboards and trunks and nooks and crannies where no child should have fit but did.

The larger bedroom had been overrun by candle-making things— molds and tallow and dyes and flowers for color and flowers for scent, and strings in various thicknesses for wicks and pieces of wood to hold things in place.

Everywhere he looked, candles in various stages, but nowhere a child.

The smaller bedroom contained orchids and potted miniature roses and gardenias, surrounding a tiny bed containing Suann's father. The elder Yellow man made as if to rise at their entrance but couldn't get more than a fingerwidth up. Suann lifted him gently, settled a pillow behind his back, explained that her father was the one who for many years had cultivated the orchids.

"Honored Yellow," Jay said politely.

"They're helping look for Cori," Suann told her father.

"You wonderful people," her father gasped.

He sounded like Mom had, right at the end, and Jay mercilessly cut off that thought. Noted that Sumi stood stricken in the doorway. Probably remembering Mom too.

No time for memories. They had a child to find.

The backyard was the same as the house, overfull of growing things to use for candle-making, overfull of places to check where a child might be curled up.

"My mother," Suann murmured to Sumi, brushing her hand over a meticulously pruned prickly bush. "Evergreen and sturdy."

Sumi straightened, flashed Jay a glance, then focused on

Suann and made an encouraging noise. She recognized his was the greater experience in this situation, and that made him stand a little taller.

"What if— what if—" Tears escaped Suann's eyes and flowed down her cheeks. "I don't have space for a memory of Cori. I should make some space, shouldn't I." She bent to pull at a massive pot.

Sumi captured her hands and drew her back up. Forced the Yellow woman to look at her. "Not yet. Just wait. Give us some time."

While Sumi provided a listening ear to Suann, Jay meticulously searched the yard— under each bush, up in a tree, behind each pot, but Cori wasn't there.

Not in the house and not in the yard— the next step was the neighborhood and then the city, unless the girl was with Nathy's mother.

Running feet brought his head around. The boys burst into the yard, followed closely by Kass and Tara and Nathy.

Not followed by Cori.

"Rest it." Jay sought Andy's gaze for a confirmation.

The boy shook his head. Suann burst into fresh tears.

Jay led the boys, Tara, Nathy, and Sumi out into the front yard and crouched to draw in the dirt. "This line is our street, and this mark is our house, see? Here is your house, Tara, Nathy, and this mark is where we are now. We need to go to each neighbor and ask them to search the way we searched here— up, down, under, behind. In spaces far too small for little girls because children have a horrible habit of folding themselves smaller than they should. Ask them if you can help them search. Familiar eyes will pass by the perfect hiding spot because it's familiar, but your eyes are fresh."

He rose and pointed. "Wil, this side of the street, that way. Andy, the other side. Kass, you go with Wil. Tara and Nathy, you take that side and go the other way. Sumi take the other. I'll go to the guardhouse."

Sumi sighed and the lines in her face eased. "Thank you," she murmured. She must have wanted to involve the guard but been afraid to draw their attention. Not altogether unreasonable, considering... everything.

He left them long enough to run to the guardhouse and notify Thom, who looked grave. He knew— better than Jay— how difficult it was to find lost ones if they weren't in the house or the yard, and he didn't have any guards available to help look for the girl.

He would find her, if she was in the city to be found. He vowed it to himself and everyone.

So he rejoined the search, but as he and Sumi and Wil and Andy and Kass and Tara and Nathy went house to house searching while Suann stayed with her father, as more of their neighbors joined them in the search, and as the sun sank in the west and the shadows ran long across the streets, his heart sank and his guts twisted.

The longer she was gone, the smaller their chance of finding her.

But they searched into the night, searched by torch and lantern light, until they were all stumbling from fatigue and no one in the Rest Third would open their doors.

Only the damned were out this late.

So Jay sent them all home and took Sumi and their boys home with him. Sat them down at the table and pushed food at them until they ate enough to please him. Briefed his sisters on the missing girl, then sent everyone to bed.

They could start again in the morning.

He slipped beneath the thin blanket and wrapped himself around Sumi. Her breathing was too controlled; she wasn't yet asleep.

"Can you—" Goddessi, he couldn't believe he was asking her this, but somehow it felt safe, in their bedroom, in the dark. "I'm out of ideas unless we ask at the temples. And they never admit to taking a child. Can you sense her?"

Sumi blinked. Stiffened. Hesitated long enough he prepared an apology.

"No," she finally said.

"You won't—?"

"*Can't.* I can't sense her." She turned toward him, buried her face in his neck.

He stroked her hair. "You can't— she's not anywhere in the city?"

"I'm not sure. I should be able to sense her if she's in either temple, but I can't."

Cori was one of his people, his neighbor's daughter, fell under his responsibility. He *had* to find her. But if Sumi couldn't feel her... "You're one of the most powerful people in the city. If *you* can't feel her—"

"There are reasons," she mumbled. "She could be unconscious. She could be shielded."

"But how do we find her if you can't sense her?"

"There are people stronger than me." Sumi burrowed in closer.

The only ones—

She meant the boys.

CHAPTER
TWENTY

S *umi*

AT DAWN, I FOUND MYSELF AWAKE AND WORRIED. *I* KNEW THE likelihood of finding Cori alive and unharmed had dwindled through the night, but we'd needed some sleep, and searching in the damned hours wouldn't get us inside the places we still needed to search.

I stretched, then I *listened* and *stretched*.

Nothing.

Please, Dark Goddess, let her be alive. Let us find her. Bring her home.

The thread inside me that led to Maldita thickened. I *pushed* away gently. Maldita wasn't mine to call on anymore.

I laid in bed with my husband, my boys safe in the room above, and knew Suann hadn't slept. Magic rose inside me, surging in response to my wave of fear.

No—

The last thing we needed right now was for Maldita to find us and take her revenge, and me using my magic only made it more likely.

I breathed and counted my breaths. *One, two, three. One, two, three.*

The boys stirred overhead, so I nudged Jay awake and whispered, "We can't do it here."

He nodded.

We dressed in silence and shadows, and met the boys by the front door. They looked exhausted, but I had a bad feeling I looked downright haggard.

The price for caring for so many people. None of them were safe from life in this city.

We walked through the city as the sun rose and shadows shrank. Faces turned to follow us.

I might be the teacher of their children, but Wil and Antero were known for their friendships with kids of other Colors— and with each other. And how could I scold them for being decent people when that was exactly what I'd tried to teach them?

But now we were being noticed because we were trying to find a missing child— and a Yellow at that. They might have understood if or was Tara or Nathy, the Green girls, or Wil— a Red— and they definitely would have understood checking each house for Andy if he was missing, since he was a Purple. But a Yellow?

Despite myself, I could hear the memory of Maldita's voice echoing in my head— *Red for blood, white for bone, black for soul. No other colors matter.*

I shivered, despite the early morning press of heat. It had never truly cooled off last night, but thinking of Her—

Jay caught my hand in his. His warmth helped push Her memory away. The boys kept on and we followed.

We walked through the streets past the markets, past the fountains, past the bath houses, to the docks where the warehouses were thick as wheat in the field across the river. Here, initially, we only saw Rest Third Guards in the streets, but as the sun rose higher, the streets filled with Oranges and Yellows who worked in the warehouses.

I tugged on Jay's hand and hissed, "Where are we—"

"Shh." He continued on until we came to the biggest of them all, a great hulking cluster of buildings, most of it a massive granary and the remainder a trade warehouse.

The building was brownwood, with the Stonefield family crest painted on the side. The massive main doors had a chain and lock. Wordlessly, Jay led us to the man-door on the warehouse and ushered us inside. I quirked a brow at him, demanding an eventual explanation for how he could get into his blood-family's warehouse.

The walls shut out the sun and I felt another chill. Foreboding. *For Cori*, I reminded myself.

Jay lit two lanterns and set them beside the door. The rest of the warehouse was gloom and shadows and sharp bits of sun cutting through from the small, high windows. We stayed near the door in the kinder lantern light. "None of this stuff belongs to us," he reminded us all, "and none of it is cheap. Please don't ruin anything you can't afford."

"And we can't afford anything." I smiled gently. When I was the damned goddess's high priestess, I had been able to buy anything. Literally.

Wil and Andy nodded wordlessly.

"They—I—" A frown twisted Jay's face, then fled. "My uncle hired me to provide security here. I think it's his way of helping us. Since my father's family is so wealthy and we're obviously... not."

"His money spends as well as the next man's." And we

needed it too much to spurn it. "And now we have a place away from home to work *push* and *pull* magic. Away from prying eyes." *Away from the demon hunters' eyes*, I meant. I wasn't sure what they knew about the boys, and I didn't want them to learn anything else.

Jay nodded and stepped back toward the door. I dismissed him from my attention— he would keep us safe from intrusions.

"You know this girl." I eyed Wil and Andy. "I can't feel her nearby. I want you to try."

They both straightened, looking dead themselves in the flickering light. *Damn us*— no bad omens.

"Work together, like you did with the flying board. Keep it quiet. Just because we're in someone else's warehouse doesn't mean the blessed or the damned won't come."

Wil nodded while Andy watched, his solemn purple eyes so like his birth-mother's it hurt my heart.

I'd taught magi and priestessi to work together in the past, but never outside their own Colors. I hadn't thought it was possible until Hana— Antero's mother— and Lena and I had discovered it with the smallest, easiest magics. The high priestess before me had actively discouraged it, and watching the boys work together, I had no idea why.

"Stand, with your feet solid on the floor, your backs straight." Something Dee's training had taught me— how to have a strong stance, and it translated well to magic, and they fell into a guard's ready stance as easily as breathing.

They adjusted slightly, set their feet, then took each other's hand.

"Start with us," I said, soothing them with my voice. "Feel the differences. How you tell one from the other. Can you *feel* each other? Me? Jay?"

"Yeah." Wil smirked at me because that was easy.

275

"*Reach* out to the walls. *Feel* everything in the warehouse. Are there any other beings?"

I knew the answer— no.

Andy shook his head *no*.

"Tell me what's in the boxes." I used my own magic, carefully, quietly, passively *feeling* what they felt, following along behind them.

"Salted fish." Andy pointed to the boxes to our left.

"Charcoal sticks." Wil nodded to the right.

"Beyond that?"

"Dried grains." Andy's brow wrinkled. "Lots and lots of seeds."

"Salted meat."

Andy pointed vaguely. "Empty."

"Shovels."

"Pipes."

Jay murmured, "The Stonefield family fortune."

Enough easing in. Time to push. "*Feel* this warehouse. The whole thing. *Feel* for Cori. Tell me if she's here." Belief was so important with our kind of magic. I wouldn't tell them I would be asking them to do something I didn't dare to do— *couldn't* do, without alerting the goddess.

"Awake or asleep, you should be able to *pull* on her the tiniest bit."

They exchanged glances. Wil's tongue came out. Andy squinted sideways and made a fist. The air thickened around us. "Not here," Andy whispered.

I lowered and smoothed my voice even further. "Good. You know where she's not. Open up a little larger. *Feel* for the river right outside. *Feel* the guards, the workers. The other warehouses."

The boys *reached*, their magics blending in a way I'd never seen. Was it because they loved each other like brothers? Or because they were young and strong and *trained*? Or different Colors? Did it matter? They were so much more powerful together than they were apart.

"Not here." Wil's voice was flat.

Not caught in the river and drowned, thank the goddess. Not in one of these warehouses for some blessed reason.

"Expand. *Feel* the crops on the other side of the river. Past the warehouses, *feel* the houses and shops and people." Now the tricky part. "Awake, asleep, unconscious—" *dead*— "you should be able to *feel* her, *pull* her just enough to recognize her."

Red hair and Purple hair shifted in a wind that didn't exist in the warehouse. *Careful now.*

"Slowly. Little by little. Let this be easy, let it be quiet. *Feel* the people and find Cori. Street by street, house by house..."

Wil stiffened, then relaxed again. "Not her."

"No." Andy glanced north. "Not in the Temple of the Blessed."

Wil tipped his head south. "Nor the Damned."

My knees nearly buckled. I hadn't thought so but their confirmation was a relief.

"Keep going, slowly. Tell me when you reach your limit." My reach— even without a boost of power from the dark goddess — stretched to the boundaries of the city.

They *reached* past the fields to the west, past the north and south walls, past the east walls and up into the mountains, past where I could follow. Their hands stretched out, one east toward the mountains, one west toward the desert. Magic streamed out of them, and I stood too close to them to tell if it was quiet. My heart thundered.

Should I stop them?

No— they were searching for their friend. No one else could do this. I had to trust them to feel their own limits, to know when to stop.

They *reached*.

Touched something.

Wil frowned. Andy shook his head. But together, they *pulled*.

My heart thundered. What they had touched— their reaction— it wasn't Cori. Something was wrong. Should I stop them? *Could* I?

Everything went white, but a white so brilliant it was blue.

The entire warehouse disappeared behind the punishing glare of a nascent sun, then a tiny dark spot appeared in the middle of the white. The dark spot grew, bringing with it a deep chill. My bones ached in a way they hadn't in months. Deeper than the ache of a winter day, more crushing even than the ache of death.

I had felt that ache before—

The boys *pulled*, their fingers curling in and the black spot grew darker, deeper, closer, bringing with it the smell of blood and fire. The thread inside me that was the dark goddess twisted sharply, slammed me to my knees.

"No!" Goddessi, no. What was it? "Boys! Let go! *Push* it away!"

My head weighed a ton. I lifted it to see the deep, swirling black spot. Raised my own hand to *push* back the black. My magic stirred sluggishly inside me, refused to answer my command.

Goddessi, no—

A moan forced its way out of my throat. My muscles locked. My magic hid. My children were in mortal danger and I could do *nothing*.

Wil's face took on a dark cast, and an evil smile— the kind I'd never seen on my boy— twisted his lips. Andy's eyes bugged out and he shook, but he continued to *pull*. They both did— as if something had taken them over.

The black reached the height of the warehouse, and now it reached out, reaching for my boys.

"*No!*" My throat was raw from screaming but I screamed it anyway. I would bargain with the dark goddess Herself if She would only hear me—

Evil was coming through that doorway, using my boys, my boys I'd asked to reach as far as they could. Evil I had to stop—

Jay was suddenly in front of me. The evil shadow slid off him like he wasn't there and I sucked a single clean breath. Started to call Her name, "M—"

Then Jay stepped between the evil and the boys. "No," he said softly, drawing his twin blades.

The darkness surrounded him, swallowed him whole.

~

Jay

Jay had watched as Sumi coaxed the boys into using their magic to find Cori. He'd watched nothing happen and nothing happen and nothing happen until suddenly something happened.

The bright and the dark coming toward them and then Sumi screaming—

He wasn't a priestess, nor a magus, didn't have magic, but he'd felt evil's touch when he'd sworn to serve the dark goddess and She had possessed him. Longest resting moment of his life. So he *knew* evil, and whatever was in that darkness was evil.

Wanted the boys.

That would not happen on his watch. No matter what it cost, he would protect their boys.

He peeled himself away from the wall, every movement like he was swimming through glue. Stepped between his family and the evil. Felt a brief burst of regret that he wouldn't grow old with Sumi, watch the boys grow up, grow into themselves. Drew his swords, comfort in his hands, even though magic could not be cut.

"No," he snarled at the dark, dared it to deal with him. *You will not take these boys without going through me.*

Must have agreed to his offer, because faster than thought, it swallowed him. Submerged him in that eerie dark glow he'd only seen in Maldita's presence.

His arms shook and his breath stuttered. Ice coated his arms and neck. The swords dipped, too heavy to hold.

Thrown into memory—

The smell of blood and effluvia in the air. Stitch in his side from running. The lingering taste of fear growing into dread. The silence of a crowd that had gone too far and just now realized it. The scene lit by torches as more and more guards arrived. The men and women of his unit—

Bodies on the ground.

Thea, a short, muscular Yellow, serious and driven, an expert with her knives, crumpled on the ground with her head bashed in, knives in their sheathes. She hadn't even had the chance to draw.

Xis, hamstrung— Jay could see it in the trail of blood the guard had left, crawling away from his attackers— Xis, a brilliant Green young man, who always had a joke when someone needed it. He'd been learning short sword, and now, with his head severed, laying next to the body, he'd never master the sword laying beside him.

Shiri, whipcord over bone and so new she called Jay by his rank instead of his name, curled in on herself, her blue skin gone gray. The priestessi had later discovered Shiri's organs had ruptured— kicked to death.

Tuulia and Wayl cut to pieces and the tanners' skinning knives discarded beside them...

Blood and brains on the ground, and all of it from his guards. His people. *He should have known, should have brought the whole unit, come himself. He'd failed them. Shame so deep he thought the only relief might be taking his knife to his own throat—*

Jay bellowed. No more—

He *hadn't* known. It had been a routine call, shouldn't have turned into a bloodbath. No one could have known—

Sumi. She'd given him shields. Magic couldn't touch him.

The ice shattered. The swords rose. He slashed, knowing it would do no good, but the darkness leaned away. Gave him a breath of air unstained by rot.

Swung again and cut the darkness. Flowed into one of the first sword patterns he'd learned and drove the evil back. Too soon, his muscles ached, joints clicked and jabbed. *Too old for this.* But he had to stand between his family and the dark. They were not here. He was the only one who could.

The light was far, far away.

Cold struck like a blow.

He heard Sumi from far, far away. "*Push*, Wil. *Push*, Andy. *Push* it back where it came from!"

Hold on, a little longer. Keep it busy, a little longer. Protect his family, a little longer.

He moved, *danced*, slashing and spinning and sidestepping the dark to keep them safe. Cut, jabbed— over and under and across, like he was fighting a crowd of men instead of a cloud of evil. Demanded more from his body than he ever had before, and since he'd learned he *could* demand more— as a guard— he kept its attention.

Then, as if it was a mango and the boys' magic a knife, the darkness peeled back, slice by slice.

The air lightened against the deep black dark. Would not think about it, because darkness still lingered and he would not let it stay.

Resting betweens, he was tired. But still he swung his

sword, his wrists aching and knees shaking and stance gone to shit.

Peel— lighter, peel— lighter.

The dark slipped away into nothing and the nascent sun faded. The warehouse returned to its previous light-and-shadow. His precious swords fell from numb fingers, clattered on the stone floor. He sank to his knees, panting.

"Jay!" Sumi had tear tracks on her cheeks and her voice rasped. She ran to him. He wrapped his aching arms around her waist, rested his head against her belly.

"You're all right?" Intended to demand, only managed tired.

"I can't believe you threw yourself at that— whatever it was."

"I had to protect you."

He felt the boys come close. Reached out and snagged their arms. "You're all right?"

"What was that?" Wilyam sounded awed.

"I think..." Jay released them. Climbed slowly to his feet. Godessi, they needed to get out of the warehouse before anything else happened. Especially if what he thought was true — "I think it was a demon."

Sumi choked.

Wil gasped, "We reached a *demon*?"

Andy punched him in the arm. "That's a bad thing."

Sumi wiped her face with her shirt and her tattoos showed faintly on the skin of her belly.

Jay felt a shiver sweep from his toes to his hair. Her tattoos—

"It wanted you boys," Sumi whispered. "It forced you to bring it here. So it could possess you."

"Like—" Jay clenched his jaw. Sought out Sumi's gaze. *Like the dark goddess Maldita possessed Her high priestess.*

Sumi nodded. Bit her lip. "Like that." She *knew*, he realized. She'd felt it and it had felt the same as Maldita. *The damned goddess might be a demon. Just like the demon hunters claimed.*

Another full-body chill shook him— almost as cold as fighting the demon. He scooped his swords off the floor, still hurting like an old man must. "You can't tell *anyone* about this," he said, side-eyeing the boys. They weren't really listening, so he clutched his blades in one hand, knelt between them. Took the moment. Looked at his tiny family and said it slowly and clearly so they could hear it in his voice. "You can't tell *anyone* that you just *summoned a demon.*"

Wilyam and Antero stared at him. They didn't realize—

"They'll kill you," Sumi breathed, stricken. "They'll hunt you and kill you as heretics, though you're only children."

Wil scowled. Opened his mouth. Andy elbowed him.

"The ones that don't want to kill you will want to *use* you." Her hands shook. "Think about how much magic, how much *power* a demon could give you."

"Power is awesome," Wil said weakly.

Andy snapped at him, "Power is *not* awesome. Not that kind."

Sumi rubbed her throat. As gruff as her voice was, it must be sore. "Think about the temple. The power of the high priestess. The Colors all fighting each other, and the way the Damned and the Blessed treat us in the Rest Third. The responsibility that comes with power…"

They still weren't getting it. "And the abuses," Jay said heavily. He sheathed his swords; he'd examine them later. "Think about that magus. The one who came to the children's quarters. Who tried—"

"All right!" Wil wrenched himself out of Sumi's arm, shoved away from Jay too.

Andy shuddered. "That was exactly it. What I felt when it

was coming for us. Helpless, weak." His voice broke. "Ashamed."

Sumi hugged him tighter. "Wil killed that man. He's never coming back."

Jay put a hand on his shoulder. "I felt it too, Andy, when I was in the dark. It tried to hurt me— to take my strength from me. But it lied to you. You're safe."

It wasn't until Wil came back to their little circle and patted Andy's shoulder awkwardly that both boys calmed.

"It's all right." Pat, pat, pat. "I won't tell anyone. I promise. I don't want to make you feel that way ever again."

"Thanks." Andy smiled faintly. "Brothers?"

"Brothers." Wil surrendered to their hugs.

Then Andy said something muffled against Jay's arm.

Sumi leaned back, her hands still around them. "What?"

Jay shifted, loath to let them go, but— "What?"

"We found her." Wil's hand clenched on Jay's shirt. "We can take you to Cori."

TWENTY-ONE

S *umi*

IT WAS A PHYSICAL SHOCK TO HEAR THEY COULD LEAD US TO CORI. "You found her?" I echoed stupidly. My magic was returning, seeping back into the hollow spaces in my middle from goddessi-knew-where, but my throat and eyes felt as if I'd been screaming and crying for days.

Jay didn't seem any better off. He winced like he'd fought the entire guard all at once.

Even the boys were tired— and I couldn't remember if I'd truly seen them tired before— but Wil's red hair lay down limp and sweaty on his head and Andy's eyes kept closing.

"Hsst!" Mouse peered down from one of the small, high windows.

"How—?" My thoughts were foggy.

"You set me to look for Enzo. Figured *he* would find *you*." She looked away, then looked back at us. "Time to go. They're

285

coming. Whatever you did— everyone felt it. Hurry up, before they surround the building."

Of course. No one could do what the boys just did and keep it quiet.

"They?" Jay side-eyed the door, staggered a little. "Let's go."

"They're one street over. Out the back!"

The boys ran for the back and Jay followed, their shuffle-lagging steps the only indicator of how tired they were. How did they recover so quickly?

My feet felt like they were on fire and my back spasmed, but I had a very bad feeling about who *they* were, and I did not want to be interrogated by the blessed nor the damned today, so I forced myself into a hobbling run.

First, get away. Then save a little girl.

By the time I'd crossed the warehouse, I thought I would die. All the phantom exhaustion I thought had healed returned — my breath hitched, my side pinched, my back screamed. Tears leaked from my eyes and I couldn't spare the energy to wipe them away.

But Jay waited for me at the door, and Mouse was guiding the boys away across the tiny street, through a deep alley, into a shadow.

"Hurry," she beckoned again.

Jay delayed long enough to break the lock. "Don't want them to think their new guard was involved," he said with a tired grin. Then he came toward me with his hands cupped like he wanted to help me run faster. "Go," I gasped. I'd get there. I'd fought a dark goddess to a standstill, not once but several times. By sheer will, I would get across the street and into that shadow.

"Surround the building!" a woman shouted. Thank the goddess the warehouse was between us— I recognized that voice.

Lena.

Betrayal stabbed me. But it also sped my feet. If the damned were here—

A brilliant white flying carpet zoomed overhead, then descended too fast.

"We claim them in the name of the Blessed!" A priestess or magus and blessed guards. Lena was outranked— but that wouldn't stop her. Shouts echoed between the buildings and then I heard Lena again.

"We were here first. We claim them for the Damned!"

"The Blessed!"

Some sort of scuffle, more shouting, more carpets overhead — then I slipped into the shadow and through a door and Mouse closed it behind me. "Hurry," she hissed. "You're not safe yet."

I nodded and followed after the others.

Lena had no choice. If she hadn't come, the damned high priestess, my blood-sister Aimi, would have known something was wrong. Heavens, even my blood-mother would have known something was wrong if the damned didn't fight the blessed for a new magus or priestess with such strength, then they'd *all* be combing the Rest Third for me.

But the bitterness in the back of my throat didn't fade.

What followed was a nightmare. We kept moving farther and farther from the Stonefield warehouse and each time I thought we might be able to rest, more carpets flew into the area, more arguments erupted between the blessed and the damned, more running and ducking and hiding.

If anyone was left in the temples, it was a miracle. And all of them looking for us.

At one point, we headed toward our house, but then the boys had a whispered conversation with Mouse and we turned away.

I wanted to cry— again— but something about that demon had returned my body to nearly dead. Numbly, I followed Jay.

Until we stopped and he led me to a flattened boulder to sit on. I swear my feet wept at the relief.

We'd made it all the way into the hills, past the poorest part of the Rest Third, and from here I could see the commotion still churning down by the river. Down by the Stonefield warehouse.

Flying carpets zipped back and forth, black and white, and gray trying to keep the peace between them. Clusters of black and white and gray on the ground too, though gray was severely outnumbered. No resting priestessi or magi to field in this circumstance. A few clumps of people were watching, but most were hiding in their homes until whatever had happened blew over.

I sat on my rock under the shade of a giant pine tree and marveled we'd gotten away at all. We owed it to Mouse. Today she'd more than paid back any lodging and food we'd given her and I would forever be grateful my boys weren't in temple captivity.

That *I* wasn't now possessed by a goddess, though I would have happily accepted Her if She had come and saved us from... *that*.

"Thank you, Mouse," I managed. "You saved us."

A grin flashed across her face, then she shyly turned away.

Jay sat beside me, rested one hand on my thigh. "We can't stay here long."

"Why?"

His shoulders lifted. "We're almost there."

I blinked at him. He didn't seem to understand I still wasn't thinking clearly.

"We're close, Mom." Wil tugged on my hand. "We have to save Cori."

Ah, bless me to heaven. Lost in my own pain, I'd forgotten

all about the girl. "All right." I stood and nearly collapsed. Everything in my body protested.

Jay steadied me. "You want to stay here?"

"No." I couldn't let them out of my sight right now. If I sat here and thought about what we'd just been through, I'd have to think about the demon, about Maldita's origins, about how the demon hunters might be right— everything I didn't want to think about. "No, I'll come."

Mouse led the way— of course she somehow knew this area as well as she knew the warehouse area of the Rest Third. The path became rockier, the trees closer, the smell of dirt and grass and sap and pine stronger.

After today, using my magic again tempted me more than ever. One, no more running from the damned or the blessed; two, able to protect myself and my kids; three, faster healing; four, if I wanted to I could just blessing *fly* over the rocks—

A maw into the heart of the mountain opened up before us, and Mouse disappeared into it, then the boys, then Jay.

Oh good. Another adventure.

I stepped into the dark, blinking furiously.

We hadn't brought lanterns or torches or any other way to light our way, but some of the caves around here lit themselves — yes.

Once my eyes adjusted, I saw light, caught between blue and green, deeper in. This area was small and the path twisted between outcroppings of faintly glowing rock. "Don't touch it," I told the boys. "In the caves that have been mined, anywhere the rock was touched, the light died."

"What is it?" Wil whispered.

"No one knows. We were too busy stripping what we wanted to stop and study anything we didn't want."

Jay's hand sought mine. I couldn't really see him— the light wasn't bright enough for more than a hint of his face, but his touch settled me. He kept his voice low, to match mine. "Boys, is Cori still here? And is anyone else here?"

Wil and Andy looked to the left, though the path wound right and I tentatively *listened* with my own magic.

The cave was a maze of rock and paths and caverns— one big one ahead of us to the right— and there was something to the left...

"She's here." Andy took the lead.

"I ain't going any farther." Mouse stayed by the opening, the whites showing all around her yellow pupils, her breathing fast and shallow. "Can't do it. The rock presses down and what if—"

"You saved us," I told her. "You brought us all the way across the city. Call out if anyone comes, and you'll keep us safe again."

She nodded and turned back toward the mouth of the cave.

Jay and I followed after Andy and Wil. Sometimes our footsteps were muffled and sometimes echoey. How had this cave formed? Some rocks looked like teeth in a giant mouth, others like squares of lace along the roof.

A cavern opened up in front of us. We all hesitated. Off to the left and up overhead, the rocks fell away. The emptiness loomed larger than the sanctuary room in the Temple of the Damned. The hair rose on the back of my neck. This much dark pressed all together reminded me a little of the dark the demon had brought with it, though this dark wasn't so cold.

We'd survived that— we could survive this.

"Go slow and mind your footing." I touched my fingertips to Jay's back so he would feel me there. "Careful now."

The only things I heard over my own harsh breathing were the scuffs of our shoes on the path. The rest of the cavern felt hushed in harsh silence as we wound around the back, ignored the misleading paths, then finally found the one to take us to the small chamber off to the right of the entrance.

Between one step and the next, I could *feel* Cori, feel her stupor, feel the sleeping drug running in her blood.

Alive!

And still we had to walk slowly through the dark to get to her. Finally we crouched next to her. My back cramped. I waited it out, then checked the girl for broken bones. She had a bump on her head but nothing bleeding where it shouldn't and nothing broken. Ropes around her wrists and her ankles, and we decided to leave them on until we could see the knots to untangle them.

Jay lifted her into his arms. I sent Wil on ahead to *feel* our way out, and told Andy to follow behind, then I took a grip on Jay's shirt and we walked back the way we'd come.

～

JAY

HE'D THOUGHT HE COULDN'T GET ANY MORE TIRED, THEN HE CARRIED A girl through the dark with only Sumi's tugs and a little rock-glow to guide his feet. Despite the extra weight in his arms, the journey back seemed shorter than the journey in.

At least until they stumbled to a halt just before the exit.

"What's wrong?" *What now? What else? Resting betweens—*

"Someone's out there." Mouse pressed against the rock as if she could become one with it. "They showed up and they're not going away."

"Who—?" Sumi staggered. She needed to rest— they all did. The kids hid it better but they too had to be exhausted from all the magic they'd done, then the running and more magic and now this—

"Dee and Robin! I *feel* them." Wil smiled and stepped forward.

Sumi grabbed him by the collar. "Wait."

Jay shifted Cori. His arms ached, his back and shoulders burned. He set his lips against Sumi's ear to ensure his voice would not carry. "We have to go out there. But we have the perfect alibi. Let me do the talking."

She nodded. Crouched to murmur into the boys' ears.

Cori in his arms, Jay stepped out into blue and purple skies, sinking sun, suspicious faces. An array of Rest Third guards surrounded the entrance— Dee and Robin and Maggie and Litka and the rest, and at their head—

"Thom." The weight of his lies— heavier than the weight of the girl he was carrying— pressed on him. "What are you doing here? What's going on?"

Thom's face fell into disappointed lines. The blue of his eyes looked more gray today. "Where have you been for the last several hours?"

"Searching for Cori." Jay hitched up the girl. "And we found her. That resting cave system is huge. We should probably ask a damned priestess to block up this entrance so we don't lose another child—"

Thom snorted. "We won't be asking the damned or the blessed for any help anytime soon. As I suspect you know."

He could pretend ignorance, but Thom knew him too well. Better to ask lots of questions. "What are you talking about? What's wrong?"

Dee took a half-step forward. "Why is she tied up?"

Thom jerked his head, signaled to the guards to stay put, and Jay followed him off to the side. And kept himself between Thom and his family— which allowed Thom to keep an eye on Sumi, so they were both happy.

Somehow Thom knew.

Jay had denied it once before and convinced the man, but that didn't seem likely this time.

"I've heard rumors you were down by the river today, boy." Thom, master inquisitor, simply looked at Jay and waited.

There was something about the human condition, Jay had learned, that made people want to tell their side of the story, to justify their actions, to share their *why*, but he'd been questioned by Thom before. He let the silence drag on, then said, "I don't know what else I can tell you. We searched the caves for hours before we found Cori. Why won't you tell me what's going on?" *Go for the throat.* "Don't you trust me?"

Thom sighed. Stepped closer. Lowered his voice. "I can't help cover for you if you don't tell me the whole truth."

Jay steeled himself against flinching or puffing up or making any reaction that would give Thom a hint he was right. "I *am* telling you the truth. Here— can you take her? She hasn't woken up yet. We need to get the ropes off and get her back to her mother— then get a healer."

Thom accepted the girl reluctantly, then looked him squarely in the eyes. "Where do your loyalties lie, boy?"

With my family. Jay swung back to the rest of the group. "Anyone have a knife? We need to get these ropes off. See if we can wake her up."

Dee came up and hugged him. "Careful," she murmured, then released him. The other guards clustered around Thom and Cori. Jay shifted back— keep attention away from Sumi, away from what he'd done, toward getting help for Cori.

Litka had a knife and Maggie had the smallest hands, so they cut the ropes. Robin chafed the girl's skin and still she didn't wake.

"A healer," Thom said, and side-eyed Mal.

The Red boy— Jay couldn't bring himself to think of Mal as

anything other than *boy*— swung the carpet from his back, rolled it out on the ground, sat.

Thom handed him Cori. Good thing Mal was skinny and Cori still young and small; the carpet meant for one would just carry the two of them.

Mal activated the carpet so it hovered waist high.

Mouse still hadn't come out of the cave, sensibly staying away from the mass of guards, and not betraying that this was one of her bolt holes. Best to get the guards away from her before someone decided to snoop in the cave.

"So?" Jay pitched his voice to carry. "What's Thom not telling us?"

Dee checked over her shoulder. Thom had turned his back on them to talk to the rest of the guards, but his shoulders tightened at Jay's words. Dee shrugged. "Someone used a bunch of magic down by the docks. Brought the damned and the blessed swarming out of their temples and fighting each other to conscript whoever it was, but they disappeared from under their noses." She laughed.

Her eyes told him it was a forced laugh, but he played along. "Resting—! And I missed it?"

"What did the magic do?" Sumi asked, while the boys concentrated on looking supremely bored.

"They won't tell us." Disgust twisted Maggie's voice. "They tried to take over the Stonefields' entire warehouse, but Grandma Stonefield had her boys bring her letters down—"

"Her typical scathing missives no doubt." Jay forced a smirk. Now that he knew they were blood-family, it pricked to hear them criticized. Even if that made no sense.

Robin flashed a smile. "Yes. So they opened up the warehouse for the guards and the magi and the priestessi to take a really good look, then closed it up again."

"Can you imagine the things in there?" Dee sounded wistful.

"Grandma Stonefield was furious. Damage to the back door. No guard on duty."

"Is there supposed to be a guard all the time?" Sumi's voice was just a little too innocent. His wife was going to get them all into trouble.

"Not all the time," Jay said abruptly. "They hired me for some night shifts. How about it, Thom? Anyone for daytime?"

"No." Thom scowled. "You didn't find anyone else in there? Whoever took Cori?"

Jay shook his head, and Thom growled, "Then let's get Cori down. Her mother will be glad to see her."

Thom and the other guards mounted their carpets and surrounded Mal. Jay wanted to ask his sisters to take the boys, but the way Thom was acting— no.

"We'll get her to a healer." Thom glared at Jay. "I'll deal with you after."

Jay nodded sharply.

The gray guard carpets rose into the blue sky and headed west, back toward the city, leaving Jay, Sumi, and the boys to make their own way back.

Downhill used a different set of muscles. It was a nice change until Jay's knees creaked and popped and then settled into a serious stabbing pain. "Sumi? Boys? You all right?"

Fatigue washed out her voice. "Why the heaven didn't they bring any spare flying carpets?"

"The Rest Third Guard doesn't have many spares. And they're heavy. And Fitz was probably tracking us once we left the city, so they hiked up. He tracks from the ground— no one wanted to go back for the spares."

Andy perked up. "Which one's Fitz?"

"The Green guard."

"Wow. Would he teach us?"

Not after today. Jay shrugged. "Maybe. I'll ask."

Sumi made a noise in the back of her throat like her back hurt. But she kept going. Asked, "Who took her? *Why*?"

"Cori? Not slavers. She'd have been shipped out by boat or caravan if it was slavers."

"She didn't run away. Didn't tie herself up in a cave."

"No, she didn't."

The boys passed them both. Ah, to be young.

"We didn't solve anything," Sumi snarled. "We don't know *anything*—"

"Sometimes cases aren't solved. Sometimes the person who commits a crime gets away. Sometimes we just don't know."

Wil and Andy glanced back, their mouths hanging open.

Andy was the first to recover. He shot Jay a devastated look. Turned his back and ran. Wil opened and closed his mouth like a fish, then shrugged and followed after Andy.

They reached the dirt road at the same time. Didn't wait for him and Sumi.

"They'll go home, right?" He finally reached the road. Waited for her to join him.

The boys had enough *reality*. He could have chosen his words more carefully to cushion the awful truth.

But he hadn't.

Rest it, he was tired.

"They'll go home." Sumi paused, bent at the waist, slowly straightened.

"Your back?"

"My back."

"Solved or not, at least we found her." Jay smiled. Small and grim but still a smile.

"True." She nodded. "I hope whoever took her doesn't take her again."

"I suspect Suann will keep her close for a while."

Sumi twisted to look back. "Mouse will be all right?"

"She was great today."

"Saved us. Thank the goddessi we're almost home."

Behind them, he heard Mouse following, all but silent.

CHAPTER
TWENTY-TWO

S umi

Night pressed on me. The hot, fetid smell of too many people and too many fires and too much desperation was a moist hand on my chest, but even worse was the touch of a cool breeze.

Summer was dying and that breeze should have been a welcome relief from the sweat, but it reminded me of the warehouse— the dark heat, and then the bone-cutting cold of the demon.

The demon who felt too much like a certain goddess.

Jay rolled over and breathed on my shoulder. "Do you want to talk about it?"

"No." Lying down helped me recover faster than I had this winter, but just *thinking* about the warehouse made my throat close up. "It felt like *She* feels."

"So you *do* want to talk about it."

"No." I turned and snuggled my nose into his chest. "It's

just..." I felt him chuckle. "What you did— I can't believe you stepped between the kids and... *that*. And I can't believe it worked."

"I have it on good authority I'm protected from magic by my own super-special magic shield." His voice was all rumbly and sexy, very much *not* like the demon.

"Whoever made that shield does blessed good work."

"Yeah, she does. *Damned* good work."

I smiled, then sobered. "Still, it shouldn't have worked. And you could have—" *died*. If he had— I'd been powerless to stop it. The memory of that helplessness sucked me hollow, set every muscle trembling.

"Shh. I'm here."

"Please, don't do that again. Please. Don't."

"I can't promise that. All I can promise—" He tried to hug away my tremors. "I will protect you. With everything I have."

"Bless it, Jay. It would kill me to lose you."

"But you didn't." His tone made it clear he was done with it. "And we learned some things." His finger traced patterns on my skin. I wondered if he realized he was tracing my tattoos. Even though, right now, he couldn't see them. The window let in just enough light to let me check.

"Those things being...?"

Jay's hand stilled. "Your shield will stand up to... *that*. Good to know. Can you put one on the boys?"

"No." I sighed and snuggled closer. "It would interfere with their magic—"

"Is that a bad thing?"

"Yes." How to help him understand? "Imagine you had a young guard who had trained all his life with a sheathed sword..."

"Er—"

"Just imagine. To protect him, his parents had sewn the

sheath shut around his sword, and made sure his teacher only used a sheathed sword. But now he's with the guard and could be fighting for his life, and can't get the sheath off. And even if he does manage it, no one ever trained him how it feels to cut. He only knows how it feels to bash."

His next words came slowly. "You're saying they need to learn everything they can about their magic. Because it might save their lives."

"They are more powerful together than anyone I've ever trained. I don't know why, and I've trained priestessi and magi to work together before. Perhaps it's their friendship or their different Colors working together or... I just don't know. But once they learned they can work together, nothing could stop them. So now I just try to help them figure out their limits and control what they do." I shifted against Jay, fitting myself to him. "Today scared me."

"Me too."

"And them."

"Not a bad thing."

"No. A little scared will make them more careful, which is good. But I can't let them stay scared, or it could turn into something worse. If they stop using their magic now, after something like that, they won't use it again until they're forced to— and then they won't be in control."

"Hmm." He rested his chin on my head. "All right. I can see that."

His warm body chased away my shivers. Yes, it was even hotter now, and sweat prickled at my hairline. But better that than the memories of the demon we'd summoned.

"So no shields for the boys," he rumbled.

"Even if I wanted to, I couldn't. Do you remember how I got enough power to make a shield?"

I did. A boy had tried to kill me, then the high priestess.

Maldita had *sucked* the blood out of the boy and then from Antero's blood-mother, Hana. And I'd been glowing from the power.

Jay's hand traced one tattoo over and over. This time he shuddered. "I remember."

"Mom!" Wil's voice, frantic. "Mom, help!"

I was out into the main room and halfway up the ladder before he called again, my ragged sleep-shirt flapping around my legs and Jay right behind me. I made it the rest of the way up, dodged around Mouse in her pile of blankets, and knelt next to Wil, who was thrashing in his sleep. Jay knelt beside me. Andy sat up and rubbed his eyes.

"Wilyam? I'm here." I hesitated to touch him. Was it just a dream? Would that make the dream better... or worse?

"No, Mom. No, don't leave me—" Tears rolled down his face.

Jay gripped Wil's shoulder, but he didn't wake.

"If he's dreaming what I did..." Andy's hands were shaking. "About that *thing*. And maybe about you dying."

"Oh no." I reached out to my boy.

He thrashed. His hand hit my face and I jerked back.

"He didn't mean to!" The whites showed all the way around Andy's eyes.

"I know." I rubbed my cheek. "We need to wake him up. Andy? I need you to—"

"Not magic." Andy glanced at Mouse, who was awake, but pretending to sleep.

"She knows. And I trust her." She'd saved us today— yesterday?— and it hadn't been by chance.

"Not magic," Andy said again. He dropped his gaze to his twisting hands.

My boys had been hurt by what had happened in that warehouse.

301

No way I would let Andy give up his magic because of it—not after the conversation I'd just had with Jay.

"C'mere, buddy." Jay held out his arms. Andy slipped into his embrace and Jay side-eyed me, then smiled. "Magic's just a tool. Like a knife or a sword. Can the knife on the kitchen table hurt anyone? Not until someone uses it, and that someone has to make a choice. Can the knife hurt you if you cut without taking care for your fingers? Yes. Can it also cut vegetables for dinner? Yes."

Wil keened, a horrible sound, twisted sideways and slammed his head against the floor. I managed to get a leg under his head and held it still. "Shh. Wil. I'm here. Shh. Andy?"

Jay scooted closer, bringing Andy with him. "He's going to hurt himself if we don't help him."

Andy wiped the tear marks from his cheeks. "Okay." He held out a hand to me.

I took it. "Start very very gently. Imagine *pushing* his bad dreams away."

His other fist clenched and he looked sideways. Reached out with his magic and brushed it across Wil.

Wil's back arched, then he collapsed in my lap. His breath hitched. He opened his eyes.

"M-m-mom?"

"I'm here."

"You were dead. It was all my fault.

"Just a dream."

"Andy?"

"Here."

Wil sat up. His eyes were dazed and a lump was coming on his forehead. I brushed his hair back from his face, and he flinched.

"Andy, maybe you could—"

"Jay? Sumi? Boys?" Dee came up the ladder, stuck her head over the edge. "Everything all right?"

Jay grunted. "Just a bad dream."

"That cave would give me nightmares." She peered at us. "You're sure?"

"Thank you, Sis."

She disappeared and I heard her muttering— probably to Robin. Maggie was working a night shift.

"Lie back down, boys. Only good dreams this time, though." I scooted between them so I could stroke their foreheads. "Chasing around in fields, buying things in the markets, running through desert sands..."

"Sands," Andy muttered sleepily.

"Feel the sands on your feet, and the heat of the sun on your faces. Let your eyes close. Go to sleep."

We watched over them while they drifted off, then I tried to get to my feet.

Everything protested— my joints, my muscles. My back spasmed.

So much for recovery.

I sat through it, blinked tears away. Jay offered a hand, helped me to the ladder. He helped me down, helped me across the main room that hadn't felt so big since I'd had to crawl along it to clean it, before his mom died, and then helped me back into bed.

I'm going to die. I wanted to moan it, but he'd take it the wrong way.

Jay crawled in next to me. "I..." He hesitated, so whatever he wanted to say must be bad.

I found the right position to be comfortable and finally my muscles relaxed. Knees and ankles still ached, but my back— thank the goddess— loosened up.

"I was surprised you didn't use your magic against that... *thing*." he murmured in my ear.

"Oh." His words were like a punch to my stomach, but I owed him the truth. "I wanted to. I couldn't. Something about it smothered me."

His breath stirred my hair. I'd rendered him speechless.

Bless it.

"I tried. I tried to call on the goddess, but—"

"The goddess." His voice dropped. "What do we do about Her?"

I stiffened. "Do?"

"It felt the same. When *that* came. It felt the same as when *She* came."

Bless us to heaven, yes it did. Were the demon hunters right? Were the goddessi really demoni? A small part of me still hoped they were wrong. "So what if they're right? Can they kill Her?"

"You don't think they know how?"

"They haven't managed it yet. Zerth had his chance. He was convinced killing me would kill *Her*. But it didn't work. Aimi killed me, Maldita passed to her. I think they don't have all the pieces. That's why they're searching out the stories."

"I will not allow them to kill you."

I smiled. "I love you too. But *if* they can kill Her— which I'm not saying they can because they obviously don't know how— what happens then? Or if they send Her back instead of killing Her? Either way, what happens to the City of Temples?"

Now Jay groaned. "I don't know. Chaos, probably. The blessed would try to take over and with no one to balance them..."

"Worse— what if they somehow killed both goddessi? It would affect everything— the magic, the power in the damned and the blessed, our very ability to defend the city."

"Guards with no magic?"

"Possibly. Maybe." I frowned. "I don't know how much of my magic comes from Her and how much comes from me. That's the thing— we just don't know what it would do to all us magic users."

"The City of Elementals could invade during the chaos. They're already here."

"Right. Even if Maldita is a demon and they do actually manage to send Her back, I don't see how our city can survive it."

"Your blood-mother would never give up her power."

"No. Aimi either, I think, though she at least seems more rational." My throat closed around the words until I wanted to claw at my own neck. If we'd been worshipping— *sacrificing*— to a demon all along... If *I'd* been giving power to a demon and so had my blood-mother, and my blood-sisters and all the priestessi and magi and even the servants with our belief in Them...

And I could see no way to get rid of the goddessi without bringing the city down around us...

Did that make me just as bad as whoever had called them in the first place?

Or... worse?

∼

Jay

MORNING PICKED THEM ALL UP AND SHOOK THEM LIKE RAG DOLLS. JAY snorted to himself at his fancy, but that was what it felt like— everything hurt, from his toenails to his teeth, after the *adventures* of yesterday.

And everything hurt *inside* thinking that the goddessi were actually demoni... and he had no idea what to do about them. *Couldn't* do anything about them, really.

Add stabbing rays of sunlight and a full bladder on top of that—

Argh.

He untangled himself from Sumi and limped into the main room.

Stopped.

Stared.

The Honored Blue, Head Guard of the Damned Third lounged at their table, drinking coffee and holding hands with Robin. Blue and yellow fingers braided together and the looks on both faces suggested they'd done more than touch fingers.

Jay snarled, "What in the resting betweens—"

Lena looked up. "Ah, bless it."

"You were supposed to sleep longer." Robin scowled.

"*What*—" he repeated— "in the *resting betweens* is *going on?*"

Sumi stuck her head out of their bedroom. "Robin? Lena?"

Dee made an appearance too. Leaned on her doorframe. Even the boys climbed halfway down the ladder and perched.

Robin jutted out her chin. "I told you I was in a relationship."

"Yes, but—" Jay spluttered. "You said— But it's different when I trip over it!"

"Congratulations," Sumi interrupted warmly, limping across the floor to gingerly hug Lena, then Robin. "I'm so happy for you both."

The boys let out little gasps, then grinned widely.

Jay couldn't make his mouth work. Happy? Everyone? "But..." Blinked. Attempted a disapproving scowl.

"Careful." Sumi tucked herself under his arm and sneaked

her fingers under his shirt to brush his skin. "Don't say anything foolish. Lena is strong and beautiful and loyal. Robin is smart and fierce and—"

"But—"

"They love each other, Jay." Dee examined her fingernails. "They have been together for months now. Robin told you. And you know you can't dictate who we love."

"That's not—"

"You can't *protect* me from her, if that's what you're thinking." Robin clutched Lena's hand tighter.

Yes, absolutely. "No." He rubbed the growing headache between his eyes. "But out there— Yellow and Blue—"

Sumi touched his hand, making obvious the contrast between brown and red. "*Color*? Really?"

"No. I just—" *Yes. Rest it, yes. Seeing them together here— I didn't really believe it before. The way people will treat them—* He waved one hand aimlessly. "I just wish it was easier."

Lena pried her hand free and rose. Lifted her belt and sword from the couch and settled them around her waist. "Love is never easy."

"We'll go." Robin jerked to her feet, jutted her jaw forward, scowled. "I can come back for my things when you're not here."

"No!" Jay held both hands up. "Please, don't go. I don't want you to leave us. That's not what I meant."

Robin had told him. But not that her lover was a Blue. And *seeing* a Blue in their house— Ack. All he wanted was to protect his sister from the stares, the whispers, the inevitable heartbreak—

"Wait. Stay. Please." He staggered to the necessary, mind churning. Relieved one pressure, at least. Washed his hands, then squared his shoulders and faced them all again. Felt backed into a corner, but he had no choice. If he stood in their way, he'd lose Robin. She had that look in her eye.

Heat ran up his neck.

And if he challenged Lena— where did *that* idiot idea come from?— she'd best him in a fight. And then Robin would leave anyway.

Resting betweens.

For his sister's sake— and to be there for her when this relationship ended, however it ended— he had to accept it. "How... how did it start?"

Dee grinned and Lena relaxed. "Told you he could be reasonable," Lena murmured, loud enough for Jay to hear. She set her belt and sword aside again, then pulled Robin into an embrace.

Robin was still scowling at him. She squeezed Lena's hand — yellow and blue fingers intertwining again— then took a step away. Faced him and lifted her chin. "I told you—"

Lena nudged her. As if Lena was the reasonable one in this relationship.

Robin started again. "I was having nightmares. About that night. The killing and the Elementals. I spied on them, then I was their friend and then— I betrayed them." Her voice wobbled. "I knew who made meat pockets with just the right spices, and who limped in the rain, and who never ate enough and who always smelled like flowers, and I cut them down—" She choked on a sob. Wiped her tears.

"You didn't tell me all that before..." Another stab of pain. She didn't trust him to help her? All that, and she'd never even hinted.

"You wouldn't understand. You've never—"

"Been a spy?" He scowled. "No. But I would have listened."

Robin shook her head. "You're not listening now!"

Jay opened his mouth to protest, then snapped it shut. He side-eyed Sumi, who nodded slightly.

Robin's chin lowered, though she looked like she still

expected him to interrupt her. "I knew Lena from before. Last winter. She reached out. We talked."

"I'd had a similar experience." Lena smiled at Robin. "I wondered if she was going through what I'd gone through. I just wanted to help."

"You did." Robin rested her head on Lena's shoulder. "And I kept finding reasons to see her. She was different from everyone else. Treated me like a person, not like a Color."

Stab, stab, stab. What *he* should have done for his sister... some stranger had done. Not fair to Lena, but he didn't feel like being fair. Where the resting betweens had he gone wrong? Rest it all.

"Lena, does she know...?" Sumi's voice was hoarse.

"You know better than that." Lena stared at Sumi. "I don't share things I've sworn not to."

"Know what?" Robin demanded. Jerked away Lena and shoved her hands onto her hips.

"You know I have things I can't talk about."

"Yes, but obviously this is about Sumi. Who is living *in my house*."

Sumi bit her lip. "Robin—"

No. Sumi wouldn't— "Don't." Jay stretched his hand out, as if he could stop her. The saying that three people could keep a secret if two of them were dead was a saying for a reason, and he and Sumi and the boys and Lena were already far more than three. Thom suspected, and Dee might know too and—

Sumi quirked a glance at him. She'd made up her mind and he couldn't change it. "She deserves to know. And I trust her."

Robin glared around at each of them, read it in Dee's face. "My *sister* already knows this resting secret, does she? Does Maggie know too? Am I the last to find out?"

Sumi winced. Blurted it out. "I was the high priestess of the

Temple of the Damned. My blood-sister killed me and took the goddess from me and Jay brought me back and now I'm here."

The room felt like someone had sucked all the air out of it.

"No," Robin whispered. "You were a servant. You said you were a servant."

Dee crossed the room. Hugged her sister. "She healed me. My back was *shattered*, Robin. She healed me. I wouldn't be walking now, if not for her."

"Healed... You have magic." Robin looked at the boys. "You have magic too?"

They grinned. "Yeah," said Wil. "But we have to be quiet so they don't come and take us away."

"Take you—"

"You know the blessed and the damned are always looking for magic users to take to the temples." Lena ran her hand down Robin's arm. "That was why they were all over the warehouse yesterday. They can feel when anyone uses magic. These three —" she shot a glance past the boys toward where Mouse was likely eavesdropping, but kept that secret to herself— "have learned to hide what they're doing. Mostly. But *whoever* did *whatever* yesterday— it was messy and loud."

Jay clutched at the wall to steady himself. Lena knew. The way she had emphasized *whoever*, the way she carefully avoided looking at anyone but Robin. She knew they'd been at the warehouse. And on top of that, she'd glanced up, but not at the boys. Toward Mouse. She knew about Mouse's magic too? And Mouse had been following after Sumi like a baby duck after its mama — Sumi was teaching the girl magic.

His girl. The one *he'd* saved—

Lena watched them all carefully. "I wonder what *did* happen at the warehouse?" She paused like she wanted Sumi or Jay to fill in the blank. "Everyone felt it."

Jay opened his mouth to tell her they'd been in the caves all day, but Sumi shook her head. She was used to trusting Lena.

But how much?

"But you cleaned our floors." Robin sounded dazed, still lost in the previous conversation. "On your knees. With a scrub brush."

"I'm not the high priestess anymore," Sumi said quietly. "Just another mouth to feed."

"You could— you could—" Robin flicked her fingers. "Magic."

"I couldn't. If I did, they would feel it. They'd come for me. And might hurt you because of it."

Robin blinked.

"Does Maggie know?" Robin bit her lip.

"No." Sumi shook her head.

Rest it, too many people knew. Jay rolled his shoulders. "I told Thom you weren't—"

"But he suspects again." Dee folded her arms. "Sometimes I wish he wasn't so... observant. He's probably asked Maggie what she knows. She's working for him. Spying on the demon hunters."

Jay's heart thundered in his ears. Resting betweens, how could he protect them when they kept secrets— took dangerous jobs—

Sisters.

"So do we tell her?" Sumi looked at Dee, Robin.

"No." They said it together. Robin glanced at Dee, who said, "She'll tell Thom, then he'll know for sure. She treats him like a father."

Jay flinched. Thom, the come-lately father he suddenly wasn't sure he wanted— especially didn't want coming between him and his sisters. No matter how well-meant.

Lena side-eyed him and said, "Any other secrets we want to speak?"

They all froze.

Eyed each other.

Kept their mouths shut.

At last, Dee said, "I think that's enough for today, don't you?"

Nods all around.

Jay cleared his throat. "Lena..."

Robin stiffened.

He forced a smile. "Welcome to the family."

CHAPTER
TWENTY-THREE

S *umi*

As if the revelation of my past life as the high priestess had been an explosion— which it emotionally was— Lena and Robin left together, and Dee followed soon after. Jay took the boys to get water, and I was on my own again.

I considered sweeping— how did all this dirt track into the house?— but made the mistake of settling onto the couch. Robin and Lena— I'd never imagined them together, but they would balance each other, strengthen each other, become more together than they were apart. And the way they looked at each other— my heart leapt to see it.

Good thing, because my body still hurt from yesterday.

Someone knocked on our front door.

I didn't move. Everything hurt, and I didn't even have dying to show for it.

Whoever knocked again.

They weren't going to leave, so I groaned and hefted myself off the couch, shuffled forward, swearing under my breath, and peeked out the window.

Suann and Cori.

I flung open the door and Suann hugged me. "They told me you found her up in the caves and you could have died up there because it was so dark and so big but you didn't give up and you found her and I'm so grateful. Thank you!"

"You're welcome." My voice was muffled against her shoulder. I tried to step back, but she clasped me tighter, so I waited, counting my breaths.

Finally Suann let me go— then Cori hugged my thighs. "You came for me."

Cori was easier. I waited her out too, then crouched down and held out my hand. "How are you feeling?"

"My stomach hurts and my head hurts." She put her hand in mine, yellow against red. Skin on skin made it easy, so I *listened*. A bit of the sedative still tainted her blood, and her stomach churned in response. The bump on her head was almost gone.

"Did you fall? Is that why your head hurts? Or did you eat something before you fell asleep?"

Her mouth dropped open. "Oh! A man gave me a sweet. He was funny. He looked like he was stuck between a Yellow and an Orange. I thought he was nice!"

I stretched my mouth in a smile. *Enzo?* "I'm sure he was."

"You didn't tell the guard that." Suann's mouth pinched.

"I forgot." Cori shrank in on herself. "I was so tired after. I think I fell asleep. Is it important?"

"It's okay." I tousled her yellow hair. "I'm just glad you're feeling better."

Suann swept her daughter into a hug and out the door. She called back over her shoulder, "Thank you again!" and hustled her girl back to their house.

I had a feeling Cori wouldn't be out of arm's reach for a long time.

After I saw their door close, I slumped at the table, but the chair bothered my back. My ankles and the bottoms of my feet hurt from walking over the uneven rocks. My knees hurt from climbing up and downhill. My hips and back—

I sounded whiney, even to myself.

So at a slow meander— half stagger, half groan, half forcing myself, and that was one too many halves, but— I took myself out and headed toward my favorite market. A Yellow woman peeled herself out of shadow and followed me.

For a bare instant I let myself *feel* her intent— follow not attack— so I ignored her. Either she was a demon hunter, so I couldn't do anything, or she was a guard because Thom was suspicious, so I still couldn't do anything. Didn't really matter which.

Carpets and pallets flew overhead, thicker than usual. Gray and black and white carpets and colors for pallets— fewer blessed and even fewer damned than yesterday, but still far too many for our resting pallet-filled skies. We broke the Rest Third with what we'd done, searching for Cori.

As I walked, my joints loosened and my muscles warmed. Eventually I felt halfway all right— was that a fourth half? Walking helped. I walked some more. Walked and turned and walked and looked up and saw—

The gates to the Damned Third.

I froze.

Not where I wanted to be.

The gates were open, as they commonly were. People passed back and forth between the Damned Third and the Rest Third as if there were no difference. The guards all eyed each other resentfully— more fallout from us— but the regular people wore smiles on either side of the wall, and those going into the Damned Third hurried their steps.

Despite all the anxiety for recent events, I felt a prickle of pride. *I* had made the smiles happen— made the Damned Third more accessible for those of the Rest Third, and vice versa.

And then we'd called a *demon*—

No— I'd left behind the damned and we'd found Cori. Now I needed to focus on turning away. Moving my feet.

The houses here shared back walls with Damned Third. They'd been freshly painted, the windows cleaned, the yards tidied. They had water piped in, judging by the berries on the bushes— those berries would have dried up and died at Jay's house.

My feet still hadn't moved. The sun beat down on my head and I flushed, uncomfortably warm. Someone jostled me, and someone else muttered, "Get out of the way," and still I didn't move.

"Sumi?" Jay appeared at my elbow, and still I didn't move. "What are you doing? What's going on? Don't you think we're kinda close—" He eyed the gates and shuffled his feet.

I'd belonged there, once. Had fought my way to the top, had taken power and done my best to better the lives of those around me. And now I was an outcast, given up for dead. Probably reviled.

Worth it, I reminded myself, *I made my choice.* Finally my feet came unstuck and we started to walk away.

A Blue girl about thirteen years old walked with her father, past me toward the gates. She exuded magic and I found myself pausing to watch her.

I wondered vaguely if she was from one of the families that commonly bought themselves free from the goddessi— those with weaker magic, easily trained or contained, who could hide it, continue living their lives.

This girl couldn't hide it.

But she and her father were doing the right thing. She would become a priestess, have power and influence of her own, some of which she could wield on behalf of her family. One day maybe even rise to the position of high priestess.

Goddess be with her

A group dressed all in white pushed— and *pushed*— their way through the crowds, past me and Jay, and surrounded the Blue and her father.

The blessed had found her.

The Blue man straightened up, put his hand on his daughter's shoulder. Looked toward the gates of the Damned.

The damned guards scowled and *someone* did some magic. Black carpets popped up into the air all over the Damned Third, heading for the gate, but until they arrived, the damned were outnumbered and out magicked by the blessed. The blessed had a magus and a priestess with them. The ebbs and flows of power around me made me nauseous. The magic reached out to me, tasted me, tugged on me.

Jay saw it in my face. He stepped between us, wrapped his arms around me.

The tugging stopped. Either their magic had decided I was nothing, or his shielding had protected me. Thank the goddessi... not that I wanted to swear by Them anymore.

I looked over Jay's shoulder. The blessed guards separated the man from his daughter and handed him a bag of coin. He shouted. Their magic surged.

The man stopped shouting. The girl stopped struggling. They both hung their heads like they couldn't fight anymore and then the blessed took the girl, shoved her onto a medium-sized carpet with the priestess. The magus and the guards all tossed down their brilliant white carpets.

The black carpets were getting closer.

"They can't—" The thread that was Maldita inside me thickened as my magic surged. I twisted in Jay's arms, fighting it back. "They can't take her. She was going to the Damned."

"They're the Blessed." Jay sounded tired. "They take what they want."

The man had fallen to his knees. His hands held the bag of coin as if it were the head of a viper, too dangerous to release. He gasped a breath, and then he wept.

The white carpets rose into the air, the guards clumped between their priestess and the oncoming damned.

"She was in the Rest Third. At the gates of the Damned." I tucked my head into Jay's shoulder. "And they still took her. From a place they had no power."

"They always have power." His voice soothed, and his hand petted my hair. "As long as they have magic, they have power. The damned chose not to engage, so the blessed had the power."

The damned stopped at the gates and the blessed flew away. I doubted any of the Resting Third guards even saw what happened.

"That's not—" *fair*. I stopped myself, but he heard the word anyway. I could feel him grin, his cheek on my forehead.

"Nothing you could have done." He set me back from him. "We've seen enough—" of the blessed, of the damned — "Are you ready to go?"

Anger closed my throat.

If I was the high priestess— if I used my magic— if I *could* use my magic without fear of Maldita hurting everyone I loved, I could have stopped them.

A year ago I would have stopped them.

But likely this wasn't the first time, and if as high priestess I'd never heard of it, a year ago I would never have known it had happened.

318

I'd made my choice, over and over, and again a moment ago. My loved ones were more important than strangers, and the workings of the blessed and the damned— fair or not— were no longer my problem.

I *pushed* my fury down deep and mustered a weary smile of my own. Took Jay's hand.

"I'm ready. Is the Yellow woman still with us? She followed me from the house."

He twitched, then spun me around in a casual circle. "I'm guessing the one to our left who is trying too hard not to look at us?"

"Yep. Demon hunter or guard?"

"I don't recognize her, so demon hunter." He grimaced. "I have the guard following me. Mal— Thom set him on me yesterday. Maybe we should introduce them to each other."

As he'd intended, my fury did not rise again, and instead I smirked at the picture in my head— the demon hunter and the young guard following *us*— the two *least* likely to cause problems in the City of Temples.

"Right, let's—"

Boom!

I staggered, then looked. *Felt.* "The granary!" The Stonefield granary. Half empty now because they were just beginning the harvest, but the whole complex— all the reserves for a bad year, all the workers inside, all the homes nearby—

My magic snapped out, touched the water in the river, ready to *pull* it to the fires as only a high priestess could do from several streets away.

Jay took my hand. His eyes were wild, like he knew what I was going to do. "No."

"We have to help!"

"We will. Come on."

I stuffed the magic back down inside me.

And then we ran.

~

*J*AY

Black smoke billowed into the sky, a column of death— the grain reserves, the seed, the workers. Everyone in the Rest Third bought from the Stonefield granary.

And Sumi knew it— she was going to use her magic, expose herself to the dark goddess.

No.

He took her hand and ran with her toward the fire, using his bulk to shield her from the people running away. Blue, Purple, Red, Brown, Green, Orange, Yellow— running away. Jay caught glimpses of a few running *toward* the fire, like he and Sumi were, guards who had trained to run toward trouble.

The skies became choked with smoke. Carpets streamed away from the complex, collided, the drivers screaming. One gray carpet flew toward the flames, but it slowed, then bucked. Something about the fire pushed it away. Maybe the heat? The driver's fear?

The granary complex contained a squat drying building, a three-story tower for storage, a small distribution area, and a framework where the flying carpets moved between. If he remembered, all built of brownwood.

Having been accidentally close by, he and Sumi had the dubious pleasure of being among the first to arrive.

Into chaos.

Flames engulfed the drying building and crept toward the storage building. They still had a chance to save the reserves.

A Green man held a Red woman back from the drying building. The Red woman strained toward it— did a family member burn inside it? Clusters of people— Browns, Reds, Greens, Yellows— stood frozen and gaping. A short, round Red woman and a taller Yellow woman led away a sobbing Green man.

They crossed in front of Jay and Sumi. Jay splayed his hand out to stop them without touching. "Where's their magus?"

The Red woman answered, "This *is* their magus."

Rest it. The one person who could legitimately use magic had curled around himself, one charred hand gripping the Yellow woman's shirt. The magus moaned.

Sumi looked at him, then at the fire, then back at him. Her lips thinned. "Start a water brigade," she said. "I'll take him."

The women nodded and handed the magus to Sumi. Gently pried the magus's fingers loose. Jay opened his mouth to protest.

"Go." Sumi's voice was soft but somehow it carried over the flames and the screams. "I'll do what I can with him."

Then the muscles near her eyes tensed— the ones that mean she was using magic.

Rest it— he wanted more than anything to pull her away from here. She'd show herself to the dark goddess and then the life they'd built together would be over. But she wanted to save lives— the lives of the people of the Rest Third. *His* people. Rest it to the resting betweens— how could he stop her when he *wanted* her to save them?

Had to trust her, though it wrenched his guts and ripped a hole in his heart.

"Be careful!" He kissed her swiftly. Turned away.

The Yellow woman hesitated but the Red sprinted toward the emergency shack set in the open area between warehouse and granary. Heaved up the overhead door to expose a stack of buckets, a hand pump, and a river tap with an attached fire-hose, hard-woven and greased and magicked to minimize the leaks. Jay yelled, "Open the tap," grabbed the nozzle end and ran with it. The hose writhed as it filled, bucked in his hands. He clamped it under one arm and aimed the gush of water at the storage building's roof.

"Buckets," he grunted at the useless fool standing there gawping at the fire. "Kill the embers!"

The Red woman knocked over the stacked buckets, cursed fluently. Set a bucket under the hand pump and jerked the handle up and down, up and down. The Yellow joined her, as if she'd been waiting for someone to tell her what to do. Heaved up the bucket and staggered after the wind-driven embers before they could catch the warehouse.

More people arrived, Mal among them, all the Colors mixed together and no one caring. Hands helped control the hose, other hands wrapped rags where it leaked. More hands heaved buckets of water onto hot spots.

A Brown man helping with the hose pointed. "The drying building—"

"Too late!" Jay yelled back, no breath to spare arguing with idiots. "Save the grain!"

Resting betweens, controlling the hose sent darts of agony into his shoulders, wrenched muscles that remembered yesterday's fight with the demon. *Ignore the pain, save the people, save the resting food.*

Smoke burned his eyes. Sweat dripped down his face. Down his back. His world narrowed to *hose-water-flames*.

Flying carpets swirled around the edges, unable to get close enough to help.

They weren't winning— just keeping the flames barely at bay.

Then rain pierced the smoke and pattered down on Jay's face, his arms, the stones under his feet, and most important, the fires.

Smoke. Sweat. Fire. *Keep aiming water.*

Rain poured from the sky, a dense mass that drenched the world.

The flames drew back, hissed into smoke, died.

Behind him, a ragged cheer.

Jay shifted.

Saw Sumi supporting the magus—wrapped around him like a lover— who had his hand stretched out toward the sky.

A healthy Green hand, no longer burned.

What had she done?

Goddessi, would the blessed and the damned believe the Stonefield mage had called the deluge? Would it be enough to hide Sumi's magic?

"Jay?" The Brown man who had been helping him control the hose wiped his own face and peered about. "Jay, is that really you? It's me— your uncle Nick—"

Jay ripped his gaze away from Sumi. Stared at the Brown man.

"I should have known it was you." Nick grinned through the ash and sweat on his face. "Only a guard could have organized us so quickly. And you realized we had to save the storage building over the drying—"

"You—" *arrogant ass.* Jay snapped his mouth shut. He was tired, cranky, and likely to make enemies if he said what he thought.

A Brown child pushed her way through the crowd and presented herself to *dear old Uncle Nick.*

"Dad! They're gone! All of them—"

Nick raised one hand. "Slow down, Tamica. What's gone?"

"Someone broke in. Everyone came here and someone saw and broke in and frightened Grandma half to death..."

Nick suddenly paled. Swayed.

His daughter continued miserably, "The histories, Dad.

Whatever the priestess did, what the magus did, all the guards to protect them. None of it mattered. They're gone."

Nick staggered. Put a hand on Jay's shoulder to steady himself. "They didn't get the proofs of ownership of the lands, the house, the fields, did they? The mage-seal copies were in the —" His eyes tracked to the warehouse. "If anyone contests us... resting betweens."

His daughter shook her head *no*, but Nick didn't seem to notice.

"Steady." Jay braced him. "No one is going to dispute anything right now. And the guard will find those papers and get them back." *Or Sumi can make another copy.*

Why did he want to help this man so much? He shouldn't. The way they'd treated his father, mother, sisters...

"The guard." Nick straightened. The hand still clamped on Jay's shoulder tightened. "That's right. You're a guard. You can find whoever did this to us and bring them before the Council. So they can be punished as they deserve."

Jay gaped.

"We'll pay you, of course." He turned to his daughter. "Ren's boy will save us. He's your cousin—"

"I'll talk to Thom." What else could he do? He was no one's savior, least of all the Stonefields. He could get Thom to assign someone else. Jay pried his uncle's hand off his shoulder, then turned away.

Spotted Sumi.

He just needed one resting minute of peace with her. One minute. Right now.

She saw it in his face. Came to him.

He took her hand and wordlessly pulled her away from the Stonefields, away from the fire, away from the magus.

Just one resting minute.

CHAPTER

TWENTY-FOUR

S *umi*

I HAD TO.

The fire was destroying the granary. People were dying. And the magus was burned and helpless. I had to help.

I took the Green man and steadied him against me, then breathed with him, murmured in his ear. Delicately *pushed* my will at him— easier, with no layers in between us.

"Calm. Breathe with me. Shh. Do you *push* or *pull?*"

His eyes closed. "*Push,*" he whimpered.

I could work with that.

"Breathe with me now. *Push* the pain away. Come on, you can do this." I ignored the heat from the fire, ignored the shouting and the water, quietly *pushed* his pain, *pushed* with him. *Pushed* him to do what I wanted. Quiet, careful, using all the tricks I'd learned here in the Rest Third.

His breathing slowed and he *pushed* with me. The man was

quite strong— I could feel it in him. That would make this easier.

"Have you healed before?"

His eyes fluttered but stayed closed. He sank further into a meditative state. "Once. No, twice. In training I helped *push* a bone straight, then one of the Stonefields' kittens was savaged by a dog. I did what I could."

"Good. The heat in your skin, *push* it away. Slowly. Gently."

He *pushed* and I steadied him. Guided him. *Pushed* and *pulled* with him, manipulating his burns until they sloughed off and new skin grew. I *looked* around us for magic. His healing rippled out, but *felt* like him.

No trace of me.

Thank the goddessi. If I could do it with small, intimate magics, could I do it with larger magics? "We need to bring moisture from the river to put out the fires."

"Can't." He shrugged, jostling my contact with him. "Can't *pull*."

I bit off a string of curses and leaned into the contact. Skin to skin. One arm around his waist, my fingers up under his shirt. The other, holding his hand, and my chin on his collarbone. As long as Jay stayed busy with the hose, he wouldn't notice this horrible intimacy. I hadn't been skin-to-skin like this with anyone but my beloved in a long, long time. "Don't think about it that way."

"Don't think." He sounded dazed.

Perfect.

"Can you feel the water in the air? Water evaporating from the river, bunching up against the mountains?"

"Yes."

"*Push* the water tighter." With the tiniest needle I could manage, I reached *through* him and *pulled* water from the river.

Pulled it toward us, overhead. Via the ground would do us no good.

He *pushed* and I *pushed* and *pulled* through him, a thing I hadn't believed was possible and never would have thought of without the boys' experiments. And still, *our* magic looked like *his*.

Then other magics joined ours— other magi, some blocks away, some closer— each *pushing* and *pulling* water into the air as their gifts allowed them, and then, between us all, we brought rain.

"Gentle," I reminded him. *Pushed* the thought out through him to them all. *We don't want a deluge. Don't want to ruin crops and cause mudslides. Just rain over the fire to put it out. Over the fire and nowhere else.*

Goddessi— using my magic again was like drinking rainbows. The sheer *joy* of it shaped it and molded it through the Green magus, and caressed the others' magic, as if I were sending sparkles into the air around us, and I felt their emotions back— shock, agreement, exhaustion. I reached out further, supported them while they supported us. Somehow it took less magic than it should have, or our combined magics did more than they should—

The last flames sputtered and died.

With a brush of my fingertips, I ran my magic through the Green man's body and made sure I'd not injured him while working magic through him. I *pushed* and *pulled* gently on his mind, blurring what we'd just done. Blurring his memory of me. Then, as carefully as I had inserted my magic into him, I slipped out.

The Red woman who had been pumping water came back for the magus, and for a moment I wondered about their relationship. Her face— she took our intimacy the wrong way, so they had some sort of understanding. Not that it mattered, but a Red and a Green, a magus and an ungifted... she untangled him from me and they embraced. Did they face any of the challenges Jay and I faced?

Jay—

He stood with his uncle and a Brown girl who shared their coloring, the shape of their chin, the line of their foreheads. Another relative? Jay's shoulders tightened and his neck flexed. Something was wrong.

Since so many magi had splashed their magic around, I dared to gently *push* at the Stonefields to let Jay go, and I walked toward him, slipping through the crowd like we were the only ones there.

Bless it, it felt good to use my magic, even if it was through someone else, so the goddess wouldn't notice. Even if it left me feeling hollow in the middle. So hollow—

Wordlessly, Jay took my hand and guided me away. He paused to search my face, frowned heavily, then tugged me after him. We walked two blocks, up and over, and then he brought me around a corner and a different world opened up in front of us.

A riot of color, carefully tended.

He drew me forward. "Our Memory Garden," he said, as if that explained it all.

Narrow paths wound their way through and here and there, and benches sat next to the path. Jay towed me deeper in, then settled us on a bench under a brownwood tree. Purple and yellow violets sprawled around the feet of the bench. Across the way, red, green, yellow and even blue orchids ran along the path, and behind them a bush of orange roses.

"A Memory Garden?" Smoke had roughened my voice.

"When a loved one passes, those who don't have the land, they plant their memories here. After a birth, they remove a memory to make space."

"But—" Trees and shrubs and flowers in all the colors, and so many I didn't recognize. Purple wisteria, a red burning bush, a green weeping willow... I craned my neck around, winced when it cracked. Hibiscus and hollyhocks and dahlias and hellebore, and all the colors mixed together.

Birds called from the trees, and one red-bellied seed-eater fluttered down to dig at the path, then strutted along it, twisting its head, looking for treats. It startled and launched itself into the air.

Bees buzzed from flower to flower, then back to a box that was probably the hive. Vaguely I wondered if my blood-sister had her bees like she had planned. Someone in the rest third knew how to cultivate them... had she found someone to teach her?

My shoulders relaxed. I leaned into Jay. We both smelled like smoke and sweat and I didn't care because the fragrance of the garden wafted around us and for a moment, we held peace. "It's beautiful." The garden was exactly what the City of Temples *could* be— a mix of Colors and carefully tended.

An old couple teetered their way through, both Yellows faded by age. They walked hand in hand, and we watched them come, pause in front of a cluster of yellow orchids, and go.

Finally Jay sighed. "The fire today," he said softly, "was a distraction. They stole the Stonefield histories."

I felt myself tensing, reminded myself to relax. I couldn't do anything about it now.

"My uncle thinks I'll 'save' them," he continued, "find their papers, arrest the perpetrators, commit justice."

I grinned. *Commit justice*— an odd phrase that summed up Jay's outlook: justice needed action. Then I sobered. While we were sharing— "I used magic today. *Through* that magus. I had no idea it was possible, but I did it."

"Will they come for you?"

"No. The priestessi and magi felt his magic, not mine."

"And the goddess?"

"Didn't stir."

"Resting betweens. I nearly lost you again and didn't even know it."

I swallowed the lump in my throat and curled my fingers in his. "Never."

Jay sighed. "I met a blood-cousin. Nick's girl. She looks like him."

"So do you."

"I suppose." Jay clenched my fingers briefly. "I don't understand the way they think."

"Do you want to?" Careful. "Do you want to get to know them better?"

Jay shifted, pulled me tighter, and avoided the question. "Thom knows who you are, or thinks he does. No other reason to set Mal on me like he has. I don't like it."

My stomach soured. More people who knew my secret. "We'll deal with it."

"I would fight them all for you."

"You shouldn't have to." I twisted to rest my hand against his chest. "Thom is a good man. We'll just have to trust him."

"Trust him? The man I thought I knew wouldn't have a boy following me through the city."

"Mal is old enough to be a guard. He's old enough to make his own choices."

His chest hitched. "It would break me to kill him."

"You won't have to." I would *not* cause him more pain. "Cruel of him, to set Mal on you. He's the guard who admires you, isn't he?"

"Not anymore. Not if Thom told him—"

"But will Thom tell the damned?" Jay might not admit it, but he needed to be liked. Almost as much as he needed to protect us— his family. I had to distract him from Mal. "Or will he ask me to use my magic? Or will he settle for glaring at me across the dinner table?"

"You want to invite him to dinner?"

I shrugged and closed my eyes. But that brought the smell of the fire back, so I opened them again and looked at the plants cultivated in memory of loved ones.

No Memory Garden in the Temple of the Damned.

His fingers traced over my arm. "Thom and Mal and the rest—"

It would eat at him unless I gave him something more important to think about. And it was time to tell him anyway. I whispered, "The magic I teach the boys? Mouse is learning too. And those thieves from the market— Tasha and Gui."

Jay groaned.

"If I didn't teach them, the thieves would have brought the priestessi down on us by now. They're quieter than before, and they keep their magic to themselves." Except I'd asked them to find the demon hunters and spy on them. I had to believe their loyalties lay with us.

Had to.

"I wish we could stay here. If we move, it will all come crashing back down on us."

Jay ran his hand over my hair. "We'll stay. For just a little longer."

Jay

He sat with Sumi in the Memory Garden for as long as he could stand his own stench. She looked like she'd not eaten for a week, but her eyes were quiet again, so the stop was worth it. He helped her up and tried to stretch. Bruised and strained muscles protested. Took more than a few steps to shift from hobbling to walking. The streets were quieter now. Everyone recuperating from the fire. Planning the future. Worrying.

Jay counted coins in his head— they'd put most of Lena's damned money aside for emergency expenses, but he should have enough to stop at a bathhouse. Guided Sumi that way, and they managed a quick shower under tepid water. When they emerged, his Sumi smelled of nothing more offensive than cheap soap. Worth the coin.

Her stomach gurgled and she looked faded, bony where she had been soft only a few hours ago. He needed to feed her. Working magic in the Rest Third somehow ate through her energy in a way it hadn't in the damned temple.

No food vendors along these streets— had they all disappeared because of the fire? Or something worse?

And where was Mal? The boy hadn't followed them into the Memory Garden, or he was getting better at hiding. Would he catch them here in the streets or at the house? And what had happened to the demon hunter spy?

Jay set it all aside when they opened the front door. Home had problems of its own.

Robin was out— no doubt with her lover. If he thought about it, it set his teeth on edge. The boys' boots slumped next to the doorway, so they were home, up in their room. Dee sat at the table, darning socks.

He should check to see if Mouse was home too... but he didn't want to see her right now. He'd guessed from their conversation this morning— was it only this morning?— that Sumi had been teaching her magic, but Sumi admitting it made it more real. Cramped his guts. Better he give it some time.

Wordlessly, he handed Sumi a bowl of early-harvest berries

and sat next to her while she ate like she hadn't eaten in months. When she finished the berries, he handed her the last two meat pockets, saving the bread ends for the boys. He'd need to buy more food tonight— tomorrow— bread from the neighbors two houses down and meat pockets from the woman who didn't sell rat.

Still quiet, they washed their hands, then gathered their own mending and plopped onto the couch. The middle sagged. He'd need to repair it— or pay someone to repair it— soon. Jay started the patch on his worst pair of socks. Gray guard socks, of course.

"Impatient stitches," Dee murmured.

Jay grinned. At least something was normal. He pretended to snarl back at her— "No one will see them under my boots—" like any other day without a fire or magic or goddessi.

Maggie came home and— for a wonder— stayed. She dumped her gear in her room and joined Dee at the table. Watched while he and Sumi slumped closer and closer to each other on the couch. His shoulder touching Sumi's made the corner of her mouth quirk just so, until he wanted to kiss her senseless, so he shifted away again. Kept darning. Felt himself falling toward her again. Smiled.

Maggie fetched her own socks and yarn, claimed her chair again, and sighed. "Prices are going up again," she muttered.

Sumi scowled at her socks. "Thrice-blessed demon hunters mucking everything up."

Maggie frowned, looked like her older sisters. She lifted her gaze from her socks and glared at Sumi as if she were a new kind of weapon— unfamiliar and dangerous.

Ugh— the way she looked at Sumi... Thom had told her *something*.

Her chin lifted. "What if they're right?"

The resting people who burned the grain and burned the magus and burned anyone they thought was in their way? The same people who had stolen histories from all the wealthy homes in the Rest Third? The ones who had tried to kill Sumi— and him — last winter? "The *demon hunters*? You think *they're* right?" When everyone stared at him, Jay realized he'd shouted. And snapped the yarn. He'd have to pick out and start the patch again. "Let's say—" *Let's say they are right and the goddessi are just demoni.* "Let's just say they were right. They tried to kill us all during that storm—"

"They tried to kill the *priestessi of Maldita*," Maggie snapped. She side-eyed Sumi. "They're welcome to them."

Yeah, she knew. Or suspected. Rest Thom to the betweens. "I was there too, and Dee and Robin—"

"They wouldn't have hurt any of us if we'd stayed out of their way!"

"They stole—"

"Prove it."

"And blew up the granary just today!"

"No one died."

Jay gaped at her. No one died? *If* that was true— and he wasn't sure it was— it was because Sumi had used her magic. Without her rain, they might still be there, throwing water on the smoldering flames of their grain reserves and seed reserves. How *could* she? "You weren't there," he snarled.

Sumi reached over and put her hand on his thigh. The muscles jumped. He closed his eyes. Relaxed his fists.

"What have the damned ever done for *us*?" Maggie slammed her hands down on the table, scattering her own yarn and needles, shot to her feet.

Dee gaped at Maggie, then cocked her head at Sumi, inviting her to answer.

"Let's say you're right." Sumi's voice was cool, composed. It was her teaching voice, and Jay marveled she could use it while he was still reeling from his little sister's attack. "Leaving aside *how* they go about it, let's say the demon hunters kill the goddessi. What then?"

"If these mystical creatures even exist—"

"For argument's sake, let's say They do."

He and Sumi had already hashed this out, but Maggie needed to think about it too.

His little sister scowled. "Then the priestessi can't use them for an excuse any more. All the sacrifices stop!"

"And then?"

"We take back what's ours." Maggie grinned sharply.

Resting betweens, he'd known she was spoiled, but *this*? Take back what was hers?

Sumi was still calm. "What is yours, exactly?"

"The..." Maggie waved one hand vaguely. "People. The servants. The animals."

"All right. *You* didn't tithe the animals, so you don't get them back. That would be stealing. But *someone* takes them *back*." Sumi's voice was dry and factual, her gaze flicking between her darning and his youngest sister. "But you *take back* the people. One of the functions of the temples is to teach magic. You don't want that anymore?"

"No! They take our best people. You— *they* took Jay! No more. Not people or our money!" Maggie glared down at the woman who used to be the high priestess of Maldita.

She knew.

Jay wanted to defend his wife, but anything he said now would confirm Maggie's suspicions. His little sister might know or think she knew, but she was still here, listening.

More than he'd expected, from her.

"So you don't want to pay the temples for anything. What happens when the pipes to the bathhouse clog?" Sumi cocked her head.

Dee watched intently.

Maggie lifted her chin. "We have people who know how to fix them."

"What if they can't?"

"They can!"

Dee snorted— she'd seen *push-pull* magic at work— but Sumi flicked a *let me* look at her and Dee subsided.

"All right. What are you going to do when your swords break? Your windows and mirrors? What will the people in the other Thirds do without those things?"

Maggie blinked. "Get new ones?"

"Where do guard weapons come from?"

Jay hid a nasty grin. He saw where Sumi was going with this. He didn't want to feel bitterly satisfied, eager to watch the woman he loved school his spoiled little sister. But she'd chosen the demon hunters' rhetoric over her own family... He should be *better* than this, rest it. He stuffed his rage down in his gut.

Breathe.

The lines between Maggie's eyes deepened. "The... market?"

"Who makes swords? Knives?"

"Er." His little sister's eyes went wide, but she closed her mouth on the words and refused to say them.

Now Sumi canted her head toward Dee, who answered for her. "The temples. The magi. The priestessi."

"Who makes the best glass?"

"The temples." Dee pulled out her favorite knife and examined it as if making her point.

Sumi went on. "What is the biggest export of the Damned Third?"

"Weapons." Jay answered this time. "Blessed Third too. Weapons and anything made with glass. Windows, mirrors, jewelry, lanterns—"

"So?" Maggie stuck her lip out. "That's them. Not us."

"What about the things the Thirds trade with other cities? What will we use to trade? How will we cross the deserts? Who will make the flying carpets?"

"We don't need flying carpets. Other cities don't use them."

"You want to *run* everywhere while you're patrolling?" Jay snorted.

Maggie tossed her hair. "Other cities use horses or camels."

Sumi inclined her head. "What will we trade for them?" She reached out and tugged at Jay's shirt. "What about linen? The bulk of the cotton? We don't grow enough to clothe us all."

"But—"

Sumi went on, implacable. "How do we get water to the fields?"

"Irrigation." Maggie smirked, sure of herself now.

"What about in the fall? Dry season is coming. The boys have started carrying buckets of water to the garden. Because the irrigation has stopped but the plants still need water, right? Who is going to carry buckets of water to each plant in those fields? The massive fields you just took from the temples?"

Dismay crossed Maggie's face, then she lifted her chin. "The Yellows and Oranges."

"Are you going to tell them that? From what I've seen," Sumi drawled, "they struggle to keep the Rest Third fields watered already."

"But—" Maggie looked at each of them. "But all those people we free—"

"*Those people*—" Now Sumi leaned forward— "and I used to be one of them— use magic *every day*. They don't carry buckets of water to every bit of field, except every few years to protect the plants from a nasty freeze."

Jay twitched— Sumi had done just that last fall, and she'd worked twice as hard as the haulers, using her magic in ways he hadn't understood.

She continued, "The magi and priestessi trainees *push* water to the fields. The apprentices clear the pipes, use *push* and *pull* magic to cool and heat the buildings."

Dee bent over to touch her toes, then straightened. Ready to start practicing fighting again. "Healers." She side-eyed Sumi, but didn't say anything more about Sumi's power. Continued, "Just because they don't help us much doesn't mean they shouldn't help *someone*."

Jay scowled. He still despised the healers for refusing to help his mother when she was sick, refusing to help Dee when she was injured. Thank the goddess— demon?— Sumi had been able to heal Dee.

"Instead of having the Rest Third struggling to live," Sumi said, "you'd have the whole city struggling to live if you outlawed magic... and those who are used to *having* are more likely to take from *you*."

"Would magic users follow laws forbidding their magic? Who would force them if not the high priestessi?" Jay clenched his jaw. And who would give that power to the high priestessi if not the goddessi?

Maggie glanced at him. At Dee. "But—"

Sumi went on. "The damned guards and the blessed guards have better weapons. The rich in the other Thirds have magi in their employ. How will they react when you try to take that away?"

"But—"

Sumi shook her head slowly. "It's not *this* or *that*. It's not goddessi or prosperity. It's *complicated* and anyone who is telling you it's simple is lying."

"But it's broken the way it is!" Maggie wailed.

Finally, she was starting to understand.

Jay rose, leaving his socks behind. Set a hand on her shoulder. "It *is* broken. And we want to fix it."

"Agreed." Sumi nodded. "But it's *complicated*. You can't tear down the temples without putting something in their place. Something *better*. So we can *all* have enough to eat and roofs over our heads and something better to live for." Now she looked away. "I don't know if anyone has the answer to that right now."

"It's like the taxes," Jay said slowly. "People complain about taxes when they forget what taxes pay for— guards and roads and fixing the city pipes, and I don't even know what else."

"It's easy to say it's broken." Dee sheathed her knife. She had furrows in her brow like she was thinking hard. "But harder to fix it. The Damned Third and the Blessed Third are used to looking to the high priestessi, but in the Rest Third, we're used to looking out for ourselves."

"We still look to certain families," Jay pointed out. He'd never realized it before his time in the damned temple, but now it was glaringly obvious. "The Yulians, because they head the merchants." His lips twisted. "The Stonefields because they control the granary. The one that burned today."

Maggie scowled.

Dee cocked her head, then nodded. "We do look to them, don't we? They make up most of the Council."

"Revolutions are easy." Sumi stood up and shifted like her back was hurting. "Look at Breadia to the north. They rebelled against their kings. Then they rebelled against the replacements. They're still in upheaval. We rarely trade with them and we probably won't until they figure it out. It doesn't make any sense to work out new trade agreements every time because your contact was killed between trips."

Jay put his hand on Sumi's back. "I didn't know that."

She smiled at him. "They keep it quiet. I— ah, overheard a couple priestessi talking about it last year." She'd made the decision herself, as the previous high priestess of the Temple of the Damned.

"And who says the City of Elements isn't using this as an excuse to invade us?" Dee said suddenly. "We have the river, the fields, the mines— if they could walk in and take it without a fight—"

Yes. Someone else saw it too. Jay nodded. "The goddessi are bad, but what would the Elementals be like as conquerors?"

"Maybe they'd treat us better?" Maggie's voice was small. "They can't treat us any worse than the blessed and damned do now."

"They could. Disarmed and at their mercy? A whole city of people they consider heretics?"

"I guess they could." Maggie rose suddenly. This time, when she stared down at Sumi, her face twisted into speculative lines. "Thank you for talking to me about these things."

"All you had to do was ask." Jay felt the last of the resentment in his gut ease. She'd listened.

The Elementals were telling one story, the guards another, but she'd listened to Sumi's story too. How would she choose between them?

Something had to change and the more people who were actually *thinking* about it, the better chance they had to push that change in a good direction.

CHAPTER
TWENTY-FIVE

S *umi*

I DREAMED, AND I KNEW I DREAMED, BUT I COULDN'T WAKE.

The granary burned, and I stood in the flames, my skin charring except for the damned tattoos. The dark goddess Maldita exploded out of the blaze and surrounded me. She reached out and touched Her tattoos, *pulled* my blood out through them, and I screamed.

The magus who had been at the granary, the one I'd worked magic through, turned a skeleton face to me, held out a skeleton hand, and when I gripped it to bring the rain, his bones shattered to dust. I *reached* for my power, but something blocked me, like at the warehouse with the *thing* the boys had summoned.

The inferno consumed *me*—blood, bone, and soul— then devoured the rest of the granary buildings and spread to the warehouses and then to the houses beyond. The dark goddess *tugged* at the thread between us, and it was no longer a thread but a scorching chain with links as large as my hand, wrapping around me—

"Sumi?"

I jerked awake, found myself floating in the sky above the Rest Third, but it was razed to the ground, buildings collapsed and bodies smoldering in the streets, and I looked farther, and it was the same in the Blessed Third and in the Damned. The city burned. Everyone I knew and loved was gone.

And I *rolled* in the power their deaths had given me— I was a *goddess*— and I *laughed*.

"Sumi!"

Fiery hands gripped my arms and I drew up all my power, ready to strike.

"Sumi!"

Jay— bless it, that was *Jay*. Alive!

I *yanked* my power back and *pushed* it down deep inside me—

And finally woke for real this time, hunched over in the bed I shared with my beloved. Jay knelt beside me, his hands on my arms. In the faint light from the window, his eyes were wide and his breaths shallow.

Goddessi, I could have killed him.

That realization had me jerking out of his grip and off the bed. My muscles protested— yesterday and the day before had been brutal— but my back merely twinged and let me keep going, so I did. Walked out of our room into the main room, trying to control my breathing.

Scrubbing at the black, black tattoos on my red skin.

I could have killed him.

My throat closed and I couldn't breathe.

Jay slipped past me, his footsteps silent. Like he was hunting. Wordlessly, he held out a cup. Without touching his skin, I took it.

I could have killed *him.*

The water jug tipped in my hand, aimed for the cup. Only a trickle. My knuckles whitened. It took all my control not to throw the jug. Instead I carefully set it down. Raised the cup to my lips and swallowed that trickle. Set the cup down. Scrubbed at my arms.

Jay stepped close. Murmured in my ear, "I am your *Shadow*."

Ah, goddessi. My feet paused.

I'd put *shields* on him. My magic wouldn't touch him. I *couldn't* have killed him. I could have done some serious damage to the house, could have brought Maldita down on us all, but *I wouldn't have killed him.*

The shakes started deep inside and worked their way out and out until my whole body trembled like a leaf in the wind.

"Something wrong?" Mouse whispered from the ladder.

"Sorry. Everything's fine. You can go back to sleep." I lifted quivering hands and rubbed my face. Felt the dark goddess's brands on my skin. Would the dark be enough to hide them?

Mouse smirked, her teeth glinting in the faint light from the shuttered windows. "Wasn't sleeping." She waited, then— "Don't look fine."

Jay watched me as if I would break into a thousand-thousand pieces.

Everyone else slept.

My shakes slowly subsided until just my fingers trembled.

"Bad dreams," I admitted hoarsely. Mouse wasn't screaming, so the tattoos on my face, my arms, my hands, must have faded. "Can't sleep."

"Usually easier *in* bed."

"Right." No. Not now. I might end up in the same bad dream, and this time not wake until I'd actually used my magic... *flames, blood*— "Really bad dreams. One of those weird ones where you wake up, but you're in another dream and you don't know what's real."

"I get that." The girl came a few steps down the ladder and perched, wrapping a blanket around herself a little tighter. She'd lived on the streets— she must have bad dreams of her own. And she was here, talking.

Something about the dark, the middle of the night, softened the reality of it, like the blanket around Mouse's shoulders. The girl had likely done bad things to survive— not as bad as I had, but it wasn't a contest.

And Jay, listening.

I could tell him, under the guise of talking to her.

"I— I thought—" I sucked in a deep breath. What bothered me most about the dream within a dream? Feeling Maldita inside me. "Bad memories."

"Yeah?" Mouse rested her chin in her hands, yellow skin on yellow skin. "Regrets?"

"Many. So many things I could have done better. Choices I made." What if I'd run away? To the south, to the City of Elementals and become a demon hunter myself, or north, where Yssa had come from, though if they'd found out I had magic, they'd have sent me right back here, just like they did with Yssa. What if I'd never fallen in love with Jay? Never left the damned temple?

Mouse interrupted my musing. "You had choices?"

"Sometimes." I snorted. "Or at least, I thought I did."

"Better than none at all."

"Sure. I guess." My knees wanted to give out. I made it to the wall, then slid down. Wrapped my arms around my knees. "Except then it's a bad choice or a worse choice."

"Survival." Mouse ducked her head and her voice sounded strange. Was she crying? I couldn't tell in the dark.

"Survival," I agreed. "Someday I hope to stop just surviving and learn to thrive."

"Yeah." The word dragged out of her like I'd pulled it from between her clenched teeth. The dark softened again, in our silence. Until her words sharpened it into cutting blades. "But don't you ever wish—"

"Wishing doesn't do any good."

"But—"

"No."

Mouse stared at me. The house creaked around us. Dee turned over in her bed and grumbled in her sleep.

Mouse said softly, "There's a woman who can get rid of memories."

"What?"

"Memories. She takes them away. Magically."

Jay made a small noise of protest, and if I hadn't already been sitting, I'd have fallen. A woman who removed memories... "Does she? Outside a temple?"

"She's not a priestess." Mouse shifted, then caught her blanket before it fell. "Can you imagine...? Not remembering? Remaking yourself into someone new?"

Her eyes found mine in the dark and the sheer *need* burned me. Goddessi, she was young—

"You should come with me," she half-begged. "We could do it together. Forget the names my father called me. Forget the guard who—" Her voice hitched, then steadied. "Forget everything we didn't like!"

I shut my eyes.

"That's enough," Jay whispered harshly. Bless it, he'd read my pain in the lines of my muscles. He knew me too well.

"No, it's all right. She asked a true question..." I gnawed at my lip, then leaned forward to ease the pinch in my lower back. "She deserves a true answer. At least as true as I can give."

Jay came to me, nudged me forward, then slid between me and the wall. His warmth surrounded me, shocked me, and I realized how chilled my arms were, despite the warmth of the night. I snuggled against his chest and wrapped him around me like my own living blanket.

"All the things that have been done to me in the name of the blessed—" the things my blood-mother had done, and those under her command while I was in the blessed temple — "and all the things that have been done to me in the name of the damned—" the damned high priestess and my blood-sisters, and all those who opposed me, tormented me — "and all the things I've done myself, even the worst things..." *As* a priestess, as the high priestess... My voice faltered and my throat wanted to close again, but I forced the words out. I had to give Mouse the truth she demanded of me, here in the dark. "The memories of each of those things *made* me. I am *me* and I make the choices I make now because of them."

"A nobody in the Rest Third?" Scorn dripped.

Jay's arms tightened briefly, then loosened when I squeaked.

A nobody? Yes— for the first time in my life, free of blood, free of duty. I grinned. "I have Jay. And our boys. There is no place in the world I would rather be."

"Not rich? In the Temple of the Damned? Not in the Temple of the Blessed?"

"No. I've been in temples and didn't much care for them. This is my haven. This is my joy." Now I stared at her as intensely as she'd stared at me. "*You* are who you are because of what you've survived, and I *like* the person you are. I can't stop you from ripping away your memories, but I can encourage you to be careful. You don't know what an untrained magic-user could do to you."

Mouse sat and stared through the darkness at us for a long moment. Then she turned and went up the ladder.

She would hear me, or she wouldn't. I'd done what I could.

Most of the ghost of my nightmare had gone. I wriggled free of Jay's embrace and rose to my feet. Held out my hands and when he took them, leaned back, trying to heft him to his feet.

He stubbornly stayed seated, and my back didn't twinge. I pulled. He chuckled under his breath at me and let me haul him up. I towed him to our bedroom and dropped his hands to close the door behind us.

He climbed into our bed, still clothed. Moonlight cast highlights and shadows onto his face, his neck, and I reached out to touch him, to remind myself he was real.

I hadn't killed him, like I'd dreamt. Hadn't hurt him, hadn't burned down the city.

Hadn't become the dark goddess.

My hands tugged at his sleep shirt. Thin as it was, I needed it off, needed to trace the hard muscles.

He grinned and obliged.

I crawled in beside him. Closed my eyes and let my fingers roam his shoulders, his arms, the planes of his chest.

"Easy," he said, and caught my hands. "We've had a couple hard days. I don't want to hurt you."

My back still didn't twinge. "You won't." I shifted until I could hear his heart thudding. *Alive, alive, alive,* it beat.

"Sumi—"

I drew my hands free. "I need you to love me—"

"I do." He pressed a kiss to the top of my head.

"Let me love you, make love with you." I stretched, kissed his lovely brown skin. "I *need* to. I'm plenty well enough and it will chase away the nightmares."

He drew back. "I just want you to be healthy."

He wanted me— I felt it, so I followed, and nibbled. This

time, I wouldn't shrink, wouldn't let him turn me away out of fear. "I *am* healthy."

His breathing changed and his fingers dug into my hips. "Are you sure?" he managed raggedly. "I won't hurt you?"

"I am so sure." But I wouldn't force him— not ever. "Unless you don't want *me*."

"I want you." His mouth found mine. His fingers slid up under my shirt, leaving hot trails of pleasure. "I *want* you."

"Stop wasting time then." I wriggled halfway out of my shirt, then got stuck. "Help!"

He laughed. "Maybe I like you stuck." He hefted me up, then lowered his mouth to my skin.

Every touch ignited fire in me— not dark fire, not Maldita's fire— but clean, wonderful tingles and blazes that didn't hurt anyone, and I reveled in it, molded myself to him, finally freed my hands. Slid them to what I needed to hold onto.

"I missed you. I— Oh!" His mouth hit a sensitive spot and my toes curled.

"Missed you too. Let me show you how much."

Jay

DAWN WOKE HIM, AND HE FOUND HIS WOMAN STILL SNUGGLED UP TO him, skin to skin. Her hair splayed across her pillow, so he buried his face in the nape of her neck. "Sumi," he breathed.

She turned. Her lips found his in the dark, and he tasted the sweetness of her mouth, the salt of her tears.

"Why are you crying?"

"I'm just so lucky. To have this. To have you." Her fingers found him.

His blood roared in his ears. Had to taste her skin, everywhere his mouth could reach. He sank into the feel of her, the taste of her, still a little careful, until she drove him wild with her mouth. Then he used his knowledge of her to bring her every pleasure— sate her, and himself.

When they were exhausted, he curled his fingers in hers. "A drink?" he asked.

"Yes please."

He rose and slipped on his oldest, softest pair of pants, only suitable for pajamas. Closed the bedroom door behind him, then sent the boys on two errands— first, to the other children, to tell them there would be no lessons today, then to the guardhouse, to tell Thom there would be no trainer today.

He grinned, thinking about the old man's expression.

But he hadn't taken time off work since he'd returned from the damned temple, so the guards would survive without him.

The boys went, and after casting a knowing smirk, Mouse followed. Jay drank, drank again, then filled the cup a third time and took it back to Sumi. Closed the door between them and the rest of the house.

"You aren't leaving?"

"Sent the boys to tell everyone we'd be... unavailable... today."

She blushed, hard to see in the pre-dawn light, but he knew her shades of red, and he saw. "They'll all know exactly what we're doing."

He chuckled. "I want to spend some time with you." Handed her the cup and watched her as the room slowly brightened around them. The tilt of her head as she drank from his cup, the line of her neck in the sun—

He waited for her to finish drinking, then took the cup away. Nibbled at her fingertips.

Her eyes brightened. "Like that, is it?"

"I'm hungry."

"Then—"

The boys clattered in the front door, obviously trying to be quiet from their exaggerated whispers. Failing.

Sumi broke into helpless giggles.

Jay sighed. "They do take the romance out of the moment, don't they? Wait here, if you can."

He stepped into the main room. "Food," he said as he gave the boys enough money for breakfast. "We're hungry and I'm sure you are too. Fresh bread, meat pockets, fruit, vegetables— anything your mom likes."

Wil grinned and snatched the money, Andy nodded sharply, then they were both gone again.

The mood had broken, and he wanted to feed Sumi before they tumbled into each other again, so he sat across from her on the bed. Stroked along her thigh, avoiding the shadows of her tattoos. Imagining them— he was just imagining those shadows. "Are you all right? You look better."

"I am." Her eyes cut down and away— not telling him the whole truth.

He waited.

Finally she sighed. "I *am* better," she insisted. "Doing—" she lowered her voice— "what I did with the magus... it felt so good. To use a part of me I'd cut off. And I checked— everyone felt *him* not *me*, so we're safe. The boys are safe, and you're safe—"

He caught her hand and brought it to his heart. "I am safe." They boys too— they knew what to watch for, in the market. He could trust them there and back, even if it did cause a pinch of anxiety to let them go alone. Carefully he continued, "I'm glad the... using your skill felt good. I'm glad you were safe. But it ate you up, what you did."

With a thoughtful frown, she nodded. "It did. It's different, doing *that* without the goddess. I've been away so long—"

"You regret it?"

"No!" She leaned forward and rested her head atop their joined hands. "Never. You've given me freedom. Peace."

"But—"

"No." She looked up at him. "I just wish they'd all go away— the demon hunters, the priestessi... not the guards, I suppose—"

"*Much* harder to eat when no one gets paid."

She dimpled at him, then sobered. "I just love being with you. With no interruptions—"

Somehow, sooner than it should have been possible, the boys came swarming in the front door. Sumi laughed. "No interruptions other than our family," she finished.

"I love being with you too," he said softly. Cupped her cheeks. Stared at her to re-memorize every line of her face, the shades of her skin, the fire in her eyes.

Something thumped to the floor and the boys cursed.

Sumi pinched her eyes shut in despair, but a laugh quirked at the corner of her mouth.

He rose and went out to the main room and she followed after him, her hand tucked into the small of his back so he would feel her with him.

Andy swiped a bunch of carrots off the floor and held them up with his most charming grin. Wil paused, broom in hand.

At least they were trying to clean up after themselves.

While Sumi directed the sweeping, Jay took the carrots and rinsed them in the last of the drinking water, then set the buckets next to the front door.

Two identical sighs met him when he turned around to look at the boys, but with better humor than he'd expected, they picked up the buckets and were gone again.

They'd found a decent variety at the market— a fresh loaf of bread, a small block of cheese, the earliest harvests. Jay set the carrots next to the rest, then fetched a plate. He took up his knife and cut. First red peppers, collecting the seeds for the boys to plant in broken cups over the winter, then carrots, a small cucumber, then slices of cheese.

Behind the rest, his questing fingers found a mango.

Small, not quite ripe by the feel of it, but close enough. He hefted it, remembered how the damned kitchen staff had taught him how to skin it, cut the seed out, score the flesh.

Sumi's eyes fastened on the fruit in his hands almost as greedily as they had focused on him when they were loving each other.

He arranged the slices on the plate. Placed one in her mouth.

She bit down and closed her eyes. Moaned quietly.

Heat surged through his body. He grinned— worth it.

More quickly now, he dumped berries into the remaining spaces, tore off pieces of bread and tossed them on top. Left the rest for the boys, then picked up the plate he'd arranged and held out one hand.

She placed her hand in his.

He led her to their bedroom and closed the door behind him.

Fed her.

Watched her expressions, teased her with sour cheese when she expected mango, or berries when she expected bread.

Like making love.

When the plate had emptied, he set it out of the way. Pulled her to her feet, then ran his fingers from her temples, over her cheeks to her chin, then down to her collar bones. Teased her lips with his.

Someone knocked at the front door.

Sumi frowned and tipped her head to the side. Looked resigned. She knew who it was, and somehow she had an idea what they wanted. That fast— somehow she knew.

Fear smashed into him. She'd used her magic so casually, as if no one would notice, no one would come looking for her. He latched on to her hand. Checked her eyes.

Red and white. Not blood lid to lid and not black.

Not the goddess.

Resting betweens, his heart couldn't take losing her again, and if she lost her caution about her magic, he would lose her. The goddess would find her, or the priestessi, or—

"It's all right." She moved closer, nestled up against him, rested her cheek on his chest. "Whatever you're thinking, it will be all right."

He touched his chin to the top of her head. *Will it?*

A breath later, the knock came at their bedroom door. Still holding Sumi, he reached out. Opened it.

Mal stood *inside* their house, looking apologetic. "Sorry, Sir. Head Guard's orders. He needs you at the guardhouse."

Jay looked past him at Robin.

"You let him in?"

She shrugged.

"Sir—"

"Why should I?" Jay demanded. Sumi tried to ease away, but he clutched her tighter. "Why should I give up my time with my family?"

"Sir." Mal rubbed the back of his neck. "He said to tell you he needs all your training records immediately. There's an audit. From the Rest Third Council. We *need* you."

"Thom is *on* the Council," Jay muttered. "He runs the resting thing. Why—?"

Mal shifted on his feet, uncomfortable.

"Go." Sumi extracted herself from his arms. When he

looked, the corner of her mouth quirked up like she was amused. "We had a good morning. The best. Go do your job."

Jay scowled even harder.

She rose up on her tip toes and kissed him, then slipped away before he could hold her. "Go," she said with a grin.

Jay huffed and glared and closed the door to Mal, but he slowly dressed in his grays, belted on his swords, slung the flying carpet at his back. Kissed her again as if she were air and he was drowning.

"I'll be home as soon as I can," he said loudly to the whole house.

And went.

TWENTY-SIX

S umi

JAY DISAPPEARED TO THE GUARDHOUSE FOR THE REST OF THE DAY, ALL night, and most of the next day. He finally came home at sunset, looking as if he hadn't slept that entire time and muttering about how Thom had tricked him by asking only for his own records at first and then all of the records for all the Rest Third Guards.

He slumped down at the table, and the boys fell on him for brief hugs. Then disappeared into their bedroom before he could send them for water again, whispering together as they often did, and Mouse descended to perch on the couch and mend a torn shirt. The girl's stitches were coming along, but she wasn't actually mending— she'd forgotten a needle and instead measured and remeasured the tear, while staring at Jay.

"Dinner?" I asked neutrally. Poor kid had only had a short time to get used to us returning the way we said we would. The way she acted each time Jay came home, her blood-family hadn't been as trustworthy.

"Haven't eaten yet," Jay grunted. "Left before he could give me any more tasks."

I brought him a split roll with a bit of fat scraped over it and mutton slices laid in the middle, took a second to Mouse, since she was always hungry, and sat down with one of my own.

Three bites in, Mal showed up *again*, knocking politely on the front door. He handed me a piece of paper— not parchment — and retreated to the edge of the yard.

It had to be for Jay.

I set the paper on the table, where Jay watched it like it was a poisonous spider. At length, Jay unfolded the paper, glanced at me, then shoved it across. It said,

Broken Sword Pub

Tonight, dusk

Both of you.

I flicked my best baffled look at him.

"A job," he explained. "Sanctioned by the Rest Third Guard." He ran his hand over his hair. "Probably not one we're going to like, or he'd have given us more details."

"Thom *knows* the details?"

"He should, or he wouldn't sanction it. Though—" he hesitated, then frowned— "for enough money he might be persuaded not to ask."

"*Thom?*" I had a hard time reconciling the Head of the Rest Third Guard with a man who could be bribed... but when I remembered he was also a son of the Yulian Merchants, it made more sense. "Right. Thom. So?"

Jay glanced at Mouse, then shrugged. "I just got home. We turn it down."

I dropped my gaze. What kind of job would Thom send to us? Especially when he had one of his guards following Jay everywhere? When he suspected me of being the lost high priestess? Curiosity gnawed at my stomach.

Jay laughed. "You want to go, don't you."

"No. You're tired." I pressed my lips together to hide a small smile. He knew me too well. "You need to rest."

Jay peeked outside. "Eat fast," he told me, his eyes brightening. "I'm not *that* tired. Though if we're late, our prospective employer will give up, and then we won't have to worry about it."

I crammed my meat pocket into my mouth and washed it down as quickly as I could without choking, then found my least tattered shirt and changed and added a knife—since it was a job. A little eating knife, easily concealed. While Jay waited for me, he talked with Maggie, then she disappeared out back, and I wondered what he'd asked her to do.

He crouched to meet Mouse's gaze. "We'll be back."

She pressed her lips together and looked away, but she was fighting a smile.

We walked through a city lit by sunset, followed by Mal, and hurried by my curiosity. A job for *us*—

The Broken Sword Pub was dim, and Jay hesitated at the door, but the handle turned under his fingers, so he stepped inside. Mal nodded to me from an alcove across the street, oblivious to Maggie perched above him on the roof.

Suddenly I wondered if my curiosity was about to get us both killed.

All the more reason not to let Jay go in there alone.

I stepped into the shadows. The pub owner handed Jay a lamp, shook his head dolefully, and climbed the stairs, his feet sure and soft in the darkness. Another lamp sat at a table pushed to the wall, occupied by a shadowy figure in a cloak.

If I used my magic, I could tear away that cloak and reveal

our prospective employer, or I could light all the lamps and lanterns, or—

The hair on the back of my neck rose. I surreptitiously looked into every shadow, but saw nothing. Magic surged inside me, ready to show me who might be hidden there, waiting to hurt us. I soothed it down, surprised it had so quickly grown strong again.

"A job," Jay muttered under his breath. He was nervous too. "The Broken Sword doesn't close for *just a job.*"

There was no real reason to believe it was a trap, but I agreed with my beloved— this wasn't *just a job.* My magic surged again and I nearly lost it. Damned tattoos rose under my skin. I shuddered, forced myself to breathe evenly. Carefully, quietly, I let the tiniest trickle of power *reach* around us, *feel* for anyone using *push* or *pull* magic nearby.

Nothing.

But my insides calmed enough I could focus again, and the tattoos no one else could see faded.

Jay watched me, waiting. I nodded.

Jay held the lamp up and we sauntered to the table as if we were the ones in charge.

The man at the table shoved his hood back.

Enzo.

Without magic, I was the weaker of the two of us— Jay was the guard. I should slide onto the bench, trap myself between the wall and the table and let Jay sit at the end, but I couldn't. My body *wouldn't.* And my magic was rising again, ready to defend me.

So instead I went to a table in the middle of the room, chose a chair and sat down. Saw the faint smile on Jay's lips as he sat next to me, leaving Enzo the choice to shout across the room or join us and sit with his back to the door.

He huffed. Joined us.

Point to us.

I wished I had a cup to wrap my fingers around, but I wouldn't eat or drink with this man... and the bartender had gone anyway. So I drew my knife, then laid it in my lap where the demon hunter couldn't see it. Kept my hands out of view. An insult and a threat at the same time.

Jay and I were silent, waiting.

Finally, when the silence had gone on too long, Enzo said, "Thank you for coming." His lips twisted. "And staying."

Point to us.

Still, I kept quiet, *feeling* for Old Magic. He'd have to say the words, make the sound, gesture—

I was almost disappointed that he kept his hands up above the table, as manners required. Enzo reached back to his belt, then tossed a bag of coins on the table. The top was loose enough to let gold spill out onto the rough wood. "For meeting me," he said, placing his fingertips together as a promise that he wouldn't magic us.

What was with everyone paying us lately? Though this would be no innocent job from an old friend. Between Lena and Enzo, we'd have enough to buy house repairs and food and weapons for *years*.

In the Rest Third. It was nothing in the Damned.

Jay growled. "And?"

The man smiled, wrinkles etching the corners of his orange eyes. "And for not killing me during this little discussion."

My hand tightened around the knife. It was going to be one of *those* discussions.

Jay left the money on the table. Did it hurt him to do so?

The demon hunters had tried to kill me in the damned temple, and this man had hounded me throughout the Rest Third. I let my irritation stain my voice. "What do you want?"

Enzo leaned forward. "How did you do it?"

"Do what?" Live in the Rest Third? Escape the temple? Avoid the demon hunters?

"Get it out of you?"

"Get—?"

"The demon."

Reflexively, I froze. Waited for Maldita to come and fill me with Her anger. The thread inside me that tied me to Her hummed, but nothing else happened.

Jay snorted. "The new high priestess ripped the dark goddess out."

I hid a wince. Not *entirely* true.

"But you shouldn't have survived." Enzo sounded aggrieved. The man really didn't like me. "No one has ever survived the removal of a demon."

Jay half drew his sword.

I put my hand on his arm, and he let his sword slide back into its sheath. Did likewise with my knife. Bared blades wouldn't help this discussion. "The dark goddess killed your father as soon as I touched him. She took him, blood, bone, and soul."

Enzo's hands clenched into fists on the table, then he forced them to relax. "She did not get his soul. He was pure and for his sacrifice went to the heavens."

Right. The dark goddess hadn't hesitated— *pure* soul or not. I doubted Enzo would believe me. And by the way his eyes bored into mine, he *needed* to know what had happened like I needed to hide from Maldita.

Pity swelled up inside me. The man *believed* so terribly hard. He didn't understand that we of the City of Temples would fight him because his holy war didn't *matter*. They were our goddessi, and he couldn't have them. Or us.

"Maldita took him and became more powerful. What he did wasn't enough to get Her out of me." My mouth was dry, my hands trembled. "My— the new high priestess *pulled* the dark goddess from me. And Maldita decided She liked her better."

Now Jay covered my hand with his. His touch allowed me to force the words out. I tasted bitterness on my tongue, but my life was better now. "Maldita betrayed me. She went to the new high priestess and tried to take *me*, blood, bone, and soul."

"She— *it*— tried to kill you?"

"She tried to take my soul. I used a spell to kill myself, rather than be taken."

Enzo stared at me, his mouth open in shock. "You— but—"

"Jay brought me back."

"But the demon should have been vulnerable during that transition. Any hunter could have killed it."

My insides churned. "No. You had plenty of them there to try, and none even noticed."

Enzo scowled. Absently, he picked up a gold coin and flipped it through his fingers. "So transferring the demon from you while you still lived... it tried to take you, probably to gain power..."

The man spoke like I was nothing, no one important, an anomaly to be understood and swept out of the way.

Jay's hand warmed mine, and the reminder of what he'd done for me, what we'd been through together, settled me. *He* settled me.

Enzo leaned back, and the coin moved between his bony orange fingers as if by magic. "But it didn't get you. You... *tricked* it. So it's *possible* to remove the thing without killing the host."

I swallowed hard. He needed to stop trying to kill people. My blood-family included, even if they hated me. "Killing the host *won't* kill the dark goddess."

He stared at me and the coin fell.

"Killing the host won't kill the demon." He pressed his

361

fingers to his forehead. "But our records say demons are vulnerable without their host. Killing the host is the easiest way."

"The *easy* way. Do you hear yourself?" Jay intertwined his fingers in mine. "Killing someone is the *easy* way? You're as bad as the goddessi."

Enzo flinched.

Then he leaned forward, hands spread wide on the table. "This is why we need you. You know it, you've been a host to it. You can tell us so much."

"No."

He rose and paced, his hands waving. "You get us the histories from the Temple of the Blessed. Everything from the Rest Third families has been worthless—"

"Worthless?" Jay lurched up. "You burned the granary as nothing more than a *distraction*. You could have killed someone. And anyone who starves next winter, are they worthless?"

Enzo stared, intense. "The downfall of one demon is worth the lives of everyone in this city."

"Why kill a demon—" I said under my breath— "if you don't save the people?"

He didn't hear me. Waved his arms. "We get the spell from the blessed histories and then we can kill the demons—"

"No!"

"Or maybe we can send them back to where they came from—"

"I'm not helping you!" I half rose, my knife in hand, and my magic swelling inside me. "Why should I? You burned our granary— and tried to kill me!"

Enzo's orange eyes burned fervently. "To be rid of the demon forever!"

Blessed zealot.

I shifted back onto my heels, as if I didn't mean to attack

him. Lied with my voice and my expression. "I'm already rid of Her."

First he looked like I'd struck him, then his face settled into grim lines. "You won't help us."

"That's what I've been telling you."

"Won't help us free you." He didn't believe me.

That was fine— I didn't believe him, either. "Don't lie now and say you care about us."

"Won't give us the key to saving your soul."

Nope. "My soul. My choice."

He pointed one clawed finger at me. "You'll see. You *will* help us. You'll see."

I folded my arms. Studied *fanatic* as if I could cure it. Maybe Viktra, the healer priestess of the damned could. Not me.

Enzo pointed at me again and this time his mouth gaped open and shut, open and shut. Then he spun, knocking over a chair, and stomped out of the pub.

Jay scowled after him like he was thinking of sticking his sword into Enzo's back.

My stomach still twisted, and I wondered what the man would do now that he was desperate, but I couldn't think that way. Couldn't read his mind.

Could distract Jay's anger. I cleared my throat. "Good thing he had that cloak to swirl dramatically around himself, yes?"

Jay snorted.

Almost... "We didn't kill him, so we get the money, right?"

Jay smiled crookedly, and his honey-colored eyes brightened in the lamplight. He scooped up the coins, then held out his hand. "Let's go home, love."

Jay

. . .

Mal followed them home. The boy wasn't even being subtle about it, hovering out of sword range but not out of bow or knife range. Audits all last night and all this morning and all afternoon and then this *job offer* from Enzo— Jay's temper snapped.

"Head home," he told Sumi, with a kiss on the cheek. "I have something to take care of."

She followed his glare and sighed a bit. Nodded. "Good luck."

Jay watched her disappear into the rapidly thinning crowds being chased off by the evening. Spun. Marched over to the boy and grabbed him by the ear. "The guardhouse," he snapped.

Towed him for three steps, then realized that one guard dragging the other along like a recalcitrant child was not the best image for the Rest Third Guards. Released the ear and snarled at him to march.

Out of habit, Mal fell into step. One of the good things about being a guard trainer— the trainees had a habit of obedience.

Even if they didn't respect him anymore and followed him around like he was some sort of spy for the enemy.

Another block in and Jay caught Mal touching the edge of his carpet. Cursed himself. He'd been so used to the old ways, he'd forgotten they were both carrying the resting things. "Fine," he snapped, replying to Mal's gesture. "We can fly."

The boy shot him a half-grin, then unrolled and had himself loaded on his carpet before Jay could even take the one off his own back.

Jay snorted. Newer wasn't always better... but the carpet would save them time and sweat. He climbed onto his own, twitched the tassels, rose into the sky. Mal joined him, and— as always— flying pallets yielded to guard-gray carpets. They flew to the guardhouse four times faster than they could have made it on foot.

Jay took his time descending, then re-rolling his carpet. He'd hoped Mal would disappear once they'd arrived, but no luck. The Red boy slung his carpet over his back, then anxiously hovered.

I'm not going to run away. Jay wanted to roll his eyes at the boy, but other guards were watching— and the boy didn't deserve their disrespect any more than he deserved Jay's. He was just following orders.

So Jay climbed the steps and went through the doors. He paused to check over the guards as they practiced, then— catching Mal's panicked look— finally climbed the stairs to Thom's office.

He knocked as if *he* had requested this meeting instead of the Head Guard— loud, confident.

"Come."

Jay did as he was bid, and found Thom alone, behind his desk. The old man continued writing whatever he was writing.

Ignored him long enough to ignite his temper again.

Finally he snapped, "I know you know."

Thom set his paper aside and looked up as if just noticing him. "Care to be more specific?"

"I don't know what you're playing at, trying to keep me away from her, sending word all you needed were my training records, then setting me on the whole resting job of copying over every resting record for the last five years—"

"You write well!" Thom protested. "The Council requested—"

"You're *on* the resting Council!"

"Someone had to do it! And if you didn't, *I* would have."

"Better me than you?" Jay demanded.

"Indeed. You work for me. Get your pay from me—"

He unclenched his jaw. "So what about sending us out on a *demon hunter* job?"

Thom flinched. "I didn't know—"

"Liar." Jay leaned over the desk. Lowered his voice. "You know who Sumi is. Was. And that's exactly why you sent us on that job."

Thom stared at him, narrow-eyed. "And what gives you that idea?"

"Only the lost high priestess has any chance to do what they're asking. And then there's Maggie. The girl isn't great about keeping secrets, spy on the demon hunters or not. And if she knows, you know. But sending that—" No word was harsh enough— "resting *shit* to us, to threaten us? How could you?"

The Head of the Rest Third Guard— and that was who now sat in the chair, not Thom the family friend— somehow looked down his nose at Jay, though Jay loomed over him. "I knew you would get it out of him. What he really wanted."

"Really."

"So? What did he hire you for?"

Jay scowled. "We didn't take the job.

"Good. So?"

"Why should I tell you?"

"I'm not the enemy, boy."

"You're forgetting who the enemy actually is."

"And who is that?"

"The demon hunters."

"Is that so? Last I checked, they weren't doing whatever it was you did in the Stonefield warehouse to cause the blessed *and* the damned to come into my Third of the city."

"That's not your business."

Thom lurched to his feet, jaw clenched. He spun to the window Jay had never seen open. Threw open the shutters. "Look," he hissed. "Look at *my business*."

Jay glanced. Thom's window looked over the Rest Third toward the river. He raised his eyebrows in mute question.

"The Rest Third," Thom barked. "The Rest Third and this city are *my* business. You put us all in danger."

"It was contained." Jay's heart thundered, remembering the cold and the darkness. But the boys had *pushed* it back. "What happened will never happen again."

"How am I to know that? Since you won't resting *tell* me?"

"I'm telling you now." Jay shuffled. Uncomfortably rubbed one hand over his face. "What about the granary? That was more a threat than the warehouse. People could have been killed. Our supplies—"

"I'm *working* on the demon hunters," Thom growled. "But I have to split my attention because one of my guard trainers is harboring a woman who could flatten the city. And won't tell me what's going on."

"It wasn't—" Jay stopped. Even worse if Thom thought the boys were the threat. "It wasn't like that," he finished vaguely. "We were just trying to find Cori."

"One little girl." Thom looked out his window. From this angle, his hair was all grayed-blue. "I have the entire Rest Third to worry about."

Jay shook his head. "She's not just one little girl. She's our neighbor, and our boys' friend. And she's important too. One little girl who is the *world* to her mother."

"The sheer numbers of people you put in danger—"

"I don't have it in me." Jay staggered to Thom's chair and sank into it. Two days straight without sleep and he couldn't stay upright any longer. "I can't think in numbers. What matters are the people who need my help *now*."

"I know." Thom left the shutters open and returned to his own chair. He moved stiffly. His arthritis acting up?

"If you can't be a hero for that one little girl," Jay demanded, "then what good is any of it?"

"That... I'm not sure I know anymore." Thom ran his hand over the wood of his desk, toyed with a pen. "But everyone out there is someone's world. Someone's little girl or someone's sister or brother or mother or father or cousin. Someone's world."

"And Sumi and her boys are mine."

"Where do your loyalties lie, boy?"

Jay tried to stand. Collapsed back into the lovely soft chair. "You know the answer to that. I've made it plain."

"Remind me."

"My *loyalties*—" Jay leaned forward. Dredged up his fury and thrust it into Thom's face like a sword— "lie with my beloved. My boys. My sisters. My family, just like they always have." He shifted back. Rolled his shoulders. "After my family, the guards."

Thom nodded but Jay wasn't done.

"Something Sumi taught me— you know, the woman you don't trust because of where she lived a year ago—"

Thom shook his head. "Who she was," he corrected softly.

"Resting betweens. She's the same person she was then. Just making different choices."

"Our choices *define* who we are."

"Yeah. They do."

He and Thom used the same words, but they seemed to mean opposite things. He fumbled for what he'd been saying before. "She taught me that my loyalties also lie with this city. This is *my* city, the whole resting thing. Those people you were just explaining to me. The ones who are someone's world. They're *my* people. So long as they don't try to kill my wife or my kids, I will do my best for them. And that includes protecting them from the demon hunters... and their allies."

Thom looked out the window again. Ran a hand over his face, rubbed the stubble on his jaw. "All right."

Jay waited, but Thom remained silent. What patience he had left deserted him. "What does that mean? You're firing me? Or you're going to trust me a little and reassign Mal?"

Thom sighed. "Son—"

"I haven't been a son to you since Mom died and you stopped coming around."

Thom suddenly looked old and tired. "Since I figured out who your woman was. And then you lied to me about her."

Jay bowed his head, just enough to imply respect. "Maybe I made a mistake there," he admitted carefully. "I'm asking you to trust me. Even if I didn't trust you."

Thom stared down at his desk. Vented a heavy sigh. "I'll pull Mal off your tail."

"Thank you." Resting betweens, now he had to get himself up. Get home.

Thom watched him, guilt around his eyes.

No— Jay refused to feel sorry for the old man. He'd made his choices. He heaved himself up, staggered, straightened.

Thundered back down the stairs and out into the courtyard. Fumbled for his carpet.

Flew home to where his beloved and his kids waited for him.

CHAPTER
TWENTY-SEVEN

S *umi*

THIS MORNING I COULDN'T KEEP A SILLY SMILE OFF MY FACE, DESPITE the early hour, despite the demon hunters, despite the blessed and the damned and the goddessi or demoni or whatever they were. Jay had made it home last night and slept like the dead, but this morning he had nudged me awake and made sure I felt cherished in all the best ways.

About blessed time.

The boys had been tutoring some of the neighbor children, the rest of the kids were coming along nicely, and one mom had sent us a jar of jam— I couldn't wait to try it. Jay had gone to fetch fresh bread from the market so we could have bread and jam to break our fast, and we would be harvesting from our gardens later.

Finally— *finally!*— everything was sorting itself out. We'd had our little confrontation with Enzo; now he should believe us and leave us alone. Jay and I were good, and his sisters knew the truth about me, and Maggie was actually *thinking* instead of just reacting.

The air was cooler this morning, though it would still be hot this afternoon. Fall came on stealthy feet, reminding me of one of the exotic cats we'd had at the damned temple. Mouse had been shivering in the breeze, so I'd sent her up to the kids' room to read, but the sun-warmed air would soon be comfortable enough, and she'd be down to join us in the yard where I was holding class. Cori knew her numbers already, and was pulling weeds while Wil and Andy recited their lessons, and Kass was head-down over his slate. Tara and Nathy hadn't come to class today, but with harvest on the way, some days their free time was short.

"Numbers now," I said.

They erased their slates and even smiled. I hoped they'd never forget how to learn; I could teach them *what* to learn, but *how* to learn would carry them all their lives—

"Sumi!" From across the street, Suann's voice, high and terrified.

I looked up. In the street, a converging mob.

I jerked to my feet, wondering if I could get the children into the house.

The mob came on, tramped into my yard and across my garden, surrounded us, and it was too late.

Demon hunters in their motley clothes, mostly Oranges and Yellows, the one who had been following me, but a few people of the Rest Third too, in plain shirts and pants as tired as their eyes. Twenty, maybe thirty strangers, but a woman near the back who'd sold me soap.

And walking next to Enzo, Green Nydia, as if she and the leader of the demon hunters were the best of friends.

Suann came out of her house, sprinted for Cori, but Nydia

held up a commanding hand. Two men in motley grabbed Suann and held her back. She went to her knees, keening.

Tears welled up in Cori's eyes and tumbled down her cheeks and sparkled in the golden light.

Nydia had betrayed us.

Like all the past betrayals— the damned priestessi, my blood-sisters... my blood-mother. I ignored my twisting guts, made an effort to unclench my fists. "Nydia?"

She lifted her chin. "How *dare* you come here? Pretend to be one of us? Try to steal our children away from us?"

"I never—"

Nydia hissed. "They told us who you are."

She knows.

Tara and Nathy absent this morning and the door to Nydia and Dansy's house shut tight and the windows shuttered— suddenly made sense.

My hands started to shake. I pressed them against my legs to hide the tremors. Magic swelled inside me.

Enzo stepped between me and Wil and Andy.

The shaking intensified.

He lifted his hands and I almost attacked then, but I saw he was prepping a spell— Old Magic— and I hesitated. He watched my face, grinned sharply. "These children will come with us now. All of them."

Nydia suddenly faltered. "A-all of them? You said *her* boys. The interlopers."

"All of them." Enzo continued staring at me, daring me to react. "It didn't have to be this way. You could have cooperated months ago."

Nydia tugged on his sleeve. "But the other children—"

He backhanded her. "Shut up!"

An Orange man took Nydia by the elbow. Her hand cradled her cheek, eyes tearless but wide— rethinking her choices.

Too late.

Enzo continued as if he'd never been interrupted. "If anyone interferes, we will go house to house and take every child we find. And then we will kill them all."

Nydia wailed.

"Knife, spell, or fists, doesn't matter which. We have plenty of people here, ready to do what they must. Not one of your children will live unless you do exactly what I say."

My skin itched. The magic in me had grown too big for my body, ready to explode. I had given up the dark goddess— and Her magic— to protect my family and now these people were here to hurt them. To hurt the children in my care. They had no idea how restrained I'd been these last months.

I was fast enough to kill them all where they stood. Before they could hurt the kids. Before he could release an Old Spell onto any of us. I *felt* each person around me. Enzo, and past him the children. Behind me, a woman who had trampled my garden. To the side now, Nydia—

The thread inside me that linked me to Maldita thickened.

"Mom?" Wil stared at me, his face pale. "Mom, we'll go."

"No." My voice had deepened, roughened. The dark goddess would come. Together we could flatten the houses, the gardens, the *people*—

"Yes." Andy sidestepped Enzo to pat my arm. "We'll be okay."

Wil shifted so one of his eyes showed behind Enzo's elbow. His tongue poked between his teeth. *We'll go to keep everyone safe. Keep you safe.*

Goddessi, he had *pushed* his thought to me. *No*, I responded the same way. *We don't negotiate with—*

We're not negotiating. We're surrendering. To protect our friends and their families.

My boy nodded sharply, then tipped his head back to

somehow glare down his nose at Enzo. He *pushed* delicately, influencing the man to *like* him. See him as helpless— which he wasn't— and innocent— which he was. "We'll keep everyone safe," Wil said carefully. "No one needs to get hurt."

Enzo nodded, his gaze still on me. "No one needs to get hurt."

Maggie came out of our house, buckling on her sword. She stopped behind an Orange woman. The Orange and several others— strangers to me— nodded amiably, then stiffened when she ignored them. "I'll go too," Maggie said coolly. "And Nydia will come with, since she's suddenly so worried about *all* our children. Worried enough to keep her own at home."

Murmurs ran through the crowd. The mob began to fracture.

How to make a mob bent on murder turn back into our neighbors? Point out what should have been obvious. "Boys? Are you sure about this? The demon hunters have killed innocents before. They use magic. And they don't care who they hurt."

The woman who had sold me soap ducked her head and stepped back, ashamed.

"They won't hurt us." Andy latched onto Enzo's hand, preventing the gestures required to cast an Old Spell, and stealing his ability to make magic.

They weren't safe yet. There were other magic users in the group.

My magic churned, still so ready to explode, but I held it tight. I couldn't trust Nydia, but Maggie? She loved the boys as if they were truly children born of her brother. I was sure of it. Had to be.

Wil nodded and took Enzo's other hand. "We're going to stay so close to their leader they won't *dare* hurt us. Won't we?" He held out his free hand and Cori took it. Her yellow eyes showed white all around and her whole body shook, but she took his hand.

Little Kass took Cori's hand, his orange hair fiery in the morning light, and Kass took Wil's hand, forming a chain from Wil to Andy, all four of them snuggled up to Enzo so close he would tread on them if he moved.

His eyebrows climbed up his forehead and his mouth dropped open. Only that bafflement— and the knowledge that Wil and Andy could— and had— used magic to protect themselves let me restrain myself.

I'd get him his blessed histories. Those mattered *nothing* compared to the lives of these kids. I'd shove them right up their—

Maggie flicked her gaze up past me, then back, so quickly if I hadn't been paying attention I'd have missed it.

Mouse— Mouse had to be watching from the children's room or from the roof, watching everything. She could follow the kids. And Suann, too— she would follow Cori. The demon hunters weren't just taking my children, they were taking them all.

"Fine. I'll get you what you want," I ground out through clenched teeth. "And you'll return every *child*, exactly as healthy as they are now. Not a slap, not a stubbed toe. Not even an insult."

Other neighbors had gathered beyond the demon hunters' group, helpless and furious.

Enzo glanced at them, then nodded. "None of the children will be hurt. I swear it." He took tiny, mincing steps, and the children moved with him.

Wil caught my eye. *We'll be okay, Mom.* Then he turned with Enzo and all of them walked away. Demon hunters surrounded him. I lost sight of him, and then Suann and the other parents fell in behind them, with Maggie bringing up the rear, where she could see everyone.

My knees gave out and I thumped down onto rock and dirt. The scent of blood filled my nose and red gushed onto my pants. My nose was bleeding and my whole head throbbed from all the magic I held, but the connection to Maldita thinned again. The boys had saved me from Her.

Saved the neighborhood.

Saved the entire city.

I'd have flattened every house, torn up every garden and memory plant for the children in my care.

Now the demon hunters had them, and I'd let them go. I'd let them *take* them all—

Just as Enzo had said, this was my fault. I should have given him the damned stories, should have stolen the blessed stories and given him those too. Should never had told him *no* and put them all in danger.

Their parents would blame me, as they should.

Jay would blame me, as he should.

I blamed me.

~

Jay

He'd just picked out the perfect loaf of bread when Mouse came running through the crowds and *slammed* into him, whimpering. He ducked his head, strained to hear her.

"How could he? How *could* he?"

Chill bumps rose on his arms and the hair on the back of his neck prickled. "What happened?"

"He *took* them, oh goddessi, he *took* them and he promised not to hurt them but he lied, he won't keep it—"

"Mouse." As if they weren't in the middle of the market with sellers hawking their wares and buyers bargaining for better prices and all of it so loud he could barely hear himself think, Jay focused on the girl weeping against his chest. Tried to lift her chin. "Mouse, tell me what happened."

"It was my father," she said dully. Winced away from him, unable to meet his eyes.

So much guilt there. Resting betweens, what had the man done?

"He came to the house. Brought all of them with. We had no chance. No chance at all."

"Mouse?" His voice cracked and his vision darkened around the edges. "Mouse, tell me—"

"They took them. Took them away to make you do what he wants."

Her voice seemed to come from very far away. "Is anyone hurt? The boys? Sumi?"

"No..." She faltered. "Not yet. He just *took* them."

Breathe, he reminded himself. Spoke the words sharp as sword-blades. "Your— Enzo. Came to the house. Took Sumi. And the boys."

"Not Sumi. The boys and— I couldn't stop him. There were so many! He'll kill them if anyone interferes."

He will hurt them, he promised not *to hurt them*— Stay on target, rest you... "He took the boys."

"And the other ones. The ones taking lessons."

The air he'd just started using exploded out of him again. "He took the kids?"

"Yes. All of them who came this morning. He took them." She moaned and buried her head in her hands. She'd had a growth spurt, he realized vaguely. Her head used to only come a handwidth below his shoulder, but now it was a fingerwidth shy of it.

That didn't matter now. He wasn't thinking right.

Swallowed hard.

He needed to get home, to see Sumi, to make sure she hadn't shattered beyond all hope, but he *needed* to do something else first.

Fingers numb, he hooked Mouse by the arm— *careful, don't hurt her just because you can't feel anything*— and looked around hoping to see another guard. Where was Mal when he needed the boy? Nowhere. But someone in guard gray leaned casually against a wall one block down. Jay stalked through the crowds that parted when they saw his face.

"Carpet," he demanded.

The guard gaped at him, but his hands fumbled for the carpet. Thrust it into Jay's hands.

Jay flipped it open and climbed on, dragged Mouse on with him. "Stay still," he told her, "or you'll fall."

Still numb, he gathered up the tassels and sent the carpet screaming into the sky, narrowly dodging shoppers, then, higher, pallets and other carpets. Flew it directly to the guardhouse where— in direct violation of every policy— he flew through the doors and into the practice room.

Shouts of alarm thundered, still so far away, but when he set the carpet down and staggered upright, silence fell.

"Demon hunters," he told them. "Stole children. Took them—"

Someone yelled, "Where?"

"I don't know. I need volunteers, to find them—"

"Jay?" Thom bellowed down from his office.

Jay ignored him. "Find them. Follow them. Don't take chances. They'll hurt the kids. If—" His heart stuttered. "If anyone *interferes*."

Every guard stepped forward and Jay nodded sharply. "Deploy in street units. A runner with each unit." Probably didn't call them runners anymore, but he didn't care. "Send up a flare when you find them—"

"Jay!" Thom leaned over the balcony.

He couldn't stop yet. "Demon hunters took my sons." *They took my sons.* "We need to find them. Now."

Thom stared. "Numbers?"

Mouse flinched and tried to melt into the flying carpet. "Lots. Counted more than twenty."

"And they threatened to hurt the kids?"

"Kill them." She choked back a sob. "Knives or spells or fists. They'll do it, too."

Thom nodded sharply. Started down the stairs.

As if released from bows, guards streamed out into the morning, unrolling carpets as they went, and Jay followed them out, still towing Mouse. Home. He had to get home before he unraveled.

"Send word," he said to Thom.

Yanked the carpet up and fled for Sumi.

Arrived far too soon, with no idea what to say. What to do more than he'd done.

Found her, crumpled in the yard with the children's slates and chalk scattered around her. She trembled like a sapling in the wind, but her eyes were dry.

Blood marked her pants. And smeared her nostrils and top lip like she'd tried to wipe it away.

He tried to find words— *should have kept them* safe *how could I not keep them* safe?— but she spoke first, her voice cracked and dull. "I'm so sorry. This is all my fault."

He stopped, stunned. "No— I should never have—"

"No." The girl he'd hauled around but had forgotten about stepped between them and squared her small shoulders. Wiped her tears, then glared at them as if *she* were the high priestess. "No," Mouse said, finally calm. "One thing I learned from Enzo—"

They both flinched at his name.

"— was that *he* chose to do what he did. No matter what my choices were, what your choices were, neither of you forced him to come here and take Wil and Andy and Cori and N-Na—Kass." She bit her lip. Swiped at her eyes and cleared her throat. "*He* chose to steal them. *He* chose to *force* you to do what *he* wants. So stop saying it's *your* fault for any of it." She lifted her proud, stubborn chin. "It's his."

Jay swept her into a hug, and just as quickly let her go. "Thank you."

Sumi slowly uncoiled to her feet. The lines of her body, the lines around her mouth told him her shame had shifted into rage.

If they'd been at the damned temple and she'd still been hosting the damned goddess, her hair would be floating, her eyes would be black, and she'd be out at the pits already, slaughtering animal after animal and sucking their blood into her tattoos.

But they weren't.

She was hiding in the Rest Third, fighting down her rage and trying very hard not to use her magic.

Sumi's eyes flicked to his— thank the goddessi, red and white instead of goddess-black. "Thank you, Mouse." She straightened, took a deep breath. "Maggie went with them. And Suann and some of the other neighbors." Her mouth pinched like she held words back.

He didn't ask. He couldn't bear it. Nodded instead. "She went with to keep them safe. Bought us some time."

Sumi side-eyed him. She didn't quite trust Maggie, and how could he blame her after the girl's behavior toward her?

"You know your boys." Gently he took her hands. "Wil has already killed once. He'll do it again if he has to. They both will."

"I know." She pulled her cold hands away. Still shaking, still keeping her magic contained. "They went with Enzo to protect their friends."

"The guards are looking for them. They're safe— safe enough—" he corrected himself— "or you'd know. Maggie..." *Think.* He rubbed his forehead and the Maggie-headache blooming there. "Maggie is playing the spy."

Sumi's eyes narrowed. "Spy?" she asked, "or convert?"

"Spy," he said, and his jaw clenched. Wanted to say more, reassure her, and himself—

A flare rocketed up, bright white against the cerulean sky. "They've found them. Mouse, the flying carpet in our bedroom—"

"Got it." The girl fled and returned as they watched the tail of the flare, and then Mal— *where the resting betweens had he been?*— was hovering overhead and beckoning to them.

He settled himself with Mouse in front of him on the carpet he'd taken from the nameless guard, and saw Sumi already up in the air on his own carpet. The face she turned to Mal made the boy blanch.

Cold, empty eyes.

As soon as Jay was airborne, Mal flew toward the smokey tail of the flare. Guided them deep into the warehouse district, not so far from where the boys had conjured the demon.

Obvious from above— Rest Third guards circled in the sky, and more spots of gray prowled on the ground, trying to contain a growing crowd surrounding a squat, sturdy building.

"They went inside there," Mal shouted across the gulf of air. "Shut the doors behind them. Maggie's in there too. I saw her go in."

"You were watching this building?" Jay demanded.

The boy faltered, looked over his shoulder as if to flee, but there was nowhere to go, not with the skies full of other carpets.

"I-I didn't know that's what they were going to do." His red eyes were wide and frantic. "I didn't know!"

Jay choked down his fury. Like Mouse had said, this was all on Enzo.

Thom flew up on his own carpet. "We can't force entry," he said as he nudged Mal out of his way. "They've too many hostages. They haven't made any demands—"

"They have," Jay ground out.

"Well?"

Jay looked around at all the people in the sky with them. Too many ears. "Follow me." He caught Sumi's eye and jerked his head. She stared at him, her jaw flexing like she was grinding her teeth down to nothing. Then nodded.

They descended, not into the madness around the demon hunter's lair but two blocks south. As soon as they touched down, Mouse rolled off the carpet. Gripped the stones of the road with both hands, like she was terrified of falling back into the sky.

"Don't like that, no I don't," she was muttering. "That's a miserable, horrible way to travel."

Sumi bent to touch the girl's shoulder. Alarm spiked through Jay— she couldn't risk any magic right now, not as angry as she was. She'd lose control.

But she straightened, and her eyes were still red-and-white. Still frozen.

Thom came off his carpet. Nearly grabbed Mouse right out from under Sumi— restrained himself and closed his hands into fists. "They outnumber us. I've got more guards coming but none of us have *magic*. We can't— *rest* it! If we give him what he wants, will he give the kids back? Unharmed?"

Mouse nodded, slow and uncertain. "I think so. If your guards don't press him."

Thom huffed in relief.

Jay turned to Thom. "That resting *job* you sent us— that was *him*, demanding we—" he stepped closer and lowered his voice— "*break* into the blessed temple and *steal* their histories."

Thom gaped at him. Found his words. "*Stories?* That's what this is about?"

"It's about killing the goddessi," Sumi said, her voice icier than winter wind. "They're fanatics and they'll do anything for their cause. Hurt... anyone." Her voice faltered and her hands flexed— fists, spread fingers, fists. "And you let them stay in our city."

"I—" Thom swallowed hard. "What do you need from me?"

Hope, perhaps, help and hope. Jay said, "Can you get the blessed to—?"

But Thom was already shaking his head. "They won't share. That's not their way."

"You can ask."

"No—" Thom jerked his chin. "*You* can ask. I can't leave this mess. But you have my authority." He stepped closer, dropped something in Jay's hand.

His ring. The one he used to seal formal letters from the Head of the Rest Third Guard.

"Then that's all we need from you." Sounded ungracious; couldn't help himself.

"Mal." Sumi watched the fliers overhead. "Give us Mal."

"Done." Thom looked as if he wanted to say something else — *be careful* or *good luck*— but instead he simply nodded. Climbed back on his carpet. Rose into the sky.

"Mal?" Jay growled. "We don't need—"

"Trust me." She turned furious red eyes on him. How could

she contain everything he saw in her gaze? "His guilt will make him useful."

Jay swallowed hard. He *did* trust her. He loved her and she loved him and they would get the boys back.

A Purple woman and an Orange man walked out of the shadows. Nodded a greeting as if he should know them. Jay struggled, then finally placed them as Tasha and Gui, the thieves from the market.

Sumi had said she was teaching them magic.

Gui cracked his knuckles. "We heard. We're going with you."

Goddessi, *more* complications? Jay demanded, "Been spying on us?"

"Not exactly." Gui shrugged, like Jay's suspicions were not his problem. "Were spying on Ezno. Took a little break— horrible timing— and then *bam*. Heard what happened. Everyone's talking 'bout it."

"We don't need y—" Jay stopped himself. They had to get into the Temple of the Blessed, borrow or copy or steal a bunch of stories, and get back out.

Sumi looked toward the demon hunters' lair as if she could see through the buildings. Maybe she could. "I'll go in alone. You wait outside—"

"No," Jay snapped. "They'll kill you."

Gui's looked shocked. "Don't be foolish."

"That's suicide," Tasha said. "And killing yourself won't get the kids back."

"No." Jay took Sumi's hand, despite her thousand length stare. "No. You won't do this alone. You can't use your magic, and you know those writings are going to be in the vault."

Shouldn't, her mouth shaped, but she didn't voice it.

He shuddered. Sumi under the control of the dark goddess again— no. Not when he could protect her. "It takes magic to get in there, right? Use Gui and Tasha as your magic. They want to help."

"No."

"You think you're the only one with something to prove?" Gui cracked his knuckles again. "That *man* is my *cousin*."

Jay ignored him. "I'll be your strength."

Her eyes flicked between them, measuring and judging. "We need Mouse, too. Fill in the gaps."

"Fill in the gaps?" Mouse straightened.

He'd forgotten the girl was there. Only barely managed not to jump. Realized— Sumi wanted to use Mouse's skills as a thief. She must be better than the other two.

Sumi nodded slowly. "Magic." She nodded at Tasha and Gui. "Strength." Squeezed Jay's hand. "Anything else." Inclined her head at Mouse. Looked up at the gray guard carpet descending on them. "And our messenger."

Jay grimaced.

Sumi's brow wrinkled. "We need three more flying carpets."

Jay scowled. "Can't afford them. Can we make them? Like the boys—" he choked.

"Tasha and Gui could probably make them. But we don't have the time. We go now."

If only. "As soon as we can."

The guard was almost on top of them. Sumi called up, "Mal?"

The boy bobbled in the air, paused. "Yes? Honored Red?"

"We need three more flying carpets. Fetch them."

He gaped down at her, like a fish out of water. "But—"

Jay snarled, "The Head Guard sanctioned our actions. And half the Rest Third is ready to riot. Just do what you're told. Even if you have to steal them off your fellow guards' backs. Find three. Bring them back—"

"To the house." Sumi settled herself on her own carpet and twitched it into the air. "We need supplies."

Mal nodded. Darted away.

The sun had already passed its highest point and seemed to speed down to the west. How had more than half the day slipped away?

Sumi had a tendency to forget to eat. He needed to feed her before they faced her blood-mother. Needed parchment and pens too.

Gui stared at the carpet Jay unrolled. Swallowed hard. "I've never flown—"

Tasha bumped him with her shoulder. "We'll practice. You'll be fine."

"It's horrible." Mouse glared at Jay's carpet. "A horrible way to go."

Sumi shivered like she was shaking off water, and some of the tension went out of her. "I didn't ask. I'm sorry, Mouse. Will you—"

"Of course I will," she snapped. "He took my brothers and my friends."

"Thank you." She glanced at each of them in turn. "We won't leave you in the blessed temple. I swear it."

Gui nodded, then Tasha. Mouse didn't— just looked scared. "Maybe they'll just let us in and back out again."

"I'm sure they will. Meet us at the house." Sumi said. Rose into the sky.

Jay glanced at Mouse, who shuddered. "Never again." Then amended, "Until I have to."

So he followed after Sumi, and if he'd believed in the goddessi, he'd have prayed for them all.

But he didn't.

TWENTY-EIGHT

S *umi*

WHILE WE WAITED FOR MAL AND THE FLYING CARPETS, I CLEANED MY face, changed my clothes, then gathered every scrap of ink, pen, and parchment in the house and packed it into a carry bag. Jay fed us a massive meal, as if full stomachs would protect us from the demon hunters and possibly the demoni themselves.

I ate grimly, trying to fill the hole at my center where the boys were supposed to be.

It didn't work.

Tasha splayed across the couch, her legs across Gui's lap, while Gui kneaded her feet. Mouse, perched on the ladder, held as still as her namesake threatened by a hunter, and thank the goddessi the magic exercises I'd given her had strengthened her abilities and she hadn't given up her magic— yet. I had a feeling we were going to need her.

"We should send Mal away after he gives us the carpets." Jay leaned against the door to our bedroom. "He's too young—"

I snorted. "More likely he'll rabbit as soon as he sees any magic."

Jay straightened. "He has orders."

"He's here." Mouse whispered.

She must have seen his carpet descending. I *felt* him coming and stood. A surge of rage blacked out my vision, so I gripped the back of my chair and waited.

When I was able to see again, Mal stood at the front door, handing carpets to Jay.

Tasha swept her feet off Gui's lap and bounced up to accept her carpet. Gui followed. Mouse just shook her head. "I'll ride with Jay or not at all."

Mal straightened so fast he could have torn his stomach muscles. "They're safe—"

"Not for me."

Jay looked at her for a long moment, then nodded.

Mal muttered under his breath about a waste of time, but Jay flung his hand out and the boy shut up. Jay moved everyone out into the front yard, then glanced back at me.

I settled the bag of writing implements over my shoulder, then followed him out.

The sun sank in the western sky, sending shadows lengthening into the yard, raking me with cold fingers. Foreboding slid down my spine and I clenched my teeth against the shiver of it.

Dansy's house was closed up tight. Lines of light leaked around the shutters. Likely her door was locked and barred, with her daughters inside. That's what I would have done, if my wife had betrayed a neighbor, then gotten herself stolen by the same people who'd taken the children.

Though the betrayal stung, I couldn't blame her. We'd not

interacted much, and no matter how good I might be at teaching her daughters, the person I had been—

I yanked my thoughts and my eyes away. Most of the other houses were empty. Fear for their children, fear that the child-thieves might return, had driven them to flee to relatives or farther neighbors.

As soon as I climbed onto my carpet, we all shot into the sky and headed for the Blessed Third gate. When it came into view, the others fell back and hovered while Mal, Jay— and with him, Mouse— and I landed.

The thread that connected me to Maldita hummed.

She was stirring.

Mouse staggered off Jay's carpet as soon as it touched the cobblestones and to distract myself, I wondered if she would repeat her display of appreciation for solid ground. She saw me watching and stood taller instead. Then winced, but whispered, "They won't let any of us *trash* in."

I straightened in reply, and stepped forward with Jay and Mal.

The wagon-gates had been shut and locked. A Brown male guard and a Green woman guard in blessed white stood in front of the man-gate. They looked us up and down, their eyes catching on the carpets in our hands, then on Jay's swords, Mal's Rest Third Guard uniform, and our faces.

"Blessed Third's closed for the evening," said the Brown guard.

Jay grimaced. "The sun's not down yet."

"Close enough."

They'd know my face. I had a bad feeling no matter which way tonight went, I could no longer hide. "We're on our way to see the high priestess."

"You're not on the list."

Jay rested one hand on the hilt of his swords and held out

the other as if he were expecting the man to clasp it. "You ready for winter?"

The Green guard eyed him warily. "Not quite yet."

"I'm one of the Rest Third Guard trainers. You heard what happened today?"

The Brown guard spat to the side. "You let a bunch of damned fools steal your children from you."

Let— my face went hot, but I swallowed it down.

"We need blessed help," Jay said smoothly, "to limit the loss of life."

"Really?" The Green guard sneered. "And them? Ain't guards."

"Sanctioned by the head guard." Jay held up Thom's ring. Though only he and Mal looked anything like presentable.

The Brown guard examined the ring, then for a long moment stared at Jay, evaluating. Shrugged and opened the gate. "Your death day."

Jay stepped through with a nod. "Hope not."

Mouse scurried through, but I paused long enough for Tasha and Gui to land. "They're with us."

The Brown guard scowled like we'd tricked him, but he didn't shut the gate. Tasha and Gui and Mal went through, then I brought up the rear. The gate slammed behind us, locking us into the Blessed Third.

First barrier passed.

We moved to the side of the road and knelt on grass. Not the thin, tall kind I'd seen growing wild in the mountains, but thick, short, dense, and *green*, under the torchlight of the Blessed Third gates. This, *this* was why my blood-mother had taken homes from decent Rest Third people and torn them down and extended her *blessed* walls—

Jay touched my hand.

The thread inside me that was Maldita had thickened to

three strands instead of one, and it sang like a plucked string, but quieted when Jay touched me.

I could do this.

We could do this.

I nodded at Jay, and the corners of his eyes crinkled in a private little smile. Then Mouse joined him on his carpet, and he twitched the tassels and rose. I followed him, as did the rest of our group. Ragged and obviously not trained together, but when I checked the guards, they'd gone back into the gatehouse and were carefully ignoring us.

Did they know what we wanted? What we intended, one way or another?

No— they'd never have let us even this far.

Sunset was slowly dying in the west, leaving behind a glow that would fade before we could make it to the temple. The Blessed Third spread out around us like the platter of treats Jay had made for us— had it only been a few days ago?

I couldn't remember flying over the Damned Third when we'd escaped the temple, but even from above, the blessed were wealthier than the rest. Bigger yards, better roofs, more lanterns than torches—

Then the temple grew before us, pale stone and pale gardens and pale roofs as if anyone cared about the color of the tiles that protected the blessed from rain and sun.

We swooped down to the temple gates and the closer we came, the more my insides buzzed. The thread binding me to Maldita grew thicker.

I did *not* want to go inside that temple, to the heart of my blood-mother's power. But I wanted to keep everyone safe. I wanted my boys back, and my students, and my neighbors, and the demon hunters gone.

The chill wind tugged at my hair and cut through my clothes like it had since we'd left the house. It was worse flying the carpets. I rubbed my hands along my arms, then took a moment to roll up my carpet. The coldest breezes seemed to come from the blessed temple itself, and the Blue guard gave me an icy look that matched the wind.

My nerves shrilled, *mistake*.

I caught Jay around the middle and when he bent his head to me, whispered into his ear, "Maybe the demon hunters were right. We should have skipped the niceties and sneaked in."

"Too late." He squeezed me. "We've been seen. We ask for help. We try it the right way first."

"That's what makes us the good guys," Mal said softly. He stepped forward with Jay, and again I found myself moving with them.

Title or no, magic or no, I would not hide behind guards for this.

"We're here to see the high priestess." I met the gaze of the Blue guard and wondered how powerful she was. I could *feel* her— a magus and a guard, and bitter—

"No."

Jay held out Thom's ring again. "We've come to ask—"

"For help," the Blue guard snapped.

A second guard, a Purple man as wide as I'd ever seen but light on his feet, came out of the guardhouse and planted himself in front of the gate. "She sent us a message for you," he said. "Read the message, Tris."

The Blue guard cleared her throat. "The blessed send their regards to the rest and advise we will not assist in a matter so clearly of your own making."

The words escaped me. "But they're *children*—"

"Not ours."

I opened my mouth. *My boys. The high priestess's grandchild and his best friend who happens to be a Blue. Strongest magic-users I've ever taught*— I'd never see them again. She'd take them

392

from me and probably leave the other children in the hands of the demon hunters and I'd never see my boys again.

If she let me live.

Horror strummed through me. Did she *know*? Was this her way of forcing me to give up my boys to her? Just another way to confuse me and keep me subdued?

If this was *her* doing, *her* planning, this night would end with death. I stepped back and bowed my head to disguise my rising rage, and tried to believe with all my heart we could still *do* this, and do it the *right way*. For Jay.

Mal tried. "The Head of the Rest Third Guard asked us to come to you, to petition for assistance." He looked between the Blue guard and the Purple guard. "A priestess. A magus. Guards. Anything."

"Get out," the Purple guard snarled, stepping forward. "Get out of the Blessed Third."

"Go back where you belong." The Blue guard stepped shoulder to shoulder with her partner. Her right hand came up and I felt her gather her *push* magic.

If I reached the tiniest bit, I could smash them both into the ground and *blast* the gate out of the way.

No.

No— Wil and Andy went with the demon hunters to protect their friends, and destroying the blessed gates wouldn't protect anyone.

No matter how good it would feel.

Wordless, I unrolled my carpet, settled onto it, and rose into the air. Gui and Tasha hovered above me, and Mal and Jay and Mouse came after. I turned as if returning to the Rest Third, despite the garbled protests, and rose higher and higher until cold bit at my nose and my ears and my fingers and I couldn't see the guards anymore.

Then I swung to the east and aimed for the center of the

temple roof and leaned forward to give it a little bit more speed. We could blessed well *fly* over the walls and land right over the vault itself—

Bong.

The carpet crumpled out from under me and suddenly I was falling.

~

JAY

TOO COLD TO STAY UP SO HIGH FOR SO LONG. AT LEAST HE HAD MOUSE to keep him warm— Sumi must be feeling the chill in her fingers, but she flew her carpet as easily as ever. Jay leveled out, waited until she did the same, then followed her when she arrowed back down.

Saw her hit something invisible. The carpet crumpled. Sumi flailed, then slid.

Tasha yelled, "It's a blessed dome!"

Sumi fell.

And his carpet was already overloaded with two— He hooked his feet over the edges, jerked it into a tight loop over Mal and dumped Mouse into poor Mal's lap.

Then leaned into a dive.

Sumi was sprawled against whatever it was, fingers and toes trying to claw purchase in the air. Sliding faster now—

He swooped below her, close as he dared to the invisible barrier.

She smashed into him and they skidded sideways and down toward the ground below—

Tasha and Gui came after them, slithered their carpets under his and tipped it back to level.

An eternity later, they all came to rest on a patch of grass in the shadow of the blessed temple walls. Laid together on the blessed grass until the worst of the shaking had stopped and a sliver of a moon peeked from behind the black mountains.

Sumi asked hoarsely, "Everyone all right?"

Mouse wiped tears off her face. "No."

"Me neither," Sumi admitted, with a half-smile for Mouse. "Still alive, then?"

"Yeah."

"That was—" Jay found himself waving his hands vaguely. "Thank you all. Thank you for not screaming, thank you for saving us and each other. Thank the resting betweens it was dark enough no one saw it."

"Never, never, *ever* again," Mouse whispered.

"What *was* that?" Mal dug his fingers into the grass.

"A shield." Sumi slowly sat up. Wrapped her arms around her knees. "A dome over the whole blessed temple complex. I had no idea that was even possible."

"Think of the *power* it took." Tasha's eyes glinted in the faint light of the moon.

"Blood, bone, and souls." Sumi sounded like she wanted to cry.

Mouse reached across the grass and patted her foot. "No one saw us... or at least no one is shouting for the guards."

But there might be guards sneaking up on them. Jay rolled to his knees and carefully scanned the area, to be as sure as he could that they were unobserved. The nearest houses sat what would be a full block away in the Rest Third. The lanterns on the nearest doors were dim or out, and the land between them and the temple seemed to be filled with more of the luxurious and *useless* grass they currently sat on. But no one was lurking along the wall in either direction, far as he could see in the moonlit dark. "What now?"

Gui stood, staggered. He caught himself on the temple wall, then snatched his hand back as if burned.

"Hurt?" Jay asked.

Gui stared down at his hand, slowly waved it back and forth as if making sure it was still attached. "No."

From where Mouse still lay on the grass, she threw something.

Jay watched it— a rock?— expecting it to hit the shield and bounce back at them, but it sailed over the wall and disappeared. "Huh."

He traded a speculative glance with Sumi. "Up and over?"

"Wait." She shook her head. Crawled to her feet, moving like she'd hurt her back again. Then tentatively set her hand on the wall. "The sheer hubris—"

Tasha choked back a protest. When nothing happened to Sumi, she swallowed and allowed Gui to pull her up.

"Come feel this," Sumi murmured to them. "Don't *do* anything, just *feel*. How it was made. What it does."

First Tasha, then Gui, touched fingertips to the rock of the wall. "Magic," Gui muttered. "Keeps out magic."

"Not natural flying things," Tasha confirmed, wide-eyed. "Not anything except push-pull magic."

Sumi's mouth quirked in a half-grin. "Mouse?"

The girl startled, then clenched her hands in the grass.

"Is it safe to go over?" Sumi arched her eyebrows. "Is anyone behind the wall?"

Mouse cocked her head. Rolled to her feet. Looked at the wall like she could see right through it.

Hm. Magic explained why she was a good thief.

Mouse nodded, then her shoulders straightened the tiniest bit. A little pride that she had helped.

Jay gathered carpets, rolled them, handed them out again. Time to go.

"Quiet your magic," Sumi told the others. Slung her carpet onto her back, then patted the wall. "The barrier shouldn't notice you, but be still all the same."

Jay made a cradle of his hands and jerked his head at Mal to do the same. Vaulted Mouse up first. She looked as if she was hanging in the dark sky, shadow on shadow, while she evaluated the ground, then nodded and dropped lightly down on the other side.

If that was *quieting* her magic, he didn't want to know what *loud* was.

But Tasha followed her over like she hadn't a care in the world. Heavier Gui half-jumped, half-climbed the rocks without waiting for help, and then sprawled across the top and held out his hand for Sumi.

Her eyes pinched like she hurt, so Jay made himself her ladder— knee, hand, shoulder, and steadied her while she climbed. Then he tossed Mal up and took his own running start. Lept, grabbed Mal's and Gui's hands and pulled himself up and over.

He landed on more of that soft, soft grass, bordering red and yellow and gray bricks— made from the local stone and clay. Past the border of the bricks lay pits and the stench of blood and fear.

Killing pits.

Jay murmured, "I thought the blessed didn't *do* blood sacrifice."

Sumi shrugged, then, when she should have winced because her back was hurting her, didn't. Jay swallowed hard. She should have winced.

"That's what they want you to think," she said. Rose smoothly to her feet as if she'd never hurt her back, never hit against the dome protecting the temple, never *died* last winter — "But their goddess is just as blood-thirsty as the other."

Jay scowled. Not hard to believe, just... disappointing. "We need to move—"

Mouse froze, fading into shadow. A white-clad blessed guard rounded the corner of the building.

Sumi held her breath, but Mal grunted like he'd been struck. Tasha and Gui thrust their hands out toward the guard. Worked some sort of magic because the Green man dressed in blessed guard white opened his mouth but made no sound. Slowly, gently, he went to his knees, mouth still gaping open and shut, eyes wide. Then his eyelids fluttered closed and he sprawled out on the path. His ribs moved, hard breath— and Jay couldn't decide if he thanked the goddessi for that or not. One fewer guard to fight now, but one more who might rejoin a fight later.

Sumi edged her way around the pits with a smooth stride he recognized— gliding as if the dark goddess possessed her.

Jay's heart clenched, but he followed her, and the others fell into line behind him.

What would this night do to her?

But the boys still needed rescue and to peaceably give them up, the demon hunters needed their resting *stories* and that meant the six of them had to get into the Temple of the Blessed and then into the vault.

A vault that he had to trust Sumi knew how to find.

So he followed his beloved away from the pits around the corner the guard had come from and when she pointed at the door she wanted Mouse to open, Jay sucked in a long, quiet breath and watched for the next guard.

More guards would come. The high priestess of Bendita was no fool.

But guards were sparse tonight, and the gardens of the blessed temple glowed under the sliver of a moon. As the gardeners of the damned had planted black flowers, the gardeners of the blessed had planted white, and each bloom, closed for the night or open to the stars, glimmered with borrowed light.

A pity the temple's residents slept, as they were missing what was likely the most beautiful thing about the blessed temple.

This time— distracted by a pretty moon-lit garden or not— he heard the guard coming and ghosted to the perfect shadow to wait. Boots crunched on the gravel path. Told him exactly where his target stepped. He let the woman take two steps past him and stiffen at the intruders, then Jay snaked his arm around her neck and flexed. Temporarily cut off the flow of blood and air to her brain.

She thrashed against him, but Tasha held her hand out, doing *something* magic, so not even the scuff of the guard's boots against the rocks made any noise.

Eerie.

When the guard went limp, he counted ten more seconds, then set her against the wall behind a bush. Waited to make sure she too was still breathing. Left her for her fellows to find because he couldn't do anything else.

Couldn't kill her. Not like this.

Mouse eased the door open and slipped inside. The others followed her. Jay took a long look around the glowing garden, then crossed the threshold into the Temple of the Blessed.

Gently pulled the door closed behind him, shutting out the night.

Closed himself and his people in with the blessed.

Heard Sumi suck in a deep breath and wondered if her eyes were blood-and-white or goddess-possessed black.

TWENTY-NINE

S *umi*

TIME DOES STRANGE THINGS.

I'd left the Temple of the Blessed— or rather, been cast out — when I was still mostly a child, but the roses and hellebore, daisies and hydrangeas, gardenias and lilies, all moonlit and nodding in the quiet of the night brought it all back to me. Even then, I'd broken the rules. Stayed up late to catch a glimpse of the gardens. Even then the ethereal glow brought me peace.

The blessed priestessi and magi and most of the guards slept early and rose with the dawn, so only occasionally did a guard stir the shadows.

And now, I was back, breaking the rules, almost as if I'd never left.

Except everything was different.

My children needed me— my boys and my students. I had companions— my beloved and those who I must now count as friends for joining me in this mad quest, even Mal. I *would* get them out again, as I'd promised. And the ties that bound me to the dark goddess thickened with every step, sang to me of blood and bone and soul.

I shouldn't have come back here, but I'd had no choice.

I stepped over the threshold into the blessed temple and the croon that was Maldita became a full-throated song.

Not a roar, not yet. I pushed my magic deep, deep down inside me. *She* didn't take me, being distracted by the ceremonies in the Temple of the Damned far across the city, but I felt her awareness of me in a way I hadn't since I'd left that temple.

I glided to the side of the room, out of the way of the others. My body felt like I was soaking in sunshine and *nothing hurt*.

Pain is a curious thing.

I'd hit the dome-shield over the temple complex and wrenched my back yet again. Breathing took thought and bending took more, but we'd gone over the wall anyway, and that had somehow helped. Now though— now I realized I'd *ached*. In my back, in my joints, in my head. A steady throbbing that flared into stabbing whenever I tested it too much.

I hadn't realized how bad it was until it was gone.

And now I didn't know if I could leave the temple and take up that constant nagging suffering again. My breath quickened and my eyes filled and I was *terrified*.

Jay set his fingertips against the small of my back, and his warmth broke through.

My feet or my carpet would carry me over the threshold when it was time, and the pain would come, and I'd deal with it then. For now, my fear had to wait. We needed to find the stories the demon hunters so dearly wanted.

I turned and gripped Jay's hand in mine as thanks, then blinked in the inky darkness of the hall. Thought about where we'd come in, and decided it was likely a side door to the kitchens. The blessed had either curtained or bricked up the windows overseeing the killing pits.

"*Pull* the faintest bit of light," I murmured.

Tasha nodded, merely a sense of movement in the dark. Carefully, she gathered herself, then pulled light to her hand.

Without waiting for my instruction, Gui *pushed* the light out into the room, and I saw with satisfaction I'd guessed correctly.

Long tables and large sinks and doors to the cold room and to storage, heavy dark curtains across the large windows, and most importantly, the doors out to the main hall.

Mouse scurried across the floor and crouched in front of those doors, *feeling* for someone on the other side. When she nodded, then slipped through, I knew it was safe.

Safe enough.

In the hall, the occasional lantern lit the way. Tasha and Gui let their light gutter out. I walked with Mouse, leading the rest, as we made our way past the branching hallways to the dormitories, past the massive double doors protecting the sanctum, along the wall that led to the high priestess's entrance across from the hidden vault door.

No lantern marked either one, and shadow sat heavily on the pale, blank wall.

I touched it, then snatched my hand away so I wouldn't be tempted. Here, I dared not use my power, or as thick as the ties were between me and the dark goddess, She would have me.

So I stepped out of the way for Gui and Tasha and Mouse.

Difficult, to step back, but the dark song inside me was stronger with every breath and I *would not* give myself to Maldita ever again.

Mal and Jay stood to either side of our group, their backs to us, ready to defend us from any guards, and I hovered behind my students so I could guide them through the next few moments.

"Anyone on the other side of the door?" I asked Mouse.

She canted her head, then shook it, *no*.

"*Feel* for poisons, for traps, for the magic of the door," I told the other two.

Gui and Tasha clasped hands, left to right, then raised their other hands— right and left— to the blank wall.

As shut down as my magic was, I couldn't *feel* anything they did, but Tasha shook her head first. "No poisons," she murmured.

Gui shifted. "No traps."

Mouse slid under their joined hands and knelt. She petted the wall, then found the spot she wanted, and brushed her hand across it, right to left. It looked— to my currently un-magical eyes— as if her fingertips disappeared into the wall itself, but then something clicked.

Tasha *pulled* and Gui *pushed* and the vault door swung open.

Silence in the darkness beyond the threshold. Chill bumps ran over my skin. This was the one place I'd never sneaked into, before the bright temple— and my blood-mother— spat me out like a rotten berry and sent me off to spy at the dark temple.

Steady.

Maldita's song was louder now, and hard to hear past.

Mouse stared intently into the vault, then mouthed the word, *Clear.*

Tasha and Gui went first, still linked and testing for traps. Mouse next, then me, and Jay and Mal last. When we were all inside, Tasha and Gui closed the door. The *thunk* felt awfully like a trap closing around us.

"Light," I breathed.

Tasha's hand lit with a gentle crescent-moon glow, then Gui

403

moved the glow out into the center of the room, and, after my nod, Jay and Mal lit the closest lanterns.

Unlike the chaos of the dark temple's vault, this one held neat stacks, orderly scrolls, racked weapons. Each item in its place.

A string twanged and an arrow came out of the corner. Languidly— but somehow still faster than the arrow— Tasha and Gui held up their linked hands. The arrow stopped, clattered harmlessly to the floor.

Jay picked it up and examined it. Black spots appeared in the air around us.

The stale, still air.

My mouth opened and I panted. Gripped Jay's arm. He stared at me, unaffected. Mousie was turning as gray as her namesake.

I could flex my power and break whatever spell this was— but that thought might belong to the dark goddess, willing me to help Her, so I shoved the thought down with my magic.

Jay hissed at Gui and Tasha.

They also struggled to breathe, but Gui scowled and Tasha bit her lip, then the pair did something I couldn't see, couldn't feel—

And air rushed into my lungs.

The black spots went away.

The high priestess of Bendita really wanted to protect her vault.

Mal looked horrified and Jay resigned. Mouse stood still, her yellow eyes wide. Tasha and Gui looked intrigued.

Temple politics were brutal, but neither here nor there for our task. "Mal, stay by the door. Don't touch anything. Gui. Tasha. *Feel* for old writings. Writings about the demoni. The beginnings of the goddessi. *Push* and *pull* the items until we identify them."

They could do this. It wasn't that different from anything else they'd done tonight. They just had to believe it, and I believed it hard enough for both of them, infused that belief in my instructions.

I'd never heard of anyone doing it before. Didn't mean it couldn't be done.

For fifteen breaths, nothing. Then a drawer shifted. Mouse went to it and reached out her hand, then jerked it back. "Magic," she hissed.

Jay stepped forward, opened the drawer. I imagined if I dared *feel* for it, it would look like the magic had slid off his hand like water off oil. He drew out a book.

"Is this table safe? The chair?"

Tasha and Gui turned blind eyes on me and nodded. They were pouring too much of themselves into their magic.

"Less," I told them, "is more. Don't exhaust yourselves."

Tasha shook her head like she was shaking off flies. Sanity returned to her gaze. She clenched the hand that Gui clasped, and he blinked.

Better.

I shifted the safe chair to the safe table and sat, then drew pen and ink and parchment out of my bag. Jay walked the book to Tasha, then at her nod, brought it to me.

A scroll moved. A dagger. Another book.

Mouse and Jay brought me everything, and I copied as swiftly as I could, letting one sheet dry while I worked on the next, and then flipping it. At the top of each sheet, I described where the words had come from, be it book, scroll, or blade, the order, and anything else I thought might help when we were done, and as both sides filled up and dried, I put them into my bag.

The bag filled. The hours passed. I didn't dare stop. I didn't dare *pause*—

Tasha and Gui and Mouse finished bringing new items and started putting them back. Jay switched to helping copy. He wasn't as fast as I, but wrote clearly enough.

If we were truly lucky, my blood-mother would never know we'd been here.

Mal's eyes closed. He leaned against the vault wall and occasionally his head nodded and a tiny snore escaped, then he jerked himself upright again.

My hand cramped, but I kept writing.

The blessed would be rising soon enough, and we needed to be long gone.

At last I said, "Good enough. This has to be enough for *them*. And if they have a truth spell, we can honestly say we copied everything we could." I'd never *heard* of an Old truth Spell, but I didn't know everything.

Jay swept up the last book and Mouse took a weapon that was either a long dagger or a short sword and they shoved them back into place. I blew on the last sheet of parchment and tucked everything away in my bag.

Took one last look around the vault.

Goddessi willing, I'd never step foot in this room again.

Mouse nudged Mal, then touched her fingertips to the vault door. She twitched and jerked her hand back.

"Problem," she whispered.

Jay groaned. "I knew it was going too well. Too easy."

"Easy?" I massaged my hand.

He arched his eyebrows at me, but Mouse spoke up. "Is there another way out? Something... something's not right about that door."

Gui reached out his hand and likely his magic. Flinched back. "Yeah. No. Bad idea."

Look for yourself, Maldita whispered to me from far away.

No. I shuddered. She hadn't spoken to me for so long, it felt

406

like swimming in refuse and I couldn't breathe for fear of a mouth full of effluvia—

No.

Jay spun. "Side door? I thought I saw—" He disappeared deeper into the vault.

"No..." I followed after him, almost to the very back, then left.

He traced a door with his fingers, half-sized, half-hidden, and all useless— until now.

Mouse wriggled between me and the door.

My pulse thundered in my ears, nearly drowning out Maldita's song.

She— Mouse, not Maldita, though it was getting harder to tell— nodded and did *something*, then the door opened. I ducked through and turned to go right, to head back to the kitchens, but the girl hissed and grabbed my wrist.

Left, then.

Mouse pulled me along the dark hall, and one of the others latched on to my belt and followed behind, and when I'd have gone straight on, she yanked me to the left again.

Then stopped.

The six of us bunched up together. Mouse took a step forward, stopped. Took a step around us to go back the way we came. Stopped. Growled a bit under her breath, then pushed me out of the way and opened the door at my back.

What else could I do but follow?

But when I crossed the threshold, the room echoed around me. I checked the map in my head—

The sanctum.

Oh, goddess, we were in the blessed sanctum, the heart of Bendita's temple. Mouse took one trembling step, then another. If I'd counted my steps correctly, we were on the dais of the high priestess.

Right, this could work. We had to avoid my blood-mother's chair, had to make our way down the steps, cross the large presumably empty room, then we'd be close to the front doors of the temple and free.

Maldita chuckled inside me. My steps faltered.

If *She* was pleased... we were in trouble.

~

*J*AY

J*AY WAS LOST.*

They'd turned and turned again in the dark, chained together by gripping hands. He couldn't see to fight and couldn't drop Sumi's belt to draw his swords because he'd lose them if he did. When they all paused, and Sumi moved first one way, then the other, then a *third*, he had a horrible feeling they were being herded. But maybe Mouse was taking them back the way they came. And the words wouldn't push past his clenched jaw—

The next door opened into more darkness. Again.

"Sanctum," Sumi breathed, shadows staining her voice.

Jay shuddered. The dark goddess was rising inside his beloved and he couldn't bear it. Then he realized what she'd said.

The dark goddess had possessed him in a room exactly like this. Had taken over his body, said the oath using his mouth, bound him to Her will-he, nill-he. He wanted to retch.

Escape first, then retch.

Sumi was shaking. Barely noticeable, but he could feel it through his grip on her belt, his knuckles brushing the back of her shirt. The room echoed around them, and he wished for a tiny bit of light.

Just to see his own feet. Make sure he didn't trip and take the others down with him.

Sumi stepped down, and he followed her, then down again, and he followed.

When she walked forward instead of down, he breathed a sigh of relief. Really, they were almost out. If they could get through this stupidly cavernous room and out the other side, they'd have a straight shot to the front doors and—

"What an *interesting* surprise," a woman said.

Torches flared bright white, all along the walls, all at the same time, and his eyes slammed closed, watering. He stepped in front of the group and drew his swords, blinking furiously to clear his vision.

A Red woman, so pale she was more faint pink than Red, dressed all in diaphanous white, stood in front of him, glowing with gentle radiance, and around her, more figures in white, though none so pale as she, and none so striking. Now, in the light, he could see the large empty room wasn't so empty. Blessed guards stood at the walls. Easily fifteen or more.

Mal, at the tail-end of their group, had drawn his sword as well, but now the blade dipped as if he was reconsidering his decision. "Jay, that's the *blessed high priestess*," he whispered.

Mouse made a whimpering sound.

"I had heard rumors," the high priestess of Bendita drawled, "of thieves coming to my temple. But I didn't believe anyone would be so stupid." She grinned maliciously. "Even if I did have my people hint *you* could enter my temple."

Sumi brushed past him. "Hello, Mother."

No!

They'd come so far. But they were outnumbered. He had confidence to spare but Jay didn't truly believe he and Mal could face sixteen— seventeen, eighteen, *nineteen*— guards. Any hesitation—

"My wayward daughter." The high priestess grimaced. "Still the root of all my problems, after so long. My greatest disappointment."

Sumi bowed. "Thank you!"

The high priestess took two steps forward. Her pale hair started to float, and her tattoos flashed black, then bright against her red skin.

"That way," Jay muttered and took two small steps toward the front of the room, aiming to the right of the main doors. Those towering monstrosities sat closed and barred. Too resting long to get open and flee through, but the blessed temple was so resting much like the damned temple that there should be a matched pair of smaller doors on each side. Covered by hanging tapestries, but likely unlocked, unbarred.

His time in the damned temple had done some good after all.

Their little group shuffled slowly toward that front side door as if the guards weren't there, ready to kill them.

"We asked." Sumi still faced her mother, stepping backward and trusting Jay to guide her. "We asked at the gates to the Blessed Third, asked again at the gates to the temple. I'd have gotten on my knees and *begged* you if it would have helped."

The high priestess cocked her head, a tiny smile on her lips. "I would have liked to see that. My most rebellious daughter, finally behaving as she ought."

"You could have seen it. But what was it you wrote? Oh— *we will not assist in a matter so clearly of your own making.* That was it."

"You should have burned the problem out, root and branch, like I've done. And will do again." The high priestess took her own small steps forward, and the guards around her moved with her.

Jay stiffened. Did the woman mean *here* and *now*? Was she planning to burn them out like she thought she'd burned out the demon hunters?

"Where are your priestessi, Mother?" Sumi drawled. "Where are the women and men you trust? You rely on? To run the blessed temple? Where are my sisters?"

The blessed high priestess faltered, then her lips pressed together. "I don't need them," she snapped, "to deal with a handful of misguided thieves."

Interesting— division there, but he had no way to take advantage of it. Had to get out, get Sumi out, get the rest of them out.

"Misguided?" Anything to take that woman's attention off his beloved.

"Misguided," she sneered. "I have spies. I know who took my grandson and why. What the Elemental demanded of you. And what you have isn't it."

Sumi faltered for a moment, but Jay steadied her with one hand on her waist. Didn't matter now— they'd done what they were asked and had to get what they had to the demon hunters. Get the boys back.

They were closer to the door. Almost close enough to run for it.

One of the high priestess's guards went off to one side and unslung his bow.

Shit—

No one could dodge an arrow, but he'd seen magic strike them down. To Gui— "Can you halt arrows? With your magic?"

Gui looked, found the same bowman Jay had. His orange eyes glinted in the light from the lanterns and the blessed priestess. "We did the one in the vault. Should be able to manage one here."

"If he lets that arrow fly—"

"We won't be good for nothing else." Gui grunted. "You'll have to keep the rest off us. Tash and me."

Sumi lifted her chin. Goddessi, she was going to do something foolish.

"Mother," she said, lifting the bag over her head. "You said you know who these are for. You know they're for the *demon hunters*."

The high priestess screamed.

Sumi yelled, "The people who believe the goddessi are just trumped up demoni! The—"

The torches flickered then roared and the room went cold.

Jay swallowed. It suddenly felt a heaven of a lot like when Maldita possessed Her high priestess in the Temple of the Damned.

"Hide," Sumi hissed, shoved the precious bag at Mouse. Then snarled at them all, "*Run.*"

Jay sprinted for the guards between them and the door. *Clear the way.* His double swords swirled in pattern, attack and protect, protect and attack.

The bow twanged, twanged again. The bowman wasn't satisfied with just one arrow. Jay ignored him, relying on his team.

From the corner of his eye, he noted Gui and Tasha stop, spin, throw up their linked hands. The arrows hit something invisible— like the dome Sumi had slammed into over the blessed temple— then clattered to the floor.

The rest of the guards surged forward.

Mal remembered he was a resting guard and started using his sword instead of letting it dangle. Some of the blessed guards headed for Jay headed for him instead.

It only *felt* like there were hundreds of them.

Jay *moved*, feet and hands and steel, inflicting incapacitating injuries as often as kills, whichever was faster. Deflect, dodge, strike, keep one eye on his team.

Block, block, slash—

He gained the wall, took one precious moment and a slice to his unguarded left arm to cut down the tapestry. Kicked open the door. Intended to keep it so they had to come at him one or two at a time.

Stab, recover, shift to the side—

Let Mouse slide through and shifted back before the guards from the sanctum could push him into the hall. One of the blessed guards must have gone for reinforcements because he could hear— could *feel* their stomping boots through the stone under his own shoes.

"Out!" He bellowed. "Mal—"

"Stop them!" the high priestess shrieked in reply.

Mal wove around him and ducked through the door, then Tasha and Gui, panting and gray. "Done," Tasha gasped. "No more magic."

"Go!" If they went, and Mouse and the boy, he could concentrate on Sumi.

Sumi, who stood between him and her mother, her hands raised as if she were ready to do magic.

Sumi, who was his life, his light, who he would lose if she allowed the dark goddess back in.

The blood from his arm started to rise instead of drip. Jay shuddered.

Sumi's hair wasn't floating, but the blessed high priestess's was. Bendita had arrived.

A Purple guard swung his blade at Sumi, and Jay lunged, parried it. The guard swung. Caught Jay's left-hand sword just wrong and the blade shattered. Jay brought around the right-hand sword and sliced into the woman's side.

She grunted, then her blood streamed out of the wound toward the high priestess. This time, the guard screamed— she knew what it meant.

Jay wouldn't wish that death on anyone. He gagged. Swung. His blade cut through her neck and lodged in her spine. Yanked once, then left it and drew his knives.

Some of the guards drew away from the high priestess like she was the worst danger in the room— which she was, if Bendita was feasting like Maldita did, and the blood streaming toward her indicated it. But the high priestess was doing something to the bowman's arrow.

The bowman grinned. Set that arrow on his string and drew — one of those barbed man-killing heads good for nothing else.

Aimed at Sumi.

Goddessi, he couldn't lose her again. *Wouldn't.*

Jay *moved—*

The guard loosed.

"*Sumi!*" Jay encircled her in his arms, spun his back to that arrow. Protected her from whatever foul magic her blood-mother had coated it with.

THIRTY

S *umi*

ULTIMATE NIGHTMARE— MY BLOOD-MOTHER AMBUSHING US WHILE glowing like a goddess, guards surrounding us, and now Mal and Jay and Tasha and Gui trying to get us out.

That and the glee I felt from the rope that bound me to the dark goddess.

I'd promised to let Jay and Mal be my sword and shield, let Tasha and Gui be my magic, so as much as I wanted to reach for the power inside me— swelling and swelling until my skin burned with it— I ignored it as hard as I could.

The high priestess of Bendita gazed at me with eyes full of death, assuring me I wasn't getting out alive. All I could do was shout to distract her from my people. Had my blood-mother hinted she'd set this all up?

Slowly, Jay moved us toward the main doors.

Too heavy. We'll never get them open in time. But no— he angled toward the man-door to one side. Better.

The high priestess sneered and the guards loomed and we needed a distraction.

Demon hunters. I knew how Maldita reacted whenever they were mentioned, and that was exactly how to fire up Bendita. I held up the bag of documents I'd copied from her vault. "These are for the *demon hunters.* You know they believe the goddessi are nothing more than trumped-up demoni, right? You—"

She shrieked and the bright goddess came in a wash of cold and dark that flung me back into that moment when the boys summoned a demon and I was *helpless* to do anything about it.

Not this time.

I handed the bag— my boys' freedom— to Mouse. She'd get it out. "Run!"

The torches shifted from glowing black to glowing white. Jay drew his pretty swords and cut down the guards between us and the door. And I faced my blood-mother as if I was going to use the magic singing in my blood.

Arrows came out of nowhere. Tasha and Gui strained, and the arrows fell. The high priestess's archer swore. The rest of the guards came for us.

Amid the grunts and choked off screams, I heard a thud and splintering wood and a door banging into the wall behind it. I risked a quick look— Jay had pushed Mal through and Mouse followed.

The demon hunters' demands would be met and the boys would be safe.

The high priestess shrieked, "Stop them!"

Tasha stumbled. I yanked her back to her feet and shoved her at Gui. Their magic was completely spent. If they kept pushing, they'd hurt themselves. "Go!" I said, and sent them to Jay. They'd done what they'd promised.

Get them out. Get them safe.

My hands came up like I was going to throw magic at the high priestess, and she hesitated.

Her pink and white hair floated on an unseen breeze, her eyes glazed white from lid to lid. Blood drops danced through the air and her black-white-black tattoos gulped them down.

Goddess, I hoped none of my people were bleeding.

The awful sounds of fighting behind me faded. The bowman handed my blood-mother an arrow. She laid her hands on it and into it she set a spell to sacrifice me to Bendita. A spell I hadn't known existed, didn't know *could* exist, but I could see it now, the brightest white in the entire sanctum.

My death and the disintegration of my soul, on the head of that arrow.

The high priestess smiled, slow and horrible, and nodded her permission to the bowman. Pointed one blazing white claw at me.

My vision went dark around the edges. She'd done the unforgivable. Nevermore would she be my blood-mother.

Gui and Tasha had made it out the door, and both were exhausted.

There was no one to stop this arrow.

And I'd chosen the path where I could not. Would not.

The arrow leaped from the bow. Sliced through the air.

I'd died to evade the dark goddess. Today I would be soul-taken by the bright goddess.

My family, safe—

Instead, was spun away in Jay's arms.

No!

Then everything happened at once.

Arrow struck flesh. World went white.

The spell flashed past us to a nameless guard. Her mouth gaped. She burst into ash and vanished.

Jay arched away from me. His hands spasmed open.

I felt the arrow split skin and muscle and ribs. Felt death prick his heart.

I twisted and cradled him in my arms and we sank to the floor.

Jay smiled. "Love you," he said, a bubble of blood at his mouth.

The archer grimaced and set another arrow to his bow.

Bluejay. My love. My everything.

Dying.

Guards coming for me, swords drawn to cut me down. And the high priestess gloating, reaching for Jay's death. For his bone, blood, and soul.

NO.

The dark goddess might consume my soul when I was done, but I would do this.

Mal and Tasha and Gui and Mouse cowered beyond the doorway. Mine, my allies, and I would shield them from my magic. Only them.

I threw my head back and *screamed* the words. Made the gestures with one bloody hand.

Thousand Cuts of Blade and *Thousand Screams of Demon* and *push* and *pull* and dark goddess power all melded together into an impossible new magic.

My *scream* echoed through the temple, through the Blessed Third, through the City of Temples. Everyone heard my pain and the eardrums of everyone in the Blessed Third ruptured.

The archer fell, cut to tiny ribbons by unseen knives.

The remaining guards fell, in a thousand gory pieces.

The high priestess of Bendita fell. Blood exploded through her pristine white gauzes, then she dissolved into glowing ash—

Every footstep outside the room *stopped.*

I rocked, held Jay with my arms and my magic and saw *everything everywhere* as if I were floating above it all.

Gui was staring at me from the doorway, a line of blood on his cheek, blood seeping from under the hands on his thigh. Whispered, "Do you know what that was?"

"Magic." Tasha's voice shook. She held her hands steady on his thigh, pressing hard, to slow the bleeding. She had a few superficial cuts and some deep bruising. I could *feel* it all without effort. "Magic like ours... but not."

Tasha shifted her hands and Mal pressed a ripped-off sleeve to Gui's thigh. "I've never seen anything like that. Never even heard of anything like that."

Gui's voice rose. "Rest it... *She* is the missing priestess. Our Sumi is the missing *high priestess of Maldita* and you knew?"

Tasha winced. "I guessed."

"Jay?" Mouse peeked in from the doorway. She was unmarked, thank the goddessi. One of us was unharmed. Her voice wobbled. "Jay?"

Gui turned her face into his shoulder. "Don't look," he murmured. "They killed him."

"What? He can't be—" Tasha stared. "Oh no."

Right now they didn't matter.

What mattered was the blood seeping from Jay's body. The arrow touching his heart.

What I was going to do about it.

I'd murdered everyone in the sanctum. What was one more unforgivable choice?

A familiar prickle came over me. I raised my black and blood eyes and screamed *Her* name. "*MALDITA!*"

Perhaps in the bright temple, the heart of the bright goddess's power, I should have called for Bendita, but I called the only goddess I knew would help me.

For a price.

I became an oathbreaker when I left Her service and now I'd be an oathbreaker again— twice foresworn. My oath to my beloved.

Make one last bargain with the Goddess of the Damned.

I *pulled* on the chains that bound us, opened myself up to Her—

And She came, between one heartbeat and the next, filling all the places that had been empty since the day I'd abandoned Her. Filling me with power. Filling the room until it hurt to breathe.

Time to ask for what I needed— but I didn't have *time*. Jay's heart faltered.

I would *not* lose him.

I reached out to every bit of power I could touch. Every bit I could steal. Hers, mine, the life of the city—

And I *pushed*.

And I *pulled*.

And I screamed.

And I—

Stopped.

Time.

❧

JAY

THE ARROW ITSELF WASN'T MAGIC. THE MAN-KILLING HEAD— NOT magic. It didn't slide around him like magic had ever since Jay had become Sumi's Shadow and Secret-Keeper.

He spun his beloved away from death, and it struck. Tore into his back, left of his spine. Not like the slice of a sword, the stab of a dagger— sharp, explosive, *now*.

But knew from the agony that he'd saved Sumi's soul.

Worth it.

What did the betweens look like? Perhaps the memory garden. Somewhere restful. Like the name. *Resting Betweens.*

Death did strange things to time. Had it been like this for her, lying on the cold, cold ground under the snowy sky?

Her hair smelled of *her*, and her body in his arms, *her*, and her soft red skin, *her*. She'd be so angry with him, but she'd have the boys and they'd have her and they'd all be okay.

He would miss her. Miss them. Wait for them.

Then—

Nothing.

THIRTY-ONE

S *umi*

THE WALLS AND FLOORS GLISTENED WITH THE VITAL FLUIDS OF THE denizens of the bright temple, come to prevent us from stealing their treasures. My hands dripped with Jay's blood.

I held *time* in my magic, *pushing* and *pulling* to keep it still.

Prevent Jay from leaving me.

Bendita appeared in front of me as if She were a real person, though no one else would see Her. White hair, instead of black, cascaded down Her back, and the shape of Her cheekbones and chin and ears and hands— She and Maldita looked like bloodsisters, if goddessi had such a thing.

"I didn't call You," I faltered.

She smiled with far too many teeth. "Yet here I am."

One goddess, the other goddess— as long as They could give me what I wanted— "His life, then," I demanded, still holding Time. Holding his quiet, quiet heart. It had only been

422

stopped for a second, but already there was *nothing* I wouldn't do to have him back.

I would break the world for him.

Bendita's solid white eyes were the reverse of mine when Maldita possessed me— black from lid to lid, the way they might look now, if Tasha, Gui, or Mouse could see me.

If Jay were alive and seeing me.

Didn't make sense— that I was possessed by Maldita but talking to Bendita, nor that I'd called Maldita while standing in Bendita's temple.

Why didn't matter.

"You have killed so many... for me?" She turned to look at the blood-spattered, body-strewn sanctum, and even if She wasn't truly a goddess, She was too *big* to be a mere demon.

"For justice." Then I corrected myself, "For revenge."

She grinned like a feral little girl. "Good."

"You may take the blood and bone and souls of my enemies," I said, "but not from my allies, nor my lover. In exchange, he lives."

She raised one eyebrow. Smirked. "I don't give *life*."

My lips trembled, but I raised my chin defiantly. She wouldn't have me, if She didn't help.

She must have read it in my glare. "I can heal his body," She admitted, reluctant. "His soul still resides in his body. Heal the body, he may yet live." She glided toward me and crooned, "But will you pay the price?"

"More than the souls of all these?" Not my allies. I might consider it, but he wouldn't, so I *couldn't*.

"You murdered the high priestess of the Temple of the Blessed. *My* high priestess. You must take her place."

I bit my lip. I'd killed so many with my twisted spell, killed the woman who had been my blood-mother. She'd been trying to kill *me* and give my soul to this goddess, but still—

Focus on now. Continue holding Time hostage, though it was trying to twitch from my grasp. A goddess and me and Jay in a tiny, fragile bubble.

"I called Maldita—"

"She has a high priestess." She waved one transparent hand. "She is content."

"I thought you were rivals." I couldn't make a bargain with *this* one if *that* one objected.

"We're closer than you think." She wound around me like a snake around a stick. "Say you'll take your mother's place."

I gasped. Her skin was hot and slick and pink like frothy blood. I wanted more than almost anything to *push* Her away. "What about Miki?" The blessed high priestess's heir.

"I want you."

My only choice was Jay's life. "I'll take my mother's place."

"Tell me you'll leave *him* for Me."

Already done— I would be the blessed high priestess and he'd never again leave the Rest Third for me. The boys needed him and his sisters needed him and even Thom and the Rest Third guards needed him.

But I had to pretend it hurt more than it already did or She would ask and ask until She found something I wouldn't give.

He would be furious with me, but he'd be alive.

Wait, wait, wait... pretend to crumble. "I'll leave him for You." I let the tears running down my face make their way into my voice. "But You won't punish anyone else. Nor ask for anything else."

She examined me, nose to nose, white eyes to black. Would She demand more?

Finally, the blessed goddess trilled, then placed Her hands over mine, and *yanked* the arrow from Jay's heart.

She ripped away my control, and Time restarted, and Jay

healed, from the hole in his heart outward, and faster than any *human* healer could have.

Bendita commanded, "Breathe for him."

Did She know he'd done as much for me when we escaped the Temple of the Damned?

I bent over him, pressed my lips to his, breathed into his mouth. Over and over, passing my life to his. Wordlessly demanding he return to me. My world narrowed to breathing for Jay.

Hands plucked at my shirt, then pulled me away.

I snarled and turned to strike.

Mouse yelped, "He's breathing on his own!" She held her hands up and backed away as if I were a dangerous animal.

Found family. I hesitated, caught between them.

Jay lay on his side, his chest moving with his breath. The pain had left his face. A faint smile rested on his lips. I could have believed I had dreamt his death except for the hole in the back of his shirt.

The blood was gone from my hands, from the floors and walls, from Jay's shirt. The bodies of the guards were gone. The ash in the air that had been the high priestess, gone. The goddess had feasted through the tattoos in my skin, but She'd been so fast I hadn't had to feel it.

Gui choked. "You're—"

My hands were as pale a pink as the previous high priestess's had been. "Bleached out. As the high priestess of Bendita should be."

"Glowing."

Of course I was. The goddessi were all the same. Give them a little blood, a few souls—

Guilt would ambush me later— I could feel it coming— but not now.

Mal gaped at me. "You really are... were... *her*."

Had been. Was. "Maldita has a high priestess. Bendita wanted me instead."

"Wow." Gui again.

I would need them to spy on the Rest Third— to keep an eye on my found family— for me. But more than that, I couldn't let them be afraid of me. "We're still... friends...?"

Tasha gaped at me, then laughed. "Surely. I haven't been friends with a high priestess before."

"I'm still... me."

"Except with *magic*."

"Yes. Except that."

"And *power*."

"Yeah."

"And *servitors*."

"All right, all right. Watch it, or I'll make *you* my servitors."

"Nah." Gui snorted. "Already halfway are. Here, ain't we? But sworn to you, not no damned goddess, nor blessed neither."

Jay stirred.

My breath caught.

He opened his eyes. Blinked. Looked up at me and smiled like the morning after love. Then looked past me at the others hovering around us. "Not the betweens?" He scowled. "Sumi? What did you do?"

"Welcome back." Would he ever forgive me? I helped him sit up, reluctantly let my hands drop away from the man I loved. "You saved me."

"Again." He rubbed at his chest, twisted like he wanted to see his own back, then stared at me. "What did you *do*?"

I tried to look innocent. White streaked hair and pale skin and bright tattoos and all.

He didn't buy it. "Sumi. I was *dead*."

"According to Her, not *quite*—"

"You didn't."

"Didn't?" He knew— thought he knew. But he didn't yet need to know everything I'd sacrificed.

"I can see you did." He scowled. Traced the tattoo on my forehead. Cupped my cheek. "You bargained with a goddess."

"I did."

"For my life?"

"As you sacrificed yours for mine. My privilege." *My beloved.*

"Fool." He kissed me, hard and hot melting into sweet and tender and only my knees protesting the cold marble floor reminded me we were in a public place.

Until Mal cleared his throat uncomfortably.

Priestessi and magi and blessed guards were filtering in from the rest of the temple; ringed Mal and Tasha and Gui and Mouse with their blessed hands on their blessed swords as if they knew what had happened. Time to introduce them to the new order in the Temple of the Blessed.

"Hold," I said mildly. Delicately— and terrifyingly easily— I clamped down on their magics and their swords. I shouldn't have become stronger. I hadn't used my magic for *months.* Except putting out the fire. Healing Dee. Quieting my own magic. Ah, well. *Should* and I had never gotten along.

"Who are you?" demanded a Blue magus. "What have you done?"

"Yes, what have you done, Sister?" The crowd parted and a pale, pale Red stamped through them as if she owned the temple.

Miki, my eldest blood-sister. As soon as she came into the room, her magic sputtered and died under my control.

She felt it. Her feet hesitated but her chin came up, ready to fight.

"Miki." *Only what you tried and failed to do many times over.* Diplomatic. I could be diplomatic. I rose to my feet and saw the glow surrounding me shining on their faces and their white clothes and their pale skins. "I killed the blessed high priestess and took her place."

Miki's gaze swept from my hair over my pale skin and bright tattoos down to my feet— more bright tattoos, and where had my boots and socks gone?— and back up. The others remained silent, waiting for her.

Finally, her shoulders slumped. "Well, damn. Best laid plans and all that."

"Mmm." Murdering the high priestess seemed to be a common *plan* among us blood-sisters, though I hadn't intended it tonight. Not that I hadn't dreamed a little.

With her acquiescence, the other blessed deflated.

The Temple of the Blessed and all its people were mine.

"I need rooms. A bath. New clothes. New guards at the gates and triple patrols around the temple. My friends will be leaving us for the Rest Third and if they need any assistance, they *will* get it. In an hour, I will meet with Miki and the head magus, and the head guard."

"Su— High Priestess." Jay's fingers clutched mine.

Leave him for Me, Bendita whispered in my head.

I will, I replied. *Soon enough. I have to finish what we started.* "Make it happen, Blessed."

"Yes, High Priestess," they chorused.

They parted for us, and I released their magic as Gui, limping between Mal and Tasha, and Mouse and Jay and I walked away from them, out through the main doors thrown wide open, out through the glowing gardens under the dark night sky, out toward the temple gates where we'd been turned away not so long ago.

My head buzzed, the blessed goddess warning me I could go no farther. I couldn't let go of Jay's hand, not yet. "Thank you. Each one of you." I banked down the blessed goddess— easier with Jay's hand in mine— and committed each face to memory as if it was the first time I'd ever seen them, as if I would never see them again.

I might not.

Gui— Orange and square-framed, his *push* magic already recovering. Tasha— his perfect foil, Purple and sharp-boned and sharp-minded, her magic slower, but so strong. Mal— the Red boy who no longer worshiped Jay, who'd been sucked into a job he hadn't wanted, who'd stood by us anyway. Mouse— the resemblance to her blood-father plain in her eyes and her jawline and her hair, but *ours* now. She would need all her courage to face the demon hunters, to face Enzo.

And Jay— my beloved, my Brown man, with soft honey-colored eyes and blunt, sensitive fingers that lit fires under my skin and protected me from the goddessi. My Jay.

"Finish the job." I touched them each on the forearm, and took an extra moment to *pull* the edges of each layer of Gui's wound together and *push* them into place, speed his healing. So easy, now that I belonged to a goddess again.

Then I brought Jay to my arms and rested my head against his chest. "Tell the boys—"

"I'll bring them."

"I don't want them here. I don't want them to belong to *Her*."

His voice rose, gruffer than before. "I'm your Shadow. We'll figure it out."

I kissed him, straining to put my love, my goodbye into the touch of his lips on mine. His heart beat— goddessi, it thundered and I hoped it never stilled again! When I could bear it no longer, I tore myself away. "I love you."

They would save the boys— and the blessed demon hunters who by now might need saving from *them*. I couldn't go, but I trusted them. My eyes filled as they turned away from me and walked through the gates.

Go, I urged silently.

The farther away from me, the safer for them.

They perched on their carpets and rose into the sky and disappeared from sight. And I— I returned to the Blessed Temple. The last place I'd ever dreamed I'd step foot again.

Bargain kept, I told Bendita.

She hummed happily.

~

JAY

RISING FROM THE DEAD *HURT*. BUT IT BEAT THE ALTERNATIVE.

It wasn't truly pain. More an odd hitch in his chest and a belief everything *should* hurt.

It hurt more to know Sumi had given up her freedom for him, even as he rejoiced when her quelling glance stilled the blessed more easily than it had stilled the damned. She looked so much like *herself* with her power blazing through her that he felt a thrill of pleasure as strong as the phantom pain.

Before he could do more than kiss his beloved and rise to his feet, the blessed bent their heads, if not their hearts, to the new high priestess. If any of them *had* hearts, Sumi would win them over easily enough.

The pale Red woman who looked so much like his Sumi that she had to be a blood-relative pointed out a Blue man and called him the Head Mage, and he turned out to be one of Thom's many relatives. She brought forward a Purple woman and named her the head guard— likely she knew Lena from the damned temple.

Then Sumi spoke, and he felt compelled to listen. "I need rooms," she said. "A bath. New clothes. New guards at the gates and triple patrols around the temple. My friends will be leaving us for the Rest Third and if they need any assistance, they *will* get it. In an hour, I will meet with Miki and the head magus, and the head guard—"

The Rest Third— the children. Wil and Andy would be devastated. Almost he called her by her name, then remembered— "High Priestess."

She let him hold her hand and they walked— all of them *walked* out of the blessed temple as if they hadn't just pilfered copies of historical documents and killed the high priestess.

But Sumi stopped at the temple gates. "Thank you," she said. "Each one of you."

His hand brought hers to his chest— he wasn't ready to let her go— but she didn't seem to notice.

"Finish the job." Sumi touched Mal on the forearm, then Tasha, then Mouse. When she touched Gui, she did *something* and he stood straighter, as if his leg had quit paining him.

Healed him, so easily.

Then she curled into Jay and he never wanted to let her go. "Tell the boys—"

"I'll bring them." They would miss their friends, but they'd be okay—

"I don't want them here. I don't want them to belong to *Her*."

Oh. She was trying to protect them, and him too. Rest that. "I'm your Shadow. We'll figure it out."

She kissed him and he kissed her back. When she pulled away, said, "I love you."

Time to pry his fingers out of hers, time to tell his heart he would see her again, time to rescue the boys from the resting *fools* who had stolen them away.

The guards made no move against them, so Jay and the

others exited the temple grounds. Sat on their carpets. Flew into the sky.

Didn't stop until they saw the warehouse.

At this, the deepest hour of the night, everyone normally would be asleep, but instead, torches lit the area. The inhabitants of the Rest Third ringed the warehouse, all packed together— Cori's mother and Kass's parents, their neighbors and friends, guards at the front and a few guards at the back. Some slept on the ground, here and there, but most watched the building that held their children, and the murmur of their words rose like a song into the sky.

A song that swelled from supportive to savage to bewildered to terrified and back again.

They made way for the descending carpets, though he could see they were reluctant to do so. When the five had landed, faces turned his way, expectant and guarded.

Before they'd finished rolling their carpets, Thom appeared, as if he'd been standing there the whole time, though Jay knew that wasn't true. "You have what they demanded?"

"Yeah." Jay glanced at Mouse.

She clutched the bag to her middle, then shifted as if to remove it.

Jay shook his head. Their Mouse deserved the chance to confront her father— if she wanted it.

Thom stepped closer and lowered his voice. "Thank the betweens. We've already calmed three riots. Blame and shame everywhere. We need the children back. Our people need to feel safe."

Jay listened to the words Thom wasn't saying. The same shame and blame the other parents felt gnawed at him too, but — "Is this wise? The demon hunters may just demand something else..."

Thom grimaced. "If they do, our people will tear them apart."

Jay nodded. Tipped his head to Mouse. "You want me to take that? Or you want to give it to him?"

She raised her chin, reminding him so much of Sumi that he caught his breath. *She's fine. She's in charge of the whole blessed third now, and she's waiting for you to finish this job.*

He turned— Thom would watch his back. When the old man sucked in a wounded breath, Jay regretted that decision.

"Son," Thom murmured. "There's a hole in your shirt. The kind of hole men don't often survive."

Jay shrugged. "I didn't."

Before he could say anything else— and this was too public a venue anyway— a Green woman pushed her way through the crowd. "*You* had it? You had what they wanted the whole time?"

His sword hilt leapt into his hand and he half-drew before Thom stopped him. "Easy, son."

Jay breathed through his nose. *In, out, in, out.* What it had cost them— "We *took* what they wanted. By force. A lot of people *died.*" *Including me.* "The blessed high priestess died, and a bunch of guards and—" He throat rasped. He was yelling again.

Thom set a calming hand on his arm. "They're just afraid for the kids."

"So am I."

This time, when he walked forward, the crowd parted before him. Mouse trailed along behind, still clutching the resting bag, and silence bloomed around them. Neighbors' faces and guard faces and his sisters' faces peppered the crowd, but he didn't meet anyone's gaze.

Not now.

If he could have, he'd have used Sumi's power to shatter the doors. Take the boys— But he couldn't, so he pushed down the fury and knocked.

Boom, boom, boom.

Right— mostly pushed down.

The door cracked open.

"We have what you demanded," Jay growled.

The door opened further.

The only thing that prevented Jay from flinging it open was the thought it could be one of the kids at the door instead of one of Enzo's minions. So he walked through calmly.

The warehouse itself was like most others— echoey, wide aisles, mysterious boxes— but the people in it captured his attention. Andy and Wil smiling mischievously— *they're okay, they're okay*— and Cori and Kass, tired but not very frightened. Maggie, when she glanced at one of the demon hunters, looked disillusioned, and when she watched the kids, faintly amused.

Enzo, exhausted. The other demon hunters flinching away from the shadows.

What had Wil and Andy done?

No time to ask. Time for Mouse to shine, if she chose. He glanced at her, one eyebrow raised.

She nodded slightly, gripped the bag strap hard, then stepped forward and took it off. Held it out to her blood-father. Let her expression and her voice show her disgust.

"Here, *Dad*. Here's what you *stole little kids* for. What mattered more than people's *lives*. What mattered more to you than your own *family*. I'm ashamed of you."

He gaped at her, and for a moment, Jay thought her words touched him.

But then his mouth hardened. He jerked the bag from her hands and riffled through it. "Good enough." Slung it over his own shoulder. Raised his voice to Thom, blocking the doorway. "We'll go now."

"Will you?" Thom shifted and let them see the crowds of parents and neighbors and friends behind him. "Might be a problem."

Enzo sneered. He muttered some words and clapped his hands together and puffed— and when he separated his hands, they held a tiny fireball.

Wil tugged on his shirt and that fireball wavered. "Don't hurt anyone. Their ghosts will come for you."

An eerie moan rose from a back corner. All the adults flinched, though the kids didn't.

Interesting.

Enzo snarled at Thom, sounding desperate. "Get them back! We're going and we'll never return to this haunted city— I swear it!"

The others pushed open the massive main doors, and crowded themselves onto a large, ragged flying carpet. Jay craned his head to see it but caught only faded oranges and yellows and reds before Enzo and all the other residents of the City of Elementals crowded on— leaving behind the Rest Third collaborators and all four children.

A growl ran through the crowd, but they stayed back, cowed by the fire in Enzo's hands.

Then the demon hunters and the blessed stories and their carpet rose into the air and shot away. Guards followed at a safe distance, and the flying carpets disappeared into the night.

Jay watched them go. "Our people will turn back at our borders?"

Then Wil and Andy clasped him around his waist and he realized he didn't care about the demon hunters. Whatever happened to them—

Anticlimactic at best. After all, he'd already been dead today.

Cori and Kass ran into the crowd, found their parents.

Guards came in, held the collaborators where they were. Robin and Dee found him, and Maggie stood nearby looking unsure. Dee pulled her into a hug that included Robin and Jay and the boys too.

"Andy and Wil were wonderful." Maggie squeezed Jay's shoulder. "The demon hunters are fools."

Wil canted his head back and smiled innocently. "We played a game of ghost," he said, and wiggled his fingers to suggest something floating. "The four of us. We made noises and moved things. Of course the grown ups didn't *know* we were playing a game..."

"Ah." That explained the adults' reactions— and that moan. Even the demon hunter collaborators looked exhausted and cowed. Thrilled to be taken into guard custody.

He herded his family over to a more private corner of the warehouse. His gut tightened up, like he was going to take a punch he couldn't avoid. "Slight change in plans."

The boys simply looked at him, as if they knew when Sumi hadn't appeared in the doorway.

Robin grimaced. "Slight?"

"Small. Tiny." He tried a grin, but his sisters hadn't fallen for his grin since they'd been children, and they didn't fall for it this time, either.

Maggie stepped back and said in a small voice, "Not because of what I...?"

"No." He swept her into a quick hug. "I'm so glad you went with the boys. Allowed us to focus on what we needed to do."

Dee rested her hand on the hilt of her sword. "Who do we need to kill?"

Jay shook his head. "Too many people have already died tonight."

"Then...?"

"I'll be gone a lot, but I'll make sure to pay my part of the house."

Robin stepped back. "Excuse me?"

"You think you're leaving us again? You're mad." Dee stuck her finger through the hole in his shirt, yanked it. "This, big brother, looks like an arrow hole."

"Where is Sumi?" Maggie stared at the door as if she could make Sumi appear.

Would that she could.

"I'm fine." He hugged Dee hard. She hugged back, then pushed him away.

"That's not an answer."

"Things got... complicated."

"Resting betweens." Robin thunked her head against Dee's shoulder.

The boys were starting to panic, even as Mouse put her hands on their shoulders and whispered, "She's okay."

How to summarize? "We'll be at the Temple of the Blessed, off and on. I was injured. I got better. But now we owe them our service. Not as long as last time, I think."

"*What?*" Dee and Maggie yelped.

Robin snarled, "That harridan?"

"*That harridan* is dead." He checked, then lowered his voice, though no one should be close enough to overhear. "You know who Sumi was before. She's that again."

Dee nodded, and Robin too. Maggie winced. "She really was?"

"She was. And the goddess wanted her back." He straightened. "I should be free to come and go. I'll come by often."

"That's all you're going to tell us?" Robin growled.

"For now. We all need to get some sleep—"

Robin snorted.

"—Dee needs to get to work. I need to talk to Wilyam and Antero. Time is on our side." *I think.*

Robin punched his shoulder. "I hate you."

"I know."

Dee punched his other shoulder. "Don't leave without saying goodbye."

Jay ignored that this might be his goodbye. "Uh huh."

"If you're going, it's important." Maggie scowled, but didn't punch him. Instead she hugged him. "I love you, big brother."

"I love you too." He reached, gathered them all into another hug. Watched them leave the warehouse together.

Together— that was the important word. He wouldn't be able to protect them anymore— hadn't been able, for a long time now— but they would protect each other.

Wil clasped Jay's hand. "Mom?"

Jay found a box and sat on it like it was a chair. Curled his fingers for the boys to join him. "She can't leave the blessed temple. But she's fine."

"The goddess got her back." Now Wil looked devastated. Andy pushed him over next to Jay and nudged until he sat, then perched beside him. They'd grown so much over the summer.

"She wanted to come, but she made a bargain." Jay thought about the hole in his shirt, the twinge in his chest. "She sent me to tell you she's fine and she loves you."

"See, Andy?" Wilyam ripped himself away, paced across the floor. "See what happens when they go without us?"

Jay caught him in a hug. "It's all right. Everything is going to be all right."

"She promised not to leave us," Wil mumbled against his shirt.

"I'm sorry." He held the boy until his shudders subsided. "I have an important question for you both. Do you want to go to the Temple of the Blessed to be with your mom? Or stay with my sisters? Your aunts?"

Wil and Andy shared a long, wordless glance punctuated by raising eyebrows, pursing lips, wrinkling noses.

"Go," Andy said.

Wil nodded. "You're going, right? You're going, so we'll go."

"It's going to be hard." Jay ran one hand over his brown curls. "She's the... she's in charge again. Bendita this time, not Maldita. We don't know the people in the temple. Don't have any allies."

Wil's chin jutted. "She's our mom. *We're* her allies. She needs us. Now more than ever."

"True." Jay tousled his red hair, then ruffled Andy's purple because he could. "She needs us."

"Mouse?"

The girl startled as if she thought he'd forgotten about her. She licked her lips. "I won't stay in the temple," she said slowly. "But I'd like to visit."

"Good. I want to hear your stories. The great Mouse—facing down demon hunters and scurrying through the night, righting wrongs."

She stared, then her breath hitched. She nodded. Flashed a grin.

"Take your time. Say your goodbyes." Jay looked over their heads to the street where Thom and Mal spoke in low voices. To where the guards were leading collaborators away. To where his sisters had gone. "We'll let your mom get settled. Then show up. In the night." He winked. "When no one can stop us. We know the way, now."

The boys beamed.

CHAPTER
THIRTY-TWO

S *umi*

I'D BATHED— SOAP AND WATER CLEAN INSTEAD OF *THE GODDESS sucked down all the ash and blood through my tattoos* clean— and dressed the first set of whites I'd donned in years— *not* my blood-mother's, instead a newly made pair Miki had bespoke and not yet worn. We were that close in size, though my hips were a little wider, my legs a little longer. Met with the people I'd needed to and then chased the rest off to bed.

After all, the blessed *slept* at night.

And I left them with their burst eardrums as a reminder of my power, even if that meant *pushing* my voice at them to make them hear. They could see the temple healer or heal the normal way or beg me for a favor.

Getting used to the pale pink skin and white-streaked hair would take time. Getting used to the goddess in my head again would take more.

The chains by which She bound me were no different from Maldita's and I was starting to share a certain nasty suspicion about the goddessi. But for now, that thought must stay hidden.

Instead, since Bendita seemed to have distanced Herself to let me sleep, I very, very quietly *pushed* a bit of barrier around my thoughts, and contemplated what would happen next, for the blessed, for my family, and for me.

After all, love is hard, and love in the City of Temples even harder.

But Jay was alive. Our found-family lived. One of the guards brought me word my boys had been spotted in Jay's arms, and the demon hunters exiled from the city. Surely I would be miserable, trapped in the Temple of the Blessed with the bright goddess and Her sticky fingers all over my soul, but we *lived*.

As long as I lived, I had changes to make. Things to *plan*.

I would never give up on Jay— no matter what I'd told the goddess— and I knew he wouldn't easily give up on me. And now we had more allies than before.

The blessed priestessi, the magi, the guards— even the goddessi were in for an awakening.

They would never know what hit them.

ABOUT THE AUTHOR

Award-winning speculative fiction author Barbara Lund has several indie-published novels, dozens of short stories, and has been traditionally published in *Daily Science Fiction* and *L. Ron Hubbard Presents Writers of the Future, Volume 37* (November 2021).

She won the Writers of the Future Golden Pen (2021), along with a First Place, three Silver Honorable Mentions, and two Honorable Mentions. She won the 24th Annual Critters Best Magical Realism Short Story.

She is currently— and always— working on new novels and several short stories.

Add a husband, two kids, and a martial arts obsession, and she keeps pretty busy.

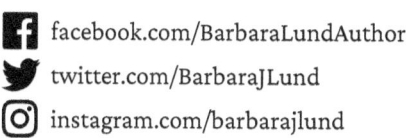

facebook.com/BarbaraLundAuthor
twitter.com/BarbaraJLund
instagram.com/barbarajlund

Also by Barbara Lund

City of Temples Series

Lost Priestess

Hidden Priestess

Found Priestess (coming soon)

Platform Eight Series (Short Stories)

Darkest Space (#1)

Recovery Space (#2)

Damaged Space (#3)

Revenge Space (#4)

Craving Space (#5)

Slave Space (#6)

Shattered Space (#7)

Relative Space (#8)

Platform Eight (Omnibus)

Crowns Peak Series

First Mage Hiding (formerly *Creeper*)

Healer (Short Story)

Second Mage Questing (formerly *Ava's Quest*)

Last Mage Standing

Doomsday Ship Stories (Short Stories)

Ship Desolate (#1)

Ship Heist (#2)

Ship Child (#3)

Ship Napped (#4)

Ship Chip (#5)

Ship Wreck (#6 - coming soon)

Stand-Alone Stories

Dragonscale Throne

Space, Lies, Syndicate

Witch's Pet (Short Story)

Reboot (Short Story)

Blood Descendant (Novella)

Sparks In The Dark: Fantasy Short Story Collection

Sparks in the Dark: Science Fiction Short Story Collection (coming soon)

www.barbaralund.com